Maraglindi
Guardian Spirit

Bob Rich

First published in Great Britain in 2021 by Sleepy Lion Publishing. (Trading name of Sleepy Lion Limited)

Text Copyright © Bob Rich, 2021
Cover Design Copyright © Sleepy Lion Publishing, 2021
Maraglindi illustration copyright © Alfredo Zotti

ISBN: 978-1-8380152-6-8

SLEEPY LION

PUBLISHING

www.sleepylionpublishing.com

Other Books by Dr. Bob Rich

Practical self-help
-The Earth Garden Building Book: Design and build your own house
-Woodworking for Idiots Like Me

Psychology self-help
-Anger and Anxiety: Be in charge of your emotions and control phobias
-Personally Speaking: Single session email therapy
-Cancer: A personal challenge
-From Depression to Contentment: A self-therapy guide
-Lifting the Gloom: Antidepressant writings

Biography
-Anikó: The stranger who loved me

Inspirational
-Hit and Run

Historical fiction
-The Start of Magic
-The Mother's Sword
-The Making of a Forest Fighter
-The Travels of First Horse: a trilogy

Science fiction
-Sleeper, Awake
-Ascending Spiral

Anthology
-Striking Back from Down Under
-Through Other Eyes
-Bizarre Bipeds: What IS humanity's role in the universe?

ENDORSEMENTS

Max Overton

I read *Maraglindi: Guardian Spirit* in its previous incarnation a few years ago, but its message has remained with me. It is a novel of Australia, but it is not limited to that beautiful country; the message applies to all men and women everywhere and in every time. Couched within the framework of Christianity, it applies equally to any religion that preaches love and acceptance. Reincarnation is a thread that runs through the story, and shows how our actions are not limited to one life but reverberate through many incarnations as we strive to learn the lessons necessary for our spiritual growth.

The protagonist, a young Aboriginal girl, Maraglindi, is born of an act of hate, but she typifies Love in its most elemental form, and all who come in contact with her during her short life are touched by this love. It changes their behaviour for the better, and each one spreads this message of love to others, enveloping families and communities. But this is so much more than just a story with a message; it is a history. *Maraglindi: Guardian Spirit* is a story set against the backdrop of Colonial Australia, where we get to experience the lives of rich and poor, privileged and deprived, the white overlords and the downtrodden, dispossessed Aboriginal

First People of this glorious country.

Maraglindi: Guardian Spirit is a book I would not hesitate to recommend, not just as a story that describes the racial discord of earlier times, but also as one that holds out a hope that things can be different. We live in times where hate is rearing its ugly head once more, so we need stories like this to remind us that hate can be overcome, not by violence and more hatred, but by love and acceptance.

Max Overton is the author of over forty books, many of them historical fiction.

Margaret Tanner

Set in 1850s Australia.

Glindi, an Aboriginal woman, gives birth to a baby girl she names Maraglindi (Glindi's sorrow).

Born amidst violent times when Aboriginal men were treated worse than their Masters' dogs, the women suffered even more. Their only use was to satisfy their owner's lust and keep his house in order.

Against this horrific background Bob Rich has woven a rich tapestry of love, hate, decency and depravity. Once you start reading you won't be able to put it down until you have devoured every word. It is quite obvious the author has done extensive historical research before he wrote this story.

Highly recommended.

Margaret Tanner is a Best Selling and Award Winning Australian author of drama-laden historical western romance.

Florence Weinberg

Maraglindi by Dr. Bob Rich pulls no punches. Set in the era of Queen Victoria, its major themes are two: Do unto others as you would have them do unto you, and, all human beings deserve equal respect and treatment regardless of sex, color of skin, age, wealth, or place of origin.

A highly superior being from elsewhere in the universe is assigned the task of leading human beings to the ideal state of perfect love. This being becomes Maraglindi, nicknamed "Mary" by the whites who cannot pronounce her name, a child of the dispossessed Aboriginal people of New South Wales. As she grows, she demonstrates to all who come in contact with her just what love and the Golden Rule can do. There is, however, one barrier to her ability to spread love, peace and understanding: the negative force of hatred and prejudice. She cannot prevail against a completely closed mind.

In and around a beautifully portrayed 19th-century village, the battle between ultimate good and evil plays out before us. There is much violence and bloodshed in this novel, but also much hope and goodness. Dr. Bob Rich's powerful work, while set in the past, is deeply relevant today, as we witness hatred and prejudice spread by persons in powerful places, through the power of modern media. We need you, Maraglindi! Come, Guardian Spirit!

Emeritus Professor Florence Weinberg is the author of eleven novels that have won eleven awards. Most of them are gripping mysteries set in an authentic historical setting.

Mary Tod

Maraglindi — the title of this new novel from author Bob Rich — embodies a promise to readers, the promise of a story that is both magical and transformative. Expect to be mesmerized by the main character, Maraglindi, and the way her life unfolds in Victorian Australia. Expect to be outraged at the way whites treated the aboriginal people. Expect to be touched by the power of love and hope. Highly recommended.

M. K. Tod is the author of many works of historical fiction, the latest being *Paris In Ruins*.

Disclaimer

When I worked as a counsellor at the Bunurong Aboriginal Health Centre in Dandenong, Victoria, Australia, all the young people called me "Uncle Bob," a title reserved for elders. I felt incredibly honoured then, and still do now. My attitude to the original caretakers of Australia is one of respect and love.

However, this story is set in Victorian times: from 1850 to 1866. People of British heritage considered themselves to be superior to everyone else, and wherever they conquered, they treated the locals with disdain, and savage cruelty. In order to bring those past days to life, I need to give my characters the words, actions and attitudes that were common then. If superficially this seems disrespectful or even abusive to some modern readers, I apologise.

Maraglindi, by Alfredo Zotti

PART 1

A Killer Horse
New South Wales,
10th day of April, 1850

Bruce MacCartney managed not to vomit as he looked at the trampled body. The man's skull was broken open, pink brains showing, and... He unfroze and turned his back, somehow.

Colin Hartley said, "He was only an Irish ticket-of-leave convict. But if your man hadn't asked me to hold off, I'd have shot the horse by now. A killer horse is of no use."

Bruce prided himself on being tolerant of everyone, but this was too much. He had to speak, he had to. "No," he grated. "He was a person with as much right to life as you or me."

Hartley shrugged. "Hell, they're a penny a dozen. I am worth thousands of pounds."

Bruce found his hands forming fists but took a deep breath. "I could buy you and sell you a dozen times over, and I'm the grandson of an Earl, but I don't consider myself better than you. Or... or that poor fellow. We are all God's children."

Hartley looked angry, but almost paradoxically, also

subservient. His lips almost disappeared, and his hands formed fists while he looked down at the ground, shoulders hunched.

Having made his point, Bruce wanted to heal the breach, even with a fellow such as this, and he had an idea. "But about the horse. I'll buy him off you."

Now Hartley laughed, his tension gone. "Once a killer, always a killer. You'll never break him, but if you want to buy horse meat, I won't object. Ten pounds do?"

Ten pounds for a magnificent stallion was more than a bargain, but of course Hartley considered the animal worthless. The best deal is when both parties are satisfied, and Bruce knew himself to be on sure ground. Mick could tame any horse. "Very well, Mr Hartley. In addition, would you care to wager two pounds that I'll end up riding him?"

Hartley again laughed. "Done!" He held his hand out for a shake.

Bruce had a great deal of distaste in his innards, shaking hands with such a travesty of a human, but that was the way to seal a bet. He did it.

"Just one thing, Mr MacCartney. We do need a time limit. A month do?"

"Very well, Mr Hartley, if you can bring him to my horse stud, alive and unharmed."

"I'll think of a way."

Gaspar rode up and halted his horse at a respectful distance from the two gentlemen. When Bruce looked at him, he said, "Sir, the axle has been replaced, and the men are reloading the wagon."

"Thank you, Gaspar. Goodbye, Mr Hartley." Bruce mounted and followed his man back to the road, so they could resume their journey home from Newcastle. Unusually for him, he had personally accompanied his merchandise, on this occasion a wagonload of cheese and six fine horses, because the wagon right now held his second wedding anniversary present for Alice: a couch and six armchairs, beautifully upholstered with a floral fabric he knew she would love. He was greatly looking forward to getting the last five miles behind him.

1

Glindi

Glindi watched Aunty Dara hold up the baby. "A girl," the wise woman said. "She's a bit pale, but then, all your other ones were too at birth." She passed the slippery little form to Glindi who squatted on the hard-packed dirt floor, over a nest of now-bloodied soft leaves and flowers. Jila comfortingly supported her from behind.

In the old days, the birth would have been in a secret Women's Place, with a hole dug under her — but now, the white man owned everything, and going out of the miserable village was risking death.

Jila helped her to stand, and Aunty Dara passed her the gourd of bitter medicine to expel the placenta.

Glindi gave a breast to the tiny new person and, allowing the baby to suck, settled on her sleeping place so Aunty Dara could clean her up. Jila left to fetch the rest of the family.

Within a minute, Atan burst in, excited, with Tari and Kohli behind him. Jila and Mick followed. Glindi could see the terrible anxiety on his face, the tenseness in his massive shoulders.

The baby stopped sucking, so Glindi sat up, lifted her upright and held her close, gently patting her little back.

Mick settled next to her and put an arm around her shoulder. He muttered, "Maybe it's all right, ey?"

The baby opened her eyes. They were a remarkable green in colour.

Mick's body turned to granite, and his breath came in short gasps. "White man's eyes," he grated, but softly.

"Mick..."

"I'm not blaming you. How could you do anything, ey? And I'm not blaming the baby. But I wish..."

"Kill Richardson. I'd love you to kill him. Rip his filthy penis off and choke him with it. Kill him slowly and with great pain."

Standing behind Aunty Dara, Jila had lifted her chin, signalling "no," as soon as Glindi started to speak. Now she said, "If you do, and they find out it's one of the people, they'll do terrible payback."

Mick gently pushed Glindi away and stood. "Don't I know that, ey?" he answered, and walked out.

Glindi looked around the hut. Flattened kerosene tins walled its single room, tied on with bits of wire Mick had secretly broken off Richardson's boundary fence, risking his life. The roof was thick layers of bark he'd stripped from a fallen messmate tree, several years ago. This was the third hut he'd covered with the same roof. The only light came through the doorway, while the tattered old feedbag curtain was tied out of the way. She, Jila, Mick and the three children slept on horse blankets Mick had brought home, thrown out because they were no longer good enough for horses.

She'd seen how the white people lived, had often worked to clean or cook for them. That was when Richardson... no, she would not think about that. White people forced you to live worse than an animal, then treated you worse than they treated an animal, too.

With a sigh, she said, "I shall call this one Maraglindi." In the language, that meant 'Glindi's sorrow.'

Mick came back well after dark when the Ancestors showed their faces above. He said, "I've been talking it over with your brother, Riso. He asked advice from the Spirits of the Ancestors. They told us they have sent this girl. She is special and has special work to do. And it's not like you chose to have this happen, ey? She is my daughter."

"You need to decide on her spirit animal."

"I have." Mick stayed silent for a while, head hanging down. "I don't think she will ever get proper skin colour. She looks like a mud frog, ey? She can be our Froggie."

That got a grin from the whole family.

The next morning, Glindi said to Tari, "Honey child, you're now old enough to learn to care for babies. You can help me to wash your new little sister." Of course, Kohli wanted to join in too, but hey, she was only three years old.

So, Glindi told Atan to take her down to the river and give her some swimming practice, and to look for something nice to eat. Kohli went off happily enough with her big brother.

Glindi soon regained her strength after the birth, and joined the other women in their daily tasks, which mostly had to do with finding food. They were digging up bulrush roots from the shallows of a quiet backwater when the baby became restless. She put down her basket, woven from swordgrass leaves and, Kohli following her, went to sit with her back against a gnarled old redgum tree. She started feeding Maraglindi.

Aunty Dara saw her and walked over. "Is the little one good, ey?" she asked.

"Something is special about her. You know, with the other three I always got sore nipples, ey? Well, this baby stops sucking the moment I'm less than comfortable. It's exactly as if she knew."

"She certainly is a quiet baby. I haven't heard her cry yet."

"You're right. She hardly ever does. Oh well, as she grows, she'll be sure to find plenty of things to cry about."

As the baby fed, Glindi absentmindedly stroked Kohli's hair, her naked back, and watched the people. Women waded thigh-deep in the muddy water, chattering while they dug up food for several days from the bottom of the river shallows. Some of them wore nothing but a fur covering over their loins, in the old way, but most nowadays concealed their breasts behind old shirts, even here where white men seldom came. Over on the shore, the children played by being useful, digging up small crayfish, mud frogs and edible roots, under Klasina's supervision. After all, she was almost a woman now, and she skilfully encouraged the bigger ones to teach and supervise the smaller children.

Glindi looked across the wide river, to the far side where grass stretched forever, and the small dots of *cattle* grazed. She had to use the English name for the animals. She sighed: once, that had been black people's country. Now, going there meant being killed. Her own nation's land stretched all the way from here to the sea, but the white man had taken it all.

She burped her baby and held her at arm's length while she wetted. Then she put Maraglindi back in the padded basket woven from cane she had slung on her shoulder and returned to the pleasant task of gathering bulrush roots.

Mick

This morning, the men had managed to get a drifting log out of the river and dragged it ashore, then chopped most of the branches off with a couple of rusty axes white men had thrown out, supplemented by the old stone axes most people still used. So, Mick was tired but feeling good. As Old

Mother the Sun reached the top of the sky, he called to his children, "Go and wash your hands," and Atan led his two young sisters to the river. Smiling, Mick watched as they splashed each other, screaming and laughing, then ran back to the hut. He noticed that some of the flattened kerosene tins making up the wall were loose. He'd have to find something to rebind them with before the winds of winter came.

Jila came from the fire with a billyful of stew made from a freshly caught fish. Glindi stood, the baby in her arms. The tiny child's green eyes found Mick and sparkled at him. Surprisingly for such a young baby, her mouth curved in a smile. Mick felt warm all over, and said to Glindi, "There is good magic in this baby of ours."

She smiled at him too. "Take her," she offered.

He cuddled the baby, and Jila served up the stew as the three children burst in.

They all squatted to eat, and Mick put the baby down on her back on the compacted dirt floor.

He'd just finished his meal when a shadow crossed the door opening. A leg covered in trousers and expensive leather boots came into view. He felt his hands close into fists, and every muscle in his body tensed. A glance showed the fear in his family too.

But a pleasant, deep, friendly voice said, "Hey Mick, are

you home?"

He felt almost dizzy with relief. He stood up and said in English, "Mr MacCartney. Good afternoon, sir."

Bruce MacCartney strode in through the door opening, having to bend his head to fit through. He nodded to Jila then to Glindi and smiled around at the children. "I've got a bet to win," he said. "You see, Mick, I bought a killer horse a few days ago, and made a bet. He's just been delivered to my stud. I'll win two pounds if he can be tamed in a month. One of those pounds is yours if you'll do the work."

A whole pound! Instantly, within his heart's eye, Mick saw all the things so much money could buy: a couple of axes and a big two-man crosscut saw, some hand tools too like a saw and a hammer, winter clothes for all the village, since now hunting furry animals was so difficult...

"Sir, I start straight away, like," he said in immediate response.

"I thought you'd feel like that. Hmm. New baby?"

Mick glanced down to see Maraglindi's eyes fixed on the white man. Her tiny mouth was half open. He bent and picked her up. She twisted her head so she could keep looking at the visitor.

"Well, well, it's love at first sight, I see," Bruce said, and held out his hands.

Mick glanced at Glindi, who gave a tiny sideways

movement of her head, indicating yes. He passed the baby over. "As long as she don't wet you."

Bruce laughed. "Hey, a farmer gets worse. I suppose her name is something unpronounceable like yours."

Mick laughed too. "I can say me name. Nothin' hard about it. Mikadaragutara."

"Heh heh, I think I'll stick with Mick."

All of them laughed, even the little girls, although Mick knew their knowledge of English was not much yet. "My women, they call me Mick too."

Bruce held the baby in his two large hands, up real close to his face. They gazed into each other's eyes. Gently, he brought her even closer and stroked her face with the tip of his nose. Then he handed her back to Mick. "This baby girl is a very special little person," he said. "Can you see the beautiful silver glow all about her, and the special one above her head?"

Mick couldn't, but he knew that this man was special too. He had never known Bruce to be unkind to anyone, ever.

"I think she is one of God's chosen ones. But you haven't told me her name."

"Her name Maraglindi. But God don't bother with no blackfella girl."

The blue eyes drilled into him. "Don't ever say that, Mick. God cares for you and your people as much as for any other person. Look, Jesus was born into a race of people others have despised and rejected through the ages. We all are God's children, both you and I. Anyway, come over to my place when you can, and I'll introduce you to Devil. He has earned that name."

The MacCartney farms were over an hour's run away. Mick set off immediately, wanting to meet this killer horse. No horse ever born could stand up to his tricks, or dog either.

Steadily he loped along the outskirts of the town, then out past the dairy farms and smallholdings — all good land his ancestors had once cared for, but now the owner could shoot him for entering, and no white man would think it any worse than getting rid of a wombat that made a hole in a fence.

He arrived, only slightly puffing, and reported to Jim Ritter, the foreman.

"Oh yes, Mick, Mr MacCartney told me to expect you. Come and look at Devil."

The big black stallion was corralled by himself in a small square yard enclosed in shoulder-height post and rail fencing. He had a half-full water trough, and the scattered remains of a pile of hay, and nothing else. As the two men approached the fence, he turned to face them, his front legs stiff, ears back, eyes wild.

"Somebody very unkind to horse," Mick said.

"He just plain hates people. Have you thought about how you're going to start?"

Mick knew exactly what to do. "Get long rope, also gloves already used by somebody. And a few people to stir him up when I say so."

"Why the gloves?"

"I have to start being bad to him. I want him smell other person. With me, always good thing. For him, people enemy. I want him think me his friend."

Ritter grinned. "You're cunning all right. No wonder you're the best horse breaker I've ever met." He went off to get the rope and gloves, while Mick stood, watching Devil.

You're a blackfella like me, he thought. *Even more black, ey? And the white man was cruel to you, too. And I have to make you like them, and to do as you're told.*

Ritter returned with a coil of rope over his shoulder. Three youngsters, Connor, Gaspar and Jake, were with him, and Bruce MacCartney himself.

"Hi there, Mick, you didn't waste any time?"

"No Sir. I here." Mick put on the gloves, uncoiled the rope and laid it out in a snake pattern on the ground. He tied a big noose in one end, and securely tied the other end to a post of Devil's fence.

The horse watched the people, nostrils distended, teeth

showing. He pawed the ground, tearing up sod.

Mick said, "Now, make some noise, wave at him. I want him run."

The three young men enthusiastically did so, and the horse went mad. He charged at them, turning at the last moment so he bashed the fence with his flank, then galloped over to the other side of his enclosure. He turned without slowing and charged back again.

As he neared, Mick swung the noose, making lazy circles around his head. When the stallion turned again, he cast the rope. The noose neatly settled around the big black head, and as Mick tugged, it tightened around the neck. Then he took the gloves off and handed them back to Ritter.

The horse screamed and reared high. He shook his head side to side, then charged off once more until the rope stopped him, bringing him to his knees.

Mr MacCartney shouted over the animal's noise, "Hey listen Mick, I don't want you to kill him!"

Mick merely smiled in response.

The one-sided battle went on for several hours. Old Mother the Sun was well down in the sky when finally Devil gave up. He stood trembling all over, with his head hanging down. Foam covered his face, and every line spoke of exhaustion.

Mick said, "A bit of a shove and he fall over, ey? All same,

Mr MacCartney, when I walk away, you wave if he move." He placed a hand on the top rail and vaulted over in one movement.

Devil watched through bloodshot eyes, but did not stir.

Slowly, ever so slowly, Mick approached him, always looking at the horse without gazing directly into his eyes. He stopped to the side, but where the animal could still see him. Very slowly he raised his hands and untied the noose, careful not to touch the sweat-covered, black-haired skin. Then he turned his back on the stallion, and equally slowly walked over to his waiting audience. He was sure he'd be safe. Despite this, he fixed his eyes on Bruce, and his whole being waited for a sound from behind, for vibration with each bare foot at each step.

At last, he reached the fence and vaulted over again.

"Well done, Mick," Bruce said. "Get a bagful of rations for your family off the cook."

"Thank you sir. I come dawn tomorrow."

He was too heavily laden to run on the way home, the cook having been generous. He'd also said, "Hey Mick, bring that bag back tomorra and I'll fill'er up for youse again." The whole little village would eat well for the next month. This was why everyone liked to work for Bruce, or for his young missus in the house. They were decent people, the both of them, not like most whites.

Darkness soon overtook him. He knew Daughter Moon would not show Her face until well after midnight, and no clouds marred the sky. As he strode along, his bare feet automatically finding the easiest footing away from the sharp stones that covered the road, Mick looked up at all the many Spirits of the Ancestors. Up there they glimmered. They had cared for this land, and the land had cared for them. He wondered what they thought about the way the white man had *stolen* it, but to think the thought, he needed to use their word for the idea. His language, the language of those spirits up there, contained no word for theft.

His nose picked up the smell of a wombat before he saw the movement. The sturdy animal scurried off into a thicket. *You're safe, little brother*, Mick thought. No need to hunt, with what he carried.

He reached the entry road into Richardsons'.

Mick stopped and looked at the tiny glimmer of light that was the homestead, a good mile away. He'd long ago learned about the white man's measures.

He put his bag onto a flattish rock, from habit leaving minimal marks of his passing, and sent the hate within his heart through his eyes. He could go in there, and not even the dogs would react to his presence. He had made friends with those dogs, long ago. As always, he was carrying his fire tools with him. He could burn the house down, and burn the evil monster with it.

But if, despite all his care, he was discovered, there would be slaughter. Jila, Glindi, the children, his parents, brothers and sisters and cousins... Besides, some of the people were in there, working as servants. Likely, Richardson was forcibly coupling with a woman, right now, and never mind his wife in the next room. Sighing, he picked up his bag and walked off toward the river.

The red glow of their fire still survived outside the hut. Within, he smelt his family and heard the soft snuffling of the sleeping children. He saw the barest light glint off Glindi's teeth as she smiled. "You brought food," she whispered. "I can smell some good stuff."

"The people will eat well while I play with that *horse*."

"I knew you were coming. Our Maraglindi woke up a couple of minutes ago, didn't cry or anything, but looked toward the door. And then you walked in."

Mick put the bag down, pulled the old sack curtain back across the doorway, and knelt next to Glindi. He reached out, and in the dark found a soft hand, very, very small. He picked the baby up and held her close.

Bruce MacCartney was right. Mick could see the faintest of glows outlining the tiny shape.

***

Satisfied with his progress, a week later Mick carried a

well-laden food bag on his shoulder, Old Mother the Sun, low in the sky, warming his bare back. Yesterday, for the first time, he'd put a halter on Devil. Today, he'd managed to lead him around with it, using a succession of apple pieces as bait. Give it a couple more days, he thought, and he'd have a saddle on the big stallion.

He strode into the settlement, by habit his eyes skipping over the squalor. In the old days, his people moved to a new place every few days, but now a tribe on walkabout was at risk of being shot, so it was here or dead. He sighed at the thought, but cheered up as people raced toward him, or more exactly toward the bag of food he carried. Grinning widely, exchanging jokes with them all, he shared out Bruce's bounty, before turning for his own hut. He handed their share of the food over to Jila. "I'm a mighty hunter, can spear a swiftly running *loaf of bread*" — said in English — "and various other strange beasts."

His family laughed. The baby smiled too and looked at him with those strange green eyes.

Atan said, "Father, one day I want you to teach me how to tame *horses* too."

"You can be sure of that. Everything I know, you will know too. And everything your father Riso knows, you'll know too. You will be a magic man one day, and talk with the Spirits like he can."

Atan seemed to grow and mature before his eyes, even if to a white man he was only an Abo boy — less than human, less than an animal even.

Mick felt happy. What you lived in, how you were forced to live didn't matter. Being with people who loved you and whom you loved was the only important thing.

2

Glindi

The year turned and turned again. Glindi sat with several other young mothers around a flat stone, under the shade of the biggest Burrawang tree. It was comfortable beneath the many arching long-leafed branches, which was just as well, because getting the nuts out of the cones had been awkward work. You didn't want a poisonous leaf to cut you. Each used a sharp piece of flint to slice the many red seeds while idly chatting. Glindi rhythmically cut one seed after another, dropping them into a finely woven cane basket by her side.

A tiny boy reached into his mother's basket. "Gita no!" she removed the stuff from his hand. "That's poisonous. Don't even think about eating it. We soak them in the river for ten days, then we'll roast them, then you can have some." She stood while saying this and picked him up. "Now, quickly, we'll go and wash it all off your hands. If you lick your hand now, you'll get terribly sick. It may even kill you." They soon returned. "Remember!" she said. "Don't you ever touch Burrawang nuts again!"

"Yes, Ma." The little boy turned and ran off. He always seemed to be running rather than walking.

Glindi looked down at her own baby. Maraglindi was

actually a couple of months older than Gita, but all the same, she hadn't even started crawling yet, never mind walking. And while other children her age happily chatted away, she only made meaningless noises, although often they sounded very melodious, almost like singing. Also, her skin was still much paler than other people's, a light brown like a mud frog's. Mick had been right about that, way back at the birth, giving her the mud frog as her spirit animal. Ah well, she was wonderful in some ways, slow in others. Aren't we all, ey?

Mick was away, far away, *droving* a mob of *cattle* for Mr Geery. He'd have *money* to share with everyone when he returned... if he returned. Sometimes, men went to work for a white man and died on the way. As she had this thought, she felt a butterfly touch on her arm. She looked down. Maraglindi's green eyes shone into hers, and a smile curved her mouth. The child cooed an odd wordless song, and, somehow, Glindi felt reassured. Mick would be all right, she knew that now.

When all the seeds were sliced up, each woman temporarily tied a lid onto her basket. They picked them up, as well as the babies as yet unable to walk. "Up you come!" Glindi said, picking up Maraglindi, and walked to the river with the rest of the group. Gita and the other toddlers ran straight into the water and started to swim around, arms and legs thrashing up a foam. Glindi lowered her own child into the cool water and supported her with two hands. Maraglindi moved her arms and legs vigorously enough, but without coordination. She floated all right, she but didn't manage to move in any direction. "Never mind, my little Froggie," Glindi told her, "as long as you learn not to sink. When you're ready, you'll do everything."

Several minutes before the other mothers, she fished her child out, dried her, and put her with her back against a tree, well away from the river. She walked to a bush by the shore, tied a thin but strong grass rope to it, tied the other end to her basket, then lifted the lid and put a big stone into the basket to weigh it down. A few more knots secured the lid. She waded then swam out to the full length of the rope, and dropped the basket, to see it sink. She started swimming back toward the shore and saw something odd going on. She couldn't quite make out what...

Screams and barks made her speed up. Those shapes were a group of white boys, laughing while their *dogs* chased the brown toddlers. She and the other women desperately raced to shore. She was the first, and when still knee-deep in water, felt a stone under her foot. Hardly slowing she bent, snatched and threw, the stone smashing into the skull of a large beast that had a child by her arm.

"You leave our babies alone!" she screamed in English. Full speed, she rushed out of the water and dived, her hands closing from behind around the throat of a *dog* that was savaging a fallen child. She stood, holding the animal, and squeezed, and squeezed and squeezed until it stopped struggling and went limp in her grasp.

She looked at the boys. A couple seemed angry, but she was beyond caring. None had moved while looking at her. She knew every one of them, knew their families. If only she could hurt them...

She threw the dead *dog* at their feet. "I tell our magic man. He put terrible magic on you for this. You suffer like my babies suffer, only worse."

They slunk away, but Glindi had no more attention for them. Gita lay in front of her, his throat torn open. Nobody could help him anymore.

All the women were ashore by now, caring for their children. Glindi went to her own. Maraglindi still quietly sat with her back against the tree, although tears wetted her face, and she'd bitten her lip so it bled. All the same, maybe being slow at moving was not a bad thing. Glindi ran to her and picked her up with a sob. She was surprised that a two-year-old child could react to the terrible act — but then, wasn't that typical of her baby? While thinking about this, she went to comfort Gita's mother.

That night, Glindi visited Riso in his hut, leaving Atan to look after his sisters.

Balini, Riso and young Granat welcomed her. She said, "Brother, a dreadful thing happened today. I promised those boys that you'll put a magic on them, so they'll suffer worse than our babies."

"I will do that. I've already been thinking on the matter."

"It'd be fitting if they were to be poisoned by Burrawang seeds. After all, they interrupted that part of our year's work."

"It would be fitting indeed. Sister, who were they, ey?"

She reeled off their names.

"Leave it with me." He turned to his family. "Granat, while I'm away, look after Balini—"

"Of course. It's my baby she is carrying, after all."

Riso just smiled approvingly.

As night fell, Riso emerged from his hut, with his face and chest bearing an intricate pattern of white markings. He lit a special fire, and when it was hot, he put a branch of green gum leaves on it. He danced around the spiralling smoke, chanting words no one else understood. Somehow, the fire didn't burn down but kept going, sending scented smoke up into the dark sky.

At last, Riso stopped. Almost immediately, the fire died down into a red glow. Without a word, the magic man turned and walked off into the night.

Maude McTaskill

As if from a distance, Maude heard Dr Daniel Horton say, "I am so sorry. Archie, Maude, I couldn't save him. He is the fourth of the seven to have... gone."

Archie took out a handkerchief and wiped at his face. "But... what caused it?" he asked.

"We don't know yet. Some kind of poison, or sickness of the alimentary tract—"

"Talk English, won't ya!"

"His guts."

"Oh."

"Can I see... see him?" Maude asked.

The doctor looked helpless, so she knew to brace herself.

Dr Horton led them along a corridor, to a double door. He opened one side to usher them in. As they entered the large back room of the doctor's house, the first thing to hit her was the terrible stench. Gerald Kline, her son's best friend, lay in a bed near the door, throwing himself around in obvious agony. The stink came from there.

The assistant bending over him gave the doctor a reproving glance. "Can you return in a few moments?" he said, his voice distorted. Maude realised he was doing his best to avoid breathing.

The three of them turned and left the room.

She imagined her Harvey, soiling himself like that, presumably without being able to control it, and shuddered. There was nothing to say.

At last, the nurse hurried out, carrying a big bundle of bedclothing at arm's length, the stench following him like a miasma. The doctor waited a further moment, then ushered them in again. Maude was barely able to spare the energy to smile at Gerald, and at the wan faces in the two other beds along the wall. Lightweight room dividers hid another bed at the end. They went behind them. Harvey — Harvey's body — looked very small under the white sheet, his face a lot thinner than a week ago, when he and his six friends had been rushed to the doctor's house while uncontrollably vomiting. She looked at her son and wanted to cry, but could not. She just felt a great stone weigh down her heart.

What was there to do? An unmeasured silence passed, then she took her husband's hand and led him out of the room, out of the doctor's house.

Gerald

Gerald sat on the edge of his bed, exhausted from the effort of having got dressed, despite Bill's assistance. The door opened, and the great stomach came in, followed by Father. That's how Gerald always thought of him. Only, this time he didn't manage to have the usual inner chuckle.

Father stopped and looked down at Gerald. "You ready to come home?" he asked, as if he didn't care one way or the other.

"Yes Father, but..."

"But what?"

"Roger. How is Roger?"

"Your dog? I had to put him out of his misery."

"Oh." Gerald managed not to cry.

"It was only a dog. You can have another one if you want."

Gerald wanted to say no, he was not only a dog, he was my friend, but Father would never understand.

"Come on then." Father turned and started walking for the door.

Gerald managed to stand, then with a cry collapsed back onto the bed.

Father turned, impatience painted on his face. "Be a man," he grated.

Gerald bit his lip and stood again. He took a step, wobbled, then slipped to the floor.

Father's roar vibrated the room. "A man shows no weakness! What are you, a milksop?"

Dr Horton stormed through the door, shouting nearly as loudly as Father, "Mr Kline, this is unconscionable!" He lifted Gerald back onto the bed even as Bill came running

in. The doctor said to him, "Get the letter of instructions."
Bill returned almost immediately and gave Father an
envelope.

Dr Horton glared at Father. "Listen here, Mr Kline. Six
of the boys have died." Gerald's heart formed a knot at this
reminder. "Your son still lives — barely. If your lack of
consideration kills him also, then you'll be a murderer."

I'm a murderer, Gerald thought, in his mind's eye seeing
the black toddler with George's dog at his throat.

The doctor and the nurse helped Gerald to stand and,
one walking on each side, gently assisted him toward the
door. Even so, he was panting, his knees shaking, by the time
they reached the front entrance. Bill stepped up into the
carriage and took hold of Gerald under the arms, while Dr
Horton lifted the lower half of his body.

Gerald slumped onto the upholstered seat, thinking, *I
don't deserve this care. Why couldn't I have died, too?*

He heard Dr Horton say, "Mr Kline, the instructions in
this note must be followed to the letter. When you reach
home, ensure the lad is gently lifted down and assisted in.
Feed him frequent small amounts of something like broth at
first. He'll soon regain his strength. I'll come to visit him
within the next day or two."

Father clambered up and sat beside Gerald. Neither said
anything until they arrived home. Then Father got down

without a word and went inside. Gerald waited a moment, then shifted sideways on the seat until he reached the door. He managed to stand and was about to lower a foot onto the step when Father returned with two of the menservants. "What are you doing?" he shouted.

Gerald pulled his foot back. "Being a man," he dared to say.

Father didn't answer. "Lift him down and escort him to the armchair by the hearth," he said and went inside.

Bartley and Smith were less skilled than the doctor and his assistant, but eventually Gerald was settled in the chair. Although everyone else was sweating, he felt cold, so Smith draped a blanket around him just as Mother came in. "Welcome home, son," she said.

"Thank you, Mother."

"You're nothing but trouble. You've caused me more grief than the other five put together."

"I—"

"Whatever made you eat Burrawang seeds? What kind of an idiot does that?"

Gerald couldn't answer this. He stayed silent.

"Well?"

"Mother, I'm sorry for the trouble I caused you."

Tildy came in with a steaming bowl. Mother snorted and left the room. "Oh Master Gerald," Tildy said, tears running down her cheeks, "I'm so glad you gunna be orright!"

"Maybe."

"Oh, you will! Look, me sweet, you's shivering! 'Ere, eat this and I'll light the fire for ya."

She put the bowl down then stroked his hair, pulled him to her. His parents couldn't spare the kindness this ticket-of-leave convict servant gave freely, from her heart. This suddenly made Gerald feel like crying. He snuggled into Tildy's softness, enjoyed the comfort, but then pulled away.

"I better not let Father see me being weak."

"Gentlefolk's crazy," Tildy answered, handing him the bowl. She went to the fireplace. "You's only twelve, and had a great scare, whassamatter with a bit'o love and carin'?"

Maude

Having heard a few days later that Gerald was at home, Maude went to visit him. She'd heard the news, but needed to hear his version from himself.

The boy huddled in a large armchair in front of a blazing log fire, despite the raging summer heat outside. Maude was shocked at his paleness, the way he had shrunk. At least he was still alive. "Good morning, Mrs McTaskill," he said, and even his voice sounded weak.

"Good morning, Gerald my dear. I'm so glad that at last you're on the mend."

"It's not fair, I ought to have died too."

"Why? What are you saying?"

"It was the Abo woman's punishment."

This didn't make sense. "What?" Maude asked.

"I'm sorry, ma'am, all seven of us did wrong, so we got struck by their magic. I didn't tell this to the doctor, or to Mother or Father, because they'd go and hurt the blacks, but I know I'm safe to tell you. Please, can you keep my secret?"

"You can tell me anything you wish to. I'll keep your secret if you want me to." Within her thoughts, she wondered if his sickness had affected his mind as well.

"We were out for a bit of fun. It was Saturday, no school, and we didn't have anything to do. So, we took our dogs out to see if we could flush some rabbits."

"And?"

"And we flushed black babies instead." She could see the horror on his thin face. "I'm so sorry! George sicced his mutt onto this little fella, then all the dogs chased them and we laughed, I mean, it seemed jus' like they was chasing rabbits. Then... then the mothers came out of the river, they was in there. One black woman threw a stone and nearly killed my dog, then she choked another dog to death. She looked at us and cursed us. Said we'd suffer worse than her babies. And my father killed my dog later anyway."

He fell silent for a long time.

At last, Maude said, "I heard it was Burrawang poisoning."

"It was, but as we went away, I realised, they was babies. People, like. Not animals. What we did was terrible. It was murder. And I don't even want to hurt animals no more."

Maude didn't think it appropriate to correct his grammar.

"Anyway, the next morning, when it was still dark, I felt this... I dunno, I needed to go to the river. I jus' had to. Not like somebody told me to, it was just what I must do. And the other boys met me there. All seven of us. We didn't speak or nothing. We went to the stand of Burrawang trees, you know, on the small hill?"

Maude nodded.

"We climbed up and collected as many seeds as we could. It just wasn't possible not to do it, I couldn't stop even when the leaves cut me. Then we ate all the seeds."

"You did know that they were poisonous?"

"Oh yeah, we been told, sure, but we couldn't help it. We jus' had to eat them. It was the Abo magic like I said. But please, keep my secret. I don't want them to be hurt. I'll never hurt another person or animal, ever again."

Maude sank to her knees next to the chair, tears in her eyes, and put her arms around the boy's bony shoulders. "May the good Lord help you to keep that vow, my dear," she whispered.

3

Atan

Atan came running from the river with the three other boys of about his age, and saw Father sitting cross-legged, his back against the side of the hut. He wore the shirt and trousers Mr Geery had given him before taking him far away to drove *cattle* to *market*. Atan was proud of knowing the English words, although "market" didn't mean anything to him.

"Come here, boy," Father called.

Atan ran over, saying, "Look, Father, I've got a big yabby. Good eating, ey?"

"You're a great finder of food, and now you're old enough to learn to be a hunter as well." He held up a perfect little spear, exactly the right length for Atan.

"A spear? My spear!"

It was straight, from a springy, tough grasstree stalk. Its hardwood point was fire-hardened in the old way, although it didn't have flint barbs.

"Not only one, I've made three spears for you." Father held up the other two. "And a launcher." The launcher was the length of Atan's lower arm, its handle just right for his hand, and with a sharp spur glued to the other end.

He wanted to hold it.

Father stood up in a smooth movement, graceful as always, the four weapons in his hand. "Come on!" He ran off to the north, toward the forest.

Of course Atan followed him, doing his best to imitate Father's long strides. Just when he thought he'd fall over with exhaustion, Father stopped, whirled, and next thing, he was up in the air, draped over a muscular shoulder. Father kept running, laughing at the same time.

They arrived among the trees, and Father went to an old, mossy fallen log. He put Atan down and pulled out his own three spears and launcher. These were proper hunting tools, longer than Father was tall, with three sharp pieces of flint glued to the tip.

He handed the small weapons over.

Atan felt his right hand join the handle of the launcher like they were the one thing, grown together, and held the three spears in the left.

Father said, "Watch me." He fitted the end of one of his spears to the spur of his launcher. In the same movement his hand lifted to his ear, then whipped forward. The spear whistled as it sprung into the air and neatly hit the centre of a red, yellow-spotted fungus. Hardly had it landed before the second spear hit the same fungus, then the third.

Father ran the fifty steps or so to retrieve his spears. "You can aim for that one over there." The fungus he pointed at with his chin was about ten steps from Atan.

Confidently, Atan fitted a spear and held his arm just like Father — but when he threw, the spear came loose and fell at his feet.

"Son, the same thing happened to me when I was a boy. Do it many times. You'll soon be a great hunter."

Atan tried again, and again, and always Father smiled and said encouraging things.

At last, the spears flew with a sharp whip, like Father's. All the same, frustratingly, they hit everywhere except into the target.

His arm was sore from all the effort when Father said, "Well done, son. We can come back again tomorrow. In a few days, you'll get the aim right. Then we'll go for distance. Then I'll teach you how to use a throwing stick. Right, it's time to go home."

They hid both sets of weapons under the old log and walked back to the village. On the way, Father said, "Never let the white people know you have weapons. It's a secret for you and me only."

They walked into the hut. "Where have you been, Brother, ey?" Tari demanded.

"Men's business," Atan said importantly, feeling very big.

Maraglindi sat on the floor by a wall, holding a rag doll

Old Mother and Tari had made for her from scraps. She smiled when seeing the two of them and sang a musical nonsense sound. Other children her age ran around, but she didn't even crawl yet. That was all right, though. Atan got down on his hands and knees and put his face close to hers. She gurgled, dropped the doll and grabbed his hair with both hands.

"Ow! Don't pull!" he said, pretending pain, but she somehow sensed the pretence and laughed with him. He gathered her onto his lap as he sat. "When are you going to walk, ey?" He held her upright, his hands supporting her under the arms, so her feet were on the ground. He could see that she was trying, but as soon as he eased his support, she slumped down onto her bottom.

"Never mind, Atan my son," Mother said. "She is different, ey? She's sure to walk and talk and wet in the right places when she is ready."

Atan laughed. "It's like she didn't know how to use her own body."

The rain started after dark that night. Atan was glad he could snuggle in his blanket, under a thick roof of bark, and listened to the gentle patter of raindrops hitting the ground outside. Old Mother and the two girls were already asleep, but he heard Father and Mother sharing bodies. He smiled to himself, glad they were happy. After all, Father had been away for a long time.

Suddenly, the baby gave a musical gurgle, then another, louder one.

It was only after this that Atan heard hesitant footsteps outside, squelching in the mud. He saw the yellow flicker of a light of some kind.

Father was on his feet, his naked body outlined against the door opening as he moved the sack sideways. "Master Kline," he said, "you are lost, ey?"

Atan heard a boy's hesitant voice. "No. I... I brought a present for you... for everyone."

"We don't need nothing. But wait a moment."

Atan heard Father putting on his white man's trousers and shirt, and the two Mothers putting on white woman dresses. Then Father was back at the doorway. "Come in, Master Kline."

Atan thought the boy was maybe his age, twelve years old, but he looked terribly thin. He wore a dark coat that seemed to shed the rain, and a wide-brimmed hat with water dripping off it. In his right hand he carried an object Atan had heard about but had never seen before: a *lantern* with a flickering flame burning within a cage with walls you could see through. The boy had a bag in his left hand. He put this down, then took his hat off.

"I came now because nobody else is silly enough to walk

in the rain," he said, still sounding scared. "I am... I'm one of the boys who, God have mercy on my soul, killed that child." He shrunk in upon himself and looked as if he expected to be attacked.

Mother said, "I know. I recognised you then. What you want now, ey?"

"I can never make up for it, but... but I want to do something. I have lots of clothes I don't need, and got them together. With winter coming, I was hoping your children will be able to use them. Please, accept this gift."

"You took a risk," Father mused aloud. "White people not like it that you do this. And some blackfellas maybe hate you and do you harm."

"I know, but I don't care. From now on, I will always do what's right, not what is safe or expected. If I can, I'd like to be friends with you people."

In the dim light of the *lantern*, Atan saw Maraglindi sit up near Father and Mother's place, waving her arms. She rolled over, her bottom up in the air, and then to Atan's surprise, she managed to stand. Wobbling wildly, she took a few steps, fell over, stood again in the same way, and continued her shaky advance toward the boy, wobbling, falling, and standing again twice more. All the family watched in silent amazement.

At last she reached him. He dropped to a knee, put the

lantern down and held out his hands. She grasped them and voiced a happy, wordless song.

Gerald Kline said, softly, "I've been blessed. Thank you."

Maraglindi

Without sound, without even words within her heart, Maraglindi thought:

Birds singing. Lovely. Dark here. Light around curtain. I can sing like birds. I want to sing like birds.

No. People still asleep. Stay quiet.

Somebody coming. Two people. New people. They come to me. They want to see me.

I can wake people. I can sing like birds.

Father sitting up. Smiling at me. I love Father.

I make more bird noise.

Outside, man says, "Mikadaragutara, you are home, ey?"

"Come in, Glaskodantil," Father calls. He is grinning.

A man comes in. He and Father hug. He says, "I am here with my sister-son Kiri." He looks at me. "That's why we're here of course, to look at your daughter. She is the right moiety." I don't know the words, but I know his heart.

Mother asks, "Is he outside? I need to go."

"No, I left him some distance away to give you time to hide."

Mother peeks out, then slips through the doorway. She

thinks, *Quickly, if he sees me it will spoil the marriage.* I don't know what this means, but I love Mother.

Glaskodantil also goes out. He comes back with the other person. He looks much more like Atan. Big boy. No beard. Thin body.

Old Mother says, "Kiri, how you've grown! And a married man. I'm going outside to light the fire."

Father picks me up and asks me, "Froggie, would you like to marry this fine young man?"

Everybody laughs. They all know I don't speak.

Kiri thinks, *Oh, she looks strange, her colour, she is so pale...* I want him to love me. Hold out hands to him. Smile. Look into eyes.

He steps forward. Looks at Father. Father says yes with his head. Kiri holds me.

I send him all the love I can. His heart glows with love. I can do this.

Father says, "Well, Glasko, looking at their faces, that's settled then?"

Again, everybody laughs.

Mick

Mick opened his eyes to see the doorway as a faint rectangle, with a bit of a breeze fluttering the makeshift curtain. He rolled to his feet, quickly dressed and walked out into the pink of dawn. Somehow, something was wrong. He heard a sound that should not have been there, a faint drumming in the soles of his bare feet. Galloping horses.

Then it was too late to do anything. Five horses charged into the collection of huts. Five hated men rode them, shouting and yelling now.

A brown gelding with Archie McTaskill on it shouldered into a hut, knocking it sideways. Screams came from inside.

A terrible, sharp sting struck Mick's chest. His already tattered shirt split in two.

Whiskey bottle in his left hand, *whip* in the right, Harry Highfield shouted, "We're having a hunt. Run, you black bastard!" Mick's blood stained the end of the whip.

Richardson, coming in last, yelled, "Nah! Not yet, it's no sport that way. Line up five bucks, and we'll give 'em five minutes' start."

The two Geery brothers rode together, as always. Each held a gun, and their eyes looked crazy. Jim Geery said, "Everyone out or we'll start shootin' into the hovels!"

Mick knew that people would be huddling within their homes, and many understood little English. So, he shouted in the Gathang language, "You must come outside or they start killing. Come out now."

People did. As they slowly emerged, Mick saw scared faces and tense bodies. Glindi walked out from their hut, already swelling slightly with the next child, carrying Maraglindi. Jila supported her with a hand on her other arm. The three older children huddled close to them. Within minutes, the terrified little crowd stood there, waiting.

Richardson nudged his horse into a slow walk and pointed his gun at Riso, then in quick succession at Tiri, Mick's younger brother Tako, Harodim, and finally at Mick.

"I have a wife and children," he said.

Tom Geery lifted his gun, and Mick saw Kohli's head explode. Red gore splashed Glindi and the other children. Kohli's body flew back against the hut, then slid to the ground.

Silence followed the bang. Then Tom laughed into it as he started to reload his gun. "One less, you black bastard. Argue, will you?"

Mick's inside froze. He'd never been this angry in his life, but it was a cold, calculating anger. "I will run," he said, surprising himself with the level tone of his voice. He then turned to the other four, and said in the language, "Start running now. If I can, I'll delay them for a short while. Go!"

They took off at a lope, toward the forest, maybe half a mile to the north.

"You too!" Jim Geery said with a sneer, pointing his gun.

Mick said, "What your Jesus think about this, ey?"

Richardson waved at Jim to stop him from shooting. He

sneered down at Mick. "Jesus is for people, not for monkeys. Now run you black bastard or I will let him shoot you."

Mick ran.

He didn't know what a monkey was, but this monkey had teeth. His three spears and the launcher were hidden under the fallen log, a few steps within the forest.

As he ran, his heart's eyes kept seeing his daughter's headless little body, slumping down. They could do nothing worse than this. He would kill them.

He reached the trees, and as soon as he was under cover, he turned left and found the mossy old fallen log. He picked up his weapons, then stopped on the north side of a tall tree. He called on the Spirits, as on a hunt. *They can't see me... they can't see me*, he kept chanting without sound, over and over.

This magic worked on kangaroos and emus. It worked on the white men. He felt the vibration of their coming through the ground, heard the hoofbeats and the men's drunken shouting. Two charged past, then two more. Being heaviest, Richardson was the last by more than a horse's length.

Mick had a spear ready, its end snuggled into the launcher. He drew back his arm and hurled true.

The force of the spear threw Richardson forward. He slid to the ground on the right side of his horse. The animal slowed, then stopped well beyond.

Mick was there in an instant. The spear had struck the back of the man's fat neck and exited through his mouth. Mick jerked it out, then turned the big body over. Blood gushed from Richardson's mouth and his eyes looked puzzled. Mick placed the point of the spear on his chest and put all his weight on it. *Through the heart. Good*, he thought. This one was for Glindi.

He knew the big mare, he'd trained her himself before Richardson had bought her. He clicked his tongue, and the horse came to him. He mounted, and then got her to run. If he'd had the time, he'd have killed the monster slowly, but four others waited...

He lay down flat over the horse's neck, holding his spears horizontally, and once more invoked the magic: *They can't see me... They can't see me...*

The other white men had spread out, riding among trees as they were. Mick used his knees to steer the horse toward Harry — payback time for the whipping.

Harry must have heard his coming, for he turned in the saddle. "Hey, Isaac, where are you?" he asked, then louder, "Richarson's off his horse!"

Close enough. Mick sat up, right arm already drawing back. Harry's mouth opened, whether to shout or in surprise, Mick didn't care. His spear entered that open mouth, with enough force that its broken tip lifted the man's hat off his head.

Harry crashed to the ground as Mick galloped past.

"Whatya sayin', Harry?" came Archie's high-pitched voice from the left. He rode into sight, and like Harry Highfield, his look of amazement was comical, but Mick wasn't laughing.

Archie lifted his gun as the two horses approached each other at a great rate. Mick had his next spear ready, but too slow. He threw as he saw the gun's recoil punch into the white man's shoulder.

The bullet went someplace, nowhere near him, but the spear flew true. Archie was thrown backward as the two horses raced past each other.

But now the Geery brothers were coming at him, side by side, guns raised. He threw himself to the right and jerked the horse's head around too. Instantly, he pulled her left. He heard the two guns shoot, almost at the same time. A frightening whistle went past him, then he rode for the brothers again.

Jim was raising his right hand. It held a short gun.

Mick fitted his last spear and threw. He saw it penetrate Jim's chest.

Tom, the one Mick really wanted, wheeled his horse to the south and kicked it into a gallop. Back to town...

No time to retrieve a spear. Mick urged his horse

forward, with kindness as always, not like the wretch ahead who used whip and spurs to torture more speed out of his mount.

Go horse! He killed my daughter! Go horse! He killed my daughter! Mick's inner chant carried him closer and closer to his quarry.

Tom was heavier than Mick, and Mick could always get the best out of any animal.

At exactly the right time, he stood on the saddle and leapt. Hands around Tom's neck, he dragged the two of them to the ground. He landed with Tom under him and they rolled over and over.

Finally, they stopped moving, Tom underneath again. Mick stared into his terrified eyes as he squeezed the last bit of life out of him.

He was unable to move for a long time, just lay in the long grass, exhaustion and grief and the last remnant of anger weighing him down.

At last, he felt the running footsteps from the north, and then his four friends were with him.

Tako said, "Brother, you have killed them!"

Mick struggled to his feet. "I have killed all five of the monsters. May their spirits rot forever."

"That's wonderful," Riso, the eldest, said. "But now what will they do to the people, ey?"

"What were they doing to the people already, ey? This rotten shit" — he kicked Tom's head — "killed my darling Kohli."

"I know, Mikadaragutara." Riso's use of Mick's full name meant serious business. "Now we must protect our people from payback."

Harodim started to laugh, although the sound was savage rather than happy. The others looked at him.

"Risobanda, your Father and his Father before him and his Father before him were magic men, all the way back to the Dreamtime, ey?"

"Yes, and I also know the magic."

"Then you've used it. These white men hunted us. We went into a secret place in the forest, and there you used your magic and turned them into black ravens and they flew away."

Tako said, "We first have to get rid of the bodies."

That was not a problem. Mick answered, "We tie stones to them and throw them into the river, well downstream. I've watched them clean their *guns* before, so I know I can do it. We clean their *guns* so it looks like they haven't been used, except for this Tom monster's, because he used it... at our place." He had to stop a moment to gather himself. "And we make sure the *horses* look exactly the way they should, no blood, but sweated up from running, then let

49

them wander off. They're sure to get to their homes some time or other. Then, Risobanda, you need to put on a convincing storytelling for the white men. And you know Sergeant Dawson is a good man. He'll be angry with them for killing a child."

"Sure. I can do that."

It was nearly night by the time the five bodies were safely at the bottom of the river, and the five men could go home.

Mick saw Glindi sitting on the ground, cuddling a small shape wrapped in one of their sleeping blankets. Her eyes were swollen and red, but she was no longer crying.

She looked up and a brief smile came to her lips. "You're still alive. Good."

"I've killed all five."

"Good."

Maraglindi was snuggling against her mother's side. Now she stood and held out her arms. Mick picked her up and was instantly comforted. He felt the tension leave his shoulders. The tiny girl took hold of his beard and turned his head. Her green eyes gazed into his, then she spoke the first words he'd ever heard her say: "Kohli happy now. I look after her." This made no sense to him whatever, but all the same, a feeling of peace and acceptance soothed his spirit.

The police came the next morning. Sergeant Dawson

rode in, with two troopers behind him. He came to Mick's hut and dismounted. "G'day, Mick."

"G'day, Sergeant."

"I need your tracking skills."

"What happen, ey?

"Five men went out yesterday, but their horses came back without them."

"Sure thing. I help. Who, ey?"

"The Geery boys, Mr Highfield, Mr Richardson and Mr McTaskill."

"Then Sergeant, I happy they lost. All cruel men."

Dawson looked shocked. "Mr McTaskill is a Church elder. Mr Richardson is one of the richest men in the district. You cannot make such a statement, my lad."

"Sergeant, I know people from what they do. These are unkind to my people. You, fair man. Hard if needed, that is good, ey? But you are not cruel."

"Thanks for the reference, lad. Now I'd like you to come to Richardson's, that's the nearest, and backtrack their horses to see where they've been."

Mick had to think fast. If he showed the white man the tracks, they'd lead back right here. Then he'd be caught for not telling the truth. Should he tell the Sergeant about yesterday's hunt, and then use Riso's magical demonstration? He knew the magic man was ready with his show. But would it be safer to mislead the police?

Dawson looked at him. "Somethin's on your mind, Mick."

Mick looked at the solid strength of this man. *He is smart. He will know if I track wrong.* Taking a deep breath, he said, "Sergeant, no need to track. I tell you what happen yesterday."

He looked around, to see the whole village in a semicircle, watching, listening. Mick touched eyes with Riso, who signalled "yes."

"Those five men. At dawn they rode right into here. I can show you tracks. They had guns and were drunk. Prob'ly drink all night. Mr Highfield hit me with a whip." Mick lifted the front of his shirt, showing the long scab over split skin.

The sergeant looked angry, clearly sympathetic to Mick.

"Mr Richardson chose five men. Me and four others. When I argued, Mr Tom Geery killed my little daughter." Mick had to stop a moment, gathering himself. He glanced at the remnants of dried blood on the ground, and on the bottom layer of the hut.

Mr Dawson's eyes followed his, and the Sergeant was now furious, as Mick had expected. He wished all white men were like this one.

"But Mr Richardson make mistake. He chose our magic man. In the forest, magic man turned them into ravens. They gone. Never people again. And they not know how to be ravens. They not know how to fly. They will slowly die, no food. That's good."

He made sure to say this in a level, matter-of-fact tone of voice. The two young troopers were clearly impressed. One had his mouth half open. But Sergeant Dawson looked sceptical.

"Oh yeah, your magic man can turn a man into a raven? This I'd like to see."

"All right. I ask, maybe he show you." Mick waved to Riso.

"Make me smoky fire," Riso commanded, speaking English for the benefit of the three white men.

While several people obeyed, he painted intricate white marks on his face and chest, taking a paste from a small cane basket hanging from a leather thong around his waist. He started to dance around the fire in slow, jerky steps.

The fire grew into a yellow roar of flames, then a couple of people threw green leafy branches onto it. Smoke billowed high and swirled around. Riso stepped into the smoke — and a raven flew free. It circled above the village once, then flew off.

It took no more than a few breaths for the smoke to clear. When all the area around it was visible, the white men could see that Riso was no longer there.

Mick said, "He know how to be raven. Also, he will change back to man when he want to. Tomorrow maybe he come back. But those white men not come back. They dead raven."

He saw that all three white men had gone paler. One trooper tried to hide the tremble in his hands, but Dawson demanded, "He could light a fire in the forest? While being hunted?"

"Of course not. But he still have magic paint. Always with him. Fire help. But when need is great, can do with no fire. Even can do with no paint. Magic comes from Spirit Ancestors. And need was great."

Dawson lifted his hat and scratched the back of his head. "Well, Mick, I've always found you to be a good bloke, and nobody should hurt children. I'll be seeing ya."

The three policemen mounted and rode off toward the town.

4

Maraglindi

It was raining outside. Water made a loud plink plink noise on the walls. I liked this sound, and the sound of the wind blowing. I liked the smell of the rain, so clean and fresh. We couldn't play outside, but I could sit on the blanket, my back against Mother's side. I love Mother. Water seeped through the wall. Only bits, here and there, but Father didn't like it. He wanted to fix it. Why? I could see he didn't like it because his glow had brown and brown-yellow flashes. I love Father.

Old Mother was spinning wool from a sheep, in the old way. She held a big lump of soft, fluffy thing in her left hand, and over and over rolled a part of it against her thigh with the right hand. She told me this makes thread. She wound the thread onto a ball. This ball was getting bigger all the time. Old Mother is very clever. I love Old Mother. She kept rolling the next length against her thigh. Father brought the wool home yesterday, after working for Bruce. Father said this wool was thrown away because it was not good enough. It was good enough for blackfella people. I love Bruce, and I could see him in my heart, with his beautiful silver glow. I knew the colour's name, because once I pointed to a cloud with Old Mother the Sun shining through it, and I asked

Father Riso what colour that was. He said that's the colour of the light coming from Daughter Moon when She is the oldest, and we now call it *silver*. I love Father Riso.

But now I wanted to play with my baby brother. He was inside Mother's big tummy. I put my face on Mother's tummy and it felt nice. I love Mother. I love this baby. It was a boy, but also it was Kohli. She was coming back because she wanted to be in our family again. I didn't know how I knew this, but that was all right. I knew it, like I can sense what people think. That's fun. Like, Atan wanted the rain to stop. He wanted to go and practise with... something. I didn't know the word he said to himself without speaking. It was a thing to hunt animals with. I could see a special glow around his right shoulder and arm, like when a person is throwing something. I love Atan.

The baby was moving downward, inside Mother. When Kohli died, when the policemen came, Mother already had a baby inside her, but then the baby had no thoughts like people's thoughts. The baby's thoughts were like the thoughts of a fish in the river, or a frog hiding, or a bird flying to her nest. But soon after, somehow, the baby turned into a person, and that person was Kohli. I love you, Kohli, who is now a boy.

I sensed Gerald coming. I love Gerald. I sat up straight and said aloud, "Gerald coming."

"My Froggie, I don't know how you can tell these things," Mother said with a smile. She gently put me to one side and stood. It was hard for her because of her big belly.

And here he was, coming in through the doorway, his coat and hat dripping with water. "G'day," he said, smiling at all of us. "Look what the rain washed in." He took off his hat and coat. Father hung them to dry on a piece of wire that sticks out from the wall. Father specially made that for Gerald, because he always comes when it's raining.

Gerald opened his bag and took out a paper bag. "Some sweets for the children," he said, passing it to Father. Then he squatted next to Atan. "Are you ready for your next lesson?"

"I knew you come, what with the rain."

"Well, it's Saturday, and there is no school for me today." He took a book from his bag. "Here is where we'd got to last time. This is the story of how God gave the Ten Commandments to Moses."

"Command... what is that word, ey?" Father asked.

***

Looking down at me from a branch of the tree, Tari said, "Come on. You can do it!"

On the branch above her, Tiki put his tongue out. "I can do it and I'm younger than you!"

He was. I'd heard Old Mother say he wasn't three years old yet, and I knew I was. But also, I was scared. I am always so awkward; I just knew I'd fall off if I tried to climb up after them.

"You can do it," my big sister said again. "Look, grab that branch and put your foot there..."

I did. Bit by bit she talked me up the tree till I sat next to her.

She let go with both hands and hugged me, but I held on, trying to be a bump on the tree.

Tiki shouted, "You can't come up here!"

He was right. I didn't even want to try.

Even higher, Moro jumped up and down to make her branch sway. But she was a big girl, bigger than Tari even.

I had to close my eyes rather than look at her.

Tari said, "She can, too! Froggie can do anything."

No I couldn't; I knew it.

Tari stood, reached up, pulled hard, wriggled on her stomach and was beside Tiki. Tiki swarmed up, and Moro reached a hand down to help him. They made their branch swing together, laughing, and I felt ready to empty my stomach.

Tari leaned over and held her hand to me. "Come on!"

I grabbed her hand. She pulled me up onto her branch. "See! She can!" Tari said to Tiki.

Moro climbed up higher still, and Tiki followed her, laughing and having fun. I wanted to go back to Mother, but couldn't say so, because then they'd all laugh at me.

Tari stood. "Up you go," she said. "I'll support you from below."

I wanted to say no, but how do you say no to your big sister?

I could now see the places to hold, places to put my feet. Tari put a hand under my bottom as I climbed, and I was up on the branch above. In a moment, she was with me.

Then Old Mother's voice came, "Tariligani! Maraglindi!"

At the same time, from the other side, Moro's mother also shouted for her.

Moro and Tiki climbed down, very fast, and Tari lay on her stomach, then hung by her hands and stood on the branch below.

I looked down and had to close my eyes. I had to grab a thin branch with each hand. I had to press up hard against the trunk of the tree. I knew I couldn't go down.

"Oh," Tari said. "Do it like I did."

I said no with my head. If I tried to speak, I'd surely cry.

"All right. Stay there, Froggie. I'll get help."

I heard the noises of her climbing down.

Old Mother again called, "Children, dinner time!"

Then Atan's voice reached me. "Froggie, it's all right.

Look at me."

I opened my eyes.

He ran hard toward the tree, jumped, then was up on my branch! He held on with one hand and hugged me with the other.

I clung to him, hard.

He laughed. "Climb on my back, Froggie, but don't choke me."

Next thing, he was kneeling on the ground so I could climb off his back.

Father stood in the doorway of our hut, smiling. He told me, "Maraglindi, you can do anything. When you're scared, do it anyway."

I said yes with my head, but inside I knew that if my wonderful big brother hadn't rescued me, I couldn't have climbed down myself.

I hated being scared. I hated being more awkward than others. But it was no good saying anything, because people would just tell me to be brave. So, all I could do was smile.

***

Mother said, "It's time. Atan, go and get Aunty Dara."

My big brother rushed out. Old Mother had a woven cane basket packed. She gave this to Tari, took the two of us by the hand and led us out, to Father Riso's hut. There,

Aunty Balini kissed us each on the cheek, saying, "You'll have a new brother or sister soon!"

I had to tell her, "It's a brother, Aunty, but it is Kohli, coming back."

Her eyes grew big and round. "Froggie, we never say the name of someone who..." Tears started running down her cheeks.

"But, but, Aunty Balini, it's true! She is coming back to be with us, only she is now a boy!"

Old Mother said, "I can never work out the things this little one says. Well, I better go back and assist."

Uncle Granat was cuddling baby Hur with his back against the wall, feeding him with a spoon, but more went on the baby boy's face than into his mouth. "It's all right, Froggie." He laughed at me with his eyes. "I know you know lots of stuff the rest of us don't. All the same, it's a good idea to only say things old people like Aunty Balini want you to say."

"Old people, ey?" Aunty Balini threateningly waved her arms, but she was also grinning.

"Where is Father Riso, ey?" Tari asked.

"With your Father Mick," Aunty Balini said. "They've gone to the forest to talk to the Spirits, to ask for a good life for this new baby. It's a mother's job to bear the baby and give birth and look after the body, and the father's job to look after the spirit. Both are important."

Atan came in. "Froggie, it wasn't so long ago that I was here, waiting for you to be born!"

"It was my whole lifetime ago," I answered, making everybody laugh. But I wanted to find out what was happening with Mother, so I sat on the ground in the corner closest to our hut and closed my eyes. I could sense that Mother was in pain, but happy. She was walking, with Old Mother right next to her. The pain went away, then came again, and again and again. I also felt the pain and fear of my new brother. He felt terribly squeezed and didn't know what was happening. I sent my love to him but didn't know if he could feel it.

I didn't realise that time was passing, until Uncle Granat said, "Hey Maraglindi, have some nice goanna." I opened my eyes, and everyone else was eating. He passed me a bit of wide palm leaf holding the still-steaming meat on a bulrush-root-flour pancake, with two cakes of roasted gymea root, one of my favourite vegetables.

I asked, "Aunty Balini, why is it so painful to have a baby?"

"Now, how could you know that... oh, never mind. It's because women are strong enough to do it. It's a proof, like the men's hunting. You need to feel the pain to be worthy."

I didn't understand this. It didn't make sense, but I said

nothing. When I finished eating, I closed my eyes again to better feel what was happening. Mother was squatting, with Old Mother behind her, supporting her. Aunty Dara was also very close. And the baby didn't like cold air, and the light, and all the noises. "He is born!" I had to shout.

"Well, well," Aunt Balini said, "We'll know when your Father Mick returns to get you."

But I knew. I could feel peace come over the new child as he started sucking Mother's breast, and so I could relax, too. I sent a loving thought to Mother and the baby.

*****

It was wonderful having a little brother and watching Mother feeding him and looking after him. I enjoyed seeing him getting bigger every day. One day, Mother said, "Froggie, you'd better come with me. We're visiting a white house."

That was exciting. I had never before been away from the people. I was happy as we walked. I chatted with mother and skipped along the road. I wore my best dress. Gerald had brought it specially for me. It was light blue, covered with white flowers all over. It made me feel like a flower, wearing it.

Mother also took the trouble to look nice and carried baby Rippie in a clean cloth sling. The glow around her contained sunshiny gold, and flashes of blue. Those swirling parts of her glow were big and strong because she felt good.

Big trees lined the dusty road. Mother said, "Little Frog, don't stir up the dirt. Walk on the grass edge, over there. And we should be practising English, so you can speak to Mrs MacCartney correctly."

"MacCartney? Like Bruce, ey?"

Mother answered in English. "Yes, this is Bruce's wife. But you no say Bruce. You say Mr MacCartney, or sir."

"Yes Ma." I noticed a kookaburra land on a branch of a big tree ahead. "What tree that, ey?" I asked Mother in the white-person words. It was fun to speak English, but difficult.

"Don't know. Some white tree. They brought their own when they came."

"Still look nice."

Mother smiled at me. "You are sunshine, Froggie. But listen. Tell me where we go now."

"To Mrs MacCartney's house."

So, we talked in English, but it wasn't easy for Mother or for me. Meanwhile, we walked fast. I was getting very tired and thirsty when I sensed someone — lots of someones — up ahead. I told Mother, "Ma, people, only many..." I didn't know the English word for "strange," so had to say in the language, "many are somehow not people."

"Now, what do you mean by that, ey?"

We went around the curve of the road to the right, past a clump of trees, then we could see. Four men on horses were herding a mob of big animals, who stirred up a lot of dust. Bruce MacCartney rode at the front, on a big, black horse.

Mother led me well to the side, in among the trees, as we waited.

Bruce stopped his horse next to us and smiled. "G'day, you're Mick's wife, aren't you?"

"Yes, Sir. We going to your lady."

I love Bruce. He is the only person I have ever met who has a pure silver glow about him; of course, apart from the colours of the swirling parts. And as well as the swirling parts other people have, he has another beautiful one over his head. Bruce is special. I could do nothing but gaze up at him.

He returned my look. "The little angel. Good morning, my wee darlin'."

"Good morning, Mr MacCartney."

"You know, this is the horse your father tamed. Don't come close, he is still very nervous."

But as I looked at the horse, and the horse looked at me, I felt a bond. This horse told me in his mind, without words, that he liked me. So, I let go of Mother's hand and stepped forward.

The huge horse did the same and bent his head until his

wet nose was just below my face, and one great black eye looked into mine. Then he surprised me: he suddenly blew a misty cloud all around my head. He told me with his way of thinking that this was how a horse showed love.

"Well, I never..." Bruce said. "You're your father's child all right." He got the horse walking again, back to leading the big animals along the road.

Soon after this, Mother turned onto a road between two tall fence posts. She told me that's what they were. We walked between two *fences*: timber posts in the ground, with shiny *wire* stretched between them. I knew about fences, but this was the first one I'd seen.

I saw some buildings in the distance. Big animals like the ones on the road grazed to the right, while the left area was empty, with long grass waving in the breeze.

"What animals, ey?" I asked, pointing at them.

"Cattle. We no have name for them. Girl cattle is cows. These cows give milk. Mr MacCartney make cheese from milk, sell in city."

I knew what cheese was, but had to ask, "What is city, ey?"

"Many, many white people live there. Many houses. More houses than trees in forest."

A forest of houses? I knew what a forest of trees was like but couldn't imagine a forest of houses.

The road crossed a short wooden bridge over a creek. Father Riso once drew a picture of a bridge for me in the dirt, in the old way we used to do, by making a tree fall over a creek. It was good to see a real one, although this was quite different, with flat lengths of wood under and something on each side to stop you from falling into the water. Mother walked off the road and carefully climbed down to the water's edge. I tried to follow, but of course my foot slipped. Why am I always doing things like that? I'd have fallen in if Mother hadn't grabbed my arm.

"Oh Froggie, you're always so awkward!" she said, but smiling.

I didn't like being reminded of being awkward, so I distracted her by saying, "Ma, you English speak, not people speak."

Mother gave that lovely deep laugh of hers. "Clever girl. All right. English. We drink water now and clean off dust. And I clean up Rippo."

Soon we walked on again, and not long after, we arrived at the back of the house. It was so big! The walls were covered with very long lengths of something flat and grey. When a dead old tree has lost its bark, it is this colour. I noticed that these flat things were put together in the same way as the flat metal bits at home, with the top of one snuggled under the one above it.

67

Mother stopped in front of a solid part of the wall. "This is door," she said in English, and rapped on it with her knuckles.

Surprise! The left-side edge of the *door* swung inward, creating a doorway like at home. Aunty Mish stood there, grinning at us. She wore a white woman dress, with a white something tied in front. She said, in the language, "Daughter of my heart, here you are. And you brought your little daughter. Good morning, Maraglindi."

"Good morning Aunty Mish," I answered in English. "Why you here, ey?"

Aunty Mish stepped aside, and Mother walked past her. Of course, so did I.

"I cook for Mrs Mac. I lucky. They best people in town."

The room we entered was larger than our whole house. The floor was shiny yellow, made from something smooth that felt cool under my bare feet. Over to the right, a hot fire burned in a sort of a box like a hole in the wall, except that it had a back, sides and top. The top must have had a hole, because the flames went straight up and there was no smoke in the room. Big iron pots hung above the flames on hooks attached to a thick iron rod. The middle of the room had a big thing, with a flat top higher than my head, standing on four wooden legs. There were other things, but they made no sense to me at all.

Before I could ask questions, Aunty Mish said, "I take you to Mrs Mac. She expect you."

"You English speak. Good," I said, copying Mother's tone of voice. Both of them laughed at that. I like to make people laugh.

Aunty Mish opened another *door*, which swung away from her. This was scary, going into a strange place. So, I clutched Mother's hand as we followed. We were in a very narrow, long room with nothing much in it. The roof above our head was flat, white, and very high. There were many *doors* on each side, and a *door* in the distance, at the end of this strange room. Beautiful light of many colours came through this *door*. The ground under our feet was soft, like walking on fur. Only, it had many coloured pictures my eyes couldn't follow.

Aunty Mish stopped at one of the *doors* on the right and did what Mother had done outside: she rapped on it with the knuckles of her hand.

"Come in!" a nice voice called.

Aunty Mish opened the *door* and stepped aside, motioning us to go ahead of her. "Here is the new wet nurse, ma'am," she said.

I liked the person in here. I gave all my attention to Mrs MacCartney, who stood beside a thing like a wooden basket on legs.

Of course, her face and hands were pinky white. She wore the most beautiful dress I could have imagined, with frilly white surrounds around the neck and wrists, and graceful folds. She had yellow-coloured hair, like the dry grass at the end of summer. Her eyes had the same colour as her man's — pale blue like the summer sky. I could also see that she was worried, and in pain, with red and dark brown in her glow.

Of course I had to make it better for her. I let go of Mother's hand and ran over. "Mrs Mac, maybe I help." I took the woman's hand and looked up into the blue eyes, sending all the love I could.

"Maraglindi!" Mother said, sounding scared.

But Mrs MacCartney smiled a beautiful smile. "What a sweet little angel you are!" She looked above my head at Mother and Aunty Mish. "Do you know, the moment she touched me, my backache went away. Is this a magical child?"

Mother said, "Yes ma'am, I notice she has a healing magic. With her, everyone feel good."

Mrs MacCartney looked down again. "What is your name, child?"

"Maraglindi."

"Mara..." she stopped and laughed. "That's too long and complicated for a little mite like you.. I shall call you Mary."

I didn't like this, because my name is special.

But Mrs MacCartney pulled on my hand, toward the basket thing next to her. Its top edge was level with my nose when I stood on tippy-toes. "Mary, have a look at my poor baby. Maybe you can help him, too, my lamb. His name is Donald."

I looked at the tiny, tiny head, smaller than Rippo's even. From his glow, I could see the problem. "He hungry. That all. Want milk." The swirling parts of his glow were very weak and small, too.

There was sadness in Mrs Mac's voice. "That's why your mother is here, Mary. I don't have enough milk, and when we tried cow's milk, he nearly died, he was so sick."

"I have more'n enough for two," Mother said.

She walked forward, Rippo still in his sling by her side. With a questioning glance at Mrs Mac, she bent over and picked up the white baby. He opened tiny blue eyes. His mouth also opened into an oval, and a thin little cry came out.

Mother pulled up the front of her top, baring a breast, and held the baby's face to it.

The sad whine stopped. The tiny white face against the dark brown breast was the most beautiful thing I'd ever seen.

There was a happy silence, filled only with the baby's snuffling sounds. At last, Donald had enough, long after

Aunty Mish had gone back to the place with the fire. Wordlessly, Mother handed him over, and Mrs Mac lovingly patted his back until he burped up a small white mouthful. Now his swirls were strong and bright.

Mother said, "Mrs Mac, I love to come. But I have family."

The lady smiled at her. "Of course, I know that. We'll find work for them as well."

"Ma'am, white people one wife, one husband. Blackfella family different."

"Oh?"

"Now I am young wife. Husband older. He has older wife. When I older, we s'pose have young husband."

I could sense the sadness. I knew that Goro had been killed, *shot* dead with a *gun*, when he was on the way to visit with his Father one day, so Mother would never have a young husband. I had heard Mother's thoughts about it, often, although this sadness was never spoken aloud. But I had Kiri. One day, I'd be married into his family.

Without a break, Mother continued, "Then later another young wife."

"Really? I didn't know that..."

"Old days, it was very good. But now, white people do not know... Can't say it."

"Do you mean, we don't understand? Anyway, how many

are there in your family now?"

"My family many parts, but not everybody live together. Like, my brothers also fathers to my children, my sisters mothers to my children. But living together, old wife Jila. Then husband Mick. He like work for Mr MacCartney. Then me. And Atan good boy, can work. And girl Tari. Maybe help Aunty Mish. And Maraglindi. She good helper. Rippie maybe play with Donald. Everybody help."

Mrs Mac laughed, a tinkling, silvery sound that made me glad to be here. "I will make sure all of you get decent pay for your work. Maybe even Rippie!"

5

Alice MacCartney

Alice looked across the dining table at her stepson and hid a sigh. His eyes were on her all the time, big cow's eyes of admiration he was simply unable to hide. Fortunately, Bruce was too loving and trusting to notice, to ever believe that Peter could be infatuated with her. The young man, a year over her twenty-four, had returned only yesterday from droving a mob of steers to market, and she wished he'd go again. She wished he'd find a girl of his own and get over this silly business. Only, she knew, for him it wasn't silly business. She very much feared that he thought of it as True Love. Forcing brightness, she said, "Bruce, have you noticed how remarkable that little Aboriginal girl is?"

When Bruce smiled like this, his eyes shone, almost with a light of their own. "Yes, longer than you have, my dear. She is a little angel, that one."

"Which girl are you two talking about?" Peter dragged his eyes off Alice and looked at his father.

"Alice's new wet nurse has a three-year-old daughter who is very special. It's hard to realise, son, that you've been away during all our changes."

"Oh yes, I've seen some new Aboriginal servants about

the place. But what's so special about this child?"

Husband and wife both started speaking at the same time, but with a bow of his head and a wave of a hand, Bruce deferred to her.

"Well," Alice answered, "she's been here only a week. The rest of her family still speak broken English like all of them, but she's been imitating me — accent, tones of voice, grammar, choice of words — and if you listened to her through a closed door, you'd swear she was a high-bred young lady of five or six, rather than a native girl of about three."

"Imitation is the biggest compliment," Bruce interrupted. The glow in his eyes was for Alice now.

"And also, anything she hears, she remembers. The first day she was here, I mentioned, just speaking aloud to myself, that I needed to write down my appointment for Donald with Dr Horton at 10 of the clock of the morning on Friday. But what with Donald taking to Glindi so well, I forgot. And on Friday I was getting in a tizz because I couldn't remember the time. And little Mary snapped out, "It was ten of the clock, Mrs Mac!""

Bruce took over. "Peter, you know my horse, Devil? This child is Mick's daughter. And, you won't believe this, that big brute, who won't let anyone but me and Mick close, breathed all over the girlie's face like she was the best thing in his life. But Alice, I'm not at all surprised at her intelligence. After all, Mick is a bright fellow."

"Oh. You don't know... Mick isn't the child's natural father. I got it out of Glindi, because I was intrigued by the lighter colour of Mary's skin and those green eyes. It was Richardson forcing her, may God forgive his soul."

Peter said, his lips compressed into an angry line, "All too many of the men do things like that. I wish there was a law..."

The door opened, and Galea came in with a tray. Young Tari walked right behind her with a smaller one. And peeking behind them, Alice saw the tiny girl.

"Mary," she called, "Meet Mr Peter, Mr Mac's son."

Shyly, the tiny light-brown girl came in, keeping out of the way of the other two who were busily collecting the used plates.

Peter leaned sideways and held out his right hand.

Mary looked at him, obviously puzzled. Alice realised, she'd never before encountered the custom of shaking hands. Then, a slight smile played over her face as if someone had whispered an instruction into her ear. She stepped forward, and gravely shook hands with him. "Welcome home, Mr Peter," she said, and Alice was amused at her perfect diction.

The driven appearance left Peter's face. He kept hold of

the child's hand and gazed down into her eyes. After a while, he said, "I don't know what you did, Mary, but thank you."

He let go and sat up. "Are you helping the others?" he asked.

The look of almost horror on her face was comical. "Oh no! I not allowed b'cause I drop things." Her speech had reverted to the natives' broken English.

"So, you have problems like all of us? My father said you're an angel."

She just stared up at him.

"All right, Mary," Alice broke in to save her embarrassment, "You can return to the kitchen, my poppet."

She whirled and ran out — knocking into the doorjamb on the way, as if to demonstrate her physical awkwardness.

***

A week later, Alice looked at her visitors in surprise. "Mrs McTaskill, how nice to see you," she said. "And Gerald, you're filling out again. Thank the good Lord you're over that terrible time."

Maude McTaskill smiled up at Alice from her five-foot-nothing stature. "Since Archie and Harvey have been... taken from me, I've formed a special bond with Gerald. He is a son to me now."

To Alice's surprise, the boy's voice had changed to have a pleasant, deep timbre. "I... I asked Mrs McTaskill to bring me over to speak with you, ma'am, because I have a request to make."

"Oh?"

"The man, Mick, and his son, Atan, and his wife and daughters and the older woman, they're with you now. But before that, before that, um... I used to secretly visit them, and I was teaching Atan to read, and told them about the Bible, bringing them to Christ."

"That's very praiseworthy of you. But why?"

There was desperation in the glance the boy cast at Mrs McTaskill, then he looked back into Alice's eyes. He took a deep breath and squared his shoulders. "I was a party to... to a murder. One of their little children. I need to make atonement. I've decided to go into the Church when I am old enough."

"How commendable of you. Shall we have a cup of tea?" Alice asked to gain thinking time and rang the silver bell.

Jila came almost immediately and went again after hearing the request.

"Oh, do take a seat. So, Gerald, I take it you'd like to continue your visits to this family?"

The two visitors sat side by side on the beautifully upholstered sofa Alice was so proud of, while she took one of the matching armchairs across the coffee table from them.

"Yes please, ma'am. Before, when they lived by the river, I used to, well, sneak there at times no one would know. Now, I can just come calling here, if I may, when it's convenient." He blushed. "And I wouldn't be no bother... excuse me, any bother. I'd just go and be with them for an hour or so each time."

"Gerald, I find your keenness most admirable. You certainly have my permission, especially..." Alice felt her cheeks grow hot as she steeled herself for what she needed to say, "...especially since it somewhat parallels my own experience."

Maude McTaskill's mouth actually dropped open.

"Oh, I wasn't ever involved in a murder, but I... I did kill someone." She laughed, half at their confusion, half in embarrassment. "Then much later, I helped to save some lives, and that's how I ended up halfway around the world, and married to the best man on earth."

Jila came in with a tray holding the silver teapot, bone china cups and saucers, milk and sugar, and this gave Alice a few more moments, all too necessary to steel herself.

She looked at these two good people, and like jumping into cold water, launched into the story of her salvation. "I wasn't always a good person. Oh no! In fact, when I was seventeen, I'm afraid I was responsible for my father's death. We had a terrible row, with me screaming defiance at him. He was halfway up the stairs, with me above. He suddenly clutched at his chest, then he fell, and... and was dead when I got to him."

She felt tears come to her eyes but steeled herself to continue.

"He was an elder of the Church, and on every charitable committee in our town, and a lawyer whose word was trusted by everyone. Often, people brought cases to him from fifty miles away, rather than to deal with a lawyer who might have been, er, less than honest in his practices. So, we lived very comfortably, and I had all I wanted — except that I always wanted more, and never felt satisfied. I'm afraid I played up dreadfully.

And then he died.

My mother had five children, with me the eldest. Not only did we lose our father, but also the source of the family's income. We were forced to sell our house and move to a more modest one. We had to let most of the servants go, and for the first time in my life, I was required to do domestic work with my own hands instead of issuing imperious orders. My father had planned to send me to the famous Girton

College for ladies in Cambridge to finish my education. My dream had been to become a celebrated actress. Instead, I needed to find a job.

My father's elder sister had a friend — a widow who lived in London with her brother, who travelled a lot on business. It was organised that I would become her companion, with my earnings contributing to my family's upkeep. It went a tiny way toward restitution for having caused my father's death. But actually, it proved to be anything but a penance. Mrs Pickering was a formidable lady and soon had me act with discipline, but her stern manner hid a kind heart. From her I learned the pleasure of acting charitably toward others less fortunate than myself. And also, she schooled me in the graces I'd been too stubborn to acquire as a spoiled child.

One day, Mr Bartley, her brother, invited her to visit him in Italy. Naturally, I was to accompany her as her companion, and this was hugely exciting. In due course, we set off on a large three-masted ship and travelled to Venice, which is an unbelievable wonder, a place with canals instead of streets, and buildings of beauty. Two months we stayed there, then returned on the same ship, which regularly plied that route.

Soon after we exited the Mediterranean Sea through the Strait of Gibraltar, we were caught in a terrible storm. Imagine waves the size of some of the hills around here, the roar of a wind so loud you could take it to be thunder only it went on and on. That big ship tossed around like half the shell of a walnut — it was a storm the like of which I couldn't even have imagined. Of course, everyone but the sailors had to be locked away into safety. My mistress and I strapped ourselves to our beds — a bunk it is called on board a ship, but a bed it was, fixed to the floor. Our cabin was on the main deck, with a large porthole, and glass in the heavy timber door. To my dismay and fright, I could see, hear and feel waves actually battering against the door! And the porthole was regularly under the water. Indeed, water soon sloshed around inside, and the ship groaned and screeched as if falling apart. The howling of the wind was audible even through the thick oak walls, and there were terrible bangs all the time.

I have no idea know how long this went on, but at last I must have fallen asleep. When I awoke, the ship was still tossing about, but in a much more regular pattern. The place stank, because Mrs

Pickering had been sick from the motion. So, I needed to resume my duties, and cautiously went outside to organise cleaning by the steward.

All three masts still stood, which was a marvel. Huge waves still marched in endless rows, swaying the ship so badly that I needed to hang on to safety ropes all the time. Eventually I found the person I needed, but as we were returning, there was a commotion on deck. The lookout had sighted something, and the captain was changing course. In a sailing ship this involves moving the sails from one position to another so they still catch the wind correctly, but don't ask me about the why and how of it.

Soon enough, I could see for myself. A ship lay in the water on its side. Two or three boats were taking people off, and the lifeboats from our ship raced over to them also. Then, as I watched, the water around the stricken ship bubbled like it was boiling, and she slipped below the surface. To my horror, two of the boats near it got sucked down by its passing."

For a long moment, Alice couldn't continue, her mind's eye seeing the disaster, her heart wrenched by the terror as if she were there all over again. Taking a deep breath, she resumed her account.

"Within a few minutes, though, I was too busy to grieve or worry. As the rescued people came on board, everyone helped in one way or another, even us passengers.

That ship was from New South Wales, on the way Home. Bruce and Peter were among the survivors. Sadly, Bruce's wife and two daughters had been on one of the lifeboats that went down. Father and son had helped them into the boat, but, like the gentlemen they are, they stayed on the dead ship to rescue others. When the ship went down, they were thrown up by some miracle. I'm told the turbulence is completely unpredictable, and such things are not unheard of.

Mrs Pickering allowed me to take part in nursing the injured. Both Bruce and Peter had broken limbs, and I spent many hours in their company. When we arrived back Home, they needed to travel to Scotland and couldn't do so unaided. My mistress released me from my duties so I could care for them during the journey. She told me that Peter would be a good catch! Little did she know... it was Bruce I fell in love with. I spent a year in his uncle's castle, after which we married."

Through her tears, she smiled at her visitors.

Mrs McTaskill said, dabbing at her eyes with lace handkerchief, "Of course I had heard all about the tragedy, but—"

"But you didn't know that I was merely a lowly companion."

"I'd never consider you to be lowly anything, Mrs MacCartney."

Gerald said, "Mrs MacCartney, I understand that you see a parallel. You did wrong in your youth and are now making atonement with your many good deeds. You're universally loved and admired."

"Thank you. Yes, like you, I made a resolution. I've dedicated my life to God's will and good works on His behalf. There'll be no unkindness to anyone if I have the ability to stop it."

***

"Father, Alice, I need to speak with the two of you." As usual, Peter's eyes were fixed on Alice, making her wince inside.

"Certainly, son," Bruce said. He led the way to his study and ushered the other two in. They sat in the comfortable armchairs that faced a view of Alice's rose garden.

"Father, I have a terrible dilemma, one that honour and

duty forbids I should even speak of. For a long time now, I've been caught in hell and couldn't find a way out. It's little Mary who has helped me. Somehow, don't ask me to explain it, she made me feel that I've got the power to do something constructive about it, and so I've thought of a solution."

"You're being very mysterious, Peter. Surely, within the safety of our family, you can divulge your secret?"

Oh no! Alice thought in despair. If he should...

Fortunately, Peter shared her view. "No, Father, it's neither appropriate nor useful. Look, we've heard rumours of war threatening with the Russians because Britain is allied with the Turks, and those two countries are squabbling over some Godforsaken piece of land. I have a considerable sum of my own money saved. I intend to use it to buy a commission in the Army and go and distinguish myself."

Bruce's lips went pale and he took a deep breath. "Peter, you may get killed... Son, I love Alice and Donald, but you're all I have left of my life with your poor, dear mother. It'd be devastating to lose you as well."

Alice noted a suspicious sheen in Bruce's eyes, so she reached over and took his hand while dealing with the turmoil of her thoughts. If only he would go! It'd relieve the daily torture of his admiration. Oh, he was a nice enough young man, and if she didn't love Bruce, she could perhaps learn to love him, but... but it'd be so good to have him on another continent! At the same time, Bruce of course loved his son, and it would be selfish of her to wish him gone.

She should be acting on the side of duty and love, rather than seek comfort and safety. She should beg him to stay. Instead, she sat there and kept quiet.

6

Maraglindi

"Try again," Gerald said. I watched the way his face became all intense when he was teaching. I love Gerald.

Atan read, "Our Father, which art... It no make sense."

"You should say, 'It doesn't make sense.' Remember?"

"All right. It doesn't make sense. Well, really, it doesn't. I mean, would you say it like that... 'which art'?"

"There is a reason. It was written hundreds of years ago, when people spoke differently. But the idea is wonderful, and this is the tradition. You can read it."

I told them, "I can say it too. Our Father which art in Heaven, hallowed be thy name, forever and ever, Amen."

The two boys laughed. Gerald said, "You did leave out the middle."

"Teach me. I want to sur... sup..."

"Surprise?"

I grinned up at him. "Surprise Mrs Mac."

So, the three of us recited the Lord's Prayer over and over, Gerald tracing the words with a finger.

The next day, straight after breakfast, I said, skipping in excitement, "Mrs Mac, Mrs Mac, can I please do something for you?"

"Go on, child."

I stood up straight, and sang to a tune I made up myself,

> Our Father, which art in Heaven,
> Hallowed be thy name.
> Thy kingdom come,
> Thy will be done
> On earth, as it is in Heaven.
> Give us this day our daily bread.
> And forgive us our trespasses,
> As we forgive those who trespass against us.
> And lead us not into temptation,
> But deliver us from evil:
> For thine is the kingdom,
> And the power,
> And the glory,
> For ever and ever,
> Amen."

To my shock, tears came to the lady's eyes. "Oh, I sorry. You crying, ey?" Then I realised I was speaking blackfella English.

"My poppet, I'm not sad. I cried because I needed the lesson you've just taught me."

Alice

Alice could hardly wait for the men to come in for dinner. As the hours dragged their feet, she endlessly rehearsed her planned solution.

Then, over dinner, she chatted, waiting for the right

moment. At last, Bruce poured port for the three of them, and she looked around. Her eyes finally stopped on the young man. "Peter, I really would hate to see you die in some foreign place, in a futile fight that actually has nothing to do with us. And also... how can I put it? God didn't give you your life back so you could become a professional killer. Because, isn't that what a soldier is?"

The look from Bruce was reward enough.

"Nevertheless, I have decided. I need to go."

"Certainly. But I've got an idea. The widow Highfield is not coping. She can't manage the men, lacks the knowledge to run things, and the whole farm is running down. I think if you made her an offer, she'd be very glad to sell."

"I like it." Bruce waved both his arms. "You're twenty-five years old, and it's time for you to have your own life independently of me. And if the price is more than you can afford, I'm happy to go into partnership with you."

"And of course you'll still be welcome here at any time," Alice said, hoping the invitation didn't sound forced or insincere. "After all, it's been your home for all of your life, while I'm only a newcomer."

"I'll think about it." Peter stood, smiled at the two of them and walked out.

Maraglindi

Father Riso took my right hand, Father the left, and they walked with me out into the dark. "Look at that Ancestor, over toward the east," Father Riso said. "At this exact time of the evening, He was in just that position when you were born. Today, you are four years old."

I gazed at the twinkling little light on the horizon, marvelling that Father Riso could distinguish it from the many others.

He explained, "Have a look. That Ancestor is one of those that stand around the shape of the Lizard, right at the tip of the Lizard's tail. See where there is a darkness between the Ancestors, long and thin and with a curve?"

I did.

"That black shape is the Spirit of the Lizard. All the animals have Spirits in the sky, among the Ancestors. When a baby is born, we look for a sign like this, and that's how we can tell when that person is a year older."

"White people have a *calendar*," I told him.

Father laughed. "Our *calendar* is up in the sky. Now, Froggie, it's sleep time."

In the morning, after I'd helped Mother to look after Donald and Rippie, Mrs Mac said, "Mary my dear, we have a surprise for you!" Aunty Mish came in carrying a platter with something brown on it, the same colour as her skin. Old Mother, Tari and Galea followed, each carrying something: plates, cups, a jug of pale liquid.

Mrs Mac smiled brightly at me. "Happy birthday, Mary. This is your special day!"

The door opened again, and Mr Mac walked in, and surprise! Father and Atan were behind him.

Mrs Mac used a long, shiny knife to cut slices from the brown thing, which she said was a cake. Even Donald and Rippie got a small piece each, and Donald soon looked funny with bits of his face the same colour as my family's.

I tasted my slice. It was beautiful, so I ate it all up.

Meanwhile, Galea went around, giving each person a cup of the pale liquid. "That's lemonade," she told me, so I knew it must have been made from the lemon tree outside the kitchen window. That was nice too, but the cake — I wanted more cake.

Mrs Mac waved her hand for attention, then said, "This sweet girl of ours is a blessing for all of us. Mary my dear, thank you for moving into my life. You are now four years old. May the good Lord permit that I will be at your fortieth birthday!"

I couldn't even imagine myself forty years old.

Mr Mac started clapping, and of course everyone followed.

About half the cake was still left, so I asked for a second slice. "Well, it's your birthday cake," Mrs Mac said and cut me one. I loved the smell. I loved the taste. I loved the colour. Maybe, eating this cake would give my skin the same colour as my family's? But even as I enjoyed the cake melting in my mouth, I knew that if that was so, Mrs Mac and Donald and Mr Mac would change colour too, and they certainly wouldn't want that.

Tari said in the language, but softly in my ear, "Froggie, I wish you had a *birthday* every day!"

So, I asked Mrs Mac if Tari and I could have some more.

She laughed. "How much can one tiny stomach hold?" She cut a smaller piece for each of us all the same.

Soon, Mr Mac said, "Well, we men need to return to work."

Atan stood very tall, having been included among the men.

As they left, I picked up the platter with the cake on it. "Careful!" Mother said, but I held it flat, and walked out the door.

Tari was right behind me, with a tray of empty cups. "You are clever, Froggie," she said. "We can have some more!"

The table in the kitchen was too high for me, but Tari helped to put the cake there, then she quickly cut two pieces. As we stuffed them into our mouths, Aunty Mish came in and said, "Hey, hey, hey, enough is better than too much!"

Tari grinned up at her. "We're growing girls!"

Aunty Mish firmly put a cover over the remains of the cake and put it away in the pantry, all the while scolding us.

"Sorry Aunty Mish," Tari and I said together, neither of us meaning it. But as I went into the corridor, suddenly I really was very, very sorry. My stomach started to hurt, and I felt as heavy as the whole house, and then I had to turn around, and rush through the kitchen and out the back door, which luckily was not latched, and vomited all the lovely cake up on the ground.

***

Winter passed, then spring, and much of summer. "You're a big girl now, Mary," Mrs Mac said, "nearly five. You're going to mind the boys all by yourself!"

That was exciting, but I also sensed her thought, *I do hope this is all right*.

"Mrs Mac, you can trust me." I smiled up at her and tried to make my face look confident. "After all, they'll be asleep in bed."

"Yes, my dove. Now, remember, if anything happens, ring the handbell and your mother will come."

"Yes, Mrs Mac."

As Mother finished getting Donald ready for bed, he

looked at Mrs Mac, saying, "Mother, story?"

Mrs Mac smiled at him. "My poppet, I don't have time for a story tonight, but it's special: you have Rippie and Mary sleeping in your room!"

She kissed all three of us on the cheek before going to her important dinner party. Mother tucked Donald in, then settled Rippie before kissing us too, blowing out the lamp and hurrying out. She was needed to serve up, and to help in the kitchen.

It was strange, settling for sleep in the big house, without Tari's body in the same bed. The light of Daughter Moon came through the window from a different angle, and the straw mattress under me was softer than the one I was used to. Also, the boys were giggling and talking with each other, enjoying the novelty of being in the same room after dark.

There was the murmur of adult activity too, clinks and knocks and someone saying something. I could sense the presence of many people. For something to do, I tried counting them, but kept making a mistake roundabout nineteen or twenty.

Then Donald attracted my attention. "Mary, Mary, Mary!"

"Yes Donald?"

"I want a drink of water."

"If your mother was with you and just finished telling you

a story, would you ask for a drink of water?"

"Yes." But listening to his thoughts, I knew this was a lie.

"Donald, she doesn't give you a drink when you've gone to bed."

"She does so!"

Rippie said, in the language, "Yes, Froggie, water!" Then he started chanting in English, "Water! Water! Water!"

Donald of course joined him.

I was sure I didn't used to behave like this when I was two years old. I knew I should ring the bell so Mother could sort them out. But hadn't I told Mrs Mac she could trust me?

I got out from under my blankets. "All right. Quiet down. I'll get you drink. Then you must go to sleep."

On tippy toes, I reached the doorknob and went out into the corridor. The kitchen and dining room doors were open, and I saw the backs of Galea and Aunty Mish as they carried something. Going to the kitchen would be the same as ringing the bell for Mother: showing that I couldn't cope after all. So, I softly walked to the front door. It was harder to open, and heavy to push, but I managed.

Outside, Daughter Moon's light made everything black and white. Carriages stood in a row, with their horses' heads in feedbags. I heard men quietly talking to the right, so snuck to the left, ran around the house, to the pump outside the kitchen window. Good, the metal cup was there as usual. I filled it, wincing at the sound of the pump, then walked more slowly back along the house, to the front door. I tripped on something, but only spilled a few drops of water.

In I came through the door, concentrating hard to avoid spilling water on the carpet.

I started to ease Donald's door open, but a bright yellow light blinded me. Mother said, angry, "Maraglindi! What are you doing?"

"Oh."

"Well?"

I could see better now. She had a lit lamp standing beside the one that belonged in the room and was tapping a foot on the ground.

"Mother, the boys wanted a drink, and I couldn't talk them out of it. So, I went and got some water."

"What were you told to do?"

I felt tears running down my face, then she took the cup from me, and she was down on a knee and hugging me to her. I sensed her love, and the anger was gone and instead she was laughing inside and everything was all right.

"Maraglindi my little Froggie," she said, "it's all right to ask for help." Then she said in English to the boys, "See, you two? You got Mary into trouble. Now say sorry."

First Donald then Rippie did so, and soon all three of us were asleep.

Another year passed.

I knelt in the long grass and held my arms out wide. "Run to me!" I called.

The two little boys, one golden, the other dark, raced toward me side by side. As always when excited, Donald squealed in a high-pitched voice that would've hurt my ears if I didn't know it was his expression of joy.

They threw themselves at me in the same instant, so that I was bowled over, the two little bodies on top of me. As we lay there, all three of us giggling, I heard Mrs Mac call, "Mary, where are you, my dove?"

I stood up. "We're playing in the garden, Mrs Mac."

"Bring the boys in, please."

I took a small hand in each of mine and we walked in. Mother waited for us in the nursery, too.

"Sit down, Mary," Mrs Mac said, while Mother took charge of Donald and Rippie.

I sat on the special little chair Mrs Mac had bought for me some time ago.

"My poppet, I want to do something very special for you. How would you like to go to school?"

I could see that the lady's glow shone an almost pure silver, with her swirls strong and bright. Mrs Mac was offering something from her heart. All the same, I felt a great weight of danger, of something awful coming. Trying not to show my fear, I asked, "Ma'am, can I still live here with you when I go to school?"

"No, my dear. You see, our town has no suitable facility..." Seeing that I didn't understand the word, "...Oh, a girl can't go to an ordinary school. There is a ladies' college in Newcastle, which is a much bigger town. And the school term starts soon. I have your father's and mother's permission, and I'll be making all the payments."

I couldn't help it. I felt tears trickle down my face. To leave home, all the people and things I loved, to go to some strange place with strange, dangerous people...

Mrs Mac's face lost its smile, and her glow had flashes of the red of pain through it. Hurting her was the last thing I wanted to do.

Mother said, "Mrs Mac said she making you the clothes specially."

"Yes, Mary, we need school uniforms for you. You and I can make them together."

7

Maraglindi

I tightly clutched Mrs Mac's hand as we stood in front of the large, shiny brown desk. Mrs Mac said, "Mrs Talbot, this is the bright little button I wrote to you about, Mary Fisher. Mary, say good afternoon to Mrs Talbot."

I didn't know where the 'Fisher' came from, but dutifully said, imitating Mrs Mac's way of speaking, "Good afternoon, Mrs Talbot."

This was a scary place. Everything was shades of brown, and heavy. Lots of shelves held lots of books. Mrs Talbot was scary, too. She looked big, sitting behind the big desk. She had a fat face, and broad shoulders, and her neck hung down in folds. She looked so serious it was almost angry, with a very pale brown glow about her head. Her gaze at me, the thoughts in her mind, made me feel like a frog or insect, and I sensed her contempt. I mean, my family calls me Froggie because my skin is the same colour as a mud frog's and the mud frog is my spirit animal, but they say that with love. This was different: cold, as if I didn't matter, as if maybe she should call a maid to sweep me out with the dirt. She spoke, and the voice was cold, too. "Are you sure, Mrs MacCartney, that one of her kind could possibly cope with educational activities?"

Mrs Mac gave my hand a reassuring squeeze.

"Oh, Mrs Talbot, would I put up the money if I didn't think so? Do ask her a few questions!"

The steely eyes in the fat face looked at me once more. "Mary, how far can you count?"

I shrank even more, then managed, "9,999, Mrs Talbot. I'm not sure what comes after that."

Mrs Mac laughed.

"Just start counting, girl."

Obviously, I'd given the wrong answer. I started, "One, two, three, four..."

When I got to twenty, Mrs Talbot actually smiled, if frostily. "The number after 9,999 is 10,000. So, what comes after 99,999?

I thought for a second. There didn't seem to be any trick. "100,000?"

"Right. And the next level?"

"One thousand thousand?"

"That would be logical, child. The name for it is one million. All right, do you know your letters?"

I nodded. "Yes, Mrs Talbot."

"Recite the alphabet."

I did so, that's easy. Then I told her, "I can also do it backward."

This was a mistake. I got a glance from Mrs Talbot that said without words, "Don't you dare to be cheeky!" She took a slate board from a drawer and pushed it across the desk. She leaned forward to hand me a piece of chalk. "Your next task is to write your name."

I wrote, as neatly as I could: MARAGLINDI.

Mrs Talbot frowned across the desk. "I thought your name was Mary."

"Mrs, Talbot, that's my white name. My real name is Maraglindi."

"No. You will introduce yourself as Mary Fisher, like Mrs MacCartney called you. Mary is a good Christian name, and in this school, you will learn to be a good Christian."

"Yes, Mrs Talbot."

"All right, Mary, you will start school a week from Monday. Come to me immediately if you have any problems."

"Yes, Mrs Talbot."

***

On Saturday, it was wonderful to watch Mrs Mac use her brand new sewing machine, the first one in town. It had Singer written on it in big letters, not because it could sing but because somebody called Mr Singer had made it. It had arrived on the regular stagecoach from Sydney over two months ago, and a sailing ship had taken it to Sydney from Home, wherever that was, and it had got to Home from Prussia where it was made. Mrs Mac had had lots of fun explaining this as she took measurements and cut material. "Here we are, all set out clearly. You need two pleated skirts, then we must make you white blouses — three I think and…" she consulted the instructions again, "…we'll also need to make a belt for the skirt. That shouldn't take too much material, should it?"

Next she cut out two blazers from the same material, and three blouses from a lovely white one, then two ties to go under the blouse collars. There were also three pinafores to wear over the uniform to keep it clean. Once all the cutting was done, she used the wonderful machine to sew it all up. Actually, it did sing as Mrs Mac worked the treadle and the needle went up and down.

"Oh, careful, Mrs Mac," I couldn't help saying as the rapidly moving needle came very close to the lady's finger. I knew, if I were using the machine, I'd be sure to get blood on the material.

Mrs Mac laughed while rhythmically working the treadle and smoothly moving the seam along under the needle.

Finally, the whole uniform was ready, and slightly too large to allow for me to grow into it. I didn't like this way of dressing. These clothes were heavy and closed in on me. The pleated skirt around my ankles would get in the way if I wanted to run. All the same, it did swirl and move very nicely. I twirled around until the skirt rose in a circle.

"All right, Mary, now I want you to sew on the badges."

What could I do? I smiled at Mrs Mac and dutifully accepted the needle, thread, clothes and badges, but inside I sighed. The badge stated, "TALBOT LADIES' COLLEGE" in black embroidery on a white shield-shape. It looked very nice on the black material. I threaded the needle easily enough, and started to sew as neatly as I could, which was not very neat. And of course, the third time the needle went through the material, it also went through my skin. I had to sigh again. Careful, I must not get blood on the precious clothes! I sucked on my finger until it stopped bleeding, then stuck a piece of lint over the hole in my skin before returning to work.

At last! I managed to sew on the third badge without further injury. So, I sneaked away and walked down to the bridge across the creek. It was such a long time ago that Mother and I had washed ourselves there! Now, the little boys were the same age as I was then. Everything had changed so much in three years! I looked along the dusty road but didn't dare to walk that way. Someone would be sure to see me if I did. Still, I knew that the creek eventually had to flow into the river. I could walk beside the creek, then turn left at the river and end up at the village.

My neat button-up shoes slipped on the sloping grass verge. Oh, I nearly fell in! I took the shoes off, and also my white cotton stockings. I tried to use the stockings to tie the shoes together, but I am so awkward! Still, I managed it after a few attempts, and hung them around my neck. It was lovely to feel bare feet on the ground again. I breathed deeply, enjoying the clean scent of flowing water, and laughed when a green frog jumped out from under my feet, into the creek with a plop. Once upon a time, I'd have jumped in after her and taken her home to be eaten. I could always catch animals, even if they managed to hide from other people.

Although I left the frog, I picked edible leaves, a few early berries, and a couple of mushrooms hiding under a stone that overhung the creek. I had no way of carrying them and solved the problem by popping them into my mouth. It was just wonderful, being a blackfella girl again for a while!

The creek kept curving left and right, all over the place. As I followed around the next left bend, my foot slipped on a bit of mud. Fortunately I landed on my hands — oh, if I got my dress dirty! I very carefully clambered down to the edge of the creek to wash my hands and took a good sip of water by putting my face underwater while I was there.

At last, after yet one more of the endless number of

bends, the view opened, and there was the wide river. I knew the village had to be to my left, and happily started running that way.

The terrible stink hit me before the village came into view. I'd forgotten about the outhouses being there. At the MacCartneys', one of Atan's daily jobs was to put a half a bucket of rock lime powder into the hole, and that stopped the smell. Here, how would people have gotten rock lime?

I passed the Burrawang trees, ran down the slight incline, and thankfully got beyond the outhouses. Now, the light breeze brought several other smells to me: fish cooking, smoke from a gum tree fire, the smell of people. I walked past the stand of scrubby trees, and there was my home.

I stopped. I just had to stop. The village looked so horrible! I remembered it as a place of joy and comfort, of friends and aunties and uncles, but what I now saw was a pitiful collection of shacks on bare, muddy ground, people dressed in rags, buzzing flies over heaps of refuse. I could feel their despair and fear and could see it in the way they moved around with frequent glances toward the track that led to the town. Oh my poor people! Why do they suffer like this? I wished I could do magic, to give my beloved people back their lives. I remembered lots of stories from Father Riso and other old people about the times when everyone was black, when people were part of country and they moved every few days to care for a different area of the land that fed them, loved them and gave them everything. Now, they were forced to stay in this one spot — this ugly, terrible, stinking spot.

But what was that? Something brown moved between two of the huts. Hey, that was the back end of a horse! I stepped forward to see better, and then saw Father, squatting with his back against the side of the hut. At the same time, now that I came back from my thoughts, I could also sense his presence. Wonderful! I ran forward.

Father stood, in that easy, graceful way of his, and held out his arms. "Welcome my little one, I knew you'd come here."

I jumped.

He caught me and swung me up high before giving me a big hug. "All the same, Maraglindi my little Froggie, you shouldn't have gone off all by yourself."

"I know. I'm sorry. But..."

"But, yes, I know. You wanted to say goodbye. Let's do that now, and then you can ride back to Mr Mac's with me."

Ride! On the big horse!

Father carried me from person to person. Some cried, some made jokes. All the women hugged me, and even many of the men, but Father Riso said something special that stayed with me for a long time: "My darling, you're lucky.

Use your luck for all of us. Now, the white people don't know that we're as good as they are. Prove it to them. Then maybe one day we can live well once more."

I thought that this was a terribly heavy weight for a little girl but signalled yes with my head. And then, Father walked back to the horse. Still holding me, he unhitched the rein with one hand, put a foot in the stirrup and easily mounted. He settled me in front of him, said, "Hold on, Froggie!" and we were off. As soon as we reached the track he clicked his tongue, and the horse sped up. Trees and bushes, and later fences and houses whizzed by and I held on tight, almost forgetting to breathe in the thrill of it.

Soon we turned in at the gate, were over the bridge, rode more slowly up to the back door, and there was Old Mother to grab hold of me as Father lowered me down.

Inside, mother gave me a slight smile, but Mrs Mac was clearly furious. "Why did you run away?" she demanded in a loud, shrill voice. She leaned down so her red face was close to mine. Strangely though, her glow was more of fear than of anger.

What was wrong? I tried to explain. "I am sorry, Mrs Mac. I... I didn't run away. I—"

Mrs Mac straightened and took a deep breath. Her face became slightly less red. "Go on."

"I'm going away. Maybe, I'll never come back. I don't

know what will happen in the future. So, I went to say goodbye to my friends and family."

"That's perfectly proper, but you should've asked. You should've told someone. I was so worried about you! You're far too young to wander about unsupervised. But never mind, you're back." I could see her glow turning calmer. "Go and have a wash, and then help your mother with the boys."

This was something I was happy to do, because I'd miss them too, terribly. All the same, as I left the room I still felt puzzled over the reason for Mrs Mac's upset. Didn't she know I was a child of the land, a part of it and the land a part of me? How could I be too young to walk to the river?

***

It would have been exciting, if only... if only I didn't feel the maggots of fear crawling around in my insides. I was wearing one of the new uniforms. Mother had brushed my hair until it shone, and I smelled sweet after using Mrs Mac's scented soap for my morning wash. I thought the new straw hat on my head looked beautiful. I walked alongside my mentor (she liked me calling her that), and wanted to be anywhere, doing anything but going to Newcastle.

"My poppet, you know everyone comes to love you as soon as they meet you," Mrs Mac said reassuringly, but how would she know? A school full of white girls... white teachers... everything and everyone strange... all I wanted to do was to turn around, to go back to Mother and safety.

Father stood by the carriage, behind the two beautiful brown horses. He easily threw my new square cane basket with the locked lid on top of the carriage, jumped up and tied it in place with a few deft knots. I wished I could be as graceful as Father.

Meanwhile, Mrs Mac stepped onto the high step, and into the carriage.

Father picked me up, gave me a hug, kissed my cheek, then passed me up to the lady.

As I settled beside Mrs Mac, I was very glad to see him climb onto the driver's seat in the front.

The journey to Newcastle took more than half a day, and all that time Mrs Mac chatted easily, but afterward I couldn't remember any of it, or the sights along the road. I felt just too worried. I knew that this wouldn't be pleasant and easy, never mind how Mrs Mac felt about it.

Last time, when coming to see Mrs Talbot, we'd brought a picnic lunch. On this trip, we stopped at a big building. I easily worked out that the sign in front said, 'Coal River Hotel.' I knew the meaning of 'coal' and river,' and guessed that now I'd find out what a 'hotel' was.

Mrs Mac handed me down to Father, then stepped down

to the ground herself. Father drove the carriage and horses around the back. Mrs Mac took me to a door with a sign on it: "WC." During the trip, we'd stopped at a couple of quiet, private places to empty our bladders, but the last hour or so had been among a scattering of houses, so I was very glad to see that this was a place for relieving oneself. Mrs Mac pointed to one cubicle, and went into the second one, shutting the door.

I walked into the tiny room but felt puzzled. I could smell Mrs Mac's wee next door, so knew this was the place I needed — but the shiny white object with the wooden ring on top looked nothing like the outhouses I was used to. Still... I could sense from Mrs Mac's thoughts that this did the same job. I pulled my skirt up and bloomers down and sat.

A sudden, loud, strange noise came from next door. Then Mrs Mac said, with laugh, "Oh, I forgot, my lamb, this'll be new to you. When you're finished, pull the chain behind you."

I wiped myself on a square of paper, one of a wad on a nail in the wall, and stood. I gave the chain a tug and had to squeal in delight as water rushed into the white thing, washing my wee away.

Dutifully I rinsed my hands, and then we went into a big room with many small tables, which Mrs Mac called the restaurant. We sat at a table opposite each other. Within a few seconds, a young woman dressed similarly to the maids at home came out through a pair of swing doors. Only, she had white skin, with brown hair and eyes. As those eyes settled on me, the woman's face hardened. Her previously many-coloured glow turned very dark.

Oh, that hate blasting at me was awful. I took my eyes off her and focused on Mrs Mac, who didn't notice anything.

"What's on the menu?" Mrs Mac asked.

Roast mutton with vegs, ma'am. But..."

"Hmm?"

"But Abos ain't allowed in here."

Now Mrs Mac's face went hard, her eyes narrowed, her glow flashing darkly with anger. "You will bring a meal for an adult and one for a child. If there is anything wrong with the food or the presentation, I'll speak with the owner. Actually, call the owner now. I wish to speak with him immediately."

The woman left with an angry flounce, and in a few minutes an older man came through the swing doors. His face and bald top shone with sweat, and I could see his anger too.

Before he could say anything, Mrs Mac spoke. "I am Mrs MacCartney, the wife of a pastoralist—"

"I know that, Ma'am. You have stayed here before, and

your husband and Mr Peter too. But——"

"But nothing. This little girl is my special protégé. She is a human being like you or I. She is to be treated like any other child, or my family will never patronise your establishment again."

And that was that. We ate a good meal, although of course white-people food, had a drink — Mrs Mac a glass of wine, while I had water — and then it was back into the carriage.

"Why did those people hate me?" I asked, doing my best not to cry.

"They're ignorant. People who feel small inside try to build themselves up by looking at someone else as less good than themselves." She stopped for a moment while thinking. "They, we and our kind, have taken everything from your people. Therefore, many Aborigines behave in ways that seem quite awful. Those who don't understand the reasons then blame the victim."

I thought about this. I knew without having to be told that the children and teachers at my new school would be exactly like the hotel people. Only, there I wouldn't have Mrs Mac to protect me.

PART 2

8

Maraglindi

In ten minutes, the carriage arrived at the school, and turned in through a pair of open double gates into a busy yard. In a quick glance, I counted eight other carriages with people around them. Other people were walking around. I saw girls of various ages talking in twos and threes, and a few — little girls like me — looking lost and sticking very close to the adults near them.

Father lifted me down and gave me a very brief hug, whispering in the language, "Maraglindi, you can make them love you like you do with everyone. I'll think of you every single moment of every single day."

Then I hung on to Mrs Mac's hand as we weaved through the groups of people, into a room where a woman sat behind a desk. We joined the end of a line of three or four girls with their parents, and almost immediately I sensed others behind us.

The girl in front of me was tall, taller than the lady beside her who had to be her mother. I thought she was maybe eleven or twelve years old and had her long blonde hair in a plait sticking out from under the straw hat. I tuned in to her thoughts, which were about some girls named Bev, Kathryn and Maeve. The tall girl was looking forward to seeing her friends again. Her glow was mostly golden. I smiled at her back.

As if aware of the probing, she turned. The pupils in the middle of her blue eyes became pinpoints, and her glow changed into the dark of hating. I clearly sensed the thought, *Ugh, a stinking Abo! And a half-caste at that.*

I'd planned to send all my love to the girl, to establish contact by touching her, but this was so shocking that I wanted to find a deep hole to crawl into. I desperately clutched Mrs Mac's hand, looking down at the floor, anywhere but at the hating, contemptuous face of the tall girl.

"What's wrong, Mary my lamb?" Mrs Mac asked in her usual sweet voice, completely unaware. She squeezed my hand.

Oh, if I could just say, "Mrs Mac, I don't want to do this. Please take me home!"

The line moved forward by one, and the tall girl turned to her front again.

We were at the desk within minutes. A sign standing on it stated, "Mrs A. J. Jardine."

Mrs Mac said, "I am here to have Mary Fisher admitted to first grade."

Mrs Jardine didn't even look up, but shuffled through

one of several piles of brown folders on the desk. She found the right papers. "Sign here please," she said disinterestedly, shoving them across. I sensed the boredom, as well as being able to see it. The whirling part of the glow above her eyes was very slow, showing that she was barley thinking, merely doing things over and over.

Mrs Mac passed the papers back.

"Please take the child to Dorm F, through the door there, on the left. The route to it is clearly signposted."

We stepped aside, and Mrs Jardine was already dealing with the next girl.

Dorm F was a big room holding ten little beds and ten little wardrobes. A child-sized chair stood at the foot of each bed. A big wardrobe occupied all of the wall to the left of the door. Three families were settling their daughters, while a fat woman stood in the middle, looking toward the door.

"Good afternoon," Mrs Mac said, "I'm Mrs MacCartney, and this is my ward, Mary Fisher."

"Good afternoon, ma'am, I am Mrs Gately, the dorm mother. Mrs Talbot has told me about this child."

"Oh good. May I ask you to take special care of her? She is precious to me."

I wanted to win this woman's friendship, so gave her my best smile. "Good afternoon, Mrs Gately," I said as I stepped forward, hoping to shake hands with the woman, and so pass love into her.

But Mrs Gately actually took a step backward. "We shall see. Now listen, child, you'll need to follow the rules of cleanliness here, you understand? I won't have any humpy behaviour in my dorm."

"Mrs Gately, this child has been living in my household for the past three years." Mrs Mac's voice was frosty. "She is the best-behaved, most intelligent, most decent young girl I've ever come across. Do give her a chance." Her voice softened. "You'll find her to be delightful, and a great help if you let her. But..." she paused, and then said in a threatening tone, "if word comes back to me that she is treated with less than the kindness other girls receive, then Mrs Talbot will hear from me immediately. Do I make myself clear?"

I sensed the thought, *Stuck up young bitch*, but the woman smiled and nodded.

After all my things were neatly packed away in wardrobe number 3, I couldn't help a few tears as I said goodbye to Mrs Mac. Then, to get away from feeling so scared of everything, I focused on the girl next to me at bed number 4. She had straight black hair and blue eyes, and very white skin. She looked at me and I sensed her thought, *Why does she look so dirty?* But meanwhile, she walked around her bed and came closer. "My name is Rosalind. What's your name?"

"I'm Mary." I knew better than to give the real one, but then couldn't help adding, "You know, my skin is clean. I just happened to be born this way. It's like, you and I have black hair and some people have blonde hair."

"I didn't know... but how..."

I reached out and took Rosalind's right hand with mine, imitating adults when they introduced themselves. "How do you do?" I said. I looked into Rosalind's eyes, and sent her all the love I could.

Rosalind smiled a broad, beautiful smile and her eyes shone. "I'm so glad we're going to be side by side," she said.

But then, Mrs Gately called loudly, "Ladies, it's time to go to the Chapel. Line up here in front of me in twos, by bed number."

I of course had no trouble with that and took Rosalind with me, but most of the other girls had to be gently shoved into place, since clearly they were unable to read their bed number. There were nine of us, bed number 10 being empty.

We marched across the courtyard, now empty except for other lines of girls, to a door with a cross above it. So, the Chapel had to be a church. Good. I loved going to church.

As we walked in, Mrs Gately said, "Take your hats off, ladies."

Six rows of chairs faced a higher area, where I saw Mrs Talbot sitting next to a man with a stern expression on his face. Mrs Gately led us up to the front row of seats. The chairs there were small, the right height for us.

The big room was filled with the muttered voices of girls and the rustling of dresses. Then Mrs Talbot stood, and the noise stopped. "Good afternoon, ladies," Mrs Talbot said, not loudly, and yet I knew that even those in the back row would hear her perfectly clearly.

"Good afternoon, Mrs Talbot," came a chorus of girls' voices.

"I welcome you back to your school. We shall have a wonderful year, and here is Father Durham to bless it for us."

The man stood, walked forward and said in a harsh voice, "All of you will stand."

Afterward, I only remembered parts of his speech, because it was so severe. All of it focused on obedience being a woman's lot, and you must do the right thing or you will go to hell, and how all women are sinful because of what Eve did at the beginning of time, on and on in a fiery waterfall of dislike for females. While standing there, listening, I remembered the beautiful passages Gerald had often read to us from the Bible, about God's love and forgiveness, and I strongly doubted that this man was talking about the same God.

At last Mr Durham stopped and Mrs Talbot took charge

again.

"Ladies, it is time to go for our evening meal. You will transport yourselves to the Dining Room in an orderly manner."

The Dining Room was even larger than the Chapel and had six rectangular tables. At a glance, I noted that each table held the girls of a particular age, and one adult woman. However, several seats were empty. At our table, there was only the one empty chair, obviously the one for the girl who was not in bed number 10.

Soon, a procession of girls came out through a pair of double swing doors, each bearing a tray with steaming bowls on it. I smelt soup. The girl approaching our table was perhaps eleven years old, with her brown hair in two plaits. She had a scattering of freckles on each side of her nose. She was smiling at Mrs Gately, then her eyes lit on me and the smile froze. Her thought was, *Bloody Hell, am I being forced to serve a dirty, stinking Abo?*

I wilted inside. I looked down, anywhere except at the girl, and jumped when a bowl of soup was thumped down in front of me.

Mrs Gately said, "Ladies, say grace with me." She recited some words, and the other girls spoke with her, but I could say nothing.

For the first time in my life, I felt I couldn't eat, until Mrs

Gately said, "Mary Fisher, what's wrong? Eat, child."

I forced the soup down, then the rest of dinner, but could taste none of it, remembered none of it. I withdrew into myself and cried within. Oh, why did they hate me so?

***

I awoke at first light as usual, although it had taken me ages to get to sleep the night before. It's so difficult to sleep when you're crying! The other girls were still asleep, the room filled with their quiet, snuffling breaths. Silently I eased out of bed. The timber floor was cold under my feet as I walked to the door, and then into the corridor that led to the back door, and from there to the outhouses.

As I opened the back door, I faced the brilliant red of dawn. It was so beautiful that I stopped to gaze at it, at the small fluffy pink clouds still lit from beneath.

This view made up for the nasty smell coming from the five doors of the brick building facing me. The middle door opened, and a tall girl came out. She wore a long, blue dressing gown, and shoes without socks on her feet. I recognised her: she was the one who'd been in Mrs Jardine's queue in front of me. I tried to shrink back into the doorway, but the tall, blonde girl had seen me.

"What are you doing here?" she demanded in an unpleasant, high voice.

"I... I need to have a call of nature."

"No. I mean, what's the likes of you doing in my school?"

"Mrs Talbot decided that I could come." Within, I felt a stirring of anger, I think for the first time in my life. I could see from the girl's glow that she was furious, but now I no longer feared her. Who was this girl to question me anyway?

"Listen here, dirty little Abo slut, you go home where you came from and—"

"No! You have no right! I'll tell Mrs Talbot. She said I should."

A whirl of movement, and I found myself on the ground, looking up. At first, there was no pain, just a numbness about my left cheek. Then a shod foot slammed into my side. The girl towered over me, and I had never seen a black glow about anyone before, except, suddenly I remembered, Father had one like this when Kohli died. The whirl of her glow at the heart, and in the middle of her body, were large and fast. She was ready to act.

"You do and you're DEAD, little slut!"

Then I was alone. The worst thing was, I'd wetted myself. The left side of my face now throbbed, and I felt an ache in my thigh too, where I must have landed on a stone. Painfully, slowly, I struggled to my feet and slunk back through the still-open door. Why did she hate me so? And why couldn't I take that hate away and make it into love?

At first, I saw nothing in the dim corridor, because of the change from the red dawn outside. Quietly, I returned to the dorm, picked up the clothes Mrs Gately had made me neatly stack on the chair at the foot of my bed last night, and tiptoed out to the washroom.

Still-dim light came in through a high window. A boiler stood in the corner, looking the same as the one in Mrs Mac's laundry, only bigger. The firebox was cold, and full of grey ash. I saw several metal basins, and a hand-operated pump. When I worked the lever up and down it made a noise and I winced, but nobody came.

I gingerly lifted the muddy, wee-stained nightdress over my head, and vigorously washed it out using one of the many cakes of soap. I squeezed it out as best I could, which was not very well, then washed myself in a new basin of ice-cold water. That was all right — it was no colder than the river at home. I dried myself on my towel and quickly dressed.

Still afraid of being seen, I hurried out again, carrying the wet nightdress in a basin, and found the clothesline. Only, it was way too high for me. Like at Mrs Mac's, a long, forked stick held up the middle. Unfortunately, I couldn't reach the line even when I pulled this prop out from under it.

I jumped with shock when Mrs Gately spoke behind me. "Mary, what are you doing?"

I turned. "Oh, good morning, Mrs Gately." My voice

sounded strange, even to myself.

"Good morning, child. Let me help you." She easily pegged the dripping wet nightdress to the line and raised it high again with the prop. Then she asked, nicely enough, "Did you wet your bed?"

"No Mrs Gately. But... but..." I couldn't continue, but started to cry. Great sobs shook my body and I bent over, hiding my face in my hands.

"Stop that. Stop that now!"

Why was she shouting at me? I somehow managed to do so.

"This is a ladies' school. Despite your background, child, you're here to receive training as a lady. Regardless of the provocation, ladies do not make a spectacle of themselves."

All I wanted was a hug, some loving comfort. I looked up at Mrs Gately, and without thinking about it, read her glow, heard her thoughts. She felt no compassion for me, only an impatience at having her morning routine disrupted, and a superior contempt. There'd be no comfort here.

Sadly, without another word, I turned and dragged my feet back toward the building.

"Mary."

I stopped and turned. "Yes, Mrs Gately."

"I did not give you leave to go."

"S-Sorry, Mrs Gately."

"Something is wrong, child. Tell me." But behind the words was the thought, *That snooty young bitch has power. I've got to be seen to do the right thing, even for the fruit of an Abo whore's indiscretion.* There was no point in telling this woman about being hit and kicked. She'd probably do the same if she thought she could get away with it.

So, I answered, "Mrs Gately, I fell over and hurt myself and got my nightdress muddy."

Somehow, I got through breakfast, but afterward I couldn't remember a single thing about it, then Mrs Gately marched us over to a classroom. Ten slightly older girls were already in the back half of the room, and a young woman stood smiling in front of a wall with a smudgy black surface. Her hair was the colour of carrots, which I found amazing.

After the nine of us sat and Mrs Gately left, the woman said, "Ladies, I am Miss Bachel, and I'm your teacher this year. We'll have lots of fun and learn all sorts of interesting things. Starting with the Grade 2s, I want each of you to stand up and tell me your name."

A voice from behind me started, "I am Jessica McGuire."

"Jessica, say 'Miss Bachel, I am Jessica McGuire'."

Obediently, the girl did so, and soon it was my turn.

I stood up. "Miss Bachel, my name is Mary Fisher."

Then Rosalind said her name, followed by the other five.

Miss Bachel said, "Lift the lids of your desks, ladies, and

you'll find a picture book there."

A brief clatter filled the room as I looked at my book, and saw that my neighbours held identical ones. The cover had "My First Reader" written on it, with many pictures in small squares under the title. I turned the pages, and saw that those pictures were repeated, one to a page, with a word for each: CAT, DOG, CHAIR and so on. Rapidly I started going through the book, finding that I already knew all the words.

Miss Bachel's voice interrupted my reading. "Mary Fisher, what are you doing?"

"Miss Bachel, I was reading the—"

"Wait until I teach you, silly child. Now, all you Grade 2 ladies, I want you to write down each word as I read it to the Grade 1s. Open your book and look at the first page."

She turned around and used a piece of chalk to write CAT on the blackish surface behind her. Turning again, she said, "That's Cat, C-A-T."

I remembered Mrs Talbot's reaction to my knowledge of the alphabet and said nothing. But within my heart, I wondered if it was possible to die of boredom.

***

The first week passed — somehow. I managed to make friends with Helena, the girl in the number 5 bed. I was constantly careful to make sure that whenever we were out of sight of teachers or other adults, I had either this girl or Rosalind with me. In the dining room and on the playground, I often caught the hateful, hating thoughts of many of the bigger girls, and they always made me cry inside.

I quickly realised that I already knew everything Miss Bachel taught — even the things the Grade 2 girls were supposed to learn. So, I sat in my seat and dreamed of home with my eyes open. Within my heart I could smell the scent of the gum trees, feel the wind on my face, played with my two little boys, hugged Mother or Old Mother or Father or Tari or Atan, who smelled of horse even in my imagination, sat on Mrs Mac's knee while the lady read me a story, copied the same words that Gerald was teaching Atan, and all the while I managed to do what the teacher ordered and seemed to be just one of the class. Every now and then, Miss Bachel spoke sharply to me for not paying attention, then I was forced to return to a few minutes of boredom, but soon went home again, replaying memories of Mr Mac on Devil, or from earlier, food gathering with the women by the river, or listening to Father Riso telling stories about the Dreamtime or of the old days before the white man.

One evening I sneaked out, wanting to be alone under the sky, and gazed at the sunset. Three men were cutting the grass on the playground, using scythes — something I'd seen at the MacCartneys' — so, watching them took me back there. I admired the rhythmic grace of their movements as they covered the big area in an orderly way.

Something different happened on Friday. Halfway through the morning a tall, very thin lady came into the classroom. She had a hook nose and somewhat browner skin than most other white people. Miss Bachel introduced her as Mrs Goldberg. The lady looked around through a pair of glinting spectacles. "I'm the music teacher, and now, you Grade 1 ladies, you'll come with me one at a time for some tests."

I could hardly wait for my turn. I loved to sing, and the sound of musical instruments always gave me great joy. Oh, to learn to play one!

I couldn't help wriggling impatiently in my seat while Clara, then Elizabeth went off with Mrs Goldberg, and each stayed away forever, until at last it was my turn. As we walked down the corridor, I only sensed curiosity in Mrs Goldberg's thoughts, no hostility. The lady looked down at me. "It's unusual to see an Aboriginal child here. What's your name?"

"Mrs Goldberg, my name is Mary Fisher. Only, my real name is Maraglindi."

"That has a lovely sound. The way you say it is almost singing."

"Oh, I love to sing!"

We smiled at each other as she opened a door. "You haven't told me yet how you got here."

"Mrs Goldberg, my family works for Mr and Mrs MacCartney, and Mrs Mac wanted me to come here."

Mrs Goldberg's mouth twitched. "And I bet that's not all a blessing for you? But Mary, we have work to do."

I glanced around. The sun shone in through a big window, onto bookshelves holding lots of very big-sized books. Many black cases of various odd shapes were stacked against the other walls. Mrs Goldberg sat on a chair and picked up a shiny brown object with a very graceful, curved shape. Looking at my face, she smiled. "You've never seen a violin before? Of course not." She took a stick-like thing from a stand in front of her and drew it across the violin. "Beautiful sound, isn't it?"

I was too fascinated even to reply, just drank in the last lingering memories of the sound.

"All right, Mary. Sing this." Mrs Goldberg produced another pure, clean note.

I enjoyed making the same sound, as clearly as I could.

This was repeated with note after note, then the lady played "Three Blind Mice," which of course I knew well, having often sang it for my little boys, and so it went for several songs, more and more complex. Most I'd never heard before, but could listen to it once, then perfectly repeat it back from memory, with a wordless "la, la, la."

At last the teacher stood. "My poppet, you're the newest member of the music group. We practise in the Chapel every Friday after luncheon. You will also start learning to play the pianoforte."

"Oh, thank you!" Before I realised what I'd done, I stepped forward and hugged her. I felt the love flow between us. I didn't know what a pianoforte was, but it had to be something that made music.

"Maraglindi, while we're alone I'll call you that, you're a very special person. There is something about you." Her long, sensitive hand stroked the top of my head.

For once, I happily ate my lunch, hardly able to wait for it to be over. Of course, today Mrs Gately had to reprimand one of the girls for eating in a messy way and took forever.

At last, I could run to the Chapel. It took a moment for my eyes to adjust to the gloom inside, but gradually, as I walked forward, I made out a group of girls of various sizes up front. They were chatting and didn't see me. Then, as I got closer, I recognised two of them with horror: the tall, blonde girl who had hit and kicked me, and the brown-haired girl who served the Grade 1 table in the Dining room, and always had such hating thoughts toward me.

With my insides in a knot, unable to hold back sob, I turned to walk out again.

9

Rachael Goldberg

"Oh, I must have a cup of tea!" Rachael exclaimed as she entered the staffroom. "Why can't girls ever do the work I set them? Why can't they remember a score?"

Caroline Bachel grinned at her. "This is the right place for a cup of tea." She waved toward the teapot wearing its cosy on the scratched table in the middle of the room. "And the answer is that you're too soft on them." She sat at ease on one of the battered, sagging couches, cradling her own cup of tea in her hands. As yet, none of the other teachers had arrived.

Rachael took a cup — chipped of course — from the shelf and poured. Unlike anyone else, she had hers black and without sugar. "I've had a disappointment," she said. "One of your darlings."

"Hmm?"

"Mary Fisher. I really bonded with her, lovely child, and..."

"But she is an Abo half-caste!"

"So? And I'm a Jew, and you talk to me. Many people treat me like I was a leper."

"You're civilised, and intelligent, and clever too. Abos are barely above animals. Not that I have anything against animals, but well, it's not the same."

"This child can sing like an angel. Anyway, I told her to be at the Chapel for practice, and she never turned up."

"Rache, you're a city girl, so you don't know anything much about them. It's just the way they are. They have no idea of word given, or appointments, or promises. I don't know why the Dragon ever allowed her in. So far, all she's done is to sit there like a cabbage. She does nothing, says nothing, just dreams with her eyes open."

"I had the distinct sense that she is intelligent. She has a fantastic memory for sound."

"So do birds, but they're not intelligent, are they?"

The door creaked open, and Sue Logan came in. As usual, she greeted Caroline and gave Rachael a wordless, dirty look.

As usual, Rachael retaliated with the most brilliant smile she could manage. "Oh well," she said, "it's time to pick up my children." She drained her cup and went out with as regal a bearing as if she were Queen Victoria herself. This was somewhat spoiled by almost knocking into Lillian Hislop outside. The older woman gave her a barely civil grunt, so Rachael said "Good afternoon, see you next Friday," and walked past with another smile she hoped didn't look contrived.

She picked up Becky from the playground, and the two

of them walked out through the gate, toward the boys' school half a mile away. "Did you have a good day, my poppet?" she asked.

"Oh, all right I suppose, Mama. Maths was interesting. Mrs Darley taught us a funny poem to remember Pythy... Pytho..."

"Pythagoras?"

"Yes, that's the one. Pythagoras' theorem. 'The squaw on the hippopotamus hide equals the sum of the squaws on the other two hides.' And you know, most of the girls still couldn't remember the real thing even after that!"

They laughed together, Rachael enjoying Becky's tinkling laugh. That reminded her of another musical voice. "Darling, have you noticed a Grade 1 girl with brown skin?"

"Oh yes, everyone has. The little Abo girl."

"Don't call her 'Abo.' That's a rude word, the same kind of thing they throw at us, like 'Yid.' She is an Aborigine, and there's nothing wrong with that."

"You surely wouldn't know from what the other girls say about her! I've heard Bev say to Kirsten that she stinks, and is a... excuse me, Mama, a slut, and..." She petered out.

"Beck, I've been right up close to her, and she doesn't stink. She is probably cleaner than many of those girls. Sometimes, Bev and her gang are quite smelly, aren't they?"

Becky wrinkled up her nose and nodded vigorously, and

again the two of them laughed.

Benjamin was waiting at the schoolyard gate for them.

Shocked, Rachael saw that he had a bruise swelling on his left cheek, under the eye. "What happened?"

"It's all right, Mama. Dennis said that all Jewish girls are, um, sluts, and that he was going to, excuse me, do something to you, Beck, so I had to fight him." He looked proud, holding up his two hands so the backs showed. Skin was missing from the knuckles on both. "He won't say things like that again. When we finished, Arthur and Joe had to help him to walk."

Becky stepped forward, dropping her bag on the ground, and gave her big brother a hug. "I hope you don't get in trouble for me," she said.

"Nah, there were no teachers around. Anyway, they tell us it's a manly thing to defend a lady's honour."

The children picked up their bags and the three of them walked on toward home. Rachael looked down on her son's curly dark head. "So, the boxing lessons from Mr Fletcher have paid off, Ben?"

"They certainly have! I didn't even have to think about it. I told him to shut his ugly mouth or I'd shut it for him, and he hit out without warning." He lifted his free hand to the bruise on his face. "Right, well, that caught me by surprise, and so I took a step back, and heard Arthur and somebody else laugh. They thought it'd be like the last time. So I went for him and hit him maybe eight times before he realised. Then he was on the ground, his face a mess. He spat out some blood and a couple of teeth and turned on his side. Then he chucked up his luncheon, and everybody laughed — at him."

"I'll make sure Simon Fletcher has some extra lessons. His father has earned them."

"He was there too, Mama, and gave me a big wink. He is a good fellow."

They arrived home, and Rachael got immersed in preparation for Sabbath Eve. It wasn't until David was singing the blessing on his children that Rachael remembered the young Aboriginal girl at school. She decided that next Friday, she'd make sure to seek her out and find out why she hadn't turned up.

Maraglindi

I lay in my bed, watching the curtained windows lighten. I needed to empty my bladder but, like every morning since the first, I waited for one of the other girls to awaken before daring to go out.

At last, Elizabeth stirred and sat up.

Then the door opened, and a strange lady walked in, smiling. "Good morning, ladies," she said loudly, "I'm Mrs

Judson, your weekend dorm mother. Rise and shine!" The glow about her was mostly silver, almost like Mrs Mac's, so I instantly knew that she was a good person.

Before the other girls managed to get out of bed, I was already peeking out the back door. It seemed safe, and anyway I could hear footsteps behind me. I relieved myself and was also the first in the washroom. I dressed in a clean uniform and neatly put yesterday's clothes in my washing bag.

Mrs Judson was straightening the beds at the other end of the room, so I quickly smoothed my bottom sheet and pulled the top linen into place. Then I ran over to the lady, asking, "Mrs Judson, may I help you?"

"My, you're a good girl. Thank you."

We worked on opposite sides of the bed while the other girls came trickling back in.

"It's not expected of Grade 1 ladies, but from next year on you'll be doing this for yourselves anyway."

"At home, I always made my own bed, and also for my little boys."

We moved to the next bed.

"Hmm? Tell me about your little boys."

My heart lit up at the thought of them. "Rippie is my little brother, and Donald is the son of Mr and Mrs MacCartney, who are the wonderful lady and gentleman who employ us.

I used to look after the two little boys a lot. They are three years younger than I am. And Mrs Mac used to teach me to read, and I even learned to write." We walked to the third bed as I said this.

"You should be doing well here then!"

"Um... I don't know." I just stopped. I could not move, because the heaviness of the present came crashing down on me. I hung my head and felt tears run down my face.

Mrs Judson straightened her back and came around the bed. "What's wrong? By the way, what's your name?"

"I... I'm Mary Fisher, ma'am. But, but no, I'm not doing well."

I felt myself lifted up, then I was sitting on a soft lap, within a soft embrace, my head held to ample breasts. I sent her all the love in my heart.

"Tell me."

When my tears allowed me, I managed to say, "They hate me! 'Cause I'm an Abo. 'Cause my skin is brown and not white. Even the teachers. Only you and Mrs Goldberg have been kind to me. And I'm scared of being hit again, and—"

"Hold up, Mary. Who hit you?"

"Oh, if I tell she'll kill me. She said so, and I could see it's real, she wants to kill me and..."

"People say things like that."

I couldn't tell her about seeing people's glow, because I

knew others couldn't, and about sensing their thoughts. "When Mr Tom Geery killed my big sister, my father looked like this girl did. I... I can see things about people."

"All right, little Mary Fisher. Look me in the eyes."

I did as she told me to.

"I have duties now, but after breakfast, you will come with me and we'll sort this out."

I sensed her thought, *This is wrong. I'll get the Dragon to sort it out all right!* I almost giggled, knowing that the Dragon had to be Mrs Talbot. I said, "Mrs Judson, I can't go to Mrs Talbot. Anyway, she doesn't like me either. She has only let me come to the school because Mrs Mac is paying her a lot of money. Please, just let it be."

"You're a strange child. Were you reading my mind? But don't answer. We're running late." She raised her voice. "Everybody, line up by bed numbers. Off we go to breakfast!"

As I did every mealtime, I withdrew into myself as soon as the brown-haired big girl pushed her way through the double swing doors with her tray of bowls holding steaming porridge. I kept my eyes down and saw nothing, sensed nothing, and so, I managed to feel nothing. When the girl went away for her second tray, I looked up to see Mrs Judson's eyes on me. The lady gave me a kind smile, then said grace.

Later, out in the playground, some girls organised a skipping game. Two girls swung the ends of a long rope in a circle, and one after another, girls skipped through to the shouted words of a nursery rhyme. It looked like fun, but I knew I'd trip if I tried. Besides, I also knew I wouldn't be welcomed by many of those girls.

So, I picked a sunny spot against the bole of a big oak tree and squatted. Within my mind, I again went home, to the wide river and the laughter and companionship of the people.

I looked up when a shadow fell over me. Mrs Judson stood there, gazing down with pity in her eyes. Her thought was, *The hate and hitting are real all right!* Aloud, she said, "Mary, I'd like you to tell me about how your people used to live before the white man came. I'm always fascinated by things new to me." She reached down an inviting hand and I stood. Hand in hand, we walked over to one of the benches against the Chapel wall and sat.

I said while we walked, "My Father Riso is a magic man. He is not my father but my mother's brother, and that also makes him my father. Um, I can't explain that. And because he is the father who is my mother's brother, he is the one who has to tell the stories to me and my brothers and sisters. And he has told me some of the old stories. You know what you white people call the stars in the sky?"

We sat down, and I happily snuggled against Mrs Judson's side. It was so wonderful, once more to have loving contact!

"Hmm?"

"They are the old people. The people who used to live, our parents' parents' parents, way back."

"Ancestors."

"And they're up there and watch over us. Some people, like Father Riso, can talk to some of the spirits of the ancestors. And that's how they do magic."

I sensed the good-natured disbelief in the lady's thoughts.

"Oh, Mrs Judson, it's really true! I've seen it! When... when I was a little girl, before we went to work for Mr and Mrs MacCartney, three policemen came, and in front of them Father Riso turned himself into a raven and flew away. I saw it! Then he came walking back, all tired, two days later."

Something like a stage trick, the lady thought. I didn't know what a stage was, and anyway, I sensed something else, something wonderful... Father! Atan! Gerald!

I jumped to my feet and raced for the closed gate of the yard. I tripped on my own feet of course, fell and was running again, barely noticing the scrape on my knee.

I'd reached halfway to the gate when it swung inward, and there was Atan, pushing on it while leading in a dappled brown horse. Gerald rode in on his black gelding, then Father on his big brown one.

With a scream of joy I threw myself at my big brother, who caught me and swung me up into the air before hugging me and putting me down. "You've hurt yourself again," he noted, looking down at the blood soaking through my stocking at the ankle, though the pain was at the knee.

Then Father was holding me, with Gerald hugging both of us from behind my back.

"I don't care," I replied to Atan, "You're here!"

All four of us laughed. "Always a stranger to your own body, my little Froggie," my big brother said.

When things settled down from the joy of reunion, I clutched Father's hand with my right and Gerald's with my left, and led them to Mrs Judson, who'd stood from the seat and waited with a smile. "Mrs Judson," I said, "this is my Father, Mick, and real good friend, Gerald, and back there looking after the horses is my big brother, Atan, and I'm so happy!"

Gerald removed his wide-brimmed hat and Father followed him. Gerald bowed slightly, saying, "How do you do, Mrs Judson. We came to bring Maraglindi a letter from Mrs MacCartney, and also because the world is a sadder place when she isn't around."

"I've only met her today," Mrs Judson answered, "but I

do know what you mean. There is something special about her. Only, Mr Fisher, may I have a word with you?" She walked away from Gerald, Atan and me, and Father followed her.

I saw them talking quietly and started to tune into their thoughts. Mrs Judson was saying, "I'm only here on weekends, and of course..." Then I lost the rest of their conversation, because Gerald playfully tugged my hair. "Hey, Maraglindi, I've got something for you." He handed me a sealed envelope. I instantly recognised it: Mrs Mac had a box of these.

With awkward fingers I opened it, trying and failing to avoid ripping it as I eased the gummed-on flap off. Then I sat back on the seat and started reading aloud, although I had to stumble over the occasional longer word:

"My dearest Mary,

Our little boys send you their love.

So do I, and your family, and Mr Mac too.

I know you will be doing well, and make everyone love you.

Please study hard and prove to everybody that a child of this land can be as good as anybody else.

You have only been gone a week, but already I miss you very much. I do know that it is the right thing for you to go to school and learn. I will be so proud of you!

    With continued best wishes,

    Alice MacCartney."

When I finished, I looked up to see Mrs Judson and Father, both looking at me with admiration. The lady said, "I wouldn't have believed it, a child of your age reading so well."

From behind me, Atan answered. "Gerald has come for the past four years, to teach me. And always, Maraglindi has learned everything as well as I did, usually better and faster. She is a smart one all right."

Father added, "In doing things with her hands and feet and that, she is not much good. But thinking and talking, she be better than many children twice her age."

"So," Mrs Judson mused aloud, "why did you say this morning that you're not doing well in class?"

I looked up at her, feeling my eyes blur with tears. But reading the lady's thoughts, I knew I didn't have to answer.

After a long moment, Father said, in the language, "Maraglindi, love, come with us. We've set up a camp by the river, and you can eat some bush tucker for lunch."

"Oh, Mrs Judson, may I?"

"Sorry, Mary, I didn't understand what your father said."

"He'd like to take me out for luncheon, on the riverside, eating my people's food."

"Of course you may. If you look around, you'll see that many children have gone home for the day, or even the weekend. Do you wish to sleep out as well?"

The thought was so wonderful that I couldn't find the words to express my delight.

Mrs Judson laughed down at me. "I'll miss you, my dear. Be back tomorrow by five of the clock — unless you want to attend Chapel of course. That'll be at ten of the clock of the morning. Now, let us go to your Dorm and get a parcel of clothes together for you."

Kirsten Petersen

"Kirsty. Kirsty!"

The blonde girl shook her head, coming back from her private world. "What?"

"Have you gone away to dreamland or something?"

"Oh Maeve, do you see him?"

She still had her eyes fixed on the young man. He was so tall — was that six foot four maybe? And the breadth of his shoulders, and he moved with such easy grace as he sprung to the ground off his fine horse. And he came with two Abo servants, so he must be important.

Then she saw a movement: that filthy Abo girl running toward them. The Abo boy picked her up, then the man.

The magic broke when he... he cuddled the man and the

girl. Oh how could he touch them? Ugh. Kirsten felt her body shudder. Then she hated the dirty animals all the more for spoiling what she knew had been instant love until then. She turned her back and said, in a voice that sounded shrill in her own ears, "Oh, I am thirsty. Would anyone care for a cup of tea?"

10
Maraglindi

Gerald had brought a thing he called a tent. He said it was what soldiers slept in when at war. The four of us set it up in no time, then I helped Atan to gather wood and start a nice fire. Birds flitted around, and I heard the quiet buzz of insects. The smell of the river, the whisper of the gumtrees, all soothed my spirits. I thanked God to be out of school! This was home, although I could barely see the other shore of the river because of its great width, but it was still home, even if a long way from the village, from the MacCartneys' place.

"Tell me!" I demanded while the billy came to the boil and a fish and a yabby baked in mud skins within the red glow. "Tell me about the boys, and mother, and... and everyone and everything."

Atan said instead, "I've trained my first horse! Father watched me, but I did it all meself."

Father smiled. "And he did a good job too."

"As for me," Gerald said, "I've come to say goodbye. That's why I just had to come."

"Oh?" I managed not to cry.

"I'm going to a town near Sydney, to a place called a

theological college, where I'll learn to be a priest. You know that's what I've been wanting to do. And when I'm fully trained, I want to work with you wonderful Aborigines, to ease life for you and stop all this disdain."

"I don't know the last word," I interrupted.

"It's when you treat a person worse because of what group they belong to, like."

"Oh. Is that's what it's called?"

Father looked at me. "You are learning about being Abo in the white man's world?"

I nodded, unable to say anything.

Atan asked, "But your magic? I don't know anyone who doesn't come to love you."

"I... I need to touch a person and send them the love in my heart. But when somebody comes up to me all hating in spirit, I can't do it. I just can't. I still love them of course, but I can't make them love me when I'm scared of them."

The billy started to rock over the fire, so Gerald lifted it off with a stick. He dropped tea leaves into it, whirled it about by its wire handle, then poured into metal cups. We waited for the tea to cool. Instead of sitting, Gerald used his stick to turn the meat, then hung his head. "Heavenly Father, please protect your dear daughter Maraglindi from harm, and place the gift of love within the hearts of those who look on dark skin with disdain. Teach them that all people are

Your precious children, and that she is more precious than most."

Awhile later, as we ate, I remembered. "Hey, you haven't told me the news!"

So they dutifully filled me in on the happenings of home.

At night, we slept close together in the tent, under a bit of netting to keep mosquitoes off. My last thought was that it was so wonderful, cuddling Father.

Emma Judson

After supervising luncheon, Emma took a deep breath to steady herself and went to the office building. She walked through the anteroom where the secretary sat during the week and knocked on Mrs Talbot's door.

"Come in!"

It seemed to her that Mrs Talbot always sat behind her big desk and always busy with some stack of papers. The hard face softened with a smile, looking at her. "Oh, Mrs Judson," she said, "it is good to see you."

"You too, ma'am."

"How is the family?"

Emma couldn't help smiling. "My daughter, Sarah, is about to have her first baby! I'll be a grandmother soon!"

"Well, well, congratulations. And it seems only yesterday that you were my best teacher."

The compliment felt nice — the Dragon was not free with them. "Twenty-one years it's been. But, ma'am, I'm here to report on a couple of matters."

"Very well. Do go on."

"Both concern the Aboriginal child, Mary Fisher. First, she is unusually intelligent."

"I know that. I did give her a test."

"This morning, she had visitors: her father and brother, accompanied by a young gentleman who told me he is going to train for the ministry. They brought a letter for her, from a Mrs MacCartney."

"Yes, that was the person who had brought her and is paying the fees."

"Well, this mite read the letter out aloud. Let me recite it to you." She did, word for word from memory, and saw the unspoken appreciation on Mrs Talbot's face. "She had to work on a few of the longer words like 'everybody,' and 'continued,' but got it all correct, and clearly understood it all. Ma'am, I don't know any second-grade children who could have done that. It's more appropriate for well into third grade."

"This is something of a surprise. I have received the first weekly report from her teacher, and I quote, 'She sits there all day like a cabbage, taking nothing in.' So, I thought it may have been a mistake to admit her, after all."

"I guess she must be bored beyond tolerance. She needs to be given work that challenges her."

"She is of the right age to be in Grade 1. I could not possibly advance her to Grade 3!"

"No ma'am, of course not. Socially, physically and emotionally she is a six-year-old. In fact, she is rather awkward in her physical coordination. But I do have a suggestion."

"Do go on."

"I'd like to come in for an hour every weekday and spend personal time with her. During the rest of the day, she can do work I set her, while sitting in class."

"Hmm." Mrs Talbot looked pensive. "I will need to contact this Mrs MacCartney person and see if she is willing to pay for the extra tuition."

"Oh, ma'am, I'm happy to do it for free!"

Now the Principal looked at Emma as if she was crazy.

"It's only for an hour a day, and now my youngest is pretty well independent, I can spare the time. And... and, well, there is something special about her. I'd feel it to be a privilege to ease her time through life."

Mrs Talbot shook her head in disbelief. Clearly, she'd never do anything for anyone without payment. She said, "I shall discuss it with Miss Bachel and send you a message."

"Thank you. Now, the second matter may be harder to

solve. This Mary Fisher is being terrorised by at least one of the bigger girls."

Emma was glad the look of steel from the Principal was not aimed at her as she said, "Do continue."

"She has been hit by someone, with enough force to make her feel afraid. This girl told her that she'd kill her if she told, and the child believes this. So, I don't know the name of the perpetrator. I've watched her. In private, or among the other younger girls, she is sociable, sparkling even. When in the Dining Room or on the playground, where she is among the bigger children, she is withdrawn, depressed, quiet, and goes away into a dream world."

"Leave it with me, Mrs Judson. A child has been entrusted to my care. It does not matter who she is or what she is. She is in my protection, and I shall protect her."

Kirsten

Kirsten looked along the aisle, delighted with the crowd packing the church. She glanced down at her beautiful long white dress, through a white tulle veil. It felt odd, but perfectly right, that she had breasts, and that she was actually taller than Father, who held her right elbow as they walked forward. Everyone smiled, and she heard appreciative whispers over the sound of the music. But her eyes were fixed on the front. Standing before the altar was the

Reverend Mr Taylor, looking the same as ever, with a young man by his side. Kirsten instantly recognised him: he was the young man who'd come to the school, but older, looking even stronger. Strangely, he was also dressed as a priest, with a cassock, surplice, and a black stole. He had a loving smile on his face, but Kirsten felt frustrated because she couldn't remember his name.

Then, from nowhere, a brown little girl ran between the two of them and held up her hands. "He is mine!" she shrilled, and to her horror Kirsten saw her groom's face and hands turn dark brown, his features coarsen until he had thick lips, a wide, flat nose and beetle brows.

Then she awoke, in her narrow bed in Dorm B. Her blankets were on the floor. Sweat covered her body. Dawn light shone between the closed curtains.

Shakily she stood and would have fallen if she hadn't grabbed the back of her chair.

Kathryn sat up in her bed. "Kirsty, what's the matter?"

"Nothing. I just had a nightmare." She put on her dressing gown and shoes and walked out to the outhouses. She hoped the little Abo slut would be there again, but no, she had the place to herself.

An hour later, she still felt shaken during Monday assembly as she took her place in the second back row of the Chapel. She spotted the Abo girl up front and was so overtaken with revulsion that she felt like delivering her breakfast all over the floor. How could any man...

Mrs Talbot moved to the front of the stage, and the room grew quiet. The Dragon stood there for a long time, silent, glaring. At last she spoke, in a voice that made Kirsten want to hide under her chair. And when she realised the subject-matter, she wished she could.

"Ladies, I am proud of our school. Many years of girls have passed through it, with credit to society, and each of you is in my personal care. Your parents have entrusted you to me. So, it is my duty to protect you from harm." She stopped and glared at the back rows. "One young person has been harmed. A Grade 1 girl, only six years old, has been attacked by a bigger child. How do I know? You have all been in Mrs Judson's care. She is the one who has noticed it. Nothing slips past her, as you well know. The cowardly attacker threatened to kill the child if she told. So, she has kept secret the identity of the bully, but truth will out, with God's help. So, at this moment, I do not yet know who the criminal is. When I find out, she will be expelled. That is all."

Throughout the morning classes, Kirsten was unable to concentrate. She wanted to scream, to hit someone, to cry — but she had to sit there with a blank face and pretend that everything was all right. The unfairness of it all choked her. She loved the school! She was proud of it, and that was why she felt so disgusted that a piece of rubbish could have been admitted. What could the Dragon have been thinking of? If it became known that Abo sluts went to Talbot Ladies' Academy, a girl might have to keep it a secret that she'd been a student there. She suddenly saw a vivid image, blanking out Mrs Hislop blathering on up front. She saw a fat, greasy man leering at her, his sneering, wet mouth coming for her face. "You're just a slut of course, hinny," he said. "Didn't ya go to school with an Abo? All they're good for is to get a good stoking, and the same to you. C'mon then!"

She jerked back from the apparition, so suddenly that her chair nearly overbalanced.

Mrs Hislop stopped whatever she was saying and glared at her. "Are you falling asleep, Miss Petersen?"

"No, no ma'am. I just... just was thinking."

"Very commendable. But was your thinking concerned with the War of the Roses?"

Thank Heaven she asked it like that, so Kirsten now knew the topic. "Ma'am, I think Richard was unfairly pictured. He wasn't the villain Shakespeare painted him." She thought this to be a good save. To her great relief, the teacher fell for it, and a lively debate started. At least, it provided an excellent distraction from her inner devils.

11

Maraglindi

I sat in class, and within minutes was lost in my memories of the wonderful weekend. Without having to think about it, I copied the numbers Miss Bachel wrote on the blackboard, while within my heart I enjoyed the memory of the letter I'd written back to Mrs MacCartney, and Gerald's deep musical voice, and Father's hard yet comfortable body I'd held all night, and the quick riding lesson Atan had given me on his horse, and picking food from its natural places, and the song of the wind in the trees...

The door opened, and Mrs Judson came in.

The two teachers smiled at each other. Miss Bachel said, "Ladies, say good morning to Mrs Judson."

The chorus of voices followed, and Mrs Judson returned the greeting.

Then came the surprise. Miss Bachel said, "Mary Fisher, you'll now go with Mrs Judson for an hour, then return here."

Oh goodness! Flustered, I put my belongings under the lid of my desk, but naturally, managed to drop my pencil on the floor. When I bent to pick it up, my notebook slid off on the other side.

A girl at the back giggled, but a stern look from Miss Bachel silenced her.

I followed Mrs Judson out. She led me to the Dining Room, where we sat at our usual table, still damp in spots from having been wiped. The place was empty of course, but the sound of chatter and clattering crockery came from the other side of the swing doors.

One of the workmen busily cleaned the windows from the outside, but my occasional view of him was merely background, like the noise of the kitchen women.

Mrs Judson took a book out of a bag she had with her. Its title was *My Grade 3 Reader*, with a picture of boys and girls playing on grass with several different trees in the background. Naturally, they were white children, and they looked happy.

The lady got me to read the first two pages. I understood it all but needed a little time to work out two words.

After we were finished with this, I asked about the trees on the cover.

"This book comes from Home. Those are European trees. See, this is a maple, this one is a linden tree, and this looks like a chestnut." She smiled at me. "Anyway, now we'll work with numbers. I'll teach you the two times table." At the end of the hour, she gave me the book. I was to read those same two pages over and over, and to write out the two times table and practise it.

During the morning break, all the other children in the class wanted to know why Mrs Judson had taken me away. They looked at my new reader with curiosity.

I answered the question "Why you?" with "Because Mrs Talbot said so." I had thought this out in advance, and they couldn't very well argue with it.

The hours and days flew after this. When Mrs Judson found out that I had read ahead in the book, she allowed me to do so, and gave me longer sections to study. By the end of the week, I did repetitive activities to a singsong version of the four times table and learned all sorts of facts about Home from the reader. I was no longer bored.

I still stayed very careful in the playground and when no adults were around. I withdrew into myself in the Dining Room, so I could ignore the waves of hate blasting at me. It still hurt to be disliked, but now I could focus on all the wonderful learning from Mrs Judson.

On Friday morning, the lady said, "Mary my dear, I've had a talk with Mrs Goldberg."

"Oh?" My insides tied themselves into a knot.

"The people who victimise you... they're in the music group, isn't that right?"

I couldn't say anything but looked down at the table.

"Here is what you shall do. After luncheon, go to that

storeroom Mrs Goldberg uses. Do you know it?"

"Yes, Mrs Judson."

"She'll meet you there, and you'll walk to the Chapel with her. She and I will ensure that no one will do anything nasty to you again. Do you understand?"

I looked up into concerned, loving blue eyes and nodded.

Mrs Judson then took out a new book, *The Months of the Year*. I found something odd on the very first page. The top of the page had "JANUARY" in big capital letters, but under it I saw children wearing heavy coats, warm hats and gloves. They were playing in some white material. "Why are they dressed like that?" I asked. "January is hot!"

Mrs Judson laughed. "The book comes from Home. There, the seasons are the opposite of ours. When it's summer here, they have winter, and when it's winter here, they have summer."

I couldn't believe such a thing.

Looking at my face, my teacher laughed. "Next week, I'll bring you some books about geography. That's the study of the world we live on."

The hour flew as usual, and soon I was back in class, copying the longer words from the new book. I also worked hard at improving the neatness of my writing, because my awkward fingers resisted the task of matching the teachers' beautiful letters.

All too soon, it was luncheon time, and we marched to the Dining Room. I couldn't eat for worry. Oh, I wished I could get out of this! It was all very well for Mrs Judson and Mrs Goldberg to promise protection, but they couldn't watch me all the time, everywhere.

"Mary Fisher, child, why are you not eating?" came Mrs Gately's harsh voice.

"Sorry, Mrs Gately," I managed, and forced down a few mouthfuls without tasting any of it.

At last luncheon was over, and I could go. I ran to the classroom building, puffing a little. I stopped at Mrs Goldberg's door, feeling the room to be empty.

I could now easily enter my dream world. Standing in the gloom, I played with my little boys, chasing them with mock fierceness as they ran screaming, but with big grins on their faces.

At last, the outside door opened and a person entered. In the dimly lit corridor, Mrs Goldberg's approaching shape reminded me of a tall, gawky wading bird, a heron maybe, or a jabiru. I managed not to giggle, but said, "Good afternoon, ma'am."

"Good afternoon, Maraglindi. I'm so glad you're here. Wait a minute." She unlocked the door and went in, and came out almost immediately, handing me two small black boxes, then ducked in again, coming out with several bigger ones. She put one down, locked the door, picked up the case and led the way out into the bright sunshine.

"What are these, ma'am?" I asked, more to fill the time with talking than for any other reason. That was much better than thinking about the coming afternoon of being hated.

"You're carrying two flutes. I have a violin — you know, the instrument I used to test you — and a viola, which is bigger, but the same kind of thing, and two clarinets."

Kirsten

"The Yid is late," Bev muttered to Kirsten, who was re-plaiting her hair.

Kirsten glanced to the side where Becky busied herself at picking out a tune on the piano, safely too far to overhear them. "Maybe she fell into a mud puddle and drowned?"

Bev giggled. "If we had such luck! Look."

The sunshine outside the door made the entering teacher into a dark silhouette. A small figure walked by her side. As they approached, Kirsten felt like screaming: it was the Abo bitch! How could one little intruder spoil everything, be everywhere, even put her nose into the music group? She wanted to yell out the kinds of obscenities she'd heard her brothers use. She wanted to bash the animal, to wring her neck — but no, then she'd have to touch her filthy, stinking skin. Ugh.

"Good afternoon, ladies," the Yid said. The other girls responded with the usual chorus, but all Kirsten could do was to open and shut her mouth, miming them. Her throat felt too tight for talking.

"I'd like to introduce Mary Fisher to you," the teacher continued. "You've all been in Grade 1, so I hope you'll have the kindness to look after her and introduce her to our way."

Predictably, Becky volunteered, all so sweet. "Come, Mary, I'll show you how to make lovely sounds on the piano." Hand in hand, the two interlopers went off.

Kirsten turned her back on them, trying to pretend they were not there. She tuned up the viola, but when her turn came to play, she just couldn't get it right. She kept making mistakes, and glancing at the Yid's face, she felt like smashing the instrument across that hooked nose. What right did a Jew have to teach in a Christian school, anyway? And when it came to singing, her own voice sounded like a crow's cawing to her. And it was all because of that little... words failed her, even within her mind.

The worst was when the Yid got the black bitch to sing to the group. Kirsten didn't want to admit it, but her voice was clear and beautiful, and surprisingly powerful for such a small child. It filled the Chapel and soared, and Kirsten saw delight on most faces. She exchanged a look with Bev, who wrinkled her nose. It was good to know that one other girl was not bewitched.

In the choir, at least Kirsten could hide in the crowd. She didn't have any solo parts in the current repertoire. But, toward the end, the Yid called her aside. "Miss Petersen," she said, "you aren't your usual today. You're a talented musician and singer, but today I wouldn't have known."

Kirsten felt like shouting, "It's your fault for besmirching the music group with that black slut!" but of course that was not possible. "I have a bit of a headache today, Ma'am," she managed.

Maraglindi

I felt like dancing on air after leaving the Chapel. Once Becky had taken charge of me, I'd loved every moment of the afternoon. Kirsten and Bev kept their distance, although if I allowed myself, I could feel the battering of their hate. So, I ignored them as best I could by drowning myself in the music. I could only reach what Becky called the keys on the piano by standing while the bigger girl sat, but then we played a lovely, lively tune together, me quickly learning the high part while Becky played the deep notes.

Before Becky had to go to her own lessons, she taught me exercises she called 'scales,' which I then dutifully played. Really, they were like the times tables, only they related to music rather than to numbers.

Thinking about this, and about the wonderful singing, I relaxed my usual caution when in the playground. Without warning, I felt something thud into the middle of my back, so hard I stumbled forward and almost fell. I turned, and barely managed to catch the movement of someone ducking out of sight into one of the senior Dorms. But, in the usual way I couldn't explain, I knew it had been the dark-haired big girl called Maeve, and that Kirsten and Bev were with her.

I saw a river pebble on the ground, a smooth, oval stone like a black egg in the grass. That was when the pain struck. The centre of my back became a deep, throbbing agony. Crying, I slowly walked to Dorm F.

Rosalind and Helena were playing a game, clapping their hands, then touching palms high and then low to a repetitive song, but stopped as I entered. "Didn't you like music group?" Rosalind asked.

"Oh, yes, I... I loved it."

"But you're crying!"

"My back. Can you please look at it?"

Helena went behind me and pulled the neck of my blouse away. "Oh, you poor thing! I'm getting Mrs Gately." She ran out of the room.

By now, I couldn't raise my arms, so Rosalind gently eased my blouse off. We'd just finished when Helena returned with the dorm mother.

"What happened to you, child?" Mrs Gately demanded, impatiently.

I turned to show my back.

"Elizabeth, Clara, run to the bathroom and bring a towel soaked in cold water, and a dry one. Now, Mary, did you fall over again?"

I managed to answer without more crying. "No, ma'am. A big girl threw a stone at me."

The two girls arrived at a run. Mrs Gately said, "Lie down on your face on your bed." She pressed the wet towel onto my back. After a while the throbbing eased, and I felt my eyes close.

A hand on the top of my head woke me. "Wake up, Mary," I heard Mrs Talbot say.

I turned over and sat up, shivering with cold and still sore, but no longer in agony. "Good afternoon, ma'am," I said. The room was empty apart from the two of us.

"Tell me, did you see who it was?"

I hadn't actually seen, but I knew. Explaining that was impossible, so, without telling a lie, I just said, "It was a big girl called Maeve. She has dark hair and—"

"Oh, I know Maeve O'Riley. This is serious. Are you sure?"

"Yes ma'am."

"Is she the one who had hit you previously?"

"No ma'am."

"All right. Tell me exactly what happened."

"Ma'am, I was in the Chapel with Mrs Goldberg, learning about music and singing, and when we finished, I was walking across the playground to come here. And usually I am very careful, but the music was so wonderful that I forgot."

"And?"

"And the stone hit me, and I turned, and she was just ducking into Dorm B."

I was glad the anger I saw in Mrs Talbot's face and glow was not directed at me. I sensed the thought, *It would just have to be the Judge's brat. I shall have to expel her now.*

"Ma'am…"

"Yes, Mary?"

"Please… don't expel Maeve from the school. Maybe somehow I can make her be my friend?"

The steel-blue eyes in the fat face drilled into me. "How did you know what I was thinking?"

Fortunately, I remembered: "Ma'am, after I was hit on the first day, you said in assembly that the person doing it would be expelled. I really don't want to cause harm to somebody else!"

Mrs Talbot's face softened, and I sensed both surprise

and warmth directed at me for the first time. However, aloud she said, "A crime needs to be punished."

"Mrs Talbot, uh, Jesus said to forgive your enemies, and to love your neighbour, and... and I don't want to harm anybody..." I reached out a hand and took hold of the Principal's. Looking up into her face, I sent all the love within my heart, and felt the response.

"Little Mary, you are a very unusual person, but rules must be followed, and once I give my word, I keep it. But what would you like to see happen?" Slowly, almost reluctantly, she pulled her hand away from mine. She picked up a small white tub. "Lie on your face again. I have some healing lotion to put on that bruise."

I did as I was told while answering, "Ma'am, I... I don't want them to hate me. They hate me because I'm an Abo, and my skin is brown, and they call me nasty names, and why? I'm just an ordinary girl like them—"

Mrs Talbot's hands made gentle, soothing circles on my back, easing the pain. She said, softly, as if talking to herself, "Ordinary you are not. If everyone was like you, little one, this world would be a better place." She continued, louder, "I do not have the power to change what girls think, only what they do. And the way to stop this from happening again is to set a firm example. I do not have any choice in that." I felt Mrs Talbot place something over my back. She then said,

"All right, sit up, and I shall help you to put your blouse on again. I think you will need help to get undressed tonight, but it should ease by the morning. I shall instruct Mrs Judson to renew the ointment then."

Wonderful. Mrs Judson would be much nicer to have around than Mrs Gately.

Gerald

Saturday. Gerald sat up and stretched. His two new friends were still asleep, Edward with a slight snore that had gone on all night every night and had made it difficult to go to sleep. Quietly Gerald got out of bed, and within a quarter of an hour was outside, admiring a magnificent dawn. Pink and orange clouds hovered above still-grey trees, and a magpie's warble embroidered the silence. Gerald took a deep, grateful breath, then returned to the kitchen.

For the past five days, a Mrs Sweeney had cooked breakfast for them, but this morning the kitchen was empty and cold. The basket next to the stove held no firewood. Gerald took it outside, found the half-full woodshed, and brought the basket back, loaded. In a few minutes he had a merry fire burning, and when the porridge started bubbling and steam curled up from the spout of the kettle, he found a large frying pan and a ladle, and made several loud bangs.

He took the porridge pot off the heat, served himself, and

had almost finished when two young men with frowsy faces entered. "Are you responsible for that noise?" Richard demanded. His shirt hung out of his trousers around his rotund waist.

"M'lord, I sounded the gong. Breakfast is at your disposal," Gerald answered with a full mouth.

Edward said, "Very good, Jeeves, my man, but for your information, it is the day beyond the culmination of our formal duties, and no obligations await us. Why persist with such unseemly haste?"

Gerald scraped his plate clean with his spoon, licked the spoon and took a good sip of tea. Then he waved an expressive hand at the window. "Glorious sunshine peeks her lovely head through yonder aperture. Awaiting us, kind sir, is the adventure of exploring Liverpool."

"Oh, stop clowning!" Richard pressed both hands to his eyes. "Any time before noon is dawn, and for the past five days, I've been forced to attend class at a time when any civilised man is still asleep. And now, not only am I roused for no reason, but am forced to listen to obsolete conversation."

Gerald got up and poured tea into two mugs. "Poor fellow! This elixir is the medicine you need. Anyway, I've cooked. One of you might be good enough to wash up." He finished his tea and went out the back door, returning to the woodshed. He'd seen a pile of unsplit logs and an axe stuck in a splitting block. He spent a pleasant half an hour splitting and stacking. The other two hadn't come outside during this time, so he returned to the house and looked for them.

He found Edward in the Library, reading one of the late Mr Moore's leather-bound books. When he saw Gerald, Edward said, "You're sure to find this interesting. It's notes and sketches about the native vegetation and fauna of the Hunter river area."

"That does sound exactly my kind of thing. I think I'll save it for a rainy day. Actually, I have some friends back home who have taught me a fair amount about that very subject."

"Naturalists?"

"In the real sense of the word. They're the local people, whose lives for ages untold have depended on just this knowledge."

"Oh. Abos?"

"Yes. Delightful people."

Edward put the book down and looked up at Gerald with interest. "You're a remarkable fellow, you know that? How can you make friends with savages?"

Gerald sat down in one of the armchairs. "There are savages in New South Wales. They've come from Britain. The original people of this land have an intriguing culture based on an incredible complexity of family bonds. They're just people, not savages."

"They're dirty, and get drunk on the smell of a beer, and can't be trusted to do a job without someone standing over them, and will never keep their word, and have no manners whatever."

How to set him right? Then with an inner laugh, Gerald found just the metaphor. "All right, imagine this. We British are currently the crown of creation here. But tomorrow, a great fleet of warships arrives, and purple-skinned warriors storm ashore to sweep all before them. Our possessions are taken from us. If you as much as raise your eyes to a purple person, you'll be whipped, killed, tortured. They rape our women, deny us education and dignity, force us to live in squalor. Maybe three generations pass. White people will be dirty, and drown their despair in grog, and why should they act in a decent and trustworthy way when dealing with the purple overlords?"

"Hmm. I do see your point. Still, I'll stick to what I feel comfortable with."

"The work of God is to go where you're needed, not where you're comfortable." Gerald stood. "Happy reading." He went outside, to explore Liverpool.

12

Maraglindi

After luncheon on Sunday, Mrs Judson had us nine girls play a word game in the dorm, because the world outside the window consisted of a constantly falling drizzle of tiny raindrops. I was careful not to do too well and exchanged the odd secret grin with Mrs Judson, who noted what I was up to, and clearly approved. The bruise on my back still hurt when I moved suddenly, especially when raising an arm, but it was a lot better. Last night I'd still slept on my stomach but actually managed to go quite a long time between awakenings.

Someone knocked on the door.

"Come in," Mrs Judson called.

One of the sixth graders entered. "Good afternoon, Mrs Judson, girls," she said. Her long, straight hair was so blonde it was almost white, and blue eyes twinkled from a round face. She carried a closed umbrella. I instantly liked her, because of the pureness of her glow.

"Good afternoon, Anneke. It's delightful to see you."

The girl smiled. "You too, ma'am. Mrs Talbot sent me, to escort Mary Fisher to her."

I stood from my chair, then winced at the stab of pain.

"Anneke, my dear, I know you'll look after her." Mrs Judson took out one of the ten child-sized oilskin coats from the common cupboard and carefully draped it over my shoulders.

Anneke smiled down at me. "Certainly. Come along, Mary." She reached out her right hand and led me out of the room.

I sent her all my love, to see the big girl look down with a surprised smile.

"What was that, Mary?"

"What was what?"

"You, um, did something special. I feel like I was inside a soft, warm nest or something."

I didn't know what to answer, so stayed quiet as we walked out into the steadily drizzle. Anneke let go of my hand and opened her umbrella, and this provided a distraction. We started toward the administration buildings.

Anneke said, "Everyone knows about you. You've had a rough time of it, haven't you?"

"Yes."

"So did I in Grade 1. You see, I couldn't speak English then. About the only person to be kind to me was Mrs Judson."

"Yes, she is wonderful. But why couldn't you speak English?"

"My family comes from Holland, also called the Netherlands. Do you know where that is?"

In my heart's eye, I saw the picture Mrs Judson had called a map of Europe. "Just above Britain, and to the right?"

Anneke laughed. "Yes, that's how it looks on a map. Anyway, my father is an expert cheese maker, and we came out to New South Wales, to a town called Bega. That's far away from here, on the other side of Sydney. My father sent me here because schools for girls are very rare, and that's why I'm staying here on weekends."

"I thought all white people speak English."

"Oh no! But I'll tell you about that later."

We entered the building and were soon at Mrs Talbot's door. Anneke knocked, and at the Principal's command, ushered me into the office.

With a wrench of fear, I saw Maeve sitting there, between a man and a woman, obviously her parents.

Mrs Talbot smiled at the two of us from behind her desk. "Thank you, Miss van de Louw. Remember what we have discussed. You are now released from duty."

Anneke said a polite goodbye, then left.

Mrs Talbot stood and ponderously walked up to where Anneke had left me, a step inside the door. She took my hand and gently led me forward. "Turn around, Mary," she said, then, "Your Honour, Mrs O'Riley, please have a look at this." She eased the coat off my shoulders, draped it over the back of an empty chair, then pulled my blouse away from my back.

I heard the scrape of chairs as the two adults stood, the sounds of steps, then the hiss of an indrawn breath.

Terrible! I wouldn't do that to a dog," the man said. "But Maeve denies that she did it."

The woman added, in a voice edged with tension, "I believe my daughter. And this poor child is an Aborigine after all."

"So?"

"So, they don't necessarily have our conception of truth and falsehood."

I pulled free and turned to stare at Maeve. Her face instantly turned a bright red.

"It wasn't me!" she said. "I was with my friends inside; I wasn't anywhere near!"

Mrs Talbot asked, "When was that? When was the stone thrown at Mary?"

Maeve paused, and I sensed her searching for a plausible reply. At last, she came out with "My friends in the music group just came in. I s'pose it was then, while she was walking out of the Chapel."

I smiled at her. "And how do you know that I'm in the music group?"

I immediately caught Mrs O'Riley's thought, *An uppity Abo who doesn't know her place.*

Maeve's face went even redder, and the glow around her became so dark and the swirls in it so strong that I thought she might jump up and attack me. She said, "Because Kirsten and Bev told me."

"I've asked Mrs Talbot not to expel you. I... If only you and your friends will stop being unkind, I... I want to be friends with everybody."

I stepped forward and held out my right hand for a handshake.

Maeve actually put her hands behind her back, and her mother stepped in the way, blocking my advance.

Mrs Talbot opened her mouth to speak, and I sensed her outrage.

However, Maeve's father spoke first into the awkward silence. "Mrs Talbot, we've sent our daughters here because of the excellent reputation of your school. I still wish to continue Maeve here if that's at all possible. And let's consider the situation. If this were a court of law, the accused would have to be acquitted. There are two people with conflicting claims, and no independent witness. So, how is this situation different?"

I wanted to say, "The difference is that your daughter is lying," but kept quiet.

Mrs Talbot nodded. "You are right, Your Honour. Very well, the principles of British justice shall prevail, but, Miss O'Riley, I want you and your friends to know that Mary Fisher is under my personal protection. And I have appointed a sixth grade lady to keep a special eye on her. The slightest hint of any more victimisation, and I will act with great firmness."

"I think that's entirely fair," His Honour answered, though the form of address puzzled me. He turned to face his daughter, who stood to leave. "Maeve, I say this to you in Mrs Talbot's hearing. If word comes to me that you're cruel to any living being, be that a child, a dog or even an insect, you'll have me to answer to!" He stepped forward, bowed to Mrs Talbot, and marched out of the room. His wife and daughter followed.

"Ma'am, thank you for your kindness," I said.

"It is my duty. You are in my protection. But also, somehow, as a result of this deplorable incident, I have realised that you are more than worth all the trouble it may take to protect you. I now understand why Mrs Judson is making a special effort on your behalf. And, Mary, what I said holds. Anneke van de Louw will keep an eye out for anything untoward. She is the ideal person to be your mentor. Now, return to your Dormitory."

Gerald

Although the sky was overcast with the threat of rain a week later, Gerald carried on his project of exploring Liverpool on Saturdays. This second time, he wandered into a back alley that led to a small watercourse, overgrown with weeds and smelling unpleasant.

About to retrace his path, a movement on the other shore attracted his eyes. Four dark-skinned men sat on the ground, quietly watching him. One held a bottle. Their clothes were ragged and dirty.

"Good day to you," Gerald called across.

Having been noticed, the four men stood. "Sir, we was doing no harm," one said.

Gerald smiled. "I wish to do no harm either, to you or to any man."

The man with the bottle said, "We bought this with money, sir. We didn't steal nothing."

Instead of reacting directly, he said, "My name is Gerald. What may I call you?"

"Sir, why you mock us?" This was from the man on the left.

"I'm sorry. I didn't mean to mock you. At home, I have friends like you, and I wanted to make friends here."

"Oh. Where you come from, sir?"

"From the Hunter River area. Oh... my friends call the river Coonanbarra."

"That is different country. They speak different, not same people as us."

That surprised Gerald. "Oh, I thought... It's not that far."

The one who had spoken first said, "Sir, we come over. All right?"

"Of course. And please call me Gerald."

The man walked back for a dozen steps, sprinted forward and jumped clear over the creek. The other three followed. This was impressive: long-legged as he was, Gerald didn't think he could have managed the jump.

The first man said, "Me name Harry. Him George, and Jim, and Toby."

"Are they your real names?"

"Of course not. White man names. But everybody call us that."

George, who still held the bottle, shyly offered it to Gerald. The aroma of rum came from it.

Gerald felt torn in two. Refusing would make them feel rejected. So, he accepted the bottle, although the smell almost turned his stomach, and took the tiniest of sips. As he handed it back, he said, "My friends, I don't drink alcohol usually, only the wine from Holy Communion at church.

The father of my best friend died, because he got drunk too often. So, I decided a long time ago to avoid the drink."

Harry, clearly the leader, answered. "Gerald, sir, I never meet a white man like you. But please. Holy… what you said, what is that?"

Maraglindi

Because of my painfully bruised back, I'd missed church on the Sunday, but on Friday at music, Mrs Goldberg said, "Mary my dear, I think you're ready to take part in the chorus at Sunday church service."

I sensed Kirsten's thought, from behind me, *Yeah, two Yids and an animal in church*, and couldn't help wincing. I didn't know what a Yid was, but it had to be something nasty.

Misinterpreting this, Mrs Goldberg patted my head. "You'll do fine, Mary. I'll place you next to Becky."

So, Sunday at ten of the clock in the morning, I stood in the second row of three, holding Becky's hand. The girl on my left was all right too and smiled down at me. It was a relief that no one from the hall would see me and, thank Heaven, both Kirsten and Bev had their positions on the other end of the line. The entire music group formed a solid block beside the piano, with Mrs Goldberg ready to play.

The quiet buzz of talking stilled. Looking between the

two girls in front of me, I saw Mrs Talbot and Mr Durham enter onto the stage from a side door I hadn't noticed before.

Mr Durham nodded to Mrs Goldberg, and I caught his thought, *It's a sacrilege, having a heathen attending my church service, but what can I do?*

Mrs Goldberg played the opening chords, and the choir sang the first hymn.

After this, I felt too much joy to pay attention to anything else. Even during Mr Durham's sermon, I heard the glorious music in my heart's ear, my spirit soared, and I thanked God.

When the service was over, the girl on my left said, "You're Mary, aren't you?"

"Yes."

"My name is Christina. I'm in third Grade. Tell you what, I've never heard anyone sing a hymn as beautifully as you." She bent to give me hug, and of course I formed a bond of love with her.

I heard Bev's mocking voice, "Hey Chris, make sure you have a good wash after that!"

We stepped away from each other. Face red, Christina snarled like a cat ready to attack, "The only filth here is in your mind, Miss Barton."

The bigger girl stepped forward threateningly, but then Becky stood beside Christina. "Try it Bev, and I'll be sure to report you," she said calmly.

"Dirty Yid!"

"Jesus was a Jew too, did you know that?"

"Yeah, and you Jews killed him."

"It was the Romans, actually. Anyway, even though your grandfather was a convict, that doesn't mean that you're a criminal — yet. So, what Jews did 1856 years ago has..."

At the mention of the word "convict," Bev's face paled. She spun around and almost ran out of the Chapel.

Becky laughed. "That's why she has to make herself feel superior to everyone."

Christina laughed too, but I didn't know what they were talking about. "Becky," I asked, "can you please explain to me what a Jew is, and what a convict is?"

We were alone in the Chapel by then.

Christina said, "Actually, my mother was a convict, and I'm not at all ashamed. She was a good girl in service, and her master forced himself on her and so she started a baby. That's my brother, Jacob. So, to avoid a scandal, they accused her of stealing and she was sent to New South Wales as a convict. And out here, she was assigned to service again, but this time her master was a Lieutenant, and a kind, good man. When his wife died, he married my mother and so I was born."

"I only understood some of what you said. My mother

was working for Mr Richardson and he attacked her and so I was born. That's the same, isn't it?"

"Yes. Mary, I knew we had some things in common."

"But I still don't know what a convict is, or a... what was it? A scandal. Stealing has been explained to me. And, um, Liet..."

"My father is an officer in the army, a soldier. You know what that is?"

"Yes, Mr Peter wanted to be a soldier, so Mrs Mac has explained that to me once."

Becky asked me, "Do you know what a policeman is?"

"Yes."

"If you break a law, they take you away. Then you go before a judge, and if he finds you guilty, you are punished. And if the punishment is being locked up, then you're a convict. Well, back in England, they had so many convicts that they couldn't put them anywhere, so they sent them out here to New South Wales."

This didn't make any sense. "But, but... then they could break the law here. How does that help them to become people who don't break the law? Maybe teaching them and giving them kindness would be better?"

The two girls laughed.

"Anyway," Becky said, "You asked about what a Jew is. Some people are Christians, right?"

"Yes."

"Others say they're Christians, but don't act according to the teachings of Jesus."

"I've noticed that."

"You know there is the Old Testament and the New Testament?"

"I do."

"All right. If you believe in the Old Testament, and accept Jesus as a prophet like Moses, but don't believe he is a God, the Son of God, then you're a Jew."

"Oh. But... but why should people hate you for that?"

Sadly, Becky answered, "Well, why should people hate you for having ancestors who have lived in this land from the beginning of time? Mary, I don't know."

***

As the weeks passed, life settled into a routine. Learning from Mrs Judson was a constant joy. I made friends with all the other girls in my grade, and one by one with the second graders, too. Becky and Anneke watched over me when no teachers were around, and I often spent my play times in the Chapel, practising on the piano.

I still missed my loved ones, and still felt the need to be very, very careful. I knew that maybe thirty older girls disliked me because I was an Abo and had browner skin than theirs, and half of these hated me. One day, three of my friends and I were playing a game that involved dancing in a circle, holding hands, when I sensed the thought, *Horrid! Glad I don't have to touch her filthy hands!* I couldn't help looking around to see a fourth grade girl I knew was called Jessica, walking past with a stormy face. The movement caused me to let go of the hands on each side, and I fell. I then sensed Jessica's glee.

That night, lying in bed, I angrily wiped my tears. *If I didn't know what they thought, I'd be much happier.* And, somehow, the next morning, I managed to keep other people's thoughts from my mind. I practised this with friends, and even with Mrs Judson, by busily thinking about other things. If I concentrated on something else, I could avoid knowing what other people thought.

That morning, I wrote a letter to Mrs MacCartney under Mrs Judson's supervision. The lady said, "Mary, the new postal service is going to start up today, isn't that exciting?"

"Ma'am, I don't know what that means."

"The regular coach that goes along the river road to and from Newcastle will carry letters to all the townships. That's why I got you to write this letter. It should get to your town by tonight, and your family and friends will be able to pick it up tomorrow."

"Oh, how exciting!" I vowed to spend even more effort

on improving my handwriting.

After this, every Monday was letter-writing day, and I got Mrs MacCartney's reply on the Thursday. Occasionally, the envelope also contained a letter from Atan, who told me that Mrs McTaskill was continuing to teach him in Gerald's absence. The smith was also taking an interest in him, so now he could shoe horses, and repair the pots when a hole burned into them. And in another letter, he wrote with pleasure that Mr Mac allowed him regular time off to spend with Father Riso, so he could learn to be a magic man.

With the coming of autumn, more and more days were wet, and playtimes had to be spent indoors. The workmen moved the big tables to the side of the dining room between mealtimes, and special activity groups were held in various classrooms. I started to learn the flute and spent even more free time in the Chapel. Miss Bachel also encouraged me to join the embroidery group she supervised, but I proved to be so awkward at this that the teacher excused me. Instead, sometimes during class, she gave me a storybook to read aloud to the other girls.

Life was easier now, because I became very good at not listening to the thoughts of others. Oh, I was still very careful, ensuring that I was always with one of my protectors, but mostly I could enjoy life the way I always used to.

On a Thursday, the letter from Mrs MacCartney contained news that put a smile in my heart. Term was to end in two weeks, and Gerald was also coming home. He'd pick me up on the way, so we could ride in the stagecoach together. That night, I dreamt of him, and woke with a smile.

Kirsten

As usual, Kirsten was the first to wake within her dorm. She hopped out of bed, and shivering, put on her blue dressing gown, tied the belt around her waist and stepped into her shoes.

Outside, the sky was ablaze with wonderful red clouds to the east. She stopped to admire the display for a moment, knowing that a day that started with such beauty just had to go well. *Holidays in two weeks!* she thought happily, while making her way to the outhouses. She'd enjoy time with her friends, particularly Susannah and Caroline, as long as she could stay away from wretched Luke and his constant harassment. But she was not going to allow him to spoil such a lovely morning.

She did her business, washed her hands and stepped outside again. Suddenly, unaccountably, she had the feeling of being watched. She flicked her eyes around, glancing in particular at the door of Dorm F, but the little Abo bitch wasn't there.

She took a couple of steps and froze. A snake lay along the path, its head raised, its small eyes watching her. Its mouth opened, showing two fangs, and a tongue flicked in and out so fast she could hardly see it.

Kirsten couldn't help it — she screamed.

She froze in place, unable to move. Her eyes were fixed on the snake.

The snake also stayed motionless, its eyes fixed on her.

She noticed that its top surface was dark brown, while the underside was pale. It had to be well over six feet long.

Time stopped. She didn't know if she'd been standing there for hours, or only a fraction of a second. She realised she'd stopped breathing and deliberately took in some air.

Then she heard a movement behind her, and almost immediately a small shape came into her view. It was the Abo girl wearing a nightdress, sprinting toward the snake!

The snake's head swivelled. The little girl dived.

Then the Abo girl was standing, her hands clasping the snake a few inches from the base of its head.

The snake's body wound itself around the girl's arm, and then her body, but it moved slowly.

The girl looked up at Kirsten, and white teeth shone in the brown face as the little girl grinned. Breathlessly she said, "They can't move fast when it's cold. Please, get Mrs Gately, and ask her to bring a coal bag. I can hold the snake for a while."

Kirsten came to life, turned and sprinted for Dorm F. "Mrs Gately! Mrs Gately!" she shouted.

The house mother put her head out of the washroom. "Miss Petersen, that isn't ladylike beh—"

"One of your girls is holding a big snake. Poisonous!"

"What?"

"She said to bring a coal bag to put it in."

By the time they rushed out, several other girls and a couple of women were approaching. The Abo girl still held the snake, but she wasn't grinning anymore. Kirsten could see sweat covering her forehead, and her usually light brown skin had gone grey. Then she saw the reason. A loop of the snake's body was around the girl's neck, and she only stopped herself from being choked by forcing her chin down. The snake's tail wildly whipped from side to side, flapping her nightgown as if by a raging wind.

She said, in a strained voice, "Somebody... pull it away."

It's me she saved, Kirsten thought, and surprised herself by jumping forward. If she'd thought about it, she'd have been revolted by touching a snake, but she grasped the animal with a hand on each side of the child's neck and pulled it away. Its strength amazed her.

Something strange happened as the backs of her hands touched the girl's skin. Her fear disappeared. In that split second, she saw that the snake was beautiful, the colouring on its body made up of a myriad of diamond shapes, each subtly different from all the others. She also saw that the little girl in front of her was a lovely child, and she felt the warmth of love from her flow into her own heart.

The tiny girl spoke again, panting in short bursts. "Thank you. Somebody else... hold his tail." To her surprise, Kirsten felt ashamed that she couldn't remember her name. It had been a point of honour not to know it till now.

Some girl — Kirsten didn't know her name either — jumped forward and caught the whipping tail after a couple of tries. The three girls held the snake, which was still throwing itself around.

"Mrs Gately. The bag. Please." The Aboriginal child — Kirsten could no longer think of her as "Abo" — still breathed with many rapid gasps but seemed completely calm. She was very much in control of the situation, and Kirsten couldn't help but admire her.

Mrs Gately came forward, rather hesitantly, and held the thick jute bag open.

"Please put it over... my hands and his head."

Mrs Gately did so.

"Now hold it. Through the bag... next to my hands." Clearly, she had more and more trouble breathing.

As soon as the woman did so, the child withdrew her

hands. She added the leverage of her hands to Kirsten's, pulled her head through the loop of the snake's body, and stepped free.

The girl holding the tail actually staggered side to side from the whipping motion.

The little brown girl now grabbed the mouth of the bag. She looked up at the dorm mother. "I'm going to pull the bag up. When I say three, please let go. Kirsten, you too."

Mrs Gately nodded.

"One... two... three!"

In an instant, the front half of the snake was within the bag.

The snake must have turned inside, because the bag suddenly bumped out right next to the girl's tightly clenched hands.

Still completely calmly, she said, "Can somebody please tie something around it?"

Kirsten removed the belt of her dressing gown and did so with three quick movements.

At this, the small child let the bagged snake fall to the ground and started to laugh. It was an open-mouthed, joyous, uninhibited sound of merriment, so musical it could have been singing. She looked up at Kirsten and held her arms wide to each side.

Kirsten felt that new love within her heart burst into an

irresistible flame. She dropped to her knees so her face was almost level with the child's, and hugged her close. She felt the thin little arms close around her neck, and love filled her being.

In a strange way, although she knew that this was merely a young girl, she felt in the arms of a Mother, wise, strong and loving. She knew that whatever she did, whatever happened, she would have this love, and nothing else mattered.

Mrs Gately's harsh voice broke into her consciousness. "Ladies. This is unseemly. Stop it now!"

Somehow, Kirsten separated from the embrace and stood. "Mrs Gately, this child saved my life. She admirably coordinated our efforts to capture the snake. I think a thankyou is more than justified."

Mary turned to the girl who had held the tail. "Miranda, thank you too."

"That's all right, Mary. I'm from a farm and know all about snakes, too. But you've done very well." Right. Her name was Mary. Now Kirsten remembered it.

"What shall we do with this creature?" Mrs Gately asked, as if talking to herself.

The girl, Mary, grinned. "Mrs Gately, if I was still with my people, we'd eat him, and make good things from his skin. We call him a kowwerree."

Kirsten shuddered at this and could see a similar reaction from everyone else.

"At Mr and Mrs MacCartney's, one of the men would cut off his head with an axe. But, you know, we don't need to kill him. Why kill somebody for no reason? After I'm dressed, I can take him outside and let him go free near the river."

The dorm mother said, "I'll send for one of the workmen to dispose of it. Now, we're running late. Ladies, quickly wash and dress, then off we go to breakfast."

13

Kirsten

As they walked toward the dining hall, Kathryn stayed as far away from Kirsten as she could and still keep to the obligatory double line. When Kirsten looked at her, she hissed, "I heard! You were all over the dirty half-caste slut!"

But Miss Dorner was just ahead, with only one pair of girls between her and Kirsten, so she could do no more than to whisper back, "I'll talk to you later."

"Don't bother!"

Breakfast was a torture. Maeve and Kathryn acted like she wasn't there, and when Bev, busy serving, passed close to their table, she stabbed at Kirsten with looks of hate. Once she made a face like she'd smelt a terrible stink.

With what felt like an extreme effort, Kirsten finished her porridge and cup of tea, but the breakfast sat in her stomach like a cannon ball. As they stood to leave, she glanced over at the Grade 1 table. Her eyes met those of Mary, who gave her a friendly smile, and suddenly, somehow, things were all right again. *All term*, she thought, *that's how I treated her, and she got through it. So, I can survive, too.* It seemed odd, but perfectly natural, for her to follow the example of a six-year-old child.

In Dorm B, as she picked up her bag of books, she felt a hard shove from behind. She had to grab onto the chair in front of her not to overbalance. She turned, and of course it was Bev.

"Sorry, Miss Petersen, I accidentally slipped," her best friend of yesterday said loudly, with exaggerated sweetness.

Not to be outdone, Kirsten managed a smile. "That's perfectly all right, Miss Barton, you're every bit as graceful as usual." Holding her head high, she took her place in line.

For the rest of the morning, Kirsten concentrated on the work as best she could. She studiedly ignored her erstwhile gang, just as they made a great show of ignoring her. And whenever the pain of their attitude got too much to bear, she briefly closed her eyes and imagined the warm hug of love from Mary. She found that she could actually recapture that feeling of being mothered, protected and loved without condition.

During the break, she separated herself from the rest of the class as quickly as possible and hurried to the Chapel, knowing that was the most likely place to find Mary. As she entered, she heard the sweet sound of a flute and the piano, playing a Mozart duet. She recognised Köchel 315, while her eyes got used to the dim light within a few steps. She saw Becky at the keys, and Mary standing by her side. They stopped mid-bar. Becky said, "You're blowing too hard.

Could you hear that extra whisper of a sound that shouldn't be there? Try again."

However, Mary called out, "Hello Kirsten!" Surprisingly she started saying this before even turning, as if she knew Kirsten was there.

Becky turned and then quickly stood, as if expecting to be attacked. Every line of her body signalled readiness to fight.

Kirsten stopped, facing her from a few feet away. "It's all right, Becky." She found the words hard to say but knew this was necessary. "I've... I've learned a lesson this morning. Mary somehow taught me how wrong I was. I... I want to offer my apologies to you, and to your mother, for all of my nasty thoughts and actions of the past."

The Jewish girl's eyes opened wide, making her into a picture of incredulity.

"When, when Mary saved me from the snake, I realised what a lovely child she is."

The little girl interrupted, "And you're a beautiful person, too."

"How could you say that when I've been so mean to you!"

Disconcertingly green eyes smiled up at her from the brown face. "Yes. You did awful things. But, oh, I don't know how to say it. What you do is not you. Now we can be friends."

"Yes, Mary. I'll be your friend. And Becky, can I please be your friend too?" Anxiously she watched the younger girl.

"Even if I'm a Yid?"

"Mary taught me this, today. You were born into a family that happens to be Jewish, so you're Jewish. It isn't something you chose. You're just a person like everyone else."

Becky held out her right hand, and Kirsten stepped forward to grasp it. Then she pulled, got the smaller girl close, and hugged her to herself. This time, rather than receiving motherly love, she felt she was giving it.

Back in the classroom, she was now able to ignore the three who were sending her messages of hate without words. When the teacher called her to read a passage from Macbeth, she did so in a clear voice, without hesitations, and with a good inflection. As she stopped, she knew it had been the best reading she had done, ever.

"Bravo, Miss Petersen," Mrs Hislop said, "perhaps you should choose a career on the classical stage."

Kathryn muttered, "Yeah, or on the hangman's stage."

Kirsten felt completely unaffected. She didn't even bother to look at her.

She still had the most difficult task left. Innards churning, straight after class she went to the office building, entered, and asked Mrs Jardine if she could speak to Mrs Talbot.

The secretary stood, knocked on the Principal's door and put her head in. She turned. "Please take a seat. Mrs Talbot will see you in a moment."

Kirsten perched on the edge of the indicated chair, wishing she could escape, but knowing there was no choice. She had to do this.

After about forever, the door opened and Mrs Talbot stood there, seeming ten feet tall. "Miss Petersen. Do come in."

Kirsten stood and forced her body to act with a confidence she didn't feel. She entered the office. Mrs Talbot shut the door behind her, then, leaving her in front of the desk, ponderously lumbered behind the big desk and eased her wide body into the impressive armchair. "Well?" she demanded.

"Mrs Talbot, I... I have a confession to make."

"Do go on."

"On the first day of term, I was the one who had hit little Mary."

Mrs Talbot regarded her with an expressionless face, for what felt like a very long time. At last, she asked, "Why did you choose to divulge it now, Miss Petersen?"

"This morning, something happened."

"I have heard about the snake incident."

"Yes, ma'am, but it's something that happened during then that nobody could have told you. It's something about Mary."

Surprisingly, the Principal smiled. She was not known for smiling. "I shall tell you what happened. You touched Mary, and suddenly you felt that you loved her."

"Oh... but how..."

Mrs Talbot actually laughed. "Because, Miss Petersen, I have had the same experience. That child is most unusual. She has the magic of love. All right, Miss Petersen, explain why you had hit her."

Kirsten hung her head, gathering her thoughts. "Mrs Talbot, I'm proud of this school. But, until today, I believed that all Abo... Aboriginal women are um, morally loose. And as a half-caste, she comes from an immoral um... coupling. And I felt that her intrusion here would spoil the reputation of the school. And so, Ma'am, I was outraged that she was a student here."

"And now?"

"And now... I know that what you're born as makes no difference. It's how you live that matters."

"Excellent. Miss Petersen, this issue shall stay between us. You are not to divulge this information to anyone."

"Um..."

"Yes?"

"Ma'am, three girls already know."

"You do not have to tell me their names. They have kept quiet about it for all term. Surely—"

Kirsten actually cut the Principal off with "But, but now they hate me!"

"I see." Mrs Talbot paused a moment. "Of course. They now see you as having joined the enemy. Very well, Miss Petersen. Look on their treatment of you as your just punishment for having assaulted a child."

That part was all right. Actually, Kirsten thought it to be very appropriate, and would certainly make their bullying much easier to bear. But... "So, Mrs Talbot, now they may tell, in order to get me expelled."

"Do leave that with me, Miss Petersen. I shall handle it."

Gerald

Gerald was in that in-between state when he knew he was dreaming, but the dream felt real nevertheless. In the dream, his legs were sore from having walked up and down mountains all too long. A blister on his left heel stabbed pain into him at every step. A big, heavy bag weighed him down, and his back and shoulders ached.

All the same, he was happy.

Ahead, the evening sun hung almost below the level of his eyes, a huge red ball, painting massive dark clouds red on the underside. The trunks of many tall trees cut the crimson disc into vertical stripes, and he saw with relief that now the ground started to slope down.

A tall, blonde young woman walked by his side, and a glance at her lifted his spirit and filled his heart. She carried a small child in her arms, and she also had a big bag on her back. Although her dress was shabby and dusty, she smiled happily at him.

He glanced behind. A long line of people followed them. All of them had the chocolate coloured skin and facial features of Aborigines, and all were carrying their possessions. Like him and the blonde woman, they looked exhausted. He saw a small child collapse, and a man lift her with a heave.

He decided to stop and said, "This is the highest spot."

"Wha... what'd you say?" Oddly, that was Richard — what was Richard doing in his dream?

He opened his eyes to find himself in his narrow, hard cot, in the back room Richard, Edward and he shared within the late Mr Moore's magnificent mansion. A red beam of dawn light stabbed right into his eyes, through a gap between the window frame and the curtain.

"Good morning, Richard. I think I must have been talking in my sleep." He sat up, getting out of the path of the blinding red light.

Edward also stirred and raised himself on an elbow. "Good morning, compadres," he said.

"Yes, well, I s'ppose we've got to get up anyway." Richard was never at his best in the morning.

"Never mind," Gerald told him, "It's two weeks till the end of term. You need to put up with only nine more early mornings after this one."

The other two students laughed with him.

As Gerald stood, he was actually surprised that his legs felt fine. No blister marred his foot. *Now, what was that about?* he thought, but by the end of his inner question, the details of the dream had faded. He went for a wash and a shave, and was dressed and ready in ten minutes.

In the kitchen, Mrs Sweeney welcomed him with a hot cup of tea, and porridge bubbling from the pot. "Always the first, Mr Gerald," she teased him.

"It's only because I enjoy your cooking so much." He put a lashing of butter on the porridge, watched it melt into an instant yellow pool, stirred it in and started to eat. "I had a funny dream," he said between mouthfuls.

"Hmm?"

"It's a bit fuzzy now, but I was walking at the head of a long line of Aboriginal people, across mountains. Something like that anyway."

"Maybe they were chasing you to make a meal of you?"

She laughed with a cackle.

"Oh, Mrs Sweeney, they're not like that at all. That's the people in the Sandwich Isles you're confusing them with."

"Well, I wouldn't know. The ones I see here in Liverpool I wouldn't trust. Sneaky, drunken savages, the lot of them."

They'd been over this issue many a time. Gerald had given up on trying to convince her.

Richard and Edward entered the kitchen and sat down. "You two arguing about Abos again?" Richard asked.

"No, I was just telling Mrs Sweeney how you sprung out of bed right at dawn."

Half an hour later, they were in the classroom. Gerald smiled to himself.

"What's there to smile about?" Edward asked.

"Going home in two weeks."

"Oh. That's fair enough."

But then the Reverend John Garfield entered and they all stood for morning prayer.

The morning passed in the study of the symbolism and deeper meaning of Saul's miraculous transformation into Paul, from the ruthless persecutor of Christians to their loving leader, and while grappling with the concepts, all thought of his dream vanished from Gerald's mind, until he settled for sleep again that night. Then, suddenly, he saw the face of the blonde young woman again. He realised that he'd seen that face somewhere before, but for the life of him he couldn't remember where or when. He hoped she'd return to him in his dream, but if she did, all memory of it was gone by the morning.

Mrs Talbot

Margaret Talbot thoughtfully looked at the four girls in front of her desk. This needed to be handled just right. "Miss Barton, Miss O'Reilly, Miss Cooper. Do you know why I called you into my office?"

"No ma'am," the three chorused after a momentary gap. Kirsten Petersen said nothing, not having been addressed.

"As you know, I am aware of everything that goes on within my school. You three ladies risk not being allowed to return next term." She was satisfied to see the dismay on their faces.

"For the whole of this term, you failed in a duty you had to this school. A lady is always truthful, and does her duty by God, the Queen, and her superiors. I am aware that on the first morning of term, Miss Petersen had hit a small child. You knew this but chose not to tell me. Why did you fail in this duty?" Keeping her face blank and calm, she laughed within at the confusion and warring emotions on their visages.

As she fully expected, Kirsten Petersen was the one to

speak into the awkward silence. "Ma'am, they kept silent out of friendship and loyalty to me. A lady is also protective of her friends, and, um... well, it would've been a betrayal had they done so."

"Yes, I can see there would have been a potential for conflict. But was there any feeling of conflict, ladies? Did you need to struggle with coming to the right decision?"

Beverley Barton took a deep breath, her eyes flicking for a moment to Kathryn, to her left. "No Ma'am. It didn't occur to us to betray Kirsten."

"Very well. Miss Petersen has confessed her crime to me. There are extenuating developments, so I have decided that I do not need to expel her. However, I expect the four of you to keep this issue confidential. If any word of it gets out, all four of you shall be banned from the school, and your parents shall be informed of the reason. Do I make myself clear?"

"Yes ma'am," came the obligatory chorus.

14
Emma

"Mary my dear, I'll miss you," Emma Judson said at their usual table in the Dining Room.

"Oh, ma'am, I'll miss you too, but I am sooo glad to be going home!"

Emma saw the brown face shine with joy, and the remarkable green eyes glinted as if emitting a light. "I know. You want to be with your little boys, and the other people you love."

"Oh yes!"

Emma just had to lean over and hug the child. "My dear," she said, "I've made arrangements for you. Now listen carefully. Your friend Gerald Kline will get here with the stagecoach at its usual time, about midday on Monday."

"Oh, I thought—"

"Well, he'll have set out from Sydney early this morning. He is on the road right now, pulled by four horses. And every four hours or so, those horses are exchanged for another team, and the passengers get a short rest, then they're off again. At night, they only get about six hours of sleep. And even then, it takes all that time."

"But, but, all the other girls will be gone?"

Some have families a lot farther away than Sydney, but yes, I think everyone will be gone by Saturday evening because their families don't rely on the stagecoach."

"So..." Little Mary was now a wilted flower in a drought.

"So just let me finish."

"Sorry, Mrs Judson."

Emma smiled. "That's all right, Mary. Don't worry, Mrs Talbot and I care for you. And here is the offer. Mrs Goldberg is inviting you to stay in her home while you're waiting, and she will take you to the hotel to meet the stagecoach on Monday."

"With Becky?"

"Yes."

"Oh, I am so looking forward to it!"

"Right, my dear, let's set you up with the three weeks' worth of study materials you'll need to take with you."

Maraglindi

I returned to the classroom an hour later. Miss Bachel and the children were busily decorating the walls with colourful drawings. I hurried to put my bundle of books away in my desk and joined into the fun. I drew two round, smiling faces, coloured one true skin-colour, which is a darker brown than my own, and one the faintest pinky-brown. I put on black hair and yellow, and wrote under it in my best writing, "I am going home to my little boys!!!!"

I started a second drawing, of Mr Mac on Devil, but this was way too hard. I just couldn't get a horse right. Seeing me getting upset with myself, Miss Bachel asked a question or two, then with a few bold lines outlined a horse and rider. I watched how she did this. Maybe I can learn how to draw? This second picture could be pinned up too, just before luncheon.

Then we had a break from routine: all the children were required to pack up their belongings before going to the Dining Room. I managed to fit the seven books into the square cane basket on top of all my clothes, made sure the precious flute was well protected, locked the lid and hung the key around my neck on its ribbon.

In the playground, I said goodbye to the several older girls who had become my special friends, particularly Anneke, then ran to be in the last music class for the term. I was the first in the Chapel and clambered up onto the piano stool to play the Chopin etude Mrs Goldberg had simplified for me.

However much I enjoyed the liquid chords of the music, I kept a part of my attention on my safety, as always. So, I suddenly knew in that way I am unable to explain that Bev was coming. Quickly, I slid off the stool and stood on the far side of the piano, next to the back leg. I wished the piano was a solid object instead of having that big empty space under it.

The doorway darkened, and Bev strode in.

With my back against the cool brick wall, I trembled. *Oh, Lord Jesus*, I prayed, *please make somebody come!*

Bev hummed a song, and for a long moment I thought she mightn't notice me. But at last the big girl casually glanced toward the piano, and I saw her eyes widen. "Hello, little Abo slut," she said.

I couldn't breathe. I couldn't move. I pressed my back against the cold brick wall. Although, for a long time now, I'd managed to ignore the thoughts of others, right now I was clearly aware that Bev was gloating inside, enjoying my terror, wondering how she could twist the knife. That was the wording of her thought.

Somehow, from somewhere, I found the strength to breathe out, to suck in some air, and managed to say, "Mrs Talbot. If you..." My voice sounded weak and pitiful even to myself.

"What about Mrs Talbot? What have I done, little crybaby? All I did was to say hello to you."

That was true. Suddenly I realised — the fear didn't come from anything Bev did. It came from within myself.

I stepped away from the wall, toward the big girl, no

longer afraid. "Why do you hate me?" I demanded, now feeling and sounding calm.

"Because you have no place in my school. Because—"

"I do have a place here. This is Mrs Talbot's school, and she is happy to have me here."

"You're just a filthy animal."

"You are the one who is being inhuman." I was now angry, and free of my previous terror. Also, as I said it, I wondered if Bev knew the meaning of "inhuman."

Bev raised her right hand and swung hard at my face.

Before the blow could land, a blur of movement came between us. Kirsten held Bev's wrist in a steel grip and shoved with the other hand. Bev landed hard on the stone-paved floor, Kirsten half-bent over her, still grasping her wrist. She twisted, and with a yelp Bev turned face down. Kirsten pulled Bev's arm up behind her back. "Mary, come here!" she commanded, panting.

I came forward.

"Do your magic on her."

"I... Kirsten, I don't know if..."

"Do it!"

"What's this magic?" Bev asked, sounding scared now.

I bent and put my hand on top of Bev's head. I said, "Bev, I only want to be friends with you. Please give me a chance. I'm... um... I'm just a little girl, not some monster or something."

Kirsten let go of Bev's arm and stepped back.

Bev struggled to her feet. Looking at her dark glow, I saw that she was still hating, still furious. She said, "Kirsten, you're a shrew and a witch. I'll—"

"Miss Barton, are you being your charming self again?" came Becky's mocking voice, interrupting her.

Several other girls entered the Chapel behind her, and I could see Mrs Goldberg towering further behind them.

"What's going on here?" the teacher demanded.

"Oh, good afternoon, Mrs Goldberg," Bev said. "I fell over and Kirsten helped me up, that's all."

I could read the teacher's thought: Mrs Goldberg didn't believe this for one moment. However, aloud she said, "Oh good. Cooperation and friendship are what makes society function. Now, ladies, I have a special surprise for you. Today being the last day of term, we'll do something different. You have five minutes to form into groups and decide on what you will perform, then we'll do an impromptu concert for ourselves. You may be in groups of two, three or four. I've supplied a selection of musical scores, set out on the seats."

As the girls browsed along the line of big black books, I stayed close to Kirsten, but Becky soon called from the other end, "Kirsten! Mary!"

We came over. Becky was looking at the musical score of a song by Franz Schubert, with violin and piano accompaniment. "This is perfect for us," she said.

"I can't read the music," I said, feeling inadequate.

"We'll go through it once. You know you can remember any melody from one hearing. Read the words, and we'll help you with any you find hard."

The three of us retreated to the back of the stage, and I read the words aloud. They sounded silly, all about a young man's love for a maiden, but I had no trouble in working them out. Then, reading the music, the two big girls sang it together.

"I'm off to tune up the violin," Kirsten said. Becky and I went over to the piano, where we waited our turn while a quartet including Christina practised. As soon as they finished, Becky played her part softly, while the two of us sang along, Kirsten joining in for the last few bars.

Our trio performed third, and I was instantly lost in the beauty of the music, my voice leading the violin, with the piano providing a subtle harmony behind us.

Two more groups played. Everyone had performed, except for Bev. Mrs Goldberg said, "Miss Barton and I have decided on a Mozart clarinet duet from Köchel 487."

I knew Bev to be a skilled clarinettist, but today she made mistakes, and the sound was harsh. As soon as she finished, she threw the precious instrument to the floor and ran out of the Chapel.

"Miss Barton!" Mrs Goldberg shouted after her, but the brown-haired girl was gone. "I shall have to report her," the teacher snapped, bending to pick up the clarinet.

I, said, "Um, ma'am, Bev has a sort of a sickness. Please, excuse her." This was true, I thought, because isn't hating a sickness?

The anger smoothed away from Mrs Goldberg's face, and she smiled down at me. "Mary my dear, there are very sensible school rules. I'm required to report insolence, and an expensive musical instrument may have been damaged." She turned to the group as a whole. "Ladies, I've enjoyed the term with you. You're all talented, with lots of potential, and I'm looking forward to helping you to make your musical ability blossom even further during next term. Do have a wonderful holiday break."

The girls chorused, "Goodbye, Mrs Goldberg." There were quick hugs, many members of the group including me, then I was alone with Mrs Goldberg and Becky.

"Maraglindi," Mrs Goldberg asked, "Is all your luggage packed and ready?"

"Yes, ma'am."

"Girls, please help me to stack up everything. Michael is about to come, in order to take all my material back to my store room."

Just then, a figure darkened the entrance. One of the workmen strode in. "Ready for me yet, Rache?" he asked.

I was surprised at the familiarity but saw from his glow that he was a good man.

"Oh thank you, yes, Michael. The three of us will give you a hand."

The man had a pull cart outside the Chapel. We quickly loaded this up and unloaded it at the other end. Then I got a surprise. Michael stayed with us as we walked to Dorm F. He easily picked up my square cane basket and led the way out.

The four of us exited through the open gates. Up ahead, Mrs Goldberg and Michael chatted like old friends, with Becky and me following.

Becky said, "I'm really looking forward to having you at my place for two whole days! Mama and I rigged up a really comfortable bed for you."

I was too caught up in my own thoughts to answer. "Oh, I do wish Bev wasn't so hating. Kirsten made me touch her, but I knew it wouldn't work. I can't fight hate, I just can't." Thinking back to that moment, I felt my eyes grow hot with tears.

Becky reached down and grabbed my hand. "You can do that to me as often as you like!"

I sent all the love in my heart and squeezed the big girl's hand.

We arrived at a timber fence, the height of my shoulders. The red brick building behind had a big sign on it: "The First Public School in New South Wales."

A big boy stood outside the gate. He had curly black hair, and his face was very similar to Becky's. He welcomed us with a wide smile. "I thought you'd never get here. Oh, pleased to meet you, Mary, I'm Ben. I've heard all about you."

"That's all very well," Michael said, switching my basket from his right to his left hand, "but how about some manners, lad?"

"Oh, sorry Mr O'Halloran. Good afternoon, sir."

"And a good afternoon to you too." Michael smiled at the boy.

I said, "Good afternoon, Ben, I'm pleased to make your acquaintance." For some reason, this got a laugh from everyone as I held out my hand to him.

"I'm looking forward to this," Ben answered, and clasped my hand in his much bigger one. As I sent my love, he said, "Oh! It's even more wonderful... What do you do, Mary?"

"Hey, what's this about?" Mr O'Halloran asked, and seeing we were stopping for the moment, put the basket down.

Ben turned to him, still holding my hand. "Mama and Becky have been telling me stories about this little girl, Mr O'Halloran."

"Yeah?"

Mrs Goldberg interrupted, "One demonstration is worth a thousand words. Maraglindi my dear, do your magic for Mr O'Halloran, too."

I suddenly felt shy and hung my head. I let go of Ben's hand. "Um... I don't really have any magic. I just love people, and I guess when they feel that, they like me too."

Becky gave my back a friendly push. "Come on, Mary. Mr O'Halloran is our neighbour, and always doing kindnesses for people. He is all right."

I held out my hand to the man. His huge hand enfolded mine. As I sent the love in my heart, he softly murmured, "So, that's what the dream was all about?"

"Oh, Michael, tell me more!" Mrs Goldberg demanded.

"This morning, I woke from a dream..." With his free hand, he touched his forehead, the middle of his body, his right shoulder, then his left shoulder. "...The Virgin Mary came to me and blessed me." He looked down at me. "And here she is."

This sounded confusing. "Mr O'Halloran," I said, "My name is actually Maraglindi, not Mary. And, um, I don't know what 'virgin' means."

At this, both Mr O'Halloran and Mrs Goldberg went red in the face, Becky giggled and Ben looked away. I couldn't help tuning in to their thoughts and realised it was something about men and women sharing bodies, like Father and Mother often did, and Father and Old Mother when Mother's woman's blood came. What was so embarrassing about that, anyway?

Mr O'Halloran let my hand go and picked up the square cane basket. "Well, are we going to stand around in the street all day?" he asked, obviously to change the topic. "I require payment for carrying this thing, like a piece of whatever cake you have in your pantry, Rache."

We started walking again. Mrs Goldberg said, "You know, the original Virgin Mary wasn't called Mary either, but Maryam. A good Jewish name, that."

Mr O'Halloran laughed. "Trust you to know all sorts of facts nobody else does. Anyway, Mary... Mara-whatever-that-was—"

"Maraglindi," Becky offered.

"Maraglindi, right. "The Virgin Mary was the mother of Jesus."

"Oh, I do know about her! Only she wasn't called that in the Bible I've read."

"Well, you must've been taught by Protestants. I am a Roman Catholic."

"Uh... I'm sorry..."

He smiled down at me. "I guess your home is different in many ways, my girl. Protestants and Catholics practise different forms of Christianity. We're different enough that many men have been killed for the difference."

Now I felt really puzzled and outraged. "But, but, how can people kill each other over different ways of worshipping the God of love?"

15

Maraglindi

I entered the second white-people home of my life with interest. It was much smaller than the MacCartneys', one of a row of similar houses. Like at the MacCartneys', the walls were made of weatherboard, but painted white. I liked the display of pretty flowers in the front yard, and the graceful folds of white lace curtains showing through the windows. We walked around to a back door, which opened into the kitchen, like at the MacCartneys'. The first thing I noticed was the smell: different from any other I'd ever met before, and quite pleasant.

Mrs Goldberg opened a small door, exposing full pantry shelves, and the smell got stronger. So, it had to be from the food this family ate. She took down a plate with a domed cover over it and put it on the table. "You cut, Ben," she commanded, and got cups and saucers from a cupboard behind her.

A kettle hung over a red glow in the fireplace. Becky had gone straight there when we'd entered, and she put a double handful of thin twiggy branches under it. By the time Ben had wedges of cake on six plates, Becky came with a teapot, steam rising from its spout.

"Ben," I asked, "Didn't you cut one piece too many?"

A man spoke from behind me. "No, one is for me."

I turned and realised where Ben's and Becky's looks came from. I slipped off my chair to the floor. "Good afternoon, Mr Goldberg," I said politely.

He was tall, even taller than Gerald, but thin, with curly black hair and laughing dark eyes. He had a funny-looking hat on his head: a small black circle. "Good afternoon, Maraglindi. You're famous within this house. I hope to hear you sing." I sensed the mutual love between this man and his family. I went to shake his hand. Once more, I passed love to a person, making him my friend.

Grinning, he put his hands around my waist and lifted me back onto my chair, then sat. "Taste the cake," he said, then turned to his son. "Ben, the yarmulke."

"Sorry, Papa." Ben ran off to return in a moment, also with a small black hat on his head.

I'd never seen a cake like this before. Unlike those baked in Aunty Mish's kitchen, it was fluffy and light. Its shape resembled a mountain with a vertical hole in the middle. Ben had neatly sliced it into wedges, showing that inside, it consisted of swirls of brown and creamy-coloured cake mixed together. I broke off a brown piece first, because that was only slightly darker than my skin, and experimentally put it in my mouth. It was delicious!

Looking at me, Mrs Goldberg said, "I'm glad you like my Gugelhupf. I got the recipe from my grandmother, who came from Austria. Do you know where that is?"

"Yes, ma'am. It's where Mozart lived."

"Excellent! But, my poppet, we're not at school now. All right everyone, here is a contest. What can Maraglindi call me in private?"

Becky spoke first. "While she is here, she can call you Mama. Then she's my little sister."

Ben asked, "Hey Maraglindi, what do your people call a respected lady?"

"Malu. That means Aunty. It's also what we call a woman who is a leader because of her wisdom. Like, Malu Dara helps babies to be born and heals sick or hurt people."

"There you are then, Mama. That's my entry in the contest."

"I was going to suggest Aunt Rachael," Michael O'Halloran said.

Mr Goldberg smiled at his wife. "She can call you Melody like I do. Well, Aunt Melody."

Mrs Goldberg laughed. "All right then, Malu Melody it is."

Mr O'Halloran stood. "And I'd better be going or Kathleen will think I've run away from home. Thanks for the cake and cuppa, Malu Melody."

Becky stood, too. "Come on, Maraglindi, I'll show you our room." She was at the door of the kitchen by the time I managed to clamber off my chair. As we walked along a corridor. I asked her, "Why do Ben and your father wear those black hats?"

Becky had her hand on the knob of a door but turned. "The yarmulke? Remember the story of when God came to Moses in a burning bush?" She opened the door.

"Yes." Her room was airy and light. Embroidered wall hangings brightened it. Seeing me look, Becky said, "Mama made them. Anyway, God said to Moses, 'Cover your head, for your God is with you.' And of course God is always everywhere, so a Jew should cover his head all the time."

"But Ben didn't have a... a yarmulke at the school?"

"We're the only Jews in Newcastle at present, and Papa has special permission from the right people in Sydney. We try to fit in and look like other people to avoid trouble. We do the right things at home but blend in as much as possible outside. Even then, we're dirty Yids, as you know."

A beautiful, many-coloured quilt covered Becky's bed, which stood against one wall. She had a desk under the window, and shelves full of toys and books on the wall opposite the bed. The bottom part of the shelves was hidden by a second bed, shorter and lower than the main one, with an embroidered cloth covering it. Becky lifted one corner of the cloth to show me how the bed was constructed. "Papa made this especially for you," she said.

The flat platform of the bed rested on two curved branches, each forming an arch. Even the rough bark still covered them. The effect was beautiful and, I thought, entirely right for a person of the land. I said, "Your family is so kind."

"Papa says, suffering can bring out creativity and love in people. It's why God allows it."

Music started somewhere. It had a loud, strident tone and made my feet twitch with its rhythm. "Oh good!" Becky said, "Ben is playing his trumpet. Grab your flute and come on!" We raced into a pleasant room with a sofa and two armchairs, and again, paintings on the wall. Mrs Goldberg sat at a square object that had to be a piano, judging from the sounds coming from it, though it looked quite different from the one at the school with its graceful curve. Ben was blowing into a shiny metal thing with a flaring end, while Mr Goldberg used two sticks to rhythmically tap on two flattish circular objects. The effect was so joyful that I had to laugh and twirl around — then of course tripped on my own feet and fell down. For once, this didn't bother me but only made me laugh all the more. The music stopped, and the family laughed with me. Mrs Goldberg said, "Beck, you take the piano. I'll get the clarinet, and Maraglindi, you can join in with your flute."

"Oh, but, but, I don't know the music."

Ben said, "It doesn't matter. We make it up as we go. As long as you keep in rhythm and do something that fits, do whatever takes your fancy."

By the time he finished saying this, Mrs Goldberg — no, Malu Melody — was back. She said, "I've heard of a new instrument invented by a Monsieur Sax in France. It's like the trumpet, Ben, but with a reed like the clarinet. That should make this kind of improvisation even better. All right, a-one, a-two, a-three," and the four Goldbergs started together. I listened for a few bars, then played a loud trill that somehow exactly continued Ben's last note.

The joy of music stopped time, until Mr Goldberg said, "Hey Melody, it's nearly Sabbath Eve!"

Everyone got very busy. Becky said, "Maraglindi, help me to set the table."

"What's this about?" I asked as I rushed for the kitchen behind her.

"You'll see. You know how Christians have a special day on Sunday?" She started to take a stack of plates, beautifully decorated with a flower pattern, from a low cupboard.

"Of course."

"For us, Saturday is the day of rest. Here, be very careful, but take these and follow me." She passed five plates to me and picked up five bowls and five smaller plates, all from the same set. "And in our customs, the day starts when the sun sets the evening before. So, now it's almost Sabbath Eve."

I felt relieved that I managed to get the plates safely to the table. Malu Melody had already placed a beautifully embroidered cloth over it, and five placemats. We put the plates at each place, with a bowl on top and the smaller plate to the side.

"Come on girls," Malu Melody said, "the men can finish this. We have cooking to do." She continued, on the way to the kitchen, "It's all ready, merely needs to be put together and warmed."

I'd never seen food like this before. We heated a light soup with small yellow dough balls floating in the liquid, and delicate patties that smelled of fish when fried, and two loaves of bread that seemed to be plaited like Kirsten's hair, and were even much the same colour.

As the red glow of sunset peeked through a window, Malu Melody lit two candles in a double candlestick with beautiful figures embossed on it, and softly said something in words I couldn't understand. Everyone dipped fingers into a bowl of water on a side table, and dried their hands on a little towel, again each saying some strange words. I copied their actions, and at least the sound of their words.

Mr Goldberg held his hands over a bottle on the table,

saying more strange words.

"Papa is blessing the wine," Becky whispered.

He poured two glasses full, and mixed water with the wine in the other three, making the contents a beautiful pink rather than the deep red. He then moved his hand over a cloth covering the bread, again murmuring something I couldn't understand.

Ben and Becky walked to stand side by side, and Becky pulled me along by my hand.

Mr Goldberg smiled at me. "You'll be one of my children this evening." He held his hands over our heads and sang a lovely, slow tune in the foreign words, then explained, "This is a traditional blessing, asking God to make you like some of the wonderful people from the Bible, and to put the light of peace onto your face."

We sat at the table, and Mr Goldberg broke pieces from the plaited bread, passing them around. This started the delicious dinner, flavoured with laughter and joy. Then it was another musical session, with me singing to the accompaniment of a surprising variety of instruments.

That night, I slept better than I'd ever done at the school. I snuggled down in the lovely bed, closed my eyes and next thing I heard was Becky's laughing voice: "Wake up, sleepyhead, it's morning." She led me to a small room at the back of the house, where we could have a wash. "Sorry, it's cold water this morning," she said.

"That's fine, but why?"

"Because today is the Sabbath, and on the Sabbath we must do no work. Lighting a fire is work."

"But last night, we played music."

"We're allowed to have fun, but only as long as it's not for any useful purpose. Practising scales is work, so that's not allowed." Becky pulled her dress on over her head. "Any moment, Mrs O'Halloran will come and cook in our kitchen, and in exchange Mama teaches reading, writing and numbers to her daughters, because they don't have a school to go to."

Indeed, a blonde lady with a friendly smile served up breakfast. Ben and Mr Goldberg arrived a minute or so after Becky and me. Ben said, "Good morning Mrs O'Halloran, good to see you again, Maraglindi. Oh, you may be wondering where we've been. We've just done our morning prayers."

Mrs O'Halloran said, "I've heard all about you, Mary. Can you do your magic for me, too?"

So of course I formed the bond of love with her as well.

After breakfast, we three children went outside, into a beautiful, sunny morning. Four children already waited there. The oldest, a boy slightly taller than Ben, said, "Wanna come to the beach?"

"I'll ask." Ben spun and raced inside, to come back in a

few minutes, carrying a basket with a white cloth covering it. "Picnic lunch," he said and off we went along the street.

I was being introduced to Kevin, Aileen, Colleen and Kieran, who was my age, when a group of big boys came out of a side street. At the front, Ben and Kevin stopped. Ben put the basket down.

One of the boys shouted, "Hey, Yids and Micks, and hey, they've got a darkie too!" I noticed that his two top front teeth were missing.

"Dennis," Ben said, "I whipped you last time. Won't you leave well enough?"

"Yea, well, it's time for a bit of vengeance, dirty stinking Yid."

Another boy spoke. "There's only two of the filth, and girls and babies. Let's get them!"

I heard Aileen say, "Colleen, get Dad." I sensed a movement past me and saw Aileen rush forward. She screamed at the top of her voice, punched the boy who'd just spoken fair in the nose, kicked another in the groin, then was through the group of them. She picked up a fist-sized stone from the ground and hurled it to hit Dennis on the chest with enough force to make him stagger.

Kevin shouted over her screaming, "Aileen, hold!" He turned to the gang. "Little boys, I don't suppose you know, we're descended from a long line of Vikings. If you go away,

I won't show you what an Irish male can do. You've seen what an Irish female can." He stayed smiling and calm, and I could see that this was more intimidating than violence would have been.

Then Mr O'Halloran was there, with a panting Colleen. What's going on here?" he demanded.

Dennis said, with a sneer, "Teach your children not to be violent. That vixen threw a stone at me!"

Mr O'Halloran said nothing, just stood there, solid and menacing, and gave him a long, long look.

The silence stretched. Then a boy turned, and they all slunk away to wherever they had come from.

16

Maraglindi

Eleven of the clock on Monday morning, I stood in front of the Coal River Hotel, the centre of a crowd of Goldbergs and O'Hallorans. "Oh, I so enjoyed my two days with you!" I told them. "Thank you!"

Mr Goldberg smiled down at me. "When you return next term, maybe you'd like to spend the odd weekend with us."

"I'll even teach you to fight," Aileen said with a grin. "I've been told that some of those bitches at the school pick on you."

"Aileen! Language!" Mr and Mrs O'Halloran said together.

But I had another problem with this. "Oh, I could never bring myself to hurt another person!"

Ben said, very seriously, "Sometimes you just have to, or they'll trample you into the ground. I learned to fight, and now they leave me alone, well, unless there is a bunch of them like on Saturday."

Kevin laughed. "Yeah, I remember. You improved Dennis's appearance quite a lot."

I wanted to explain something but didn't know how to put it into words. "I... um..."

The others stopped speaking and patiently looked at me.

"Well, um, if you hurt them, then they want to hurt you back, and then you want to hurt them back, and it just goes on and on."

Sadly, Mr O'Halloran answered, "And if you don't defend yourself, that only encourages them to do more, and worse."

"Mr O'Halloran, they killed Jesus, but He still said love is better than hurting them back."

"You're a good girl, Maraglindi, but I guess I'm not made of the stuff of martyrs. If anyone is about to hit me, I get in first so they can't even land the first one."

"Yeah, like I did to those bullies on Saturday," Aileen added.

I was about to answer when Colleen shouted, "Hey, the coach is coming!"

I looked along her pointing finger to see a cloud of dust above the rooftops to the right. Almost immediately, I heard a deep rumble, then four horses rushed past, pulling the big, black stagecoach. As they wheeled through the open double gates, I barely saw a flash of Gerald's face beaming at me through a window. I'd have run after the coach, but Malu Melody grabbed my arm.

"Wait up, Maraglindi. Your friend will want to attend to a call of nature after the long ride. He has seen us, and will be sure to come out here, the very moment he is ready."

I jumped up and down in impatience and lost my balance. I'd have fallen, except for a strong steadying hand from Kevin. "Thank you," I said, smiling up at him. "My big brother always says I do things as if I didn't know how a human body works."

"Well, maybe you've come visiting us from another planet?"

"Sorry. I don't understand."

Kevin stomped his foot. "This thing we're standing on is a ball that moves around the sun. There's other balls too, and maybe you were some strange-looking thing-person on one of the others, maybe Mars or Venus, and blundered here."

Everyone laughed at this, as Gerald emerged at a run through the open double gates.

***

I desperately needed to relieve myself.

The coach had followed the wide river for several hours. At first it was exciting, and so wonderful to sit beside Gerald. Four other people travelled inside the coach, as well as a young man beside the driver up front. Sadly, all the passengers looked at me with disapproval, so for a long time I pulled myself into a little space, chatting with Gerald in half-whispers.

Then he said, "Maraglindi, my poppet, sing me a song."

"But..." I flicked my eyes to the hard, closed faces of the people on the opposite bench. That lady would look like a nice grandmother if her expression didn't make it seem like she'd smelled something bad. The man next to her kept his eyes out the window, and when he turned his head within the coach, he looked through me in the same way as the hating girls at school often did. On the other side, a young man seemed as if he'd like to throw me off the coach, and perhaps only Gerald's broad shoulders stopped him. And the man in the dark suit on Gerald's other side sat as far from him as possible, as if he might catch some illness second hand.

"That's exactly why I want you to sing. Remember, years ago, the tune you made up for the Lord's Prayer? I think the words of Jesus are most fitting right here, right now."

I closed my eyes, because I knew I couldn't possibly do it while looking at these people's hating expressions. Instead, with the eyes of my heart, I saw Mrs Mac, with tears running down her face.

I sang. The first line was hesitant, but then, as always, the music took over. My heart lifted, and my voice soared to Heaven.

"...Forever and ever, Amen," I sang, and opened my eyes.

The young man was half leaning forward. His mouth hung open, and a probably unnoticed tear trickled down his cheek. The lady now had a smile on her face and looked ready to cuddle me. But the other man still gazed out of the window, his face like granite.

"Little girl," the lady said, "that was wonderful."

Speaking at the same time, the young man told me, "Thank you. I feel blessed."

The man on the other side of the lady turned his face away from the window. He swivelled his head, his eyes passing over me as if I wasn't there and fixed a gimlet gaze on the young man. "It's just monkey imitation," he said. "Birds can sing, but they've got no mind, no soul."

The young man looked away, but Gerald said, "Sir, do you then think that Aborigines are no better than animals?"

"Nah. They are animals. Shouldn't be allowed on a coach." Once more, he turned to look outside.

Gerald spoke, loudly enough to make ignoring him impossible, but with perfect politeness. "Sir, I have a horse. He is definitely an animal. All the same, I'm sure he is intelligent and has a mind, and has emotions and a soul."

The man fixed his eyes on Gerald this time. "If there wasn't a lady present, I'd tell you what to do with your opinion. Why don't you discuss it with your priest?"

Gerald laughed, to all appearances unoffended. "Because

I'm training to be one myself. I'm on my way home for a break from the theological college."

The lady asked, "Child, what's your name?"

I knew which one to give. "Mary Fisher, ma'am."

"Mary, please sing for us again. It'll help to pass the time."

So, one after the other, I sang all the hymns from the weekly church service. I sang nursery rhymes I'd used to amuse my little boys. I repeated the performance from Friday afternoon's impromptu concert, then without words the beautiful Jewish melodies from Sabbath Eve.

In between, Gerald gave me the odd sip of water from a bottle he had in his bag. That was all very well, but, I thought, what goes in has to come out. I couldn't stop wriggling, and crossed my legs as hard as I could, and it was becoming more and more of an agony.

The lady looked at me, and suddenly laughed. She turned around and sharply rapped on the wall behind her. "Driver!" she called.

"Yes ma'am," came the faint answer.

"Please stop for a minute or so, near a place of some privacy."

There was no answer, but a few minutes later, beyond a curve to the right, the coach slowed so its dust cloud overtook us, then stopped.

The lady struggled to her feet. "Come with me, my lamb,"

she said, "Us females have some business to transact."

As I took her hand, I passed her all the love in my heart.

***

The holiday flew. I played with my little boys and read them stories. Every day, I studied with joy from the books from Mrs Judson, and worked on the mathematics problems she'd written out in an exercise book. I played music on my flute, to everyone's admiration. Atan taught me to ride a black filly, Devil's daughter, whom Mr Mac called Hecate. This joke upset me when it was explained. "She is not a witch but a lovely little girl," I insisted.

"You're right," Mr Mac said, laughing. He stroked his chin, something he always did when thinking. "She and you make a matching pair."

Shortly before dawn on the third day at home, a wonderful thing happened: Father Riso called outside, and when Old Mother opened the door, Kiri and his father Glasko stood behind him, smiling widely. "We got the message all right," Glasko said.

Kiri gazed down at me, love in his eyes. "I've so missed you, little one!" he said as I ran forward and jumped into his arms. He then walked away, to give Mother a chance to keep out of his sight. I kept my arms tightly wound around his neck and breathed in his clean smell, knowing from his thoughts that he'd washed in the river before coming to us.

When he brought me back again, Mother was gone, as required by custom. Father Riso had explained to me that a prospective husband must never glimpse his future mother-in-law, in case he fell in love with her instead. After all, she was closer to him in age than a baby or young girl, who had a long way to go before her woman's blood came.

Tari ran off to the main house to fetch breakfast.

Holding me, rubbing his face into my hair, Kiri said, "I'm going to have another baby! Suba is with child!"

This called for a celebration, but after a while Father said, "Atan and I've got to go and work on the horses." Kiri and Glasko went with them.

All through the day, I felt a warm spot in my heart for a faraway baby who'd one day be the child of my family, my child in a way.

Two evenings later, Glasko and Kiri started on the long and dangerous walk home. I couldn't sleep for a long time, worrying about their safety. I knew they'd have to walk all night, then hide during the daytime because to be seen by a white man could mean being killed. Then they had to walk hard for another night so they could arrive before daylight. Why couldn't the world be safe for my poor people?

Over breakfast, Atan told me a story Father Riso had taught him about the Dreamtime — not one of the secret magic man stories of course, but something I needed to know as one of the people.

"You know, Froggie, that Bayami, the Great Sprit, made everything?"

"Naturally. Of course I know that." I realised he was telling this story to distract me from my worry and loved him all the more for it.

"Yeah, it was boring and lonely for him with nothing and nobody, so he made Old Mother the Sun, and she shone her beautiful light around, and that made him happy. But she said it would be better for that light to shine on something. So, he made all the land, but there were no trees, no plants, no animals, no rivers or lakes, no nothing."

I'd seen pictures of a desert in a geography book from Mrs Judson. I imagined all the world like that and had to shudder.

"So, Bayami came down and walked around. He took soil from one place and piled it up somewhere else, and so there were mountains and hills and valleys and deep holes, and that looked better. Old Mother told him that those holes needed something to fill them, so Bayami made the great sea to circle all the land, and Old Mother shone her light on it, and clouds came, and rain filled those holes with water, and that was good."

I was thinking how similar this story was to the creation

story in the Bible. That had never occurred to me before.

"But the water needed to go from one place to another, so Bayami made the Rainbow Snake, Yuulangga, who went from the mountains to the lakes, and to the sea, and so we had rivers. But everything was still bare dirt. So, Bayami said to Old Mother, "Shine your light everywhere over the land and make some plants for me." She did, and plants with beautiful flowers grew everywhere. So, both Bayami and the Old Mother were pleased, and danced with each other up in the sky. But then Bayami said, "Hey, those plants are good, but they're all so small. We need tall things too, to reach into the sky and give shade." So, Old Mother went around again, and here and there she shone her light, and trees grew there, all different kinds."

"I like trees," I broke in.

"Yeah, well, but they stay in the one place, just like the plants do. So, Bayami sent Old Mother around again, and this time, wherever her yellow glow shone, little animals came. There were beetles and butterflies and frogs and lizards and mosquitoes—"

"Oh, she could have left the mosquitoes out!"

We both laughed.

"...and then she went around one more time to make the big animals. And Bayami needed one special animal to be the father of them all, and that was Kolwa, the eagle, because he can see everything.

"And Old Mother and Bayami also made plants and animals in the rivers and lakes and the sea. And each kind of animal had its Spirit above in the sky. But then there were so many different kinds of living things that Bayami wanted somebody to look after them and care for them and love them, so he made people. And when those people died, Bayami invited their spirits to go up in the sky, so they settled around the spirits of the animals."

"Yes. The Spirit Ancestor who tells me my birthday is at the tip of the Lizard's tail."

"There you are, then, Froggie. And sometimes, Bayami feels the need to make special people, and you are one of them."

I gave him a big hug for that. "You know what? I'll write this story down, only I'll have to do it in English because I don't think there is writing in the language. Then I'll show it to Mrs Judson and my other friends at *school*."

✱✱✱

I stood in front of a mirror, inspecting myself in one of the new winter uniforms Mrs Mac wanted to fit on me before sewing it up on the Singer machine. It was warm and comfortable, but heavy. The round black felt hat nicely matched the pair of black gloves.

There was a knock on the door, and when Mrs Mac gave permission, Atan entered, looking awkward in these surroundings. "Ma'am," he said, "the stagecoach is in. There are two letters for you, and one for Maraglindi."

I eagerly accepted the letter, wondering who could have sent me one. With a smile, Mrs Mac passed over the letter opener, so I sliced the envelope open, and looked at the signature first. "Oh! It's from Kirsten!" I read it aloud.

29th day of April, 1856

My dearest Mary,

I thought to surprise you with a letter, because you have so wonderfully changed my life, and I am now doing your work of spreading love and tolerance at home. It is not easy!

We have a servant who used to be a convict, but now has a ticket of leave. That means that he is free, and can work for money, but cannot ever go back Home. And he made a mistake, and my Father beat him for it.

Before our fight with the snake, I simply accepted this as normal, just the way things are. But now I know that it is wrong. If Jake the servant had hit back to defend himself, he would go to jail, back to being a convict. So, I realised, it is cowardly and wrong for Father to hit him. If Jake was a truly free man, Father would not be able to do so.

As a female, of course I could not intervene, but later got very brave and asked to speak with Father. I said I love and respect him but had learned a lesson in school (I did not say the lesson came from you!) and that I wanted to share it with him. You can be sure, I trembled inside! But I explained that all men, even convicts, are the beloved children of God, and that it is wrong to treat them in a way we would not want to be treated ourselves and asked him if he could please discipline Jake in the way he would discipline one of my brothers who had happened to make the same mistake.

At first, he looked very serious, and I was afraid that he was angry with me. But then he gave me a big hug and thanked me!

So, Mary my dear, a big thank you to you in turn.

With fondest regards,

Kirsten.

I had trouble with "intervene" and "discipline," but Mrs Mac explained these words to me, then gave me a glowing smile and a hug. "Isn't it wonderful?"

"Yes. Kirsten is wonderful."

"Well, that's not quite... what I meant was... let me think. You know, when you drop a stone into a still pond, you get tiny waves spreading in circles. They go a long way. That's what you're doing. Wherever you are, you get people into the way of love, and they then spread the same message elsewhere. I think Mr Mac is right. You're one of God's angels."

I felt my face go hot. "Oh no, ma'am, I'm not anything special. I'm just a little girl."

"And I'm so glad that this little girl is in my life."

17

Maraglindi

After a few days back at school, it was like the holiday had never been. There were only two changes from first term: the weather worsened, so more time was spent indoors, and I slept many weekends at the Goldbergs'. We enjoyed Sabbath Eve, I played with the O'Halloran and Goldberg children, and we created lots of joyful music. Of course, Malu Melody brought Becky and me to sing at Sunday Chapel service each time.

Mrs Judson helped me to write down the story of how Bayami the Great Spirit and Old Mother the Sun created all living things. I carefully made a neat copy to send to Mrs Mac by mail, and another to show to Mrs Talbot. Unfortunately, there I ran into trouble. She sent a message for me to come to her office. When I stood before the big desk, she said sternly, "Miss Fisher, the story of creation is in the Holy Bible. This is a pagan myth, and untrue, because it is against the word of God."

Standing there in the glum room, as so long ago before the start of school, I hung my head, and knew better than to answer. But within my heart, I knew that there is a white person truth and a blackfella truth, and both can be true at the same time. It hurt when Mrs Talbot crumpled up the story, fruit of over two hours of painstaking copying, but I managed to stop my tears.

In the dining room, and during playtimes, I still had to be very careful about my safety. To make it possible to endure the hate, I once more formed the habit of keeping out the thoughts of others. But one rainy afternoon, I wasn't careful enough. Without realising it, I allowed myself to be separated from my protectors. Standing under the roof overhang outside the Dining Room, I idly looked out at the steady downpour, within my heart's ear hearing the patter of water on the walls and bark roof of the shack by the river. Suddenly a great shove against my back drove me out into the rain. I almost fell from the force of it. My hair and shoulders were wet before I turned. The Grade 4 girl called Jessica sneered at me. "Dirty little bitch. That might wash the filth off your skin."

I felt no fear, or even anger. "And what will wash the filth out of your heart?" I answered. I stood in the rain, getting wetter every second, and gazed up at the bigger girl.

"How dare you speak to me like that!"

"How dare you push me out into the rain?"

Jessica moved forward, then must have thought better of getting wet herself. She turned and disappeared inside.

Slowly, sadly, I squelched my way across the sodden grass

to Dorm F and changed out of my dripping wet uniform. With all the water in the thick material, it was almost too heavy to walk in. I still felt no fear or anger, only a deep, aching sorrow. I knew I should report Jessica to Mrs Talbot, but... that would do harm to someone else, and how could I bring myself to do that?

The next morning, I woke to a terrible pain in my left ear. Also, my head hurt above the eyes, and to my shame, I couldn't stop my nose from running. I started to sit up but simply lacked the strength. Unable to move, I lay in a haze, distantly hearing the other girls going through their morning routine.

"Why are you still in bed, child?"

I opened my eyes, to see Mrs Gately's angry face looking down at me.

"Ma'am, I..." A terrible, racking cough cut off my speech, and my throat felt like knives were slashing it into pieces.

The dorm mother put a hand on my brow. "You do have a fever. You're ill. I guess you'd better stay here, nuisance as it is."

The room emptied, and I closed my aching eyes.

I don't know how long I'd slept, when a deep voice woke me. I saw only the ceiling when I looked, and raising my head was too difficult.

The man said, "Influenza almost always kills them.

Aborigines don't have our toughness of disposition. So, just keep her clean and comfortable, and say a prayer for her soul."

Mrs Talbot replied, for once sounding upset, "Oh no, I cannot allow that. Doctor, what would you do to assist her if she were a white child?"

"Hmm. As you well know, ma'am, it's dangerous enough for any small child. Force her to drink lots of fluid. Only feed her a nutritious, thin broth like chicken soup. Encourage her to cough up what's in her lungs. If she has severe pain anywhere, put a hot towel on it. And prayer is still a good idea."

I managed to whisper, "Thank you, Doctor."

I heard two sets of footsteps on the timber floor, then Mrs Talbot's broad face came into view, followed by a face framed by a grey beard. I said, "My left ear and above my eyes. Hurt."

"I shall order hot towels from the kitchen," Mrs Talbot said, and moved away.

The doctor called after her, "And could you also provide a basin, please?"

I heard Mrs Talbot walk out the door, to return almost immediately, then she was gone.

The doctor helped me to sit and held one of the basins from the washroom in front of my mouth. "Cough, er, Mary, and then spit in here." His strong arm behind my shoulders felt so good that I snuggled against it. I put my right hand on the one holding the basin and sent him all the love I could.

"Oh? My goodness... Cough, my dear." His voice was friendly now.

Right then, I didn't need to cough, so I pretended to, but that one artificial cough started a chain of terrible barks that shook my whole body and sent knife-stabs of pain into my left ear. When it was over, a horrible greenish-yellow goop half-filled the basin, I dripped with sweat, and felt too exhausted to keep my eyes open.

Days and nights passed in a haze. Occasionally, I was aware of people coming and going, of being helped out onto a chamber pot, of Mrs Judson sponging me all over with a soft, warm, wet cloth. Then even that stopped. There was no pain, no misery, just a deep peace. *I am going home*, I thought.

***

I faced a huge, glowing Presence I couldn't describe. She just was, and She was there for me. That was my Guide and Mentor, I knew that much. I was still Maraglindi, with that little person's thoughts, feelings, and memories, but I knew myself to be much more. Only, what that greater more might have been was beyond my comprehension.

The Person's thought came. "You're doing well, but must return. Your work is not yet done."

The pain, the hurt of being hated, the suffering of my people struck me. "I don't want to go back," I sent the thought to Her, without knowing how.

"You know better. Pain is merely a tool for the distillation of the spirit. You need to experience this pain, so you can help others through it, onto the Right Path, the path of Love."

***

"Mary sweetling, please don't die... Mary sweetling, please don't die..." I heard a beloved voice saying, over and over. I took a breath and managed to force my eyelids open.

Mrs Mac's blue eyes shone down at me. A teardrop was caught on her blonde lashes. "The good Lord be thanked," she whispered.

As I drifted back to sleep, I heard the doctor's deep voice. "Ma'am, your love and prayers have worked a miracle. She is through the crisis and will now certainly recover."

When I awoke, I felt hungry. I tried to sit up, but fell back, too weak to do so.

Anneke was reading a book by my bedside. Watery afternoon sunshine dappled the ceiling with the pattern of the lace curtain over the window. "Welcome back to life, Mary," Anneke said, her blue eyes sparkling with pleasure. She stood and propped me into a sitting position with a couple of soft pillows.

I looked around. My bed stood in a room I'd never seen before. A plain brown carpet covered the floor. In fact, everything in the room was various shades of brown.

Anneke stepped away from the bed. "I have to report that you're awake." She hurried out of the room, the door softly closing behind her. She returned within a few minutes, with Mrs Mac behind her. So, that had been real, not a dream. Mrs Mac carried a steaming pot, and my mouth watered at the smell of chicken soup.

Alice

Alice MacCartney sat on the stage next to the Principal, gazing at the audience. *Well, girl,* she thought, *you wanted to be a thespian. Here comes the performance of your life.* She looked at Mrs Talbot, who gave her a slight nod of encouragement.

Six rows of girls faced her, in increasing order of size from front to back. A woman sat at each end of each row. Glaringly empty was the third chair in the front row — Mary's chair.

A tall figure blocked the light of the entrance, and Alice saw Mr O'Halloran walk in. She'd met him several times during the vigil over Mary. As he advanced, a susurration of whispers and squirms followed him. Soon, she could see the tiny child gently cradled in his arms. Mary had her arms around his neck, with her face pressed against his cheek.

Poor girl. She was skin over skeleton, with those beautiful green eyes far too large for her face. Although warmly wrapped, she still seemed more like a doll than a child.

Ever so gently, Mr O'Halloran settled Mary in her chair, gave the stage a slight bow, and walked out.

Mrs Talbot stood and took two steps forward. The noise in the hall ceased. "Ladies," she started, "We have a visitor. Mrs MacCartney has a reason to address you. I know you will accord her your full attention." As she turned for her chair, her lips twitched in a slight conspiratorial smile. She and Alice had talked several hours about the approach to take.

Alice swallowed, stood up as gracefully as she could, and advanced to the edge of the platform. She looked around, using silence to focus her audience. Then she launched into her speech.

> "Ladies, you all know the story of the crucifixion. Judea was a conquered country, a despised minor colony of Rome. A Roman could command a local to carry his packages for a mile, without payment. Jesus said, "Walk the extra mile," by which he meant,

instead of complaining, instead of feeling hate and resentment, accept it and maintain your dignity. A Roman could strike a local, who was not allowed to hit back, and had no legal protection. Jesus said, "Turn the other cheek." Again the message was to accept, and maintain your dignity, your inner peace.

For this, He was killed. He had to be killed, because the Romans had a puppet king who served them well, and it was convenient to maintain him there. You see, Jesus had inspired so many people that Herod's authority was becoming undermined.

Jesus guided people to love. All the same, He was killed, because those who closed their hearts with hate would not hear, couldn't be reached by the message of love. He was killed in great pain and suffering, because that gave Him the experience of what pain is like, so He can be there for us in our pain and suffering.

But then, a miracle happened, and He came back to life again.

My dears, we, here in this school, are privileged. The same sequence of events has happened here, including the miracle."

She paused for effect and looked around. She had them — not a sound could be heard. All eyes were on her.

"Judea was a conquered country. New South Wales is also a conquered country. Instead of the arrogant Romans, here you have the arrogant British — us. As in Judea then, here too, the locals, the original owners of the land, are treated with contempt and disdain.

And, a person with the gift of love has been born to these poor people. The first time I'd met her, I was in pain. The touch of her hand, and the pain ceased. If you approach her with friendship and openness, you will receive the gift of love, and have the blessing of God placed into your heart. I know, Mrs Talbot knows, because this has happened to both of us. It's happened to many others among you young ladies.

At the same time, if you approach her with hate, you'll receive nothing, because as with Jesus, hate is a barrier against the love of God.

Jesus was killed.

Our giver of love was killed too.

She died as I watched, despite everything we tried. Her breathing stopped. The doctor looked for a heartbeat, and found none.

I prayed to God, and she came back to life. She came back, because she still has the mission of teaching us love.

You all know who I am talking about. Little Mary
Fisher, here in the front row, still barely alive."

Mary was shaking her head from side to side, and her lips
formed a silent "No." However, the rest of the audience
were spellbound, and Alice saw many heads nod to her
points.

"Some among you have received the gift of love
from her. Others have approached her with hate and
lost out as a result. I ask you now to come forward
in an orderly way, and to allow her to give you the
gift of love."

Two girls in the fifth row stood. Alice recognised the tall
blonde as Kirsten Petersen, one of the several girls who had
lovingly taken turns to care for Mary during her illness. She
firmly held the hand of a shorter girl with curly dark hair and
led her forward. Tension and reluctance were writ on this
girl's posture, the way she walked.

They stopped in front of Mary, whose face lit up with joy.
She reached out an almost translucent hand. Alice heard her
say, "Oh, Kathryn!"

Kirsten gave the other girl a slight shove, and even seen
from behind, the curly-haired girl's body relaxed. She leaned
forward and hugged the brown-skinned little child.

Others left their seats. After a while, a Grade 6 girl tapped

Kathryn on the shoulder. Kathryn stood, and as she turned, the light from the high windows glinted off tears on her face.

At first, Alice was concerned that the exercise would be too taxing on Mary, but she saw that she actually gained strength from all the love she gave out.

Time passed, in orderly turmoil, and at last all the girls were back in their seats.

Mrs Talbot advanced to stand beside Alice. She said, "Jessica Holmes. You did not come forward."

A girl stood up in the fourth row, her face bright red, head hanging down.

"Speak up, Miss Holmes."

"Ma'am, I..."

"Do go on."

The girl looked to one side, then to the other, as if wanting to run. At last, she raised her head. "Ma'am, I don't deserve grace."

A movement up front caught Alice's eyes. Mary was standing. She wobbled a little, then walked to the aisle. She held her hand out to enable the Grade 2 dorm mother to steady her, then stepped away, and reached the fourth grade line. She made her way into the row, then stopped in front of Jessica. Her voice sounded clear as she spoke. "Jessica, there is nothing to deserve. All I want is to be your friend."

"But, but, I nearly killed you!"

Mary reached out a hand and touched the bigger girl's.

Jessica dropped to her knees and held the small child to her.

Cheering erupted in the hall. But as she looked on, Alice saw someone in one of the back rows stand and bolt for the door. There was a brief scuffle, and, as every head turned backward, Michael O'Halloran again entered, firmly holding the arm of a brown-haired girl.

"Miss Barton, what is the meaning of this?" the Principal demanded.

Fruitlessly attempting to pull free, the girl stared defiantly at her. "I will not be made to touch that filthy animal!"

"So far, nobody in this room has been made to do anything."

"Then tell your gorilla to let me go!"

"Miss Barton." The ice in Mrs Talbot's voice stopped man and girl into a frozen tableau. "You. Will. Not. Speak. With. Such. Insolence."

The girl still looked furious, but her voice moderated. "My apologies, Mrs Talbot. I know I'll now be expelled, then my father will give me a whipping, and truly, I don't care!"

Kirsten Petersen stood up, in the fifth row. "Mrs Talbot, may I speak?"

At a nod from the Principal, Kirsten said, "Bev, Maeve has also chosen not to go to Mary. But tell me, why are you so frightened of the grace of God?"

"Frightened? I... I'm disgusted at—"

Kirsten cut her off. "You're disgusted at your own imaginings. Of all people in the world, I should know, because I used to share them until I learned how silly they were."

"You're a traitor!"

"No. I've learned from experience. You are stuck, trapped in a sick hell of your own making."

Mary was back in her seat. Alice hadn't even noticed her return. She now spoke up, and so silent was the crowd of girls that her quiet voice was clearly audible. "Mrs Talbot..."

"Yes, Miss Fisher?"

"Please forgive Miss Barton. Please don't expel her. I don't want her to touch me. I don't want her to suffer."

"Miss Fisher, Miss Barton needs to be punished. Not because she has refused grace — as Miss Petersen has stated so well, that is its own punishment. She needs to be punished for insolence and rudeness, and for acting in a way no lady should. Now, Miss Barton, return to your seat. You shall come to see me in my office after luncheon."

Alice admired the effortless way in which the Principal re-exerted control. Mrs Talbot now touched her on the hand, directing her back to her chair with a flick of the eyes.

Alice complied, and watched the orderly emptying of the

hall. The only exceptional feature was Mr O'Halloran carrying Mary back to her sickroom in Mrs Talbot's quarters. She was sure that this Monday assembly would not be forgotten in a hurry.

Maraglindi

I lay in my bed in the brown room, exhausted after my first outing, although Mr O'Halloran had carried me there and back.

I felt my cheeks burn, like when I was suffering with the fever. What sacrilege, comparing me to Jesus! Oh, how could Mrs Mac do that? Of course, I understood the reason, and I had picked up some of Mrs Talbot's thoughts and knew that the two of them had planned this together, but... but... to put me in the position of a deity... this was wrong.

The door opened, and Mrs Mac came in, her face beaming, her glow a bright silver. "Mary my dear, that was wonderful."

I managed to raise myself on an elbow. "Yes Mrs Mac, it was. Only, only..."

"Hmm?"

"Only, you know, I am not like Jesus at all. Really, I am not!"

The lady sat on the bedside chair and offered me a cup with a tendril of steam coming from it.

I sipped the warm, sweet tea. "Well, ma'am, really. Jesus was the Son of God, and perfect, and I'm just a little girl and fall over my own feet and make mistakes and sometimes I'm scared or even angry, or can have unkind thoughts, and if I was like Jesus, I'd know everything already and wouldn't need to be taught, would I?"

Mrs Mac laughed. "My dove, have it your way. You can have your opinion and I'll have mine. What you just said is all true, and what I'd said in Chapel is all true as well."

The door opened and Mrs Talbot entered. "Mrs MacCartney, you did very well. And Miss Fisher, you did very well, too. I am pleased."

Mrs Mac turned to her. "Mary and I were having a discussion. She has demurred at my parallel."

Mrs Talbot raised her eyebrows. "Indeed? Miss Fisher, it is not a child's place to disagree with her elders."

"Oh, Mrs Talbot, I agree. But, but... If I was like Jesus, then it would not be anybody else's place to disagree with me! So, what you said proves I'm not Jesus."

Mrs Mac laughed her silvery laugh. "Mrs Talbot, I think our young friend has the better of you there."

I thought of another point. "Mrs Mac, um, Mrs Talbot has never met Mr Mac. But Mr Mac also spreads love wherever he goes. He is always kind to everyone and is a shining light who inspires people. Isn't that right?"

Mrs Mac's glow brightened even more. "My dear, you're right about that." She turned to the Principal. "My husband is a truly exceptional person. Mary's description is correct. He'd die rather than hurt another person. And... and I've never thought to compare him to Jesus."

"Very well," Mrs Talbot said after a thoughtful pause. "I will consider myself bested for once."

I felt the heat of embarrassment go from my face and sipped more of the lovely tea. "Thank you," I said to them. "I really don't think that I'm any more divine than any other person. Didn't Jesus say we're all children of God?"

Gerald

About thirty Aboriginal men, women and children faced Gerald in a semicircle in the stable behind the Moore mansion. Harry had made a beautifully crafted cross from two tree branches, which was mounted on the back wall, behind Gerald.

Gerald looked around at his congregation and met their smiles with one of his own. He said, "My friends, it is Sunday, the day the Lord has set aside for a day of rest. It's the day when we worship Him and thank Him for all the good things in our lives. And there are always things to be thankful for, even in the middle of the worst suffering. I love you people for the way you can have fun and joy, although your life is full of suffering and pain."

"All through the ages, everywhere in every place, there has always been suffering. Sadly, you people know all too much about that, and being treated badly, but let me tell you, this is not God's doing. Often, people are misguidedly cruel in God's name, but this is wrong. God is Love. Anyone who believes otherwise is simply mistaken."

"Now, I ask the children to lead us in our first hymn."

Mavis, Harry's older wife, led the eight children to stand in front of Gerald. They turned to face the congregation and started to sing.

> "Praise the Lord, my soul; all my inmost being, praise his holy name.
>
> Praise the Lord, my soul, and forget not all his benefits —
>
> who forgives all your sins and heals all your diseases,
>
> who redeems your life from the pit and crowns you with love and compassion,
>
> who satisfies your desires with good things so that your youth is renewed like the eagle's."

The tune was of their own making, and Gerald knew they had no idea about the meanings of many of the words, but the singing was delightful, and more important, it gave the people joy.

The children returned to their parents, and Harry joined Gerald. He spoke with passion for a considerable length of time in the native language. Naturally, Gerald couldn't understand him, but knew the content, having helped Harry prepare his speech yesterday. It was all about the poison in the bottle, the white man's curse that made men into beasts and destroyed the dignity of the people.

Gerald was amused at a difference. Almost all the women showed their agreement, with little sideways movements of their jaws at Harry's points, but several men put a surly, closed look on their faces. He noted these and made a mental list for further work with them.

An hour later, the church service was over, and his friends dispersed. He of course needed to attend the real church, the one for respectable white people who'd have been horrified at the thought that their God could care in the slightest about the welfare of Abos.

Indeed, the Reverend John gave him a dirty look, although he had reluctantly agreed to the use of the stables as a black church. Gerald had challenged him: did the Church not spend a lot of money on sending missionaries to all sorts of heathen places in Africa and the East? Why should it not look after the worthy heathen on their own doorstep, without any cost?

18

Maraglindi

Weeks passed while I slowly regained my strength. At first, I stayed in the brown room, but rarely alone. Mrs Judson, Mrs Goldberg, sometimes even Mrs Talbot spent time with me, supervising the lessons I slowly resumed, insisting that I eat frequently. During breaks and after school, an endless succession of girls vied to be allowed entry. I played word games with them. Some, like Anneke, told me fascinating stories. I sang with increasing strength.

At last, I returned to the dorm, and to classes, and to the regular lessons with Mrs Judson, and weekends at the Goldbergs, and music group on Fridays, and singing at the Sunday church services. It was wonderful to be popular, to be greeted with smiles, to be included in the games and fun of the others. Bev and Maeve still hated me, but I was relieved that Mrs Talbot hadn't expelled Bev. I felt safe enough, because wherever I was, the other girls now continually sought my company.

At the end of term, Mrs Mac came in her carriage to fetch me. And, surprise, the driver was Atan!

The rain started about halfway home. Mrs Mac and I were comfortable enough inside, but I knew that even with a hooded oilskin coat, Atan was getting wet sitting up front, and I also felt sorry for the poor horses. When I said this, Mrs Mac laughed. "If they were at home, they'd be out in the home paddock in the rain, eating grass!"

All the same, the carriage got slower and slower as the ever more muddy road sucked at the wheels. When at last we reached the bridge over the creek, water actually covered the road.

Atan stopped the carriage outside the back door, and Mother stood in the doorway with two little faces peeking out from behind her apron, and rain or no rain, life was wonderful.

For two weeks the rain fell. Sometimes it poured, sometimes it was a mere drizzle, but it never stopped. The creek flooded farther, cutting the house and its surrounds off from the rest of the world. At Father's request, Mr Mac allowed the people to shelter in the barns, and with the house animals in the stables, because the flooding river had destroyed the village. They still got about in boats made from bark in the old way. They caught fish, and also drowned animals floating by. I was proud of our skills: when white people were helpless, we could still cope. The people even managed to light fires, although Mr Mac was very strict about where and how, knowing that the people were not aware of the dangers of a fire near stored hay. I learned about all this from Father and Atan, who worked very hard at keeping the MacCartney animals alive, and also acted as go-betweens between Mr Mac and the people. I also spent joyful time with Father Riso, who did his job of teaching me about our people's way. I had fun playing with the children of my own kind.

The rain stopped at last, but the roads stayed impassable even two weeks later. At last, one morning, Mrs Mac said, "Mary my poppet, I've found a way for you to return to school."

Jesus be thanked, that was no longer frightening. I looked up at the lady. "How, Mrs Mac? Will we fly? Or swim?"

Mrs Mac laughed her silvery laugh. "No. You will sail. And Gerald will be with you."

The next morning, after my tearful farewell from my loved ones, Father put me into a bark boat. Atan passed my cane basket to him before hopping in himself. They rowed us downstream along the wide waterway the creek had become. It soon widened even farther into a mighty lake with the tops of trees sticking out of it. I was completely disoriented until I saw the feather-duster shapes of the Burrawang trees. Father said, "Good. The water is getting lower. Last time, all you could see was the very tops of the Burrawangs."

As we floated downstream, we passed the roofs of

houses, like red iron islands. Father turned the boat left, toward the shore, and we rowed up a water street to a makeshift jetty. Gerald already stood there, with his case by his side. "You're in time," he called out. I don't think the steamer will be long."

Father handed me up to Gerald, who gave me a big hug. "What's a steamer?" I asked.

"It's a new kind of ship. One came all the way from Sydney, to help with relieving people affected by the flood. It's been upriver once, bringing us supplies, and is now returning to Newcastle. Then it'll load up and return."

All the same, we were part of a crowd that waited for a long time, according to Gerald half an hour. Then Atan shouted, "It's coming! Look upriver."

I heard someone say, "They've got better eyes than most other animals." Father's glow immediately darkened, and his face got that closed look when he was controlling his fury. But, through long practice now, I managed not to read his thoughts, or that of anyone else. Sadly though, the comment made me lose all interest in the steamer.

When it arrived, it turned out to be a very big metal box-like thing, with a tall chimney that spewed stinking black smoke into the sky. On each side it had a huge rotating wheel that churned up the water behind it. Unlike the sailing ships I'd often seen in Newcastle, this ship had no beauty, no grace.

Men threw ropes, a sort of a bridge was formed from planks pushed out from the steamer, and in due course Gerald and I joined the procession that went on board the ship.

We arrived in Newcastle an hour before dark, and that night, I slept in my bed in Dorm F.

***

The last term was full of joy. As summer warmed the world, Miss Bachel sometimes took us on excursions. On one occasion, we visited the busy docks where towering sailing ships came for coal. Another time, we explored the riverbank, and here I could tell my friends about my people's lore, and ways of getting food from the plants and animals of the riverside.

The music group prepared for an end of year concert, and Mrs Goldberg gave me a solo singing role. It was a relief that Bev had stopped coming to the music group, and yet... and yet I was also sad that she had denied herself the joy, just to stay away from Kirsten and me.

In addition, Mrs Hislop, the Grade 5 teacher, organised a Nativity play, with parts for every girl in the school. I was one of the adoring children, and merely had to stand around wearing a turban and a long, flowing robe.

I still regularly exchanged letters with Mrs Mac, and one Thursday's letter bore exciting news: she was going to have another baby!

The last day of school was sad, because after this, Anneke would be gone from my life. As we said goodbye, I told her, "I'll write letters to you."

"That's pleasing, Maraglindi. I intend to write to you, too. And there is something else. You've taught me how to forgive, and how to love better. I'll carry on your work in Bega."

That brought tears to my eyes. "Anneke," I answered, "I'm only a servant. It's God's work, not mine."

I also said goodbye to the other nine sixth graders, but then sadness was forgotten because, as I walked out of the Dining Room, I sensed the approach of my loved ones: Mother, Mrs Mac, Tari, Donald, Rippie, Old Mother, Atan and Father.

The double gates were open, with three carriages already inside. As I raced toward the entry, I saw the familiar pair of brown horses, with Atan's and Father's joyful faces above them. Father neatly turned the carriage, stopping close by the fence.

"Surprise, Froggie!" Mother shouted from inside the carriage. "Mrs Mac arranged this with the *school* lady."

Mrs Mac climbed down, to be greeted with respectful

smiles by several girls. She bent to hug me. "My little poppet, Donald and I shall spend the night in Mrs Talbot's quarters. Your parents were sure you'd want to camp with them by the riverside."

"Oh yes!"

"Come on then. We'll get some clothes for you." She led me to my dorm, and we returned with a small bundle within a few minutes. Straight after this, Father and Atan drove the carriage out. Mother and Old Mother carrying the little boys, my family went to the Office to meet Mrs Talbot. Carriages kept coming and going away again after the passengers got out of them. Families stood around in chattering groups. I noticed dark glows and closed faces on many of the parents when they saw the Aboriginal family walking past, but chose to focus my attention on my own group. It was so wonderful to hold Tari's hand with one of mine, and Mrs Mac's with the other! It was so delightful to see the look of wonder on Rippie's and Donald's little faces!

Mrs Jardine ushered us straight in. Mrs Talbot actually smiled as we crowded before her desk. "Oh, Mrs MacCartney, Mrs Fisher, um... welcome."

Mrs Mac said, "How do you do, Mrs Talbot? I have brought all of Mary's family, as we arranged. They prefer to camp by the river, so you'll only need to accommodate me and my son, Donald."

"Well, well, the room where we nursed Mary is available, as you know. However, there is one thing. Thanks to your good work, almost all my young ladies now accept Aboriginal people, but their families will more than likely be prejudiced. So, please do not take this amiss, but I shall need to seat them in an inconspicuous place."

I spoke up and could see surprise on all the adult faces. "Mrs Talbot, may I speak?"

"Yes, Miss Fisher?"

"My family will like that. They'll be much happier sitting out of sight. And ma'am, you're right. As we walked here, I could feel the... the... I don't know the word. Anger?"

"The word you are seeking is probably 'disdain.' But Mrs MacCartney, would you occupy a place of honour with me?"

I could see that Mrs Mac was clearly torn two ways. She said after a pause to think, "Very well. And also, I'll make a point of associating with my people when possible. Hopefully, that will carry on the good work."

When we went outside again, the grassy area had been transformed into an open-air theatre. Lots of chairs, including those from both the Chapel and the Dining Room, stood outside in neat arcs, facing a clear space. I saw a big collection of girls in front of the Chapel steps and remembered my instructions. "Mrs Mac, Mother, Old Mother," I said, "I need to go and dress for the play."

At three of the clock of the afternoon, dressed in my robe and turban, I marched with the other students to the open space. The seats were occupied, with many empty chairs for the girls, all of whom stood in a neat, organised array behind the stage area. Several teachers were with us, to keep order.

Being one of the smallest, I stood at the front, but even so could not find my family at first. Mrs Mac, with Donald on her lap, sat beside Mrs Talbot in the front row, and waved to me. Naturally, other parents were waving too, everywhere. But where were the others?

Oh, I am silly, I thought. I closed my eyes to shut out the presence of strangers from my consciousness and found my family in the entry to the Chapel, out of sight but able to see and hear everything. I rose on tippy-toes and waved toward them, but a stern look from Mrs Gately stopped me.

The nativity play went as well as at the last rehearsal, although several of the girls with speaking parts forgot to shout their lines. Then most of the girls went to sit with their families, while the music group congregated in the Chapel.

Carrying Donald, Mrs Mac caught up with me and took my hand. "Everyone has seen Mrs Talbot honouring me," she said. "Now, let us show these people that I in turn honour your family."

Father and Atan had pulled the family's chairs to one side so that the music girls could go into the Chapel. As I stopped, Becky raced out, and gave me my flute. "Oh," she said, "Introduce me."

I did so and was amused at one thing. Atan couldn't take his eyes off Becky, his glow went all golden like sunshine, and the swirl over his heart grew like a green flame. *Too bad*, I thought with an inner chuckle. He had his family waiting for him, and no white girl could possibly take Dini's place.

But then, the two of us had to follow the others of the music group to the stage area.

The musical performance went off perfectly too, although the sound was far less impressive than in the Chapel. I performed my solo, with a great deal of relief when it was over. Then it was back to the Chapel. As we arrived, I heard Mrs Mac say to Mother, "Come on, Glindi. We have missionary work to do."

Gerald

Gerald celebrated the last day of the year at Moore College by wielding an axe with a will. The pyramid of split wood by his side was now above the level of his head. He placed a nice, even-grained billet of wood on the splitting block, lifted the axe and flicked it to the precise spot he wanted. The billet split in two. He stacked these halves neatly on top of each other and split them both with a mighty blow that left the axe stuck in the block. With economy of movement, he picked up the four pieces of wood and threw them on top of the pile.

"Bravo! Bravo!" Richard cheered mockingly from the back veranda, where he sat at ease, on a chair with only its rear legs on the ground, and the back against the wall. He was nursing a mug of ale. His feet rested on the rail, above the level of his head.

Gerald grinned. "That's why I have broad shoulders, my friend, while you have a broad waist."

"Comfortably cuddly, my boy, comfortably cuddly. After all, I don't want my mother to think that I was starved while at school."

"Don't let the Reverend John hear you call it a school."

"Hmm. No. Well, after this evening, the good reverend won't hear me say anything until next February."

Gerald set up another billet and quartered it with two economical blows of the axe.

"Time for luncheon, gentlemen," came Mrs Sweeney's voice.

Richard put his feet onto the floor and stood. Gerald walked to the well, taking his shirt off on the way. He worked the lever of the pump till the water started flowing and washed the sweat off his body and face. He put his shirt back on, knowing that the heat would dry him before he got to the table.

It was cool inside, and too dark to see for a moment. Edward and the Reverend Garfield were already at the table. As soon as they sat, Mr Garfield said grace. They started to eat.

Immediately after his last mouthful, Mr Garfield stood and looked around at his students. "Gentlemen, you have survived the first year of your training. Well done, all three of you. Only, Mr Kline, you need to work on correcting your tendency for unconventional thought. You, Mr Morrow, need to use your heart as much as your head, and you, Mr Jolly, need to remember that the easiest path is usually not the best one."

Having delivered these homilies, he stood and walked out of the room without a backward glance.

Edward looked at the door as it closed behind him. "Who is he of all people to advocate more heart?"

"All the same," Gerald answered, "Those were apt observations. For my part, I intend to continue on my unconventional path."

19

Maraglindi

The years flew by. I fell in love with Mrs Mac's baby girl, Althea, and in the weekly mail, often sent her stories I wrote, to be read to her by her mother or big brother. By the time I started Grade 5, Mrs Judson said she could teach me no more, so, Mrs Talbot took over my instruction. Although she only had time to devote to this task on Tuesdays and Thursdays, she set me so much private work that I was busy much of the time. I sat with the other girls in class every morning but learned about fascinating things like geology and ancient history. Every afternoon, I assisted in the Grade 1-2 classroom, reading to the class, and working individually with girls who experienced difficulties. In the playground, I deputised for the teachers in keeping order and friendliness. In the music group, I became Mrs Goldberg's main assistant, since of course Becky was gone.

I'm told that I became famous among the people, so when it was time for Atan to get married, the ceremony was organised at the MacCartneys' during the summer holiday between my Grades 5 and 6. Normally, Atan and Father Riso would have gone to his betrothed's family, but instead, Dini's entire village paddled down the river in bark boats.

The ceremony was simple. Dini's family sat in a circle, with Dini and Atan in the middle, facing each other. A small heap of dry sticks and tinder was set between them, ready to light. Dini's Father — her mother's brother — walked into their presence from around the house, carrying a firestick slightly longer than his arm, with the tip glowing redly. He touched the firestick to the tinder. Atan and Dini leaned forward and blew until a flame arose. When the fire burned brightly, they were husband and wife. The marriage would actually only be confirmed by the birth of their first baby. That was the third and final step. This firestick ceremony was the second. The first had of course been soon after Atan's birth, when Dini chose him as her husband-to-be.

Now it was time for the white wedding, which took place in Mrs Mac's beautiful rose garden, with the people of the two settlements looking on in a wide semicircle on the lawns beyond. Dini's family sat with everyone else, because, naturally, white people thought it wrong for one woman to have more than one husband.

Over the past week, Mrs Mac had enjoyed herself a lot in planning the occasion. She, Mr Mac, Mr Peter and his wife Mrs Sarah, Mrs McTaskill, and our family sat in chairs facing an improvised altar. Looking uncomfortable in very neat clothes, Atan stood between Gerald and Father Riso.

Dini walked out of the house, holding her father's arm.

She looked beautiful in a white, flowing dress. I managed not to giggle — three days ago, that dress had been a bed sheet. But looking at Dini, you'd think she was a young girl, not two years younger than Mother, and the mother of two children.

The couple reached the altar. Father Riso gave Atan a slight push, and he stepped forward to stand beside his bride.

Gerald delivered a beautiful speech about marriage joining two people into one, serving each other and serving God. I had to smile: Dini and her family were not at all interested in the white people's God. I knew, though, that Atan would talk them around in time, copying the way Gerald had done it for him.

Kissing in front of everybody was part of the ceremony, very strange for blackfellas, then it was time for a feast. All that was very nice, except... except that from now on, I would only see Atan very rarely, if ever. In the old days, we'd have met many times during the wanderings of the two hunting groups, and for the yearly ceremonies. He'd have been Father to my children, and Tari and I Aunties to his. But now...

After the ceremony, the men organised a traditional dance. They didn't perform the sacred dances of course, but had fun entertaining the white people, and the women and children.

The next day, Mr Mac and all his white workers rode out, to escort Dini's village back to their home. Mr Ritter and Father stayed behind to look after the animals. The local blackfella men stayed on to assist them.

Tari and I hid in our room to cry because our wonderful big brother was now out of our lives. Soon, there was a knock on our door, and Gerald saying, "My dears, may I come in?"

"Oh, Gerald," Tari said, "yes please."

He filled the little room. Gently he separated the us, and sat between us with an arm around the shoulder of each. "He's been a part of your lives, ever since you've been born," he said.

"Even when I'm at school..."

"I know what you mean, Maraglindi. It's the same for me, too. I now live and work a good day's ride away from home, but my heart is still here with Mrs McTaskill, and you delightful people." He continued after a long, comfortable silence. "It is the way of the world, my poppets. People grow up and move on. But he is still with us, in our hearts."

***

At the end of the holidays, I returned to Newcastle, to be one of the nine senior girls in school, and treated by everyone almost as one of the teachers. I exchanged letters with Mrs Mac, Atan, Anneke and Kirsten, and spent most weekends with the Goldbergs.

Grade 6 received weekly lessons on the Bible from the Reverend Mr Durham. As always, his every word expressed disdain for females, and his interpretation of God's message was one of harsh judgment. His was the one class in the week I didn't enjoy. At last, on the fourth Thursday of the term, I spoke up. "Mr Durham, may I ask a question, sir?"

"What is it, Miss Fisher?" He managed to give the title a twist that made it sound like an insult.

"Sir, I've noticed that so far we have concentrated on tragic events from the Old Testament. At home, I study the Bible with the Reverend Mr Kline, and he focuses on the wonderful stories from the life of Jesus. Will we also learn from those, later in class?" I had thought this out carefully, ensuring that he'd have no opening to accuse me of insolence.

He stood even straighter than usual, and his face grew thunderous. "I am the one who determines the subject matter. The object of these lessons is to teach you young women" — said with the usual sneer — "God's word on your role in the world. For that, I choose lessons from the Bible that are apt, and put the fear of God within you."

Of course, I could say nothing in reply, but silently,

within my heart, I said, *You're wrong. It's the love of God we all need, not the fear of God. Would that Jesus had blessed you with it.*

Grade 6 made frequent excursions to places like the newly established Library, to study the plants and animals of the seashore, and for luncheon in a restaurant in order to experience proper public manners. On these occasions, I found myself to be out of the heaven of acceptance and liking, back into the hell of disdain and hatred. At the Library, the lady behind the counter looked at me. Her aura expressed distress as she said to the teacher, "Please make sure this one doesn't damage any books!"

Mrs Carter replied with a lot of indignation, "You're mistaken. I'll have you know, Mary is my best student. I shall go further. She is the most brilliant student I've ever taught."

The Librarian said nothing, but almost against my will, I read her thought: *Oh yes, and I'm Queen Victoria.*

At another time, we went to the open-air market where the local farmers sold fruit, vegetables, eggs, milk, cheese and butter. As Mrs Carter and the nine of us walked along an aisle between two rows of improvised stalls, a man came the other way. His gait was not quite steady, and he glared around in an angry way. He looked at the class and his eyes stopped on me, in the second pair behind Mrs Carter. Then he looked back at the teacher. "Hey, you're from the school for sheilas, ain't ya?" he demanded. His voice was slurred.

"We are from Talbot Ladies' College," she answered. I could see the fear in her glow, and also in the way she held her body.

"You hire them out? I'll 'ave the darkie. They's juicier."

"Sir, how dare you! Leave us alone!"

"Or what, biddy? You jealous I don't want an old prune like you?"

A burly farmer stepped from behind his table and got between the man and Mrs Carter. "You're pissed drunk, fella," he said. "Leave these ladies alone or I'll surely flatten ya."

"Whatdya mean, ladies? They got an Abo with them!"

The farmer's eyes flicked to me, then he focused back on the drunk. "Yea, sure, that one is a half-caste Abo. But you got no right to speak like that to the teacher, or the other young ladies. Now begone before I lays into ya."

Mrs Carter chose to make her purchases from this man with proper gratitude, but I stayed sad: he'd also dismissed me as not being worthy of respect.

After this episode, Mrs Talbot organised Mr O'Halloran to accompany the remaining Grade 6 excursions. His height, bulk and broad shoulders provided ample protection.

There was also an amazing happening. A week after the start of third term, I enjoyed a game of throwing ball with a group of other girls. I missed my catch more often than anyone else, but this bothered no one. As Rosalind hurled the ball with full force, a Grade 2 girl ran in front of her, and the ball struck the side of her head.

The little girl fell to the grass, unconscious. Her arms and legs twitched.

Two teachers raced to her. Mrs Hislop knelt next to the girl and turned her onto her side.

Rosalind was crying. "I'm so sorry! It was an accident! She came from nowhere, and—"

I put my hand on her shoulder. "It's all right, Roz. Nobody is blaming you. It was an accident."

Rosalind quieted down. "Mary, oh please, help her!" she asked.

I joined the teachers and knelt beside them.

This child, Felicity, had been one of my special charges since the start of last year. She had difficulty learning, and difficulty staying still for more than a few moments. Every afternoon, I helped her with her work.

Now, I took hold of the little girl's hand and focused all my attention, all my love on Felicity. As I looked, I saw the glow about the girl's body, the spirit, leave and hover above. The twitching arms and legs grew still. Her chest stopped rising and falling.

I somehow felt myself join that hovering spirit and gathered it into my embrace. "It isn't time for you to die yet," I sent the thought. "You will heal. And this knock will make you be better than you were before."

The glow returned to her body, and the tiny hand in mine became pink as blood started to flow again.

Felicity rolled onto her back and opened her eyes. "Oh, my head hurts," she mumbled, then closed her eyes again. This time, however, her chest rose and fell with regular, healthy breathing.

Mrs Talbot came with one of the workmen, who picked the child up and carried her away.

For the next several weeks, I spent all my spare time in the brown room again, only not as the patient this time. And when at last Felicity was ready to return to the classroom, everyone noted the miraculous change: she could now concentrate, and sit still, and her work improved.

But otherwise, the weeks and months and terms passed, filled with the steady routine of school. Then finally, even Grade 6 was over, I had teary partings from Mrs Judson, the Goldberg and O'Halloran families, the eight other girls of my class, and the many younger girls I had formed special bonds with, and even Mrs Talbot.

Mrs Mac took me home for the last time.

20

Maraglindi

Life settled into a new pattern. Donald and Rippie went to school during the week, my brother being protected because Mr Mac made substantial donations to the school, and Mrs Mac regularly called on the mothers of other boys. I had the joy of teaching Althea, who picked up the pleasure of learning from me, and was a bright child who soaked up skills and knowledge.

There was a great surprise at Christmas time: Mr Mac bought an upright piano, similar to the one in the Goldberg home, and I became Mrs Mac's teacher in playing music. We soon played duos, me on my flute, she on the keyboard.

One afternoon, Mrs McTaskill came calling with a strange lady. I was reading Althea a story, gently leading her to make a connection between the words and the pictures in the book. Donald and Rippie were of course at school.

When Mrs Mac and the two visitors entered, I stood, and the little girl followed my example.

The stranger was clearly in pain. The glow about her had many flashes of red, and she walked in an awkward way. She seemed old, even older than Mrs McTaskill.

Mrs Mac said, "Mrs Johnston, please meet my delightful

young friend, Mary, and my dear daughter, Althea."

I stepped forward, and before the lady could think about it, grasped her hand and sent a loving wish for the pain to ease. This lady was fat, with big, heavy breasts. They pulled on her back, causing the pain. I couldn't fix the cause, but at least the red in her glow faded, and she stood more at ease.

"Don't know what you done, Mary," she said, "but thank you. Maude did say you'd help me aching back, like."

I noted that Mrs Johnston spoke like the white men working for Mr Mac rather than like a lady. Also, she wore rougher clothes than Mrs Mac or Mrs McTaskill. Naturally, neither of these things bothered me.

Mrs Mac rang the bell, and Old Mother came almost immediately. "Jila, please bring us some tea, and a nice drink for the girls," she ordered.

Mrs McTaskill said, "Well, I've done it. I've sold my farm to Marge here and her husband. It's been too much for me to run, and the men never pay any mind to a woman. And I've bought the Tomkins' place. It's in town, and with only a small bit of land, and I'll live there comfortably."

Mrs Johnston took over. "Me husband was foreman on a farm over Maitland way, and I made sure we saved money, like. So, now we can move up somewhat, and run our own farm. And Maude's been generous with allowing us to pay her off over time."

Old Mother came in with the drinks, and freshly baked biscuits, which delighted Althea who always loved sweet things.

As she added milk to her tea, Mrs McTaskill said, "Anyway, dear Gerald now lives too far away to visit me except on special occasions, and Atan is gone even farther, and so I'm at a loose end, but I've had a thought. I shall set up a small school for girls."

"What a good idea!" Mrs Mac sparkled at the thought. "It's sad that there are so few schools for girls."

"I never had a chance to learn me letters." Mrs Johnston looked sad. "Wish I could go and learn meself, but I guess I'm too old for such things."

"Maybe not. Tell you what, Marge, you can help in some way, and pick up the learning while you're there. But Alice, I was hoping that young Mary could assist me regularly, and perhaps you yourself might find some time. If you're involved, the school will gain respect."

My heart grew warm. What a wonderful thought, to teach little girls again. But then, a worry intruded. "Um…"

"What is it, Mary my dear?"

"Well, um, I'm an Abo, and the people of the town think we're no better than animals. They're unlikely to allow me to teach their daughters."

Mrs Mac shook her head at me. "My poppet, we

conquered the formidable Talbot Ladies' College. We can certainly conquer this town."

Mrs McTaskill said, "We needn't have you on show. Maybe Mrs MacCartney can loan you to me to help around the place, and what that help consists of is our business. As far as the parents are concerned, I do the teaching. What business is it of theirs if your help is in a professional capacity rather than a menial one?"

Mrs Mac gave me a loving look. "I've been thinking that, wonderful as it is to have her around, Mary is wasted, just being my companion. And yes, Maude, I'll be delighted to be a part of your venture."

Derek Johnston

Derek sat with satisfaction at the table of his own kitchen, unbelievably, in his own bloody house. Marge plonked the porridge in front of him, alongside a big mug of tea. He sloshed a good dose of whisky in the tea, grinning with a smile that could split his face as he stirred the mixture before bringing it to his face. Then it was worth drinking, like.

His wife may've been a fat old bag, and no way could he raise it for her anymore, but hell, she had her head screwed on. She was the one what saved all the money all these years and got a good deal outa that old Mac-wassherame. *Me own bloody farm! Yeah, right, five fingers is better than that bag'o lumps and wrinkles, but shit, me own bloody farm!*

He finished breakfast in minutes, then out the door and whistled for Brownie. He saddled the horse without havin' to think about it, then rode over to his land. *Bloody hell, I'm gentry, who'da believed it?*

The sun was coming up as he reached his property, swigging a nice mouthful of whisky on the way. His four men were not around yet, so he dismounted, marched up the steps of their quarters, and pushed the door back hard enough to bang against the wall. "Bloody hell!" he roared. "You blokes wanna pack yer bags and go, or what? It's the middle of the day!"

He grinned inside but showed nothing on his face as they scrambled up. Ticket-of-leave ex-convicts, the lot'o them, so no worries 'bout them arguin'. Five minutes and they faced him outside.

"You ain't workin' for some old biddy no more. We got animals, and they need carin' for, like. So, 'op to it. You got any problems, I'll tell ya what to do, but you bloody do it, and on time. You got me?"

"Uh, Mr Johnston," the tall one on the left said.

"Yeah?"

"I wouldn't mind breakfast, like."

"Tomorra, you can have breakfast before work, if you do it before I'm here, right? Now get to it. When the animals are happy, I'll be happy, then you can eat all you like."

By nine o'clock, all the chores were done. Fifteen more minutes and Derek sat with them as they started eating. He pulled out the bottle of whisky from his pocket and poured a good dose into each fella's cup. "Right lads, you earned it. Stay on me right side, and you'll be fine. Let me down again, like, and I'll break every bone in your bloody body, and you can go. There is heaps of convicts starvin' out there, right?"

He set up two men to kill and butcher a sheep, the other two to clean up after the milking, then rode home to look after his brand-new pigs.

Life was bloody good, if only he had some young slut to have a go at.

***

As the new boss rode off, Conor Ryan said in Gaelic to Liam Murphy, "Wish the fat bastard knew what a bath is for," as they both leaned on their shovels as soon as he was out of sight.

"You know from the redcoats back home, it's only the gentry who keep clean. An Irish peasant is as good as an English gentleman."

That was worth a laugh. But stinking English peasant or not, the fat bastard did have power over them, so Conor returned to shovelling cowshit. The milking sheds were clean by the time the bastard returned, then he kept them busy all day with a short break for a quick bite about noon.

Working for Mrs McTaskill got them spoiled, so Conor was tired as he washed just before crawling into his bunk. Timmo Brown, the little Cockney fella, said, "At least he's free with his whisky. Mindya, dunno how he can hold so much and not fall over."

"Rotgut stuff," Conor told him. "What my father made back home was whisky."

"Back 'ome? Forget that lad. They's dead to us, and we to them, thanks to His bloody Majesty and his rotten gentry. 'Least we don't hafta call the fat bastard Milord." Timmo was snoring as usual in five minutes.

Maraglindi

The new school opened within a month. Mrs McTaskill and Mrs MacCartney welcomed mothers who brought their daughters, while Mrs Johnston and I stayed in the background. The white women hardly gave me a glance as I brought freshly baked scones and tea to them.

The school started with eight girls, ranging in age from seven to twelve. The oldest two only had the barest idea of how to read. They could print their names, and count to ten. The others had no relevant knowledge at all.

Once the mothers were gone, Mrs McTaskill got the girls

to sit in a semicircle in the large, sunny lounge room and said, "Ladies, now I have a special treat for you. My friend Mary will read you a wonderful story."

I came in bearing a thick, heavy book: the English translation of the seventh edition of the fairy-tale collection by the Grimm Brothers. It had only recently arrived on the stagecoach.

One of the bigger girls, taller and possibly older than I was, looked scornful. "Abos can't read!"

Mrs Mac looked sternly at her. "I'll have you know, Miss, that Mary was the best student Mrs Talbot's Ladies' Academy in Newcastle has ever had. She attended that famous school for six years, and has more knowledge than most adult white men."

Mrs McTaskill added, "And I feel very fortunate to have her assistance. Anyway, let her prove it to you. Mary my dear, read."

I opened the big book and read the story of Cinderella. After the first few sentences, my audience sat spellbound, I noted tears in several eyes at all the right parts, and there was a cheer at the triumphant end.

After this, Mrs Mac took the two oldest into a small room, Mrs McTaskill went with the middle two into the kitchen, while Mrs Johnston and I stayed with the youngest four. I happily performed my well-practised task of teaching from the first reader, with Mrs Johnston quietly taking it all in, and, I sensed, learning far faster than the children.

When a little girl succeeded in a task, I touched her hand and sent her the love of my heart. By luncheon, all four were my friends.

By design, at first the school only operated during mornings, so Mrs Mac and I returned home, happy with the outcome.

Within a week, I conquered the hearts of the older girls, but then asked them to say nothing to their parents about my role. I dreaded the thought of more conflict. Mrs Johnston and the older two girls learned very rapidly, and soon their education became my special task.

Derek

Derek swore as rain drenched him on the way home. Barely the start of March, and it was Autumn already. At last he got there, unsaddled and brushed down his horse, then fed and locked up the pigs. Then he still needed to squelch through the bloody wet grass to the back door.

Marge was waiting with dinner of course, but also a young half-caste Abo was with her. Derek felt his prick stir in his pants, looking at her. He hadn't had a fuck in ages. Bloody hell, he could just about feel his hands on her little tits, not like Marge's saggy bags. All the same, what was an animal doing in his house? He opened his mouth to tell the little bitch to get the hell out, but to his surprise Marge smiled at him. That was rare enough to pull him up.

The fat old bitch said, "Derek, meet me friend Mary. She's a marvel, fixes me achin' back, like, every day."

"How do you do, Mr Johnston," the little bitch said, all la-di-da like she was a lady or something. All the same, looking at him, she almost held her breath like he was a bad smell. She turned to Marge. "Mrs Johnston, Mrs MacCartney will be expecting me home. I shall see you at Mrs McTaskill's brand new school! Goodbye, both of you."

Marge then walked with her to the front door like she indeed was a lady not a monkey.

Well, if the little slut was one of the MacCartneys' servants, Derek knew he needed to go easy. Real nobs, them, and no one said one bad word about them. Get them offside, like, and he knew he might as well leave town.

All the same, when Marge returned and ladled him a good helping of mutton stew, he demanded, "What was that little Abo monkey doin' here?"

She flared up at him. "Let me tellya, she is Mrs MacCartney's special companion, and been to school and all, and can read and write, and she is teachin' the girls at Maude's new school!"

"She's a half-caste Abo slut, and they's only good for one

thing."

"You do anythin' to her, and may God strike you dead!" She stormed out of the kitchen, leaving her stew untouched.

Maraglindi

9th day of August, 1863

Dear Anneke,

I was delighted to get your letter. It has been too long since we have seen each other, and I certainly wish to keep in touch with you.

Dermot is obviously a very discerning young man to be paying suit to you. And you are right: if only I could meet him, I could tell at a glance if his heart is true, and if he really loves you. You know that I can see a glow about people, and it tells me a lot of things about them. The first time I met you, I knew you were a good person because of the pure silver of your glow.

Can you believe it? I am now older than you were when we first met, and you are now a lady of 19, thinking of marriage and children? You will be such a fine mother!!!

Yes, Mrs McTaskill's school is still doing well. We now have fifteen students, and of course Mrs Johnston who is a dear. She and I have become very close friends. It is sad. She has had two sons and a daughter, and both the sons are dead, and the daughter is married and living in Sydney so that they never see each other. And of course, the daughter cannot read and write, so no letters have ever gone between them for all the years they have been apart. But we are getting ready: Mrs Johnston is keying herself up to write a letter, in the hope that the daughter will find somebody to read it for her.

She is lonely, because she lives in the big house with no company except for her husband, so I have been spending time with her, helping with the chores, continuing her education. She is actually an intelligent woman, except that she has the mannerisms that make people judge her otherwise.

But I REALLY do not like her husband. Fortunately, he is out on the farm working all day, and so I rarely meet him. But HIS glow is all dirty. He drinks whisky all the time, and stinks from it. I don't know how such a nice lady can be married to such an awful man. I make very sure I am never left alone with him, because he frightens me. He is one of those like Bev Barton was, if you remember her.

But, as I said, I hardly ever encounter him. He works with his men, and by all accounts his farm is doing better than when Mrs McTaskill had struggled with it as a widow. Men take no notice of what a woman tells them!

Slowly, carefully, Mrs MacCartney has been introducing me to a few other ladies and converting them to the view that Aborigines are just people who happen to have ancestors from this land rather than Europe, but this is scary. You know how much I hate it when people react to me and my people as if we were animals. (And in fact, many of those people like animals! But they say this as a form of insult and dismissal.)

Anyway, Anneke my dear, good luck with your romance, and I will pray to God for a good outcome for you.

Your devoted friend,

Maraglindi.

I smiled as I addressed an envelope and carefully put my letter in it. Of course, a corner folded back and I had to pull it out and try again — why am I always so awkward? Then I added it to the pile of three letters Mrs Mac already had waiting to be taken to the inn for the stagecoach. I then skipped to the kitchen, because a letter from Malu Melody some months ago had contained a recipe for Gugelhupf, and Mrs Mac had just managed to find a suitable cake form, and today was the day for baking the first one.

***

Mr Mac appeared very serious one Saturday afternoon. "Mary my dear, I need to speak with your entire family. Can you please get them together in half an hour in my study?"

Instantly worried, I ran to obey. When Father knocked on the door and we entered, Mr and Mrs Mac, Mr Peter, and even Donald and Althea were already there. Chairs waited for the Fisher family.

Mr Mac cleared his throat, and for once seemed unsure of himself. "We've become great friends over the years," he started, "but now, there is a problem." He paused and looked around. "I've received a letter from Home. My uncle has died, and he has no surviving family. I'm the closest relation. He has held a high position in Scotland, with large estates, and my duty is to return there. Peter will combine our two farms and continue here."

My heart broke with the pain. To lose the Macs! Donald, Althea, Mr and Mrs Mac...

But Mr Mac continued, "I want to give you a choice. If you like, you may come with us and stay on as part of our household. You could make a new life for yourselves on the other side of the world."

Sadly, I knew this to be impossible. What about Kiri?

Tari's betrothed, Darra? And to be away from the land that was our mother and father and part of our being? And there was the rest of our far-flung family. Can a person exist outside of place and people?

Old Mother, Father and Mother exchanged a glance, and I sensed that they thought the same. Father said, hesitantly, but with firmness, "Mr Mac, sir, thank you for the honour. But, but, blackfella way is very different from white way. You go anywhere. Land is something you buy and use and sell. One piece of land is all the same as another piece of land. For us, well, land is life. If we go from our country, we are not alive."

He stopped and there was a silence. Then Mrs Mac said, "Mick, I think I understand, but… not really. Surely, you'd get used to a new place?"

"No, ma'am. Even if we stay here in New South Wales, but outside our country, it would be like dying. We are part of country, and country is part of us. I can't say it better."

Mr Mac stroked his chin. "I think you've said it most eloquently. Well, you're welcome to stay on, and to do the work you've been doing, and I'll ask Peter to increase your pay to take account of long honest service and increased responsibility. Even all the white workers respect you."

Donald started to cry, and an instant later Rippie followed. I pulled my little brother close, and he snuggled against me. He managed to say, "I can't live without Donald!"

Those two had been inseparable for ten years, for all their young lives.

Mrs Mac wiped her own eyes with a lace handkerchief. "I knew this'd happen. Glindi, Mick, Jila, I have an offer. I'd like to take Rippie and Mary with me. They're young. They can adapt to a new life and continue as part of our family."

Althea's glum face lit up as if the sun shone from it. "Yes! I want Mary!"

Donald jumped up and gave his mother a big hug, while at the same time, Mother started to cry.

I stood. What I had to say was too important to be said while sitting. "I love all of you with all of my heart. You've been my life, and made me into what I am, and if I live another hundred years I'll love you and be full of gratitude for you. But, all the same, I... I cannot go." I couldn't help it; I was overtaken by deep sobs.

Mr Mac stood and reached me in two long strides. His strong arms pulled me close, and I buried my face in his jacket. "Why not, Little Angel?"

I pulled away so I could look up into his eyes. "I have a betrothed young man and his family. As Father said, I belong to the land. And I have duties. Mrs Johnston needs me. If... Heaven help us, if we lose Rippie, Mother will need me. And, and, sir, ma'am, my destiny is in this land, in this place. I cannot explain why, but it is so."

Mother said, "It breaks my heart to lose my son, but he has to follow his heart. His heart tells him to go with you."

***

Six months passed in preparation. Mr Peter, Mrs Sarah and their children, Charles and Anna, moved into the MacCartney house. He appointed Mr Ritter as his manager at the other farm, and Father as his foreman to replace Mr Ritter. He told the workers that if they objected to working under an Aboriginal boss, they could leave. They all stayed. So, Mr Ritter moved into the big house there, and our family moved into his — much smaller than the main house, but huge and luxurious compared to our cottage.

After a heart-wrenching parting, Father drove the MacCartney family — and Rippie — to Newcastle in the carriage, with two of the workmen following on a large cart with their several sea chests, and boxes of their treasured possessions.

While I had long ago established a loving relationship with Mrs Sarah and her children, it wasn't the same. I was always welcome in the big house, and loved playing with Charles and Anna, and I taught them many things. However, they were not Donald and Althea. It was painful to see Mrs

Sarah in Mrs Mac's place, to see Mr Peter where Mr Mac should have been, and to be without my little brother.

A letter from Mrs Mac arrived from Sydney, posted on the day the great ship departed for Home. I prayed for their safety, knowing of the disaster that had killed Mr Mac's first wife and daughters.

I drowned my sorrow by becoming even more involved in Mrs McTaskill's school, and in Mrs Johnston's company. That good woman said, "Mary, my dove, every day you ease my aching back. Every day, you teach me new things, and to speak and act like a lady. You fill my life in the way no other person has, ever. So, now for a change, my dear, you need me and I'm here for you." She pulled me to her, and I lost myself in that comfortable embrace.

Mrs Johnston became active in the affairs of the church. She told me, this was to carry on Mrs Mac's work of bringing tolerance to the community, so they'd accept Aborigines as worthy of respect.

So, life settled into its new pattern as another year passed. I was thrilled and even frightened at changes in my body: my woman's blood came, my breasts started to grow, and I shot up in height. Soon, I'd be marrying Kiri, and the thought filled me with joy.

21
Maraglindi

As always, I enjoyed church. I loved the singing, and prayer lifted me into a different space where time stopped, and all suffering ceased, and I felt a warm glow within my being that I knew was God. In church during the service, even more than at other times and in other places, I saw a glow around each person. When they came in, most of them had many colours I've learned to associate with pain, anger, envy, and sorrow. Some — the ones who looked around in a bored way and went through the ritual without understanding — stayed that way. Others, like Mrs Johnston on my right and Mrs McTaskill on the left, lost the red and dirty green and blue smudges of their glow, and approached pure silver.

I loved the cadence of the ancient words, the measured pace of the service, and above all the way that here, and only here, I partook of the Holy Communion, was accepted as a child of God, as good as these white people, here by right and welcome.

I could even manage to ignore Mr Johnston, sitting on his wife's right side. His aura did not change. Even now, on a Sunday morning, I smelt the whisky on his breath. While he had washed his hands and face this morning, I could also smell the sour stench of his body.

Determinedly, I pushed my awareness of his presence away, and knelt with the rest of the congregation to pray.

After the service, Mrs Johnston called me over to say, "Mary, could you please do me a favour? Be a dear, run on home and start preparing dinner. I've got to help to plan the fair. I expect it may take a couple of hours."

I smiled at her, said my goodbyes and did as I was asked. Soon, I was in the kitchen, cutting up vegetables. As always, I had to be extremely careful with the sharp knife, my awkward hands threatening to cut myself rather than the carrots and parsnips.

I was so involved in my task that I did not sense anyone or hear any sound. But then my nose picked up the stink of whisky and unwashed man.

My stomach tied into a knot of terror as I turned.

Derek Johnston stood in the doorway, leaning against the doorpost. The leer on his face frightened me even more, and I couldn't get any air. To my own surprise, I found my right hand clenched around the handle of the knife, with the blade pointing toward the man.

"My, my, little Mary, you sure look pretty in that dress," Mr Johnston said.

"I... I've got to get on with the cooking," I managed.

"Do it. Thass righ'."

I forced myself to turn my back on him, facing the table again. I picked up the next carrot to slice.

Without warning, I felt beefy arms enfold me, and the miasma of his foul breath enveloped my head. His hand effortlessly snatched the knife out of mine, and I felt his erection pushing against the middle of my back.

"No!" I screamed.

"Shut yer mouth, little Abo slut," he growled.

I felt the cold steel of the knife against the spine in my neck. Bizarrely, I had a momentary vision: Jesus nailed to the cross, with a crown of thorns forced onto his head. But then, I realised I was feeling the back of the blade as he sliced down, through my dress and the back of my bloomers. The knife flew into my line of sight and clattered against the back door, on the other side of the table.

He let me go for an instant, ripped the dress, then spun me around. My face was level with the top of his protruding stomach and the stench made me gag. I lifted my hands and pushed against him, without effect.

He laughed, then I was bent backward and his lips swallowed mine. One large paw mauled at my exposed breast.

I brought up a knee and thrust at his groin. I clawed at his face with both hands.

He pushed me away, then I felt a mighty slap that should

have ripped my head off.

For an instant I sagged, held up only by the painful grip of his left hand on my upper arm. I felt his right hand tear at my underclothes, then he lifted me onto the table.

Black spots swam in front of my eyes and the room spun.

Derek must have thought he had me cowed, because he let me go and undid the clasp of his belt. He lowered his trousers.

Overwhelmed by horror, I looked at his manhood, bright red and huge.

Then somehow I found the strength to act. My right hand shot out, index finger stiffly extended, and I punched the tip into his eye.

He staggered back with a bellow, but swung an arm at the same time.

I went flying through the air, flying, where time seemed to stop, then painfully landed on the floor. The right side of my face was not there. No feeling. Then the lava of pain struck as I felt myself lifted up once more, then a steel cord encircled my throat, and blackness came.

Derek

Panting, a shutter of pain closing his left eye, Derek stopped squeezing. He let go of the girl's neck to see her head flop forward lifelessly.

The little Abo slut died on him. Damn the bitch to hell.

He threw her back onto the table, among the litter of vegetables. Her firm little breasts stuck up, with a little strawberry tipping each, and a cute black bush decorated the spot between her legs. He stroked her, enjoying the firm, still warm flesh. "Bugger, I'll have 'er anyway," he said as his cock rose again.

It was a struggle, but he got in and satisfied himself.

Hell, killing a darkie was no big deal, nobody would bother about it — except for Marge of course. She'd made a pet of the little animal. He'd better eliminate arguments for as long as possible. Lucky that Jack fellow was allowed to go home to the riverside on Sundays.

He pulled up his trousers, hoisted the small, light brown body onto his shoulder and went out the back door. One hand over his throbbing left eye, he carried her over to yesterday's job, the cauldron half-full of sheep guts. He dumped her in there, and when her arms and legs flopped out, fetched his butcher's knife and hacked the body into suitably sized bits. Then he relit the fire under the cauldron.

The pigs would be happy.

Once the fire roared into life, he returned to the house, tidied up the kitchen as best he could, then took the remains of the girl's clothing to throw on the flames.

Mick

Mick came home from supervising the settling of the animals to find Glindi, Jila and Tari in a near-panic. "Maraglindi is not home," Glindi said to him instead of a greeting.

Mick ran over to the big house, but the servants hadn't seen her, and Mrs Sarah could only say she'd been talking with Mrs Johnston after the service at the church. After that, Maraglindi had hurried out, and Mrs Johnston took part in the meeting to plan the fair, as Mrs Sarah also had.

So, he raced outside and whistled for his horse. Not bothering to saddle, he rode bareback over to the old McTaskill house, urging the mare to speed.

He couldn't bear to lose another daughter, particularly his Froggie, the most precious person within his heart.

Naturally, he rode around to the kitchen door at the back and could hear shouting even as he sprung to the ground, telling the horse to stay. It was Mr Johnston: "For the hundredth time, how the fuck would I know where your bloody pet is? Get off me face or I'll bash yours in!"

Mick battered on the door, ready to do some face bashing himself to defend the lady, never mind the consequences.

The door swung open, and the stinking, fat white man glared at him, legs apart, hands forming fists. "Yeah, what'ya want?"

"Mr Johnston, I need to talk with your lady." Instead of looking down, he squarely glared into the man's eyes.

"Insolent bastard, ain't ya? Jus' because the MacCartneys... oh, fuck off me property!"

"Sir, it's an emergency. I need to talk with your lady. And my next stop is Sergeant Dawson." Mick knew several things this slob would want to keep from the Sergeant but hadn't anticipated the reaction. Johnston went pale. Sweat suddenly covered his forehead, and his aggressive stance collapsed.

The man barged forward past Mick and stomped off.

Mrs Johnston came into view. "Mick. Come in. Thank the good Lord you came when you did. I was surely about to be beaten."

Even in his distress, Mick noted her way of speaking with pleasure. Like his, hers was thanks to Maraglindi. "Thank you, ma'am. My daughter is missing." He walked in and she shut the door.

"I know. I've been frantic with worry for her. Got home from the meeting at the church. Only about half the vegies were cut up, and she was nowhere. That's not like her!"

"No, ma'am, it isn't. Me and my family are worried sick. But did you see your husband's reaction to me mentioning the police?"

"Oh, Derek and the police have no love for each other,

that's for sure. But what could have happened to darling Mary?"

He looked around the kitchen. "What has changed since you've come home?"

The table was partly covered with a variety of vegetables, with a kitchen knife among them. A cooking pot held sliced carrots, celery and parsnips, and there were also slices scattered on the floor.

"No. Well, the food on the floor was Derek being angry. He swept a hand through them."

"Seems to me, she was cooking for you, then something interrupted her. In here, I can only think of one person who..." He couldn't continue, couldn't speak for the horror of the thought.

"But still, where is she?"

"I don't know, but I'm off to the sergeant."

***

Dawson listened. "In the old days, Mick, killing one of yours was treated as no crime, but the government of Britain has ruled that Aborigines are to get the same law as anyone else. There is now even a Protector of Aborigines in Victoria, though not here, worse luck. Y'know I've always done my best to protect you."

Despite the worry eating his insides, Mick smiled at him.

"Sergeant, I saw no evidence of anything, but only Mr Johnston could have done whatever was done..." he had to stop a moment, "...and, and..."

"Wait a moment." The sergeant went into his house, and Mick heard him talking with his wife. Not an easy job, he thought, having to work even on a Sunday evening. When the man emerged, they walked to the stable where Mick gave him a hand to saddle his horse, and they rode over to the Johnstons' again. Half an hour of talking and looking produced no results, so they rode back into the town, and to the pub. It was officially closed of course, it being Sunday, but a crowd of men lounged in the back garden, each with his drink.

Sure enough there Derek was, under a tree by himself. He had a patch over his left eye. The two of them walked up to him. Talking stopped, every eye on Mick and the policeman. Most of these men looked hostile, seeing an Abo there, but Mick didn't care.

"What'dya want?" Johnston said.

Sergeant Dawson looked calmly down at him and spoke loud enough for everyone to hear. "I am investigating a possible murder."

"Congratulations. That's yer job, ain't it?"

"Mr Johnston, a young girl is missing, and her last known location was at your house. So, I'm asking what you know about her."

"What young girl?"

"My daughter, whom you know as Mary," Mick said.

"Well, I don't know no nothin' 'bout her. Saw her last in the church, didn't I? Anyway, so what, she's only an Abo."

From the corner of his eye, Mick saw several men relax, nodding.

The sergeant said, "Since an Act of Parliament by the House of Commons in England, they are to be treated before the law as any other person. Anyway, please come with me to answer some questions."

"Nah! I don't know nothin'. Look, mate, I'm a farmer, right? Every other bloke can take time orf on Sunday, but animals don't know 'bout days of the week. Me men are havin' a day orf, so I was workin' after church, lookin' after me animals. So I don't know nothin' 'bout what went on in me house. So, arrest me or piss off!"

Sergeant Dawson's mouth formed a thin straight line, but he obviously controlled his annoyance. "This is not finished with, Mr Johnston. Do know you're a suspect for murder." He turned and walked back to the road, Mick following.

They parted, and Mick next rode to the village. He sought out Riso and Jack. "Risobanda, Jirdankoni, I think that horrid stinking Derek Johnston has killed darling Maraglindi."

"Oh no!" Riso's hands started shaking.

"Jirdankoni, you work for his wife, ey?"

"Yes."

"Tomorrow when you go back, scratch around, look at whatever you can, see what you can find. The police are on our side."

"I will do that."

"And Risobanda, please consult the spirits."

"Naturally."

Having done everything he could, Mick slowly rode home.

Derek

Derek found it hard to walk straight, but 'sorright, mate. He could hold his grog. Jus' a nuisance, the dirt track weaving around like that. Still, here was his front gate. Mission accop... accomp... he got there. He managed to click the catch and swung the gate inward with its usual screech. One day, he'd have to grease it.

Steps. One step. Two step. Three. Four.

Facing the door, he scrabbled around in his pocket for his key. Where the hell...

He kicked the door and nearly lost his balance and had to hang onto the doorknob.

A girl spoke behind him. "Drunk again, Derek?"

He turned, with his hand still holding the doorknob. It was that little Abo slut. Suddenly, he went cold all through his being. Breathing became a terrible chore. He felt his left eye throb worse than ever, and the right one bulge out of his head.

She stood there, in the same dress he'd ripped off her, but the dress was all right. So was the girl, with her tanned skin and mop of black hair. Although it was still quite dark, he saw her startling green eyes. If he raised his free hand, he could touch her, as she stood at the edge of the landing.

"But... you are dead!" he managed at last.

"That's right, Derek. You killed me. Then you raped my dead body. Then you fed me to the pigs. Do you think I'll let you be in peace?" There was a lilting laugh in the young voice.

How dare the little darkie? Letting go of the doorknob, he swung a mighty punch at her.

His fist went through nothing. He overbalanced, and was falling, falling. He saw the gravelled path coming for his face, slowly, taking forever.

Then darkness swallowed him.

***

It surprised Derek to be up high. The roof of his house was level with him on the left, with the dawn sky red beyond it. He looked down at a sprawling shape at the foot of the front stairs, a broken doll with its head at an impossible angle. *Hey, that's me!* he realised.

He became aware of a silver glow behind the house. He could sense it as if the house wasn't in the way. He didn't know how, but he extended his awareness, and saw Jack the Abo servant entering the back door with a basket full of firewood. He'd never seen anything as beautiful as the glow enveloping the fellow: silver with colours from the whole rainbow. At the noise of the back door closing, a spark of silver lit up within the house as well. He shifted his attention, again without knowing how, to see Marge sitting up in bed. She also glowed, but the silver was tainted with flashes of deep red. She yawned, then said, "I wonder where the old bastard is? Drunk in the ditch I suppose."

She struggled out of bed, and for the first time in many years, he looked at her and really saw her — sagging, heavy breasts pulling her spine into a painful curve, sagging belly, wrinkled face. In the past, this'd have disgusted him, but now, suddenly and to his surprise, he felt a great warmth of pity, compassion and even love overcome him. He wanted to hug her, but knew that would never again be possible.

A Voice that was not a voice spoke within his mind. "Come," it said.

The broken body on the ground twitched one last time.

Derek faced a darkness. At the end of it, as when a door is opened into summer, he saw a brightness that drew him.

He sped toward it.

In an instant that took an eternity, he faced a Being, a Person with no shape, nothing he could describe except that It was beautiful, and glowed with a brightness that made Jack's silver aura a mere spark. Derek felt very small, and very dirty, and very afraid. Was this God? Or Jesus? Or Saint Peter?

"I s'pose it's hell for me?"

The Voice answered, in meaning without words, "Forget that nonsense. There is no hell or heaven. There just Is. But tell me. Why do you feel that you deserve hell?"

"I..." He couldn't continue the thought, because without warning he became little Mary, struggling in Derek's grip, smelt his stinking breath, felt her horror and anger as he ripped the clothes off her...

Thankfully, the terrible experience stopped, and he was in the Presence again. "I'm sorry," he managed.

"What will you do about it?"

If he still had eyes, if he still had tears, he'd have been crying, but he didn't understand the question.

The Voice explained, "You must return. You must choose a life, and if it's your intention to pay for your crime, that life must allow you the choice to do so."

He thought for what felt like a long time, but could have been an instant. "I should suffer like she did... But also, I should have the power to hurt someone like I did, and not use it. In one life..."

"You'll have many lives. You can do both, at different times."

A second Presence appeared in Derek's awareness. It enfolded him in Its glow, and he became a baby in mother's arms, safe, loved, cherished. All the terrible pain and guilt ceased.

Something was familiar about this Mother, then he knew. "Mary?" he said with his thought.

"You knew me as Mary. My true name in that life was Maraglindi, but I've been many beings in many places."

"I'm sorry..."

"I know. Now you must look back over all of your life, not only its end. When you've finished, you will be born again. And then we shall meet. I'll be in your life, and you will have a chance to choose right."

PART 3

22

Kirsten

Kirsten sprinted through the grass, raising her dress with one hand, while screaming with all her might, her singing-trained lungs making a sound she hoped would carry all the way home. Between breaths, she heard Luke's pounding steps behind, but then clearly he thought better of it. She risked a backward glance to see him move away toward the trees.

She was safe, for now.

Panting, a stitch in her side, she slowed to a walk, but still hurried home, feeling incredibly tired with the release of tension. But now, there was Father...

The day had started so well. Kirsten was happily practising her violin when the door flew open, and her friend Susannah barged in. She shouted over the music, "The mushrooms are out!" She waved a cane basket around. "Come, it's pleasant outside."

Kirsten put the instrument on its rest, and the bow onto the music stand. "You're a nuisance," she said, but smiling. "I need to practise for church next Sunday, because the Reverend Mr Taylor told me at yesterday's service that he wishes to introduce a new piece by Handel. We've transcribed if for solo violin. It's complex enough to need a month of practice, and I have a week."

"Oh, all this highfaluting stuff! You know you always excel with your music. The sun is shining now, the mushrooms await us, and both our cooks will be delighted."

Looking down on top of her friend's dark head, Kirsten smiled, put on her bonnet and scarf, and followed Susannah out. They passed Mother, sitting at her loom, who said, "Do return for luncheon!"

"Yes, Mother. I expect to be an hour." She fetched a basket of her own from the kitchen.

Indeed, the sun shone outside, taking the chill of early spring off the air, but soon they were in the cool shade of the not-quite forest that formed the boundary between the two families' properties. They rapidly filled their baskets with mushrooms, to Susannah's constant chatter, as she skipped from topic to topic.

"Shush a moment," Kirsten interrupted. "Did you hear something behind us?"

They looked and listened. "What kind of sound?" Susannah whispered.

"As if someone trod on a twig or something."

But if there had been a sound, it certainly didn't repeat, and they continued until their baskets were overflowing. Then each turned for home.

Kirsten almost reached the edge of the trees when

something stirred ahead, and then a gloating face looked at her as the person she hated the most blocked her path.

"Luke. You've been stalking us, haven't you?"

"My love! My bride-to-be!" he mocked.

"I'd rather turn papist and be a nun!"

"What a waste that would be. No, you shall do as your father desires, like a good, obedient girl."

"I will never marry you! I will not!"

"You'll soon learn not to be so defiant!" He stepped toward her, threateningly.

Fear clenched her insides as she saw the viciousness in his eyes, but she made sure to show none of it. "That's precisely why you're the last male I'd ever marry. I have no desire to be a punching bag."

"All so fancy! You should never have been sent to be spoiled in that school. You don't need all that education to breed my sons!" He stepped closer again.

She had to do something. As his big paws reached for her, she shoved the basket full of mushrooms into his face and swung her left hand hard, fingers bent. She felt her nails rake his cheek as she sprinted past him, lifting her dress up with one hand.

Thank the good Lord, she'd escaped, this time.

"Were you screaming?" Mother demanded as she burst in. "And where is your basket?"

"I was attacked, Mother. Oh..." She couldn't help it, Kirsten started sobbing, tears cascading down her face, chest heaving.

"You're a lady. Take a deep, slow breath. Now." Indeed, Kirsten managed to gain some self-control. "Who was it?"

"Luke. He threatened me, and would've mauled me, but I threw the mushrooms at him and scratched his face."

Mother looked shocked. "That's very... unwise to do to your fiancé. When you are his—"

Kirsten shouted, "Mother, I will not marry him!"

Mother looked around in instant fear. "Shush! Someone may hear and tell your father."

Again, Kirsten took a deep breath, to gain time to think. "Mother, he is violent. He'd have... have violated me if I hadn't resisted."

"Surely not! He is gently bred."

"He is very good at acting the gentleman, but I know him. Ever since I was six years old and he seven, every time I was home from school he bullied me dreadfully. And when my bosom started to develop, this... er, involved my femininity. And like many times before, today he threatened me with what'd happen when he owns me, as he thinks is certain."

"Your father is very keen to complete the joining of the two families."

"Don't I know it? Haven't I heard it a million times, both

from him and from Mr Mogden? But Emil and Meredith are married, and so are Sebastian and Joan. Isn't that enough?"

Mother again looked around furtively, obviously terrified of having the conversation overheard. "You know *Kapten* Petersen will not be contradicted."

"Please. I. Will. Not. Marry. That. Violent. Savage." Kirsten whirled, and retired to her room where she could cry her heart out in private.

Luke Mogden

It's not fair! Luke lifted a hand to his cheek and looked at his fingers. They were bloody. The vixen had scratched him proper.

Of all the girls around, why did he have to be madly in love with the only one who didn't behave like a woman should? Mother, his sisters, Mrs Petersen — every woman he knew — were genteel and subservient, as the Bible commanded. He could have any girl he wanted: that little Susannah was cute enough, and he knew she fancied him, and Caroline, and Margaret, and all the others. *After all, as the only son of the town's founder and richest man, I'm a good catch!* he thought. He'd often heard the matrons say so when they didn't know he could hear them.

He vividly remembered when he was six, and Father told him, "Captain Petersen and I have decided, when you're grown, you'll marry this little darling." He'd looked at the tiny girl with golden hair and blue eyes, and he asked what being married was.

"Like Mother and I. Living together, having children together."

He liked the idea, and she did too, then. They played fine, until she went off to that fancy school. Why in the Devil's name does a girl need schooling? The others could barely read and write, and still they managed every womanly task.

He walked into his home. Father was there and asked, "Your face. What happened?"

"Good morning, Father. I was careless and a branch whipped it and scratched me."

"Go to the kitchen and get Patty to put her salve on. You don't want permanent scars."

Luke forced a laugh. "I could say I got them duelling."

Once in his room, he continued brooding. He'd tried everything he knew to properly subjugate her, but nothing worked. So, it was a brilliant idea to take her virginity, get her with child, then she'd have no choice but to marry him. It hadn't occurred to him that she'd be physically able to resist. He needed to plan this out with more care.

Gerald

"Your Grace, I came as soon as I received your message," Gerald said to Bishop Tyrrell, wondering what it was about.

"Mr Kline. You've served your time as a deacon, and we have performed your ordination. Normally I'd assign you a church of your own, but..."

The old man sat behind his imposing desk while Gerald was required to stand, enduring the hostile gaze. He waited for the Bishop to continue.

"But as I have stated before, you should not have gone to Moore College."

"Your Grace—"

"I train my own priests, to my standards and methods!" the Bishop thundered.

"Your Grace, as I've said previously, I simply didn't know. I had the calling to serve, wrote an application, and they accepted me. Had I known of your dislike of them, I certainly—"

"Dislike? Kline, you make this seem as if it was my personal foible. They know not what they do!"

Gerald hung his head, feigning humility he didn't feel. "You have my sincere apology, Your Grace, but what's done cannot be undone. Please pardon an honest mistake."

Bishop Tyrrell ignored this plea. "I have a request from

the Reverend Christopher Taylor in Griscombe. He is old and needs an assistant. You shall be his deacon."

"My thanks, Your Grace. I'll do my best. Only, where is Griscombe?"

"On the coast, a farming and fishing village with some twenty occupants, and their families and servants. Jackson has a map for you. It's two days' ride south of here, so you'd better hurry in order to be present for next Sunday's service."

Naturally, Gerald didn't share his thought that people other than wealthy male landowners were also deserving of being counted, but said goodbye, with the further thought that bishops should act Christian. He bought a spare horse, and rode home at the best speed possible, alternating mounts. He bought a packhorse to carry his few possessions, the two purchases using up most of his meagre savings, and started the three-day ride at dawn. He hoped he'd be able to sell the two new horses and spare tack in Griscombe.

He arrived about noon on Saturday, and found the vicarage beside the church, which was a plain timber building, distinguished by its cross and by a burial ground visible behind it. He dismounted and tied up his tired horses by a water trough, gave each a double handful of lucerne hay, then strode over and knocked. A fat, middle-aged woman opened the door. "Yes?"

"Good afternoon, I'm looking for the Reverend Christopher Taylor."

"Oh sure, and you're at the right place. Who will I tell him it is?" The Irish brogue was obvious. Ex-convict, Gerald surmised.

"Reverend Gerald Kline, his new deacon," he answered, smiling down at her.

"Oh, do come in, sir, do come in." She stepped aside, ushering Gerald through the door. By the time he followed her along a corridor to a door at its other end, his eyes had accustomed themselves to the relative darkness. The small living room was also dim, with curtains drawn. "Sir," the woman said, "your new deacon has arrived!"

The elderly man stood with difficulty, a smile splitting his white beard. "Welcome. Thank you, Annie. I'm sure the gentleman is hungry. Please bring him something." He turned back to Gerald. "I'll be so glad of your assistance! Vigorous youth is what this place needs."

"Sir, I'll do my best. Oh, I am Gerald Kline."

"Do take a seat, Mr Kline."

"Please, sir, Gerald."

"Very well. So, you've just finished your training with our esteemed bishop?"

Gerald laughed, ruefully. "No. I spent three years at Moore College—"

"And that's a crime in his eyes! You have my sympathy. All the same, if I like your work, I shall recommend that you take over my parish."

Annie came bustling in with a tray holding a bowl of beautifully aromatic chicken soup, a plate with bread, and butter in a small dish, and placed it on a low table by Gerald's side.

"Thank you," Gerald said. "Mr Taylor?"

"I've eaten. Enjoy your luncheon. Annie, please fetch Harvey. Gerald, please prepare a sermon for tomorrow, and you're welcome to share my supper this evening."

Gerald had expected this assignment. He blessed the food and its provider, thanking God for the hospitality, then set to with a will.

Soon after, a broomstick-thin man of perhaps forty years of age entered, and was introduced as Harvey Croft, the verger. The three of them made arrangements for Gerald's housing and other practical details, and Harvey also promised to spread the word about the two horses for sale.

Gerald brushed down and settled the horses in the backyard of the cottage that'd be his home, then worked on tomorrow's sermon before visiting the vicarage for supper.

Kirsten

Kirsten sat beside Mother in the landau coach Father was

so proud of. Even Mr Mogden didn't have an imported coach. Given the fine weather, the hood was open, so she could see Father's ramrod-straight back as he drove himself. *Isn't pride the first of the seven deadly sins?* she thought with an inner grin. Those deadly sins had been one of the favourite lessons of the Reverend Mr Durham at school, and one he exhibited as well. Didn't all men?

Father neatly parked the landau, and Tom took the reins. He'd been riding behind. Father helped Mother to dismount, while Kirsten easily sprang to the ground, carrying the violin in its case, never mind the awkward skirt.

They met up with Emil, with Meredith beside him holding Jonathan, who smiled and gurgled upon seeing Kirsten. She held out her arms, and her sister-in-law passed the baby over. She kissed the tiny, smooth cheek, but Mother nudged her, so she relinquished her prize. Sebastian and Joan arrived then, she big with child. They went inside.

A tall, broad-shouldered young man stood beside Mr Taylor at the front, also wearing a cassock, surplice, and a black stole.

Kirsten had to gasp; she knew him! But where... As if transported into the past, she was eleven years old once more, back at Mrs Talbot's Academy, watching this young man ride in, and dear Maraglindi running toward him. Only, at that time, she'd still hated Maraglindi.

They settled in their usual seats of honour at the front, with the Mogdens on the other side of their two daughters, and... she shuddered, Luke beside his father. The hypocrite, coming into God's house after attempting to ravish her. She was pleased to note the scabs of her defence on his right cheek.

She gazed at the face of this new minister. He was not handsome, far less so than Luke, but a quiet, strong confidence shone out of him. As way back then at the school, Kirsten felt an instant attraction.

Mr Taylor introduced him as the new deacon, Mr Kline, then sat down and allowed the young man to conduct the entire service. However, it was the old minister who signalled her to come forward with her violin. She did so, quickly setting up her music book, then tuning the instrument while standing beside the organ. Sitting at the keyboard, ready to pump the pedals, Mrs Lorien whispered, "One, two, three, four," and they launched into the first hymn. Kirsten led the singing, as always. Then she played the new piece from Handel. Not having been able to practise too well, thanks to wretched Luke, she was dissatisfied with her performance, but no one else appeared to have noticed.

Mr Kline administered Holy Communion, and she was disgusted at the thought of sipping from the same chalice as Luke, so she dipped her wafer into the wine instead.

Later in the service, Mr Kline stood to deliver the sermon.

"My friends in the Lord, I humbly accept my role as Mr Taylor's assistant in guiding your spiritual welfare. For my first talk to you, I've chosen Matthew 5:43-48 as my inspiration. 'You have heard that it was said, "Love your neighbour and hate your enemy." But I tell you, love your enemies and pray for those who persecute you, that you may be children of your Father in heaven. He causes his sun to rise on the evil and the good and sends rain on the righteous and the unrighteous. If you love those who love you, what reward will you get? Are not even the tax collectors doing that? And if you greet only your own people, what are you doing more than others? Do not even pagans do that? Be perfect, therefore, as your heavenly Father is perfect.'

Well, my friends, I have trouble being perfect, but I can do my best. So can we all. What the Lord tells us is that we should love everyone, regardless of what they do. But this doesn't mean we should accept bad deeds. If I were to do evil, I'd betray God. You'll hate what I do, but this shouldn't get in the way of loving me, as one of God's children. Your duty is to lead me out of my evil actions, not to reject me because of them."

He further developed this theme, and Kirsten felt he was talking personally to her. *How can I lead Luke out of his violence, his sense of entitlement?* But she knew nothing could do that, and helplessness enfolded her like a shroud.

She glanced at Luke. He looked bored, even contemptuous. Spoiled brat as usual.

After the service, the two ministers stood at the entrance to greet each member of the congregation. Kirsten looked up at the new deacon — unusual that, she being taller than most men. "Mr Kline, welcome to Griscombe. But I've seen you once before, when you visited Talbot Ladies' Academy."

His brown eyes opened wide as he gazed at her. "I also remember your face! Fancy that!"

Then Luke crowded up, the healing scratches on his face plain to see. "Mr Kline, this young lady is Miss Petersen, my fiancé, and I'm Luke Mogden." He held out a hand for a shake, and Kirsten saw him squeeze hard. But Mr Kline merely smiled, and the two young men held each other's hands until Luke's face paled, and he disengaged.

23

Jack

At dawn on Monday, Jirdankoni, universally called Jack, arrived at work. He liked old Mrs Marge, and often had the pleasure of a talk with Maraglindi, but now worry ate at him from inside. If that man had harmed Froggie, Jack would kill him, even if he hanged for it, or more likely beaten to death. He carried in a basketful of firewood and lit the kitchen fire. He swept the floor, and fetched more firewood for the inside fireplace, then restoked the kitchen fire and shut it down. The kettle on top was singing its gentle song when Mrs Marge said from behind him, "Good morning, Jack. I suppose you heard, Mary is missing."

"Yes, Missis. We all worry."

"Something else. My husband never came home last night. After breakfast, I'll visit the police, so when you're ready, please harness Brownie to the sulky and take it to the front."

"Sure. I do now." He led the sulky out the gate within minutes.

On the ground in front of the entrance was Mr Johnston's body, neck obviously broken. Jack tied the reins to the gatepost, then sprinted back to the kitchen door. "I found your husband," he managed between breaths. Half an hour later, he was at the sergeant's house. Mr Dawson tied his horse behind the sulky and hopped up beside him, asking a lot of questions on the way. Jack told him what he knew, which wasn't much. When they arrived, Dawson looked down on the body. "Drunk as usual, I guess. He fell in an awkward way and found his way to hell. Good riddance."

"Yes, good riddance is right, Sergeant," Mrs Marge said, "but it also causes problems. Who will run the farm now?"

The policeman shrugged. "I'll send a couple of men and a cart, and have the body taken to the churchyard." He waved a hand as goodbye, mounted his horse and rode off.

Jack carried on with his usual tasks, but also checked Mr Johnston's part of the yards, which he usually kept away from. Eventually he got to the pig enclosure. With horror, he saw the bones of a small human in their feed trough.

Marge

Two funerals on the one day.

The one in the morning attracted such a large crowd that the Reverend Mr Hutchins decided to hold it, as he said, under God's sky. Blimey, the families of every student at the school, and all the usual people what came to church, and in a separate group, all the Aborigines, and even a great many strangers, came to honour poor darling Mary.

Mary would've approved of having the celebration of her short life out in the open. She would've approved of white people listening with sympathy to her father's simple words from the heart, and to Peter MacCartney's beautiful words. He told several stories of her life at the Talbot Ladies' Academy in Newcastle. Marge knew of these events, but clearly most of the audience didn't. She saw amazement on faces as Peter reported on how she'd come back from death, and how she'd brought a little girl back to life herself.

To Marge's surprise, then Sergeant Dawson strode forward. "Ladies and gentlemen, little Mary was a remarkable girl. But also, she was the child of a remarkable people. I know them better than most of you, and let me say from the heart, they are not 'animals,' but people like you and me, and better people than some. Until now, our Aborigines have been forced to live in squalor, paid a mere fraction of what a far less skilled white person gets for doing the same work. What people do in other places is their business." He nodded at the minister. "Let us make our town an example of God's work and treat the brown members of our community with respect, as a memorial to Mary."

She certainly would've approved of that. So did many of those present, though certain faces became closed and rejecting. And, of course, those who stayed away would be against any such idea. She wished Alice MacCartney were still around to lead a team to do what the good sergeant said.

The afternoon funeral was much different. Their farm workers were there, and a few of Derek's drinking mates, and Sergeant Dawson because he had to, and that was it. Nobody thought to say anything good about Derek. She got a surprise all the same. After the grave was covered, she walked toward her sulky, to see Peter MacCartney waiting beside it. "Marge," he said, "have a cup of tea with us. Sarah and I have a proposition for you."

The house was very quiet when they arrived, without the background sound of servants, the mutter of distant talking. Sarah greeted her, with the two children sticking very close on each side. All three had red eyes, and the children kept sniffing.

"Welcome, Marge," Sarah said. "As you know, all our servants are Aboriginal, and right now they're conducting their own memorial service for darling Mary. God bless them for honouring her in their own way, it's only proper." She led Marge to the kitchen and made the tea herself.

After some polite chatter, Peter came to the point. "We know from experience that farm workers take no notice of a woman. Besides, Derek had a lot of knowledge you don't."

She nodded.

"Sarah and I have examined our finances and we can

afford to help. I'm writing a letter to my father, and, knowing him, he'll want to do everything possible to make things right for everyone concerned. That includes you, as well as Maude McTaskill and her school. Meantime, if you agree to sell your property to us, we'll pay you what we can and keep up your payments to Maude. My friend, Richard Windeyer in Tomago, has mentioned an ambitious young employee who is looking to advance, and recommended the fellow. I'll hire him as manager, under my man Ritter's supervision."

Marge felt tears of gratitude. "Peter, Sarah, thank you. Little Mary is still making us all into better people. I think when your manager comes, I'll ask Maude to move in with her and help more with the school."

Sarah said, "She'll miss Mary's teaching skills, for sure. I thought I'd volunteer to help out. Not that I can replace her, but we'll manage."

Mick

After Maraglindi's white funeral, all the people walked to the MacCartney property, and they also did a proper send-off. Mick lit a small fire. People brought several green leaved branches, and he fed them to the fire a handful at a time, and everyone waved some of the smoke onto themselves.

The storytelling went on in the meantime. Everyone said something about their lives with the dear girl who was now gone. Only, her name was never spoken, or her nickname, or even her white name.

Riso started. "She was my daughter, but also my teacher. I'm a magic man with secret knowledge, but I didn't know many things she knew even as a baby. She taught me that all people have good in them. Even white men who do terrible things only do that because they have wrong ideas inside their hearts. When they wake up to their true nature, they become good. I didn't know that." He looked around and caught Mick's eyes with his. *Yes*, Mick thought, *Riso is right about... the girl.*

"When she was home during the great flood, it was my chance to teach her about our ways, which was my duty as her father. But also, she taught me many things about where these white people come from. The world is much bigger than we ever knew, and many strange things are in it. And knowing these things is important for us. So, as you all know, I've been passing on this knowledge from her to all of you."

Riso squatted. Mick put another handful of green leaves on the fire while standing. "This girl of ours didn't know how to walk, how to wet in the right places, how to talk, until much later than other children. But she always had a gift, even as a baby. She could touch you and look at you, and peace came. The first time she spoke, it was to me. This was after a white man... killed another of my daughters. I killed that white man and his friends, all five of them. And when I returned, she used the first words of her life. She told me that her sister was all right, and she was looking after her." Mick stopped, to allow people to think about his words. "Riso told me, many years ago, she was specially sent to us by the spirits, and this shows me he was right. She was a great spirit herself, and much as we miss her, we know she watches over us, even now."

Then Glindi, Jila and Tari, then all the male and female elders, and eventually even the young children, each told stories about their lives with the dear girl who was now gone.

The long circle was done at last, and Riso stood again, this time as magic man. "I've spoken with the Spirits. This person who came to share her life with us for a time was sent to us for a purpose, which is our purpose but also much more. The work she had to do in this life was completed, so she needed to go. She now has other work to do, but the Spirits said, we will be part of that work also."

24

Gerald

As part of getting to know his new home, on Saturday morning Gerald went for a walk to explore the beautiful coastline. He started southward, climbing each hill to see the views. At noon, he ate his carried luncheon, then returned along the firm sand the retreating tide had left, and clambered over the rock outcrops framing the succession of beaches. He wished he had one of the local natives with him to teach him about unfamiliar plants and animals, but during his week here, he hadn't yet met any.

A hill to his left cast the long shadow of late afternoon when he saw something untoward ahead. A man was bent over a lady on the sand. Had she fainted? Gerald started running, and, in a shock soon saw that she was struggling. The man had a knee in her midriff and was tying her hands together with a rope. A scarf covered her mouth.

Gerald broke into a sprint. The man turned at the sound of footfalls, in the last second before Gerald knocked him off the lady.

The woman had to be Miss Petersen, given the blonde hair showing outside her bonnet. The man was the young fellow claiming to be her fiancé, whatever his name was.

Gerald shouted, "What do you think you're doing?"

The other man stood and charged at him.

With his longer arm, Gerald shoved an open palm into his face, stopping him, then stepped close, and spun him around by his jerkin. He picked him up by grasping his clothes from behind. Three or four running steps as he lifted him high, then hurled him into a coming wave breaking on the sand.

The man managed to stand, though bent over while coughing up seawater. Then he charged Gerald again. As he launched a punch, Gerald grasped his arm, twisted, then again picked him up, and threw him into the next wave. The man stood again.

Gerald said, making sure to sound calm and amused, "I can keep this up all day, you know. And you do realise, you could hang for assaulting a lady?"

The girl behind him spoke. Still keeping a corner of his eye on his opponent, Gerald glanced behind. She was standing, though sand clung to her clothes. She held the scarf in her left hand. "He thinks he is safe from the law, with his father the Magistrate."

"And the founder of the town, and the richest man. Fellow, you might as well move on. Making me your enemy was a bad move." He walked out of the reach of the next wave, water-filled boots clearly slowing him. All the same, he assumed an arrogant bearing.

"You can be the Prince of Wales for all I care," Gerald told him, "It's my duty to protect a lady from assault. And please note, I did you no violence, merely prevented you from doing harm. I could've bashed your face into a red pulp, or broken your arm, but just cooled you down somewhat." Actually, the impulse was there to properly rough up such a ruffian, but Gerald held it in firm check.

The fellow bent to unlace his boots. "Perhaps you can be forgiven for jumping to the wrong conclusion." He kicked one boot off and worked on the laces of the other. "Being a stranger, you don't know. I was merely exercising my rights."

"No!" Miss Petersen shouted. "You have no rights to me, and never will!"

"We're as good as married! Our fathers will it so."

Gerald could see this deteriorate into a fruitless, no doubt well practised shouting match, so he interrupted. "If you give me your word to not attack once more, perhaps we can sit up on the grass, and the two of you can explain the situation to me?"

"His word? The word of a spoiled brat is worth nothing!"

The young man opened his mouth for a retort, but Gerald spoke first. "Please, both of you. May we declare a truce for now?"

"Very well," he said, while she nodded. With Gerald still

keeping a vigilant eye on the young man, they walked across the soft sand to the grass, and sat, each facing the other two in a triangle. "I'm sorry," Gerald said. "I know we briefly met last Sunday, but with so many people, I don't remember your name."

"Luke Mogden. And it's mutual."

"Gerald Kline." He leaned toward the other man and held out his right hand, ready for instant action. However, a brief, polite handshake followed. He turned to the girl. "I know you're Miss Petersen. Now, please, I'd like to suggest some rules of engagement, so we can have a fruitful conversation. One person speaks at a time, and no interruption. Then the other, with mutual respect. Do I have your agreement?"

"Who are you to lay down the law?" Mogden demanded.

"I am not. But what I see is conflict and enmity that has obviously lasted for years. Whatever the two of you have been doing to handle the situation has failed. I hope the three of us can design a new approach, and this is the way to do it."

"You have a great deal of wisdom for a man not much older than we are," she said. "Very well, I'll do my best not to interrupt when he raves on."

Gerald grinned at her. "No, Miss Petersen. When he states his point of view, which is as deserving of being heard as yours. Remember that part of the approach is mutual respect." He turned to look at the other man. "Mr Mogden—"

"Oh, I'm Luke. Mr Mogden is my father."

"I understand Miss Petersen's outrage at being attacked, so perhaps you'd be kind enough to start, and explain your reasoning to me."

"Very well." He stopped, obviously considering his words. "Our two fathers decided to weld our two families together, years ago. My two sisters are married to Kirsten's two brothers, and we shall wed when she turns twenty-one. I've thought of her as my wife for the past fourteen years. It's arranged, and foreordained, and will happen."

Miss Petersen interrupted, "But—"

Gerald interrupted her in turn. "Ma'am, please, it's Luke's turn. You'll have every opportunity to respond when he is finished."

Unexpectedly, she gave him a brilliant smile, and his heart jumped in his chest. "Nobody has called me 'ma'am' before. I'm Kirsten."

"Thank you. Luke, please continue."

"She was sent off to this school in Newcastle, and naturally, returned for holidays. And from the first occasion, she took special delight in humiliating me, vying with me with the superiority of her learning, instead of acting like a female should."

The girl again opened her mouth in obvious outrage but stayed quiet when Gerald waved a hand.

"This went on for year after year. When we became older, I realised I loved her with my whole being, but all she did was to reject me, act with defiance, always knowing better and flaunting her unseemly independence. I was about thirteen when I consulted my father about it. He said, you train a recalcitrant woman the way you train a recalcitrant horse: use the whip until the horse knows who is boss, then make friends using kindness. So, that's what I've done, but to no avail. All I want is to love her and have her love me and treat me with the respect that's my due. Then all will be well."

"Kirsten, please respond."

Blue fire blasted from her eyes. "What a load of codswallop! I also remember my holidays from school. Every moment out of sight of adults, you mercilessly bullied me, painful pinches and knocks and hair pulling, and harsh words, and threats of worse to come when we're married! What makes you think that's the way to win a girl's love? And when we got older, the squeezes and groping and attempts to slobber on my face. Do you not think a female has feelings?" Her face grew red, and Gerald had trouble to lift his eyes above her heaving chest. He could see that Luke wasn't even trying.

Gerald turned to the young man. "Luke, what I interrupted was more than attempts at discipline, justified or not. It was more than bullying, but assault, and if my guess is right, you intended to have your way with her against her consent. That's definitely a hanging crime. You may think of her as your wife, but legally, she isn't. Could you please respond?"

He felt a stab of sympathy, seeing the tortured look on his face. "I can't sleep for thinking of her. Other girls make eyes at me, but I have no interest in them. Kirsten obsesses me, and I must have her as my wife. I've tried everything, so thought if I can get her with child, she'll be forced to marry me, like it or not, then I could implement my father's advice."

Gerald felt shocked to the core. For once, he didn't know what to say, how to react.

Kirsten's hands formed fists, and her lips disappeared into a thin line. She looked ready to explode. "I wish I'd scratched out your eyes!" she said, softly, but with immense power. "Do you not realise, this is the death knell of any possibility of peace between us? What if I were to tell your father, with Gerald as my witness?"

That was a telling blow, Gerald could see, but Luke rallied. "I'd tell him of your unfeminine behaviour, and that

I was doing no more than anticipating our future."

Gerald managed to gather his wits. "As I said, that may be your excuse, but the wedding ceremony is not a mere formality. It is a contract, and a set of promises before God, and permission from Her Majesty and her government for the sharing of life. It's a solemn and important event. Before it, you're single man and woman, and what you attempted to do is a hanging crime. And since your father is the Magistrate, I have no doubt he knows this."

"But—"

Gerald didn't allow him to interrupt. "I don't know your father. He may be the kind of man to put family loyalty before loyalty to Queen and God, and he may hide your crime. But even so, he'll understand Kirsten's refusal to marry you. And so will her father."

"I was... am, desperate." Luke looked at Kirsten with beseeching eyes. "I want you. I need you. If... I can't live without you."

"Luke, I share Kirsten's outrage. This was a most unwise plan. Please, promise the two of us, whatever happens in the future, there will be no attempt at ravishing her."

"But what shall I do?"

"You hinted at suicide. That's also a sin God has forbidden. You are here, now, in this situation, because God is teaching you a lesson. Please, think about what that lesson is. Spend weeks on the question if necessary. I'm available to talk with you, at any time, and shall be your friend and support. But from this moment on, no violence of any kind aimed at Kirsten, or I will ensure that, whoever your father is, you shall suffer the consequences."

Luke sighed. After a long silence, he said, "But why can't she behave like every other female? Doesn't the Bible require them to be subservient and genteel?"

This was an issue Gerald had debated with many others, and knew himself to be on sure ground. "I've studied the Bible more than most people. It's my profession after all. I know what you said is the popular interpretation, but I disagree. Still, let's accept it for the sake of argument. The same passages also lay injunctions on the father of a girl, and the husband of a wife. People conveniently ignore those parts. Beating your wife is definitely against Jesus' teaching. Cruelty to anyone, be it wife or child or servant, is against His message."

"But everyone does it, don't they?"

"I won't when I am married. I'd like you to read the marriage service for yourself, and you'll see what it requires of both parties."

Kirsten interrupted. "All this is beside the point. I've had fourteen years of hateful treatment, and I know it'll continue even worse if we get married. You may say what you like now, but when you have absolute power, you'll use it. And yes, Gerald, suicide is against God's law, but death is better than being an abused slave!" Once more, she was a picture of anger.

Luke sprung to his feet. "I don't need to continue with this nonsense! Kline, I won't hold your interference against you, this time, but know you're out of your depth in this situation." He stomped off, over the hill and out of sight, carrying his boots.

Gerald also stood. "Kirsten, I'd better escort you home for your safety."

She led him to a path, then along a dirt road with deep wheelmarks. "I never had the opportunity to collect the seashells I came for," she said with half a laugh, then they were both silent until approaching a substantial house. "Address my father as Captain Petersen if he is home," she advised. "A mere mister is an insult to him."

They reached the house in the last light, so all Gerald took in was its imposing size. Kirsten opened the front door and ushered him in. "Father! Mother!" she called out.

An Aboriginal woman dressed as a maid rushed up. "Miss Kirsten, your father looking for you."

"Oh dear. Thank you, Tillie. That'll make him even angrier." She strode along a dark passageway, Gerald following, into a large room already lit by a chandelier holding a circle of lamps. A woman with grey hair and Kirsten's lovely facial architecture stood, looking toward them. "Mother, let me introduce my rescuer to you. This is—"

"Rescuer? Why did you need rescuing? Again..."

"Yes, Mother, again. This is the Reverend Gerald Kline. Gerald, please meet my mother, Mrs Margareta Petersen."

Gerald bowed. "Ma'am, I made sure to escort Miss Petersen home for her safety, but now I can leave her in good hands. I hope to see you tomorrow in church." He turned to leave.

"Hold!" a gruff male voice shouted, and what had to be Captain Petersen strode through a door at the opposite end of the room. "I heard some of what was said. Explanations are in order." The man was middle-aged but vigorous. Though considerably shorter than Gerald, he looked strong enough to rip a man's head off. His bare upper arms were as thick as Gerald's thighs. He was all muscle, no fat.

Gerald hid his nervousness and looked Kirsten's father in the eyes. "Sir, we briefly met at church last Sunday. I am Mr Taylor's new deacon, Gerald Kline."

"Indeed. Now, what's this about needing to rescue my daughter?"

Mrs Petersen clutched her hands together, shoulders stiff, mouth half open, a picture of terror.

"Captain Petersen, I was walking along the beach when I noticed a man with his knee on a prone woman's midriff. She was gagged with her own scarf, and he was in the process of tying her wrists together. So, naturally, I went to her aid. The woman was Miss Petersen."

The captain's anger was very different from his daughter's. His face went pale rather than red, and he seemed to grow as he became very still. "I hope you didn't kill him, but left him for me to dispose of," he growled.

"Sir, as a priest, I avoid violence, and merely stopped harm. I implemented the lesson of my sermon from Sunday and managed to have the three of us start a conversation. Unfortunately, he stormed off when his explanation of his behaviour failed to convince Miss Petersen."

"Who is this knave?" The man's hands formed fists and opened in rhythmic repetition.

"He introduced himself as Luke Mogden."

"WHAT? But, but he is her intended!"

"Captain, I'm a stranger in this community. I have no emotional entanglements with anyone, owe no favours yet, and so can be dispassionate in my judgments. By his own admission, this young man intended to ravish Miss Petersen, deliberately, as he said, to get her with child—"

"I'LL MURDER THE VILLAIN!"

"Sir, please hear me out. Despite this, I consider that he

is not the brute this action makes him appear." *I need to steer the situation to benefit for all... somehow,* he thought. He decided to take a risk, and confront this man about his role, but it was a struggle to hide his instant fear.

Kirsten shook her head and opened her mouth.

"I know, Miss Petersen, you disagree, but please allow me to continue. I think, on the basis of our conversation, he is no better and no worse than any other young fellow who has been given a certain faulty interpretation of the world and our place in it. He has done wrong, yes. By law, he should hang, and I made that clear to him. *Now for it!* But, Captain, the fault doesn't lie with him alone, personally, but, sir, also with those who have taught and advised him all his life."

Mrs Petersen lifted a hand to her heart. Captain Petersen looked as tense as a tiger ready to attack.

"Sir, ma'am, you may recall, last Sunday I said that all of us need to do our best to give God's love to all, and to lead those who do evil out of their mistake. That's what's needed here. This is what I attempted to do, so far unsuccessfully. We certainly must protect Miss Petersen, but I shudder at the tragedy for this whole community if Luke is tried, convicted and executed. There is a better way."

"What were you doing out alone anyway, especially after last time?" Mrs Petersen asked of her daughter. Actually, Gerald was wondering about that, too.

Kirsten opened her mouth to answer, but her father shouted, "Last time? What's this?"

His wife covered her mouth with a hand and looked even more terrified.

Kirsten however stood straight and tall. "Have you seen the scabs on his face? I did that, when he accosted me in the woods between us and the Pilburys'."

"Did you not think to tell me?" Like Kirsten on the beach, he showed extreme fury by going quiet.

Kirsten took a probably involuntary step back, but steadily said, "Father, it's known to be unwise to cross you, and you've been very keen on having me marry Luke. So, Mother advised me to stay silent about it."

Captain Petersen flicked a glance at Gerald, who was sure his reaction would have been very different, except for a stranger's presence. A long silence grew, with a weight like a shipful of cannon balls. At last, the man said, still in that slow, soft, measured way, "Young lady, you must never do that again. If I need to hear something, you tell me."

She cast her eyes down. "I promise."

"I don't understand why he'd bother. Eighteen months, and he could do with you what any husband does with a wife."

"Father, I will now keep the promise I just made. For all of my life, he's been torturing me and bullying me and threatening me. This is just the latest and worst episode. I hate him with all of my heart and beg you not to make me into his possession! I'd rather die!" Tears flooded from her eyes, and she bit her lip in an obvious attempt at self-control.

Gerald spoke up. "Captain Petersen, may I make a suggestion?"

"Do go on."

"I think that your family, with me as witness, should talk with Luke and his parents, and bring this matter out into the open. As you implied, sir, honesty is the only proper path."

"Hmm. That's an odd request. The women don't need to be involved, but you and I shall go." Mrs Petersen looked relieved, but Kirsten again rebellious.

"Sir, I disagree. This is very much a women's matter. We need Miss Petersen's personal account, and we need their wisdom in finding a solution."

Clearly, the captain had never before considered the idea that women could have wisdom. And, clearly, he was not used to anyone disagreeing with him. Blue steel eyes bored into Gerald. "You're a very unusual young fellow, aren't you?"

"Sir, I study the words of Jesus, which is my professional duty. I make up my own mind on any matter. And I fear no one, in any circumstances. This is because I almost died in a terrible way once, and God gave me back my life, so it is His, not mine."

The Captain's aggressive stance eased. "The motto of my life has been, 'One God, one ship, one captain.' I'm responsible for the welfare of my family."

"Certainly, sir." *I need to challenge him again.* "But responsibility needs to be informed with all the relevant information. Because your wife was afraid of you, because, all her life, your daughter knew better than to tell you about Luke's bullying, you were unable to protect her, and you were enforcing an unwise course of action. That one God is the God of love, not of fear."

Once more, the lady looked terrified, while the captain shook his head in wonder. "No person has ever spoken like that to me before. Truly, either you're a fool or a hero."

Gerald still managed a calm face and steady voice, but it was difficult! "Neither, sir. Look, Captain, in my childhood and youth, my most important advisors were two ladies. I gained a great deal by learning how women think, and I know their particular viewpoint to contain more wisdom than that of men, especially concerning the way people act toward each other. Because of this, I'm a very good judge of character. I'm confident of my safety. You're an honourable man, and currently you are open to examining a new view of life. I'm sure you won't act vindictively." *Nothing like stating something to make it come true*, he thought.

Again the captain slowly moved his head side to side. "Well. I never... Mr Kline, you're the yeast in the bread. I can see interesting times for Griscombe!"

The fist inside Gerald's stomach uncurled, and he grinned at the other man. "Sir, the Person whose servant I am was also a rebel, and keen on upsetting the prevailing order."

Captain Petersen looked at Kirsten. "Naturally, you shan't marry that jackanapes."

She gave that brilliant smile again, hurried to her father, and hugged him.

The brawny arms closed around the girl, then he gently pushed her away. "Young lady, you still haven't answered your mother. Why were you unaccompanied on the beach?"

"Caroline and I were gathering seashells for decorations, but she wrenched her ankle. I supported her as far as her house and handed her over to Hazel. I did consider going home then, but was sure Luke wouldn't have seen me — mistakenly as it happens. He must be following me around like a wraith."

Gerald offered, "If he watched you taking your friend home, he'd have attacked as soon as you were alone, whatever the direction. So, it's lucky you returned to the beach."

"Mr Kline, so you consider that confronting Luke should

involve both my wife and his mother?"

"Yes, sir, I honestly do."

Captain Petersen rang a hand bell. An Aboriginal man entered within seconds. "Tom, hitch the horses to the landau. We're going on an immediate night visit to the Mogdens."

"Yes, sir." The man whirled and ran out.

25
Luke

Saltwater drying on his skin produced a terrible itch in many places. Luke stripped, put on short undertrousers, then went out to the pump for a thorough wash. Back in his room, he dressed again in anticipation of supper, then took his wet clothes to the back quarters. "Maisy!" he called.

The ticket-of-leave woman came running.

"These need a wash." He shoved the clothes at her.

"Yes sir, Mr Luke," she said, looking puzzled.

He stuffed the boots with random bits of small clothing and stood them on the windowsill for the night breeze to dry them.

All this while, fruitless thoughts chased themselves through his mind. *Damnation, some wretched peasant of a preacher besting me. How dare he lay hands on a gentleman? If he hadn't interrupted, Kirsten would now be irrevocably mine. Instead, I've probably lost her for good.*

He took down his sword, hanging in its scabbard above his bed, drew it, then put it back. Nothing like adding murder to his list of crimes! *If I'm to eliminate the fellow, it'll need to be with subtlety. Perhaps set fire to his house in the small hours of a night?* Round and round his thoughts went, getting darker and darker.

Without warning, the door banged open, so vigorously it crashed into the side wall. Father stood there, with an expression on his face that made Luke want to disappear. "You shall come to the living room, now," Father said in an unnatural voice, as if speech were an effort.

"Certainly, Father. What's wrong?"

Father didn't answer but strode ahead.

Luke realised what was wrong, within seconds. In the light of the many beeswax candles, he saw Captain and Mrs Petersen, Kirsten, his own mother — and that peasant preacher. Looking at Captain Petersen's face, Luke suddenly needed to empty his bladder.

Father said, in his measured, flat Magistrate voice, "There is an accusation against you that you attacked Kirsten, with the aim of ravishing her. Answer."

"It's a lie," Luke blurted out, the first thought in his mind, constricted by the snake of terror as it was. His own father might hang him!

Kirsten's hands curled into two hooks, and he could see, all she wanted was to strangle him.

The preacher fellow said, "Ladies and gentlemen, this is Miss Petersen's and my word against Luke's. We—"

He cut the yokel off. "A girl's opinion is worth nothing. And a peasant like you against a gentleman?"

Father said, "You're wrong. But before the law, we need evidence. Mr Kline, can you offer any?"

"First, sir, I shall clear up a misapprehension." How could the knave sound so calm? "In front of God, and in front of the law, a peasant is as good a witness as a prince. But, in fact, I am a younger son of a landholder with substantial wealth."

Father asked, "Kline... Any relation to Ebenezer Kline?"

"Yes, sir. He is my father."

"A hard man, but straight as a die. Only, he looks like he enjoys the table overmuch."

The fellow laughed. "That's the reason I exercise lots and eat in moderation. But, second, I can offer circumstantial evidence. Luke, I tossed you into the sea a couple of times, did I not?"

Luke pretended disdain while hiding the shaking of his hands by forming fists. "As if you could do that!"

"He did!" Kirsten shouted.

"Would you like me to demonstrate how I did it, right here and now? Only, the landing will be somewhat harder." The preacher stepped forward, and Luke stepped back in automatic response.

"If Miss Petersen and I are right, there will be saltwater-laden clothes and boots within this house. Mr Mogden, would you be so kind as to investigate?"

Father rang the bell. Ryan came in almost immediately. And sure enough, within a minute filled with silence, and Luke's racing thoughts, Maisy entered with the still-wet clothes, and Ryan with the boots.

"So," Father said, "Not only are you a villain worth hanging, but also a liar."

"Father, Captain, yes... that was a lie. How could I admit that a mere priest could beat me? But the rest is their lie."

The fellow smiled at him, as at a friend. "Can you please give me a reasonable explanation why I, a new arrival in the community, would attack a complete stranger?"

"Do I know? Maybe you're crazy!"

"Our explanation makes sense. If you saw a man attempting to tie up a lady, would rescue her?"

Kirsten spoke up. "Mr and Mrs Mogden, this farce has gone on too long." She looked at the bloody priest with admiration. "Gerald has talked my father out of immediately murdering Luke and has said there is a better way than having him tried and executed. But please know that under no circumstances will I marry him!"

Father's calm broke. "How could you do such a thing?" he roared.

Luke could say nothing for the moment, but the preacher talked into the silence. "Mr Mogden, I managed to get the three of us on the beach to have a conversation. As part of that, Luke explained his logic, such as it is. At thirteen years of age, he came to you for advice on how to deal with a girl who is not meek and subservient. You told him, the same way you deal with a spirited horse: use the whip until the horse knows who is boss, then use kindness to make friends."

Father now glared at the fellow in a hostile way. *Good.*

"Miss Petersen was outraged. She told him that cruelty is no way to win a girl's love. I'd now like to ask the two ladies a few questions, if I may. Mrs Mogden, Mrs Petersen, suppose, when you were a small girl, six years of age, a boy kept pulling your hair, hitting you, using harsh words, and promising more of the same for the rest of your lives together, would you consider him as a friend or as an enemy?"

"Did you do that?" Mother demanded.

Luke felt outrage fill him but managed a halfway to calm answer. "She came home from that school. She was merely a girl, and a year younger, and yet, everything I knew, she had to know better. Every bit of counting or reading I could do, she had to do better. Young I was, but I knew this was wrong! How could I not be upset?"

The fellow said, "Perhaps that should've driven you to study harder at school. What she demonstrated was that she was not 'merely a girl,' but one of God's children, blessed with intelligence. You should've used her as inspiration, and competition, to push you to achievement. Now, ladies, here is a second question. Suppose that Luke had succeeded in ravishing Miss Petersen and got her with child as he had told us he intended."

Luke was terrified again, looking at the faces of the two older men, particularly the captain.

The priest glanced around at everyone, then continued. "Imagine this was done to you, by the man you were bound to marry. What would be the foremost thought within your mind? Mrs Petersen?"

"I'd... I'd have a very strong urge to kill myself."

Mother nodded.

Kirsten said, "That's exactly what I'd have done."

"Captain, what was your reaction to Kirsten's disclosure a short while ago, in your home?"

"Murder. I was ready to tear him into pieces, slowly, and feed him to the sharks!" He looked as if he was ready to do that, right then.

The preacher looked into Luke's eyes. "You can see, I've saved you from a terrible fate. You've professed great love for Kirsten. And yet, your plan would have killed her. And her father would've killed you, and then no doubt hung on the gallows, for he is too honourable to hide such an action. Your sisters are married to Kirsten's brothers, and your two families are foremost in this town. So, you'd have destroyed the very fabric of the community."

He looked Father in the eyes, then the Captain. "And we can expect much the same consequences if Luke is arrested and executed. The destruction would spread. As I said to the Petersen family earlier, there is a better way."

This man... this... Gerald Kline, is saving me!

Then he looked at Luke. "If you'd done what you planned, you'd be facing your Maker, and be judged. What would be the judgment?"

He was forced to admit it. "I'd go to hell."

"Yes, but Jesus is the God of love. If you become truly repentant, and use the rest of your life to do good and avoid evil, there is hope for you. And I'm here to advise and assist you, if you'll accept it."

Kirsten said, "But even then, I'd rather die than marry you. It's too late."

To Luke's astonishment, Mother spoke up. "And that's at least partial punishment for a great wrong."

Gerald smiled at her. "I suggest the entire episode be kept a secret shared only by us within this room. However, should Luke do any violence to anyone, under any circumstances, or treat any person, male or female, with disdain and lack of respect, then we can hold it as a stick over his head. Mr Mogden, I don't believe there is a statute of limitations for rape?"

"There isn't."

"I also suggest, Mr and Mrs Mogden, you require Luke to spend time in discussion with me, so I can counsel him in reforming his ways."

Father said, "Mr Kline, you have my admiration. Thank you for, as you said, preventing disaster." He turned to Luke. "What's your response?"

Luke couldn't look him in the eyes, but said, softly, "I apologise, Father, Mother, for bringing disgrace to the family. I apologise, Kirsten, for what I've done over the years. But please, can you try to love me?"

For the first time that evening, Kirsten stopped looking like a Valkyrie. "I accept your apology. But I shall never be happy in the kind of life you imagine natural for women. I... I look at the ladies I know, terrified of displeasing their husbands in the slightest. Many have a lot of wisdom, but are prevented from exercising it, except in petty domestic matters." She looked around, defiantly. "You arrogant males think women are stupid, unable to consider whether a contract is worth signing, unable to manage property. It is not so, and I'd rather stay single than be a possession. Truly."

"Mr Mogden, I also have something to add about horses," Gerald said. "I have a friend who is the best horse trainer in my hometown. He is magic with animals, and never, ever hurts them. I've never seen him use whip or spurs, and horses he trains are both spirited and obedient. I'd like to introduce you to my horse, Gita. This man Mick trained him, and you'll see what I mean."

"Gita? What an unusual name for a horse." Father looked at him in some puzzlement.

"I named him that to honour a person who... died because of a wrong I did as a child. Because of what happened to the human Gita, I decided to become a priest, so he has shaped my whole life."

26

Kirsten

3rd day of October, 1864

My dear Kathryn,

I am in love!

A new deacon has arrived to assist our old priest, and I immediately recognised him. You may not remember, but at the start of our 5th year in school, he came to visit dearest Maraglindi. Only, that was before the snake episode, so I still considered Aborigines to be disgusting.

This man is all goodness, and actually thinks that women deserve respect and have wisdom and should never be beaten, and I just have to think of him and I have a warm smile that fills my whole being.

What is more, he has freed me from the odious Luke!

As I have often confided to you, Luke's every action toward me has been one of aggression, disdain, intimidation, in the belief that he owns me. He has carried this one step further, and assaulted me twice, as it turns out with the intention of getting me with child, so then social opprobrium would force me to agree to marry him. Can you imagine? And he keeps saying he loves me!

The first time, I escaped after scratching his face. The second time, he was ready for my resistance, and had me trapped. Then Gerald — oh, that is the deacon's name — came along, and they had a brief tussle. Luke had not a chance. Gerald just picked him up, and threw him into the sea, twice. He then surprised me by convincing the two of us to have a conversation. It was polite enough, until Luke saw he was getting nowhere in justifying his actions, and he stormed off. Gerald then escorted me home, and more surprises followed. He enabled me to disclose to Father the long history of Luke's abuse, and talked Father out of immediately murdering Luke, and even convinced Father that women need respect, and should be governed through love, not fear. Mind you, I do not know how long this lesson will stay with Father.

We then went to Luke's family, where Gerald got his father on our side also — unbelievable. Luke was tried there and then, and found guilty, and thanks to Gerald, the three females present had a say. He then basically saved Luke's life by getting us all to agree to a course of action: as long as Luke behaves and is repentant, Gerald will teach and advise him, and he is safe from the law.

And the betrothal is off!

Unfortunately, there is a fly in the ointment. After church yesterday, when Gerald delivered his second inspiring sermon, I confided my love for him to Father. He dismissed any idea of marriage to a penniless priest. Only a few days ago, this would have devastated me, but, should Gerald also be inclined to favour the idea, which by the way I do not know, I am sure he can talk Father around. I cannot imagine anything he cannot do, but that is no doubt the distortion of love.

Kathryn, please pray for me, and wish me success.

Your devoted friend always,

Kirsten Petersen.

Gerald

With help from Mr Taylor and Harvey the verger, Gerald had a list of five widows in difficult circumstances. Currently, he was up high on a ladder, fixing a leaking roof for a Mrs Gwinnel, when he heard his name called. Luke was sitting on his horse and waved to him.

Gerald waved back.

Luke shouted, "I was on the way to visit you. I guess we can make it another time."

"I'll be finished here in a few minutes, then Mrs Gwinnel will pay me with a cup of tea, and scones with jam and cream. Please join us."

The young fellow looked unsure for a moment, but then dismounted and led his horse in through the gate, which he shut behind himself.

The woman came bustling out, looking flustered. "Oh, Mr Luke, welcome." Two small faces peeked out from behind her apron.

Luke nodded to her, very much gentry to scum, and strode over to stand at the foot of the ladder. "I'm surprised to see you do menial work," he said.

Gerald tied another sheaf of straw securely into place. "The Lord Jesus was a carpenter. And acts of kindness are God's work, far more so than sermons and prayers."

"You're an unusual fellow."

Laughing, Gerald secured the next sheaf. "My teacher in the theological college was very critical of my unconventional ways of thinking." He tied the last sheaf in place. "Well, I think I'm done." He descended the ladder, jumping easily to the ground from six feet up. "That should hold, Mrs Gwinnel, but do feel free to call me if there are still problems."

"Sir, thank you. I have set up a table and chair at the back of the house, facing the view, and my Steve is just fetching a second chair. Please follow me, gentlemen."

The tea was welcome, and the scones were excellent. The view was beautiful, with two hills framing the deep blue ocean. Gulls wheeled in the distance. "It's pleasant, living near the sea," Gerald said to Luke.

When the woman was out of hearing, the young man gave him a tortured look. "Thank you for saving my life and public honour the other night. You offered to counsel me. Surely I need it!"

Gerald nodded with a smile.

"I can't sleep! I lie there all night, and my mind goes round and round, driving me crazy about Kirsten. How do I make her love me?"

What a fool! But Gerald needed to hide his judgment. "My friend, you cannot make another person have certain feelings. You cannot force love, or even liking."

"I cannot think of anything but her!"

Gerald considered how to approach this problem. "The word 'love' has several meanings. One distinction is between giving love and taking love. Giving love is, 'Your happiness is of paramount importance to me. I love you so much that I'll sacrifice anything for your welfare.' The second is 'I want to be happy, and so I want you to sacrifice everything to make that possible.' Which is your love?"

"Ouch. You're like a surgeon who will cut off a man's leg to save his life."

"Excellent analogy. I guess that's my proper task."

They sat side by side, both looking at the view. Gerald enjoyed the scones, but Luke was clearly too preoccupied to take a second one.

"So, the only way I could win her would be to undo fourteen years of my, er, misguided action. And nobody can go backward in time."

Now Gerald felt like hugging him, but that was of course way too unconventional. "Do you know the folk tale of Bluebeard? It's one of the stories in the Grimm Brothers' collection."

"Can't say I do."

"This nobleman married a succession of women, and each disappeared. Then he partly bribed, partly coerced a neighbouring lord to marry his youngest daughter to him. The girl was terrified, but," Gerald grinned at Luke, "was the kind of proper submissive female you favour, and the wedding took place. Bluebeard then gave her a set of keys, and said she had the run of the castle, except for one room. She was not to go into there under any circumstances. All the other rooms were full of wonderful things. Guess what."

"She went into that one room."

"All right, Luke, what made me think of this story?"

"I can have any woman I want, except the one I may not enter, right?"

They both laughed at the double entendre. "If Kirsten were gently compliant, and regardless of her feelings obediently allowed you to do whatever you wanted, you wouldn't give her as much as a passing thought. Sure, she is beautiful, and intelligent, and talented — I heard her violin playing in church, twice now — but to you, she'd be just another girl, and you have a bevy to choose from. Am I right?"

"Maybe."

"I put it to you, you're not in love with her, have never been in love with her. Rather, your obsession is about breaking down her resistance. Here is a prediction. Suppose that between your two fathers and you, the marriage is forced on her, then you break her spirit. After that, the two of you will have a lifetime of unhappiness together, and within months you'll be seeking solace anywhere except with your sad, broken wife. You'll quickly hate to be in her company, and of course it'll be mutual. I can't think of a worse hell on earth."

"So, what am I to do?" Were there tears in his eyes?

"Nothing for now. Go home, think. And there is still the

question I asked on the beach. Why did God give you this burden to bear? What's the lesson you're being invited to learn?"

"I've been thinking upon that. There may be many lessons. I think one is not to accept what everyone does, but, like you, question it from the point of view of... don't know how to put it... what you asked the two ladies on Saturday night: 'If you were in this position, how would you feel?' So..." His rather incoherent speech petered out.

"Congratulations! That's straight from the Bible. 'Do onto others as you would have them do onto you.' Adopt that as your motto, and cruelty becomes practically impossible. Go on, have a scone."

Luke did. "But still, how do I get Kirsten out of my mind?"

"Well, it's a habit of perhaps eight years' standing. Look, when I was a child, I participated in something terrible. For years I beat myself up with guilt, but got through that, as I said, partly by having two ladies mentor me. The other part was, I went out of my way to do acts of kindness to the people whose child... died because of me and my friends."

"I don't know how to translate that to my situation."

Gerald laughed. "Neither do I. Pray for God's inspiration."

"Oh, I've never taken much interest in religion, it's just,

you know, background, a social duty."

Gerald stood. "I'm glad you're here. Wrestling that ladder into place was quite a task by myself. Maybe you'll be kind enough to help me return it to the inn?"

After the ladder was returned, and each young man mounted his horse, Luke said, "I almost forgot. There's one more thing. Every Wednesday morning, Captain Petersen trains the young men in manly arts: fencing, shooting, wrestling and the like. It's where I meet my friends. Only..."

"Only, facing up to the good captain is somewhat frightening?"

Mutely, Luke nodded.

"I'd be delighted if you introduced me to the group, but I'll need directions. The other night, the captain had his man drive me home in his carriage."

"I'll come and fetch you myself, if you can be ready by seven of the clock tomorrow morning."

27

Atan

Atan had made a liniment from oils he extracted from tea tree and gum tree and was gently rubbing it on the strained hind leg of Mr Gardiner's favourite mare, Chocolate, when he heard a sound behind him. A mounted man was looking in through the barn door. "I was told you was here," a voice from home said.

Atan released the horse's leg, patted her flank, then ran out into bright sunlight. "Gaspar! You're here, all the way from home?"

Gaspar looked sad. "Your father sent me, lad." He was one of the MacCartney farm hands. "There is a law now to protect your people, but he still reckoned a white man would be safer." He dismounted. "I have terrible news, and there's no easy way of saying it. Your sister Mary is dead."

The world stopped. Everything around became sharp, and clear beyond clear — Old Mother the Sun in blue sky, the dusty green of the grass, the brown of the bare ground — Gaspar's gelding stomping a foot, a cicada's chirping in the distance, the breeze ruffling the leaves of the oak tree — the smell of dust and horse manure. Atan couldn't move, couldn't speak, was surprised he was still breathing. At last, he asked, "How?"

"A bloody fat, stinking, drunken savage killed her. He died the same day, somehow. I think God struck him down, and may he rot in hell. I've met two saints in me life, and that was Mr Bruce and her."

"You're right there." If anything could help, Gaspar's reaction did. "I'll just make sure this mare is all right, then show you to the men's quarters. You'll want a wash and a feed."

Within minutes, he helped Gaspar to unsaddle, rub his horse down, and turn him loose in the pasture. Then he went to speak with Mr Gardiner.

"Sir, I've just had a visitor from home."

"I know. You look like bad news."

"The worst possible. My young sister has been... murdered. I must speak with the Spirits of my people."

Surprise showed on the boss's bearded face. "I thought you were a Christian?"

"Sir, I am both, and my friend Gerald says it's the same truth. But I must honour her."

"Atan, lad, you're my best worker. Come back when you're ready."

"Thank you, sir."

He went to the paddock and whistled for his own horse, Kolwa, mounted bareback, and rode the two miles home.

Even in his grief, he appreciated the difference from the village he grew up in. Here, the people were allowed to move anywhere along the river, in the old way, so everything was clean and sweet-smelling, and it didn't take much work to make the temporary shelters from the old materials. Mr Gardiner and the other landowners gave good white-man clothes to their employees and their families, and there was a special washhouse on each property for looking after these. It was all thanks to Mr Gardiner's decency.

Dini was out on the water in a bark boat when he arrived. She saw him, waved, and started paddling for shore. Three other women, each in a boat, followed her. Old Glibi, though the whites called her Gladys, was minding the children. Nikali was of course at work.

The other families gathered, seeing him ride up in the middle of the day, but he waited for Dini's return.

When the four women arrived from the river, he said, heavily, "A white man has killed Maraglindi. She has returned to the spirits."

A great wailing arose. The people of this village had only met Froggie once, during his wedding, but every one of the people everywhere knew and loved her. She was their shining star, the Spirit who chose to grace the people.

After due expression of sadness, Atan stripped off his white-man clothes, covered his groin in the old way, and

382

painted the sacred patterns on his skin with the white paint. Then he walked off, carrying only his fire tools. On the way, he picked up his throwing sticks, shield, spears and launcher from their hiding place, and continued to a secluded glade within a stand of gum trees a half-mile away. In this sacred place, he lit a tiny fire, added green leaves, and allowed the smoke to enfold him. He cleared his mind, and asked Froggie to come.

A sound disturbed his peace. He opened his eyes. Two white youngsters were looking at him with contempt and amusement. "Bloody savage, what the hell yer doin'?" one asked. They both had guns.

Atan stood. He knew these yokels: sons of farm workers, frequently drunk and violent. "G'day, John and Pete. A man has just come, bearing news that my sister has died. I am honouring her spirit, and she is here with me, and you better beware what she can do."

"Bloody monkey, can't he talk like a boss-man, hey?" Pete taunted.

Atan sent a wish: *They can see her! They can see her!*

John's gun fell out of his hands. He was looking beyond Atan, his face blank, mouth open.

In contrast, Pete lifted his weapon and fired. The bang sounded huge and was followed by the laughter of a family of kookaburras as they flew to safety.

A huge, glowing Presence stood beside Atan. She was recognisably Maraglindi, wearing a blue dress, but she towered among the trees, with her head nearly touching the high branches.

"Kneel," she commanded.

The two white boys dropped to their knees.

In a soft, even voice she said, "From this moment on, I require you to do no harm to anyone, or even any animal, for all life is sacred. Especially, do no harm to my people. Now go from this holy place."

The two boys stood and ran, leaving their guns lying on the ground. Well, they had no more use for guns, did they?

Maraglindi's spirit and Atan exchanged a loving look, then she was gone.

Sven Petersen

Wednesday morning, Sven waited for his students in the barn as usual, betting with himself that Luke wouldn't dare to show his nose.

Sebastian was first. "Good morning, Father."

"Good morning, son."

"I've heard a rumour that the arrangement between Luke and Kirsten is off!"

"It's true enough, but how did you come by it?"

Adam Pilbury strode in, saying, "Good morning. Where

is Luke? I'm keen to equal the score with him after last week!"

Sebastian replied, "Servants' mutter," but Sven waved him to silence. Other young men arrived, then he lost his bet: Luke walked in, with young Mr Kline by his side.

After greetings, Sven demanded, "Mr Kline, I didn't think proficiency in fighting to be compatible with a priestly calling?"

The tall youngster smiled down at him. "Sir, it promises to be good exercise, and gives me an opportunity to meet fellows my age. Anyway, Luke invited me, and I was happy to accept."

"Now, Luke. You came."

The fellow swallowed with noticeable nervousness. "Yes, sir."

"Rumours are already flying. Would you care to make a public announcement?" All eight of his students had arrived by then.

"Very well... My... my engagement with Kirsten has been cancelled." He rallied, and grinned around. "You can tell your sisters they're welcome to swoon over me."

"Why? Father, what happened?" Emil asked.

Sven had a momentary battle to honour the agreement of silence, but then said, evenly, "That's a confidential matter, but be it known to be true. Now, men, limber up."

He went through the stretches and warmup exercises himself, watching with approval as young Kline copied the others. The boys paired up for fencing. He said, "Mr Kline, come here."

"Captain, please call me Gerald."

"Have you ever used a sword?"

"Only wooden ones as a child."

I thought as much." Sven gave him the heaviest practice sword, to suit his strength. "Note the blade is blunted, and this wooden plug covers the point. All the same, a vigorous blow with it can still break a bone or sever a neck, so due care is needed."

"Yes, sir."

Sven taught him the basic moves, noting he learned fast and was very well coordinated.

After an hour, everyone had a drink of water, then he organised them for unarmed combat. He got Emil to oppose the two youngest: Adam and Doug, and paired Gerald with Sebastian, the best wrestler apart from himself.

"Gerald," he explained, "your aim is to have your opponent's shoulders touch the ground for a count of three, by any means."

Sebastian feinted a punch and jumped forward for a grapple. To Sven's surprise, Gerald dived backward, placed both his feet in Sebastian's midriff, and pushed hard. As his opponent landed on his back, Gerald rolled and jumped, his knees thumping on Sebastian's chest, and banged his shoulders down. The other bouts had barely started, and this one was over.

Everyone stopped. Gerald stood, and, grinning, reached down a hand. Sebastian accepted it, and they shook hands. All the same, Sven saw his son's displeasure.

"Where did a priest learn a trick like that?" he asked.

"Sir, in my hometown, I made friends with the local Aborigines. They also enjoy wrestling, though with them it's secret men's business. I was privileged to be admitted to their inner circle, and they taught me."

David Bell said, "I wouldn't have thought them to have the intelligence."

Gerald smiled at him. "They're people like anyone else, and they vary in every way like other people. Some are not all that bright, but others could run mental rings around any white man. And their culture is marvellous and fosters both learning and physical prowess."

"Culture? What culture?" Llewellyn Roberts said contemptuously. "They were letterless, used stone tools, couldn't even farm the land like a peasant."

"Now is not the time to discuss this, fellows," Sven said. "If you're interested, it seems to me Gerald will be happy to explain — some other time and place. Now, back to training."

After Gerald bested even Emil, Sven got everyone to rest again, then faced him himself. Clearly, the young man was wary of being caught, and evaded close contact, keeping them apart with sudden kicks and punches. Sven kept advancing, waiting for his chance. Then Gerald launched a kick at his midriff, and Sven grabbed his ankle. One twist, then he used his greater strength and weight to win the bout.

As they shook hands, Gerald said with a laugh, "Sir, I can see, a long line of Viking ancestors has a benefit."

"So does having been a sailor. That's no life for milksops. You learn to fight, or you go under to the pirates in the Malaccas, or from Algiers, or in the Caribbean."

"Fascinating. I'd be delighted to hear a few stories sometime."

"Not now. Shooting is next."

As usual, young Douglas McKendrick and Luke excelled. Gerald had to be taught the basics, and wisely spent more time loading and unloading, dismantling and assembling than actually shooting.

After the training, all ten of them had a good wash, enjoyed a pitcher of beer each, then the nine youngsters mounted their horses and rode off to the inn in town for some friendly chatter.

28

Christopher Taylor

As had become usual after Sunday service, the two priests shared luncheon. On other days, Gerald paid Mrs Gwinnel to send one of her children with a hot meal.

Christopher enjoyed the young man's intellect, decency and originality, and looked forward to another interesting discussion. "Well, Gerald," he said with a smile, "I've heard of your work in reforming our community. My information is that you've saved Kirsten from young Luke's depredations."

The young man looked surprised and stopped spreading butter on his slice of bread. "How did you find that out?"

Christopher laughed. "Annie tells me about everything that happens. You can be sure, in both the Petersen and Mogden households, every servant's ear was pressed to the doors."

"Hmm. It's supposed to be a secret, but it's true enough. That misguided young man thought to win her affections by forcing her in order to get her with child!"

"And my information is that you then upbraided Samuel Mogden and Sven Petersen for having trained him to that line of thinking."

"Upbraided is too strong a word, but basically, yes. I introduced some new ideas to them: that women have wisdom, that cruelty as a tool of management is wrong, whether applied to horses or humans, and although I didn't refer to the Bible, that you reap as you sow."

Christopher wished this youngster was his son. Well, in a way, he already was. "Gerald, you have my admiration. Perhaps we can design a sequence of sermons that subtly and slowly develops these themes."

Annie took the empty dishes away and brought out some fine sweetmeats. When Gerald wasn't looking at her, she gazed at him with something like motherly love.

Gerald sat back. "Mr Taylor, I meant to ask you. Where are the natives to this place? I've seen Aboriginal servants at the Petersens', but no others."

"That Aboriginal family is Kirsten's doing. About a year before she completed her schooling, she begged her father to hire decent Aborigines to work in their house. Tom and his family come from some fifty miles away. But the tragedy of the local natives happened before the start of my tenure here, when Samuel Mogden established Griscombe Station as a young man. Apparently, there was quite a large local community, and he dispossessed them. You remember this doctrine of terra nullius, that they had no rights at all, and that the land was considered empty? Well, they speared some cattle, so he had them hunted, so they killed some of his men. He poisoned their waterholes, hired a small army of ruffians, and killed every man, woman and child."

Gerald looked sick. He placed both his hands over his heart, and his eyes glowed with unshed tears. Then he wiped his right palm along his trouser leg. "I've shaken his hand! How could he be such a monster? How can I even talk to him in the future?"

"My dear boy, how would Jesus?"

"You're right. But Jesus would require repentance from him. Has he shown any?"

Christopher had to think about his response. "Imagine you have a bull ant nest in your backyard. They take every seed you plant. Whenever you go outside, you risk painful bites, and they even invade your house. So, one night you go outside with a hot kettle and pour boiling water into their nest, getting rid of the problem. Given the ways of thinking of the time, not too long ago, no doubt that's what he considered he was doing."

Gerald sighed. "That way of thinking is all too common, even today, and not only applied to natives. Anyone not quite the same as your own tribe is either a tool to be used, or an annoyance to be removed." Still-tortured eyes looked at Christopher. "Please, advise me. How can I remove the horror and disgust from my heart, so I can work with the man?"

"There is a prior issue."

"Hmm?"

"How can you work with the man while ensuring your own safety? You'll be no use to anyone if you invite his enmity. Jesus couldn't directly challenge Herod."

Gerald

Tuesday afternoon, Gerald was having fun assisting Mr Clarke, the schoolmaster. This was one of the tasks Mr Taylor found particularly challenging, but within the first few days, all twelve lads were happily following Gerald's instructions.

The sound of galloping horses made him look out the open window. Three lathered horses pulled up. Their riders jumped to the ground, each carrying a gun. They tied their horses to the rail in front of the school building on the run, and burst in. One trained his weapon on the teacher, another on Gerald. The black eye of the gun looked Gerald in the face, and he stopped breathing for a moment. He held his hands up, palms facing forward.

The third man smiled, seeming friendly, which was bizarre in the circumstances. He was mid-thirties, and apart from the dust of the road, looked neat.

All three men also had revolvers holstered on their belts.

The smiling man said, unhurried, apparently polite and gentle, "Nobody will get hurt, provided my directions are followed to the letter. I'm Ben Hall, and I'm acting from necessity."

Like everyone in New South Wales, Gerald had of course heard of the notorious bushranger, credited with more violent crime than any other.

"A bunch of police is following us. I reckon they'll be here within ten minutes. And the big-heads in Sydney have decided, my mates and I can be shot anytime, anywhere. So, naturally, we need protection."

He glanced out the window, but his two offsiders continued their vigilant attention.

I assume all of you have a horse in the back?"

"The boys all do," Gerald answered. "Mr Clarke lives on the premises and stables his horse at the inn. I live within walking distance, and mine is at home."

"Thank you." He looked at the teacher. "You will now go to the inn and get them to send men out to the fathers of each of these boys. The fathers will come, and each bring one guinea to help us finance our survival. They'll also supply replacement horses for the three of us, in good condition and with our saddles transferred to them. Then someone needs to get this young fellow's horse, and saddle those of the boys, and his and yours."

Gerald decided to take a risk. "Mr Hall, may I make a point?"

"Nothing like a gun to make a fellow polite, right? Not often I get called Mr Hall."

"Not so. I respect every person. Anyway, just because these boys are in school doesn't mean their fathers are wealthy. Some can no doubt afford a guinea, but I know others to be struggling as it is."

Again, the bushranger gave that bizarrely friendly smile. "Your politeness has won me over. Very well, the town shall pay six pounds for the safety of twelve boys and two teachers, how is that for a bargain?"

The man threatening Mr Clarke waved his gun toward the door. The teacher scurried out, and, despite his thick girth, actually managed something like a run to the inn, about a hundred yards away. Before he got there, another group of riders arrived in a hurry. Clearly, they saw the three horses, marking the fugitives' location.

One shouted, "Ben Hall, we know you're there! Come out unarmed, now!"

Hall smoothly lifted his gun and shot. The man tumbled from his horse, and the other four quickly rode off to each side.

Reloading, Ben said, still in that amused, gentle voice, "You don't need to be smart to be a policeman, that's clear."

A loud bang sounded, and bullets whistled inside, with four holes appearing in the far wall, two on each side.

Gerald said, "Boys, lie on the ground under your desks," but he himself kept standing, given the gun still trained on him.

Ben shouted, "Let it be known, this is a school building, with twelve boys inside. Do you really want to shoot them?"

The boys unfroze and obeyed, without objection from the bushrangers.

A yell came from outside, "What do you want, Hall?"

"I've given instructions to a teacher. You can assist him. I want the fathers of these boys to come. The town will donate six pounds to the Ben Hall Welfare Fund. When the fathers arrive, I'll have further instructions. And if you get too active and disobedient, I don't really need the other teacher, or as many as twelve boys. Three is the minimum for my purposes, so everyone shall do as he is told, or we start reducing our collection."

Hall winked at Gerald, saying softly, "I'm bluffing, but they don't know that. I have no intention of killing anyone but police, and that only 'cause I'm defending myself."

Gerald wasn't convinced, but smiled, pretending agreement.

An endless half-hour passed before the first father arrived. Since there was no more shooting, the boys returned to their seats, with a mixture of fear and excitement on their faces. The two silent offsiders took turns guarding Gerald.

Ben instructed the gathering crowd outside, "Two men may take that carcase away," and two of the ostlers from the inn did so, using a handcart, eyes constantly on the schoolhouse window.

To his surprise, Gerald saw Mr Mogden and Captain Petersen among the group of nervous men standing in full view outside. He was certain neither of them had a son in the school.

At last, Ben shouted, "Right. The teacher will return, bringing the money."

Mr Clarke's return was slow and reluctant, but to his credit, he re-entered the building, and handed over a small calico bag. Ben Hall counted the coins, then put his loot in a pocket.

Again he shouted, "The horses belonging to the twelve boys and two teachers, and the three fresh horses for us, will now be led in front of this building. I want to see a man properly tighten the girths, so there is no slippage. Take our tired mounts to the inn in exchange for their replacements." When this was done, he continued. "I want the four policemen to come forward, without weapons, on foot."

"You think we're crazy?" a shout came in return.

Ben grinned. He pulled his revolver from its holster,

aimed at the roof toward the back of the building, and shot a hole in it. "That's one less boy this town has to feed," he shouted.

Several of the boys giggled, but Gerald was horrified to see the faces of the fathers outside, each wondering if the supposed victim was his son.

"You policemen can protect yourselves by standing close to the locals," Ben suggested. Softy, he said to Gerald, "Surely anyone smart enough to know the day of the week could think of that?"

"Right. We're coming out. Everyone, move at least fifty yards away. Any trouble, and I kill someone." He organised six boys to exit first, then one of his mates beside Mr Clarke, the other next to Gerald, then the other six boys, with himself among them. The two oldest boys were nearly adult size, and he walked between them. Each outlaw held a revolver to the head of one of the captives. Gerald found this more than uncomfortable, even if it was supposedly a charade.

They all mounted. Ben shouted, "We shall ride out of town. In an hour's time, we'll allow the teachers to escort the boys back. If there is any sign of pursuit before that, we kill all the boys, so you gentlemen had better hold the police on a tight rein."

Off they went at a canter. Ben caught up with Gerald.

"I've treated you all well, haven't I?"

"Some of these children may have nightmares for the rest of their lives. Others may be tempted to follow your example. I don't like either of these alternatives."

"I've been acting from necessity. Now look, this is the last thing. In a moment, the three of us will gallop away. I ask you and your group to keep riding ahead for a while before turning back. If they do catch us, more policemen will die, and probably fathers too, never mind me and my mates. It's up to you."

Gerald considered it, but only for a moment. "Very well. I give my word."

"From what I've seen of you, that's good enough for me." He spurred his horse, and the three bushrangers sped up, and within seconds their dust cloud swallowed them.

29

Samuel Mogden

Samuel didn't allow his face to show the fury eating his insides as he stood outside the school building. It was directed as much at the idiot police as against the savages inside. Thank Heaven young Kline happened to be in there, with his intelligence and level head.

His own three policemen stood back, rifles ready, but at no time did they have a clear target. When one had aimed, Samuel shook his head.

Beside him, Henry Bell muttered, "Oh God, I hope the shot boy wasn't my Richard!"

Another idiot. Samuel said, curtly, "I counted twelve boys come out and ride away."

He took out his gold-plated American pocket watch and checked the time. Ten minutes had passed only, though it felt like ten hours. Truly, that animal could kill the boys regardless, but he certainly would if chased too early. Samuel nodded to the leader of the remaining police interlopers, and the man hurried to him. "Where are you from?"

"Sir, Hall committed a robbery in Maitland, and we've been chasing him since."

"You shall return there and tell your superior that I'll pay a hundred pounds to any man who kills him, including police."

The man's eyes opened wide, greed writ on his face. "Sir, we could go after him now!"

"You shall not. I value the sons of my friends." It was gratifying to see the effect of his statement on these members of his fiefdom. "However, you'll have fresh horses in exchange for your tired ones. After the stipulated hour is over, you may go and do your best." He was confident this yokel had no chance of catching an obviously intelligent and wily foe, but he might as well try.

They waited. Samuel checked the time again — just over half an hour. They waited some more, then Sven's black servant came galloping back. "They're coming!" he shouted.

It took another ten minutes for the boys and teachers to walk their horses into view. They dismounted, each father rushing to his offspring. Old man Clarke practically fell off his horse, and his hands trembled, but Kline looked calm and relaxed. He strode up to him and Sven, with his horse following of his own volition, the reins draped over his neck. "Mr Mogden, Captain Petersen, all is well. Oh, and let me introduce my best friend, Gita, to you." He waved back at the gelding.

Samuel remembered, this was the horse trained without whip or spur. Although the young fellow was smiling,

Samuel detected something odd — a reserve? It disappeared as he looked at Sven, but was there again as the brown eyes settled on him.

"Mr Kline, congratulations on handling the situation. I suspect the safety of those boys is largely your doing."

"I don't know... Mr Mogden, that Ben Hall told me it was all bluff, that he had no intention of harming anyone except the police, and that shooting them he considers self-defence. Indeed, he merely pretended when you out here thought he'd shot a boy. My concern is that several of our charges may idolise him and end up as lawbreakers themselves. I feel we need to take preventative action and have already started on this during the return ride."

"Nevertheless, I consider you to have earned a reward." He took the guinea he had ready out of his pocket. "Here."

The young man took a step backward. "Sir, please add it to your tithe to the Church."

Was that a modest avowal of duty merely done... or something else?

Gerald

Gerald was planting out vegetable seedlings in his backyard, behind the fence he had erected to protect the new garden. Gita looked over the fence at him, or more likely at the delicious little plants he'd have liked to sample.

A man from the inn stopped beside the other fence, between him and the street. "Good morning, Mr Kline."

Gerald stood. "Good morning, John."

"Sir, a letter has arrived for you."

He quickly rinsed his hands in the half-bucket of water by his feet, wiped them on his trousers, and took the envelope the man offered. "Thank you."

He went inside, stoked the kitchen fire to a good blaze and filled the kettle for a cup of tea, then opened the envelope. Inside was another envelope folded in half, and a note from his previous superior.

The Reverend Mr MacDonald had written:

> "Gerald my dear young friend,
>
> This has arrived for you, so I am sending it on with my compliments. A new deacon has come to take your place, but let me merely say that you are sadly missed.
>
> Your friend in the Lord,
>
> Alexander MacDonald."

Gerald made his cup of tea, and, before opening the main letter, went to the larder for one of the biscuits Mrs Gwinnel had sent two days ago. He immediately recognised dear Mrs McTaskill's writing and smiled. Unfortunately, the smile didn't survive the first few words.

19th day of September, 1864

Dearest Gerald, son of my heart,

I have the saddest possible news to impart.

Yesterday, our beloved friend Mary was murdered.

As I have informed you in previous letters, I have sold my farm to a Mr and Mrs Johnston and established a school for girls. Mrs Johnston has become a friend and assistant in running the school, although she and her husband are of common stock. Naturally, my acceptance of her was a result of dear Mary's influence in our lives.

However, Mr Johnston had a habit of alcoholic overindulgence, and his hygiene was badly deficient. I disliked the man, but nevertheless failed to realise his monstrous nature. There is incontrovertible evidence that he has killed our young friend. I am merely surmising the reason, but my thoughts on this matter make me shudder.

Inexplicably, Mr Johnston was also found dead this morning, and I have no doubt this is God's instant retribution.

My dear Gerald, it pains me to be required to inform you of this tragedy, but this sad duty is among the first acts I am discharging after hearing the news. It is somehow of help to me, as if you were here in my company, holding my hand, sharing my sorrow.

May the good Lord cherish and protect you in everything you do,

Your second mother,

Maude McTaskill.

It couldn't be true — Maraglindi, dead? And foully murdered? Perhaps raped?

Gerald had no idea how much time had passed, except that the cup of tea in front of him on the table was cold, and the fire in the stove had gone out. He thought back to his first meeting with her. Terrified but determined, he'd sneaked out with presents for the Aboriginal children, and trudged through pouring rain. He approached the first hut in the sad settlement by the river — and made lifelong friends. And the best of them was the infant who'd never walked until that moment, but had made the effort to totter up to him. And when she touched him, he knew he was forgiven, and his heart filled with love for this tiny little mite.

And now this angel was dead, at only fourteen years of age.

He bowed his head over his crossed arms and sobbed.

When he had no more tears, a realisation came to him. Kirsten had known Maraglindi at school, and his young friend had put love in the hearts of everyone there. She'd want to be informed of the tragedy. He drank the cold tea, but couldn't eat the biscuit, so returned it to the basket in the larder. He had a wash, changed into neat clothing, and saddled Gita.

About an hour later, he was knocking on the Petersens' front door. Tillie admitted him and escorted him to the living room, where Mrs Petersen received him.

"Ma'am, I am here on a sad duty. I need to inform your daughter that a mutual friend of ours has died."

"Oh? I didn't know you had mutual friends."

"A very special child from my hometown was a student at Talbot Ladies' Academy, and I know for a fact that everyone at the school came to love and admire her."

"Wait. Kirsten has told me stories about a part-Aboriginal girl who saved her from a snake, and later returned from the dead?"

"That's her. She's been a very special person in my life, and... and has left us. I received a letter about it today."

To his astonishment, the maid spoke behind him. "Oh no! Maraglindi?"

He turned. "Yes."

"I get Miss Kirsten." Tillie rushed out.

Kirsten came hurrying in moments later, shock on her face. "Gerald. Is it true? Maraglindi...?"

"I'm afraid so." He managed not to cry again, somehow.

"How?"

"Some despicable white man murdered her."

Kirsten collapsed into an armchair and started to cry. Gerald found this fitting and appropriate, against social norms as it was.

Mrs Petersen said, "Kirsten, control—" but before she could complete her sentence, a scream sounded, then a great crash somewhere in the back of the house. "What in God's name?" she rushed out.

Gerald couldn't bear to see Kirsten's devastation, so walked over, and cradled her head against his side, stroking her golden hair. She leaned into him, and he had the uncanny sensation that Maraglindi was there, with them in the room, and saying in his mind, "Do it."

Kirsten stood, reached up and put her arms around his neck, pulling his head down. He felt her bosom pressing against him, then her mouth was on his lips and his whole being ignited with an almost holy love for her.

Within his mind, Maraglindi laughed with joy.

A friendly giggle intruded on his consciousness. Tillie stood in the doorway leading to the back of the house, a broad grin on her brown face. "I no tell," she said. "Please come to kitchen."

When they got there, Mrs Petersen was ministering to an

older Aboriginal woman, who had her hands in a pot of cold water. The back door was leaning out at the top, hanging on its bottom hinge, with the top edge splintered. Gerald smelled a nasty burnt stink, and looking up, saw that the timber panelling above the stove was singed and still smoking.

"What happened?" Kirsten asked.

"Mila is a hero," her mother answered. "Fat in the frying pan caught alight. She picked it up barehanded, charged through the closed door and dumped it in the water trough. It's still burning out there, but safely contained."

The brown woman, Mila, grinned. "House no burn," she said. "Hands will heal." She said something to Tillie in an Aboriginal language, but different from home. The younger woman ran off and returned with a small jar.

Mila pulled her hands from the water. Gerald sucked in his breath at seeing the damage, but Mrs Peterson said with a sigh of relief, "Good, that'll heal. None of the flesh has actually burned away."

Mila smiled, as if she wasn't in pain, though Gerald was sure it had to be agony. "Emu oil help. I still have some. Tillie..."

Tillie fetched a small towel, gently dabbed the poor hands dry, then equally gently applied some sticky fat from the jar. "Jiko getting Mr Petersen," she said while doing this.

Kirsten softly explained, "Jiko is her son, about ten years old." Then, behind her mother's back, she soundlessly mouthed, "I love you."

"I love you," Gerald copied, meaning it with all his being. He was far less keen on talking to her father about it.

Kirsten

After the ministrations were done, and Tillie took over kitchen duties, Kirsten said, "Mother, I'd like to talk my tragic news over with Susannah."

"I don't know... Luke may have reformed, or maybe he could have second thoughts."

Gerald offered, "I could escort Miss Petersen to wherever she needs to go."

Mother gave him a considering look. "I know you for an honourable man, Mr Kline. If I have your word."

"I'll be a bodyguard to a princess, ma'am."

Outside, Gerald walked over to the gate of the home paddock. His horse came running and blew a mist cloud over his head. Gerald said a few words, and the horse returned to placidly grazing near the three other horses there. Remarkable. Kirsten remembered him saying at the Mogdens' that this horse had never been treated unkindly. She wished for the same relationship with him.

She led him north, across the paddock where she'd fled

from Luke. Gerald sighed. "Poor Maraglindi. If anyone deserved a long life, it was she."

Kirsten remembered that wonderful feeling, a short time ago. "When... when Mother had to leave the room, and you were comforting me, she was with us. I thought how I'd love to have you hold me close, and she said, 'Do it,' so I did. Do you think me a shameless—"

He cut her off. "No, I don't. And at that exact time, I also felt her presence, and heard her say the same words. And when you kissed me..." his face grew red, "...I heard her give that typical laugh of hers."

"I did too! She has blessed our love."

"She has. Now all we need is your father's blessing, and I suspect that'll be much harder."

They reached the copse of gum trees and followed the well-defined path toward the Pilburys'. She stopped right in the middle, her heart beating a pitter-patter.

He looked down from his greater height with sad eyes. "Kirsten, my love, I promised your mother." How different from Luke, from any other young man she knew!

She took his hand and continued walking. "There are disadvantages to having an honourable man around!" They laughed together.

She let go of his hand before they emerged into the open again, and soon she was introducing him to Mrs Pilbury,

Susannah, her younger brother Adam, and younger sister Martha.

Adam said, "I know Gerald from the weekly training sessions with your father. He's beaten both your brothers at wrestling, and even gave the Captain some trouble."

"Not much at shooting and fencing yet," Gerald answered modestly.

"We're actually here because we both have a source of sadness, and I need Susannah's counsel."

Mrs Pilbury asked for clarification, so Gerald explained, "Ma'am, I have... I had a very dear young friend who was a student in the school Kirsten attended. We both love... loved her. I've received a letter from home that she has died."

Adam offered to show Gerald around in the meantime, while Susannah took Kirsten to her private room. Susannah already knew a lot about Maraglindi, so Kirsten described the events of today, saving till last the visitation from the girl's spirit, and her approval of Kirsten and Gerald's mutual love. "She sounded so happy," she concluded.

"From what you've told me, she was one of God's angels temporarily among us. Of course she is happy, having returned home."

"I haven't seen her since I've left school, but we did exchange occasional letters."

Susannah smiled at her. "You don't even need to do that

now. Ask, and she'll come to you."

What a surprising idea! Kirsten closed her eyes, and said inside, *Maraglindi?*

Nothing visual happened. She didn't hear an inner voice. However, a great peace filled her being.

Susannah whispered, "I also feel her. Maraglindi, thank you."

This time, Kirsten heard that joyous laughter again, and clearly, so did her friend.

"I have a problem, too," Susannah said. "Luke has been making very friendly moves toward me, and of course I'm engaged to James."

Kirsten felt horrified. "I wouldn't go within ten feet of that fellow!"

"He swears by all that's holy that he's learned his lesson. He will never as much as say an unkind word to a female, for the rest of his life, and since he can't have you, he needs solace. Just a young lady to talk with to cheer him up, and I've always cheered him up, he says."

"You do have that effect on everyone. Lucky James isn't a local. As long as you don't let Luke get too close, there is no harm in friendship — if he is really capable of that. I do reserve judgment. But even apart from propriety, make sure he is never alone with you."

30

Gerald

As the congregation filed out after Sunday service, Gerald gathered all his courage, and said to Kirsten's father, "Captain Petersen, I'd be grateful to have an opportunity for a talk with you in private."

The calm blue gaze fixed on his face. "Very well. Ride out to my place tomorrow morning, about nine of the clock, and I'll give you half an hour of my time."

"Thank you, sir." Then he had to force himself to shake Mr Monster Mogden's hand, too, with a respectful smile.

He had difficulty getting to sleep that night, kept awake by visions of Kirsten's face, and worry about her father. He endlessly repeated his arguments, then worried about his effectiveness after a sleepless night. At last, he said aloud, "Maraglindi, help me!" Instantly, a feeling of peace enfolded him, and next thing, the glow of dawn woke him. He actually arrived early for his appointment.

Captain Petersen led him to an office, but instead of settling behind the imposing desk, took one of four armchairs, and waved Gerald to another. Then he calmly looked at him.

"Sir... your daughter and I have discovered that we love

each other. I seek your permission for us to marry."

"Hahaha, I guessed right. I thought that'd be it. Gerald, I find you a very admirable fellow, and like you a lot. However, marriage is out of the question."

"Sir—"

The captain spoke over him. "I have two reasons, and you may debate each."

Knowing this man's reputation, Gerald appreciated the permission. "Thank you, sir."

"First is Kirsten's welfare. I do love my daughter."

"Naturally! Anyone would. Oh, I do sound like a lovelorn swain."

Again the captain laughed. "You do. But consider. Kirsten has been raised as a lady, with servants at her call at all times, a carriage with driver any time she chooses to go somewhere, all the best clothes, best foods, best whatever she may fancy. All right, the first blush of love makes everything heaven, but imagine her in ten years. She may have five children and has endured the life of a poor woman for all that time."

With a shock, Gerald realised, he hadn't given this problem any thought.

"Look at Christopher Taylor. He can afford one serving woman in the house, and a manservant twice a week for the rough work. He has nothing. The parish owns the vicarage.

When he retires, he exchanges houses with you, and basically lives on the town's charity. Unless you can advance to bishop, you'll share his fate."

"I have no chance of becoming a bishop, or interest in it. I want to serve people, not boss them around." They both laughed.

The captain nodded. "That's my assessment of you also. Well, do you want to subject Kirsten to a lifetime of poverty?"

Gerald hung his head, seeking inspiration. At last, he said, "Sir, actually the choice is not mine, but Kirsten's. I have an unconventional idea."

"I've noticed. Do you ever have conventional ones?"

"Often, sir. The other day, I was alone with her for a moment, and felt a desperate desire to kiss her, but refrained."

The captain grinned.

"The best teacher is experience. If she agrees, she could carry on the activities of a poor woman for a set time, say six months. She can quit any time. If at the end she is still willing to take me on, then I'll repeat my plea for her hand."

"Voluntary Cinderella?"

"Just so, sir."

"If you can talk me out of my second reason, which is unlikely, then we can put the idea to her. See, I've learned my lesson: women are capable of thinking."

This interview was a lot more friendly than Gerald's imaginings of it.

"Listen, lad. Poor people have the freedom to marry for love, if they find it. For my class, it's as much a commercial arrangement as a union of two people."

"I know that, sir. Both my brothers, and all three of my sisters were, er, traded that way."

This got a guffaw from the captain. "The result is typically perfectly satisfactory for the merchandise, haha. Provided both play the part society imposes on them, they learn to be comfortable with each other, and it helps when they share children and property. But, even if my daughter were happy to exchange a life of comfort for one of hardship, I need her to maintain and extend my family's power and wealth."

Now Gerald was on home ground. All his planning was on this issue.

"Sir, I look at my father. He has tripled his father's wealth in my lifetime, and yes, the marriages were part of this. But is he happy? He is perhaps the most dissatisfied person I know, possibly apart from my mother. They both endlessly look at what they lack, rather than what they have. This is the wisdom behind some of Jesus' teachings, although people usually draw the wrong conclusions from his sayings."

"I was wondering when you'd bring religion into it."

"Sir, I am not a fanatic, but a student of a great Teacher. When Jesus said it's difficult for a rich man to enter heaven, he actually didn't mean the wealth, but the attitude it leads to. Wealth is an obstacle because it becomes an addiction. The more you have, the more you want. You manage to have an acre of land? You want ten. If you have ten, you think you need a hundred. You can only satisfy this desire by competing against other people. Even if you're invariably honest, your gain is someone else's loss, exploitation and often suffering. So, you cannot serve this master and also give the love of your heart to all who live, and to their Master. However, if you have wealth but refuse to be addicted to it, God will welcome you in heaven."

"I've never heard it explained like this before." The captain looked thoughtful. "That saying about the eye of the needle has always sounded like something thrown out to keep poor people in their place and not covet wealth."

"Yes, that's how the princes of the church use it, and priests follow. But Jesus befriended rich people and poor, regardless, so he couldn't have intended that. He was, as I said, against greed, not against happening to be rich. Joseph of Arimathea was a rich man, and yet he has been venerated all through the ages."

"All right. Where are you going with this?"

Back to battle. "Sir, I believe you are already the second wealthiest man in town, and—"

"Keep this in confidence, but actually I'm the wealthiest." He was grinning again. That's if you take my fishing fleet into account. I run five ketches, with Sebastian as my commodore."

"I'd greatly appreciate going out sometime!"

"Well, well, you need to talk that over with him. But I hear you saying, hey Sven, you have more than enough wealth and influence, why bother to gain more?"

"Yes, sir, that's exactly my point, but I'd have put it more diplomatically."

"Because it's the way of the world. It's what is expected, and if you don't go forward, you go backward. I wouldn't have my level of comfort if I hadn't played the game well in the past."

"Hmm. But when is enough enough?"

"You are an awkward fellow! If people stopped playing this game, what would they do for fun?" The captain's laugh was infectious, and Gerald joined in.

"You know my answer. We little humans were not created to exploit each other, to grasp all we can, to play games, big or small. We were created to worship God by looking after His creation, other people being foremost in this."

Captain Petersen stood. "Gerald, I don't know when I had such an enjoyable morning. We must have further discussions when the occasion arises."

"And your answer, sir?"

"I'll think upon it."

That was a great deal of movement from the original flat refusal!

Kirsten

Kirsten and Mother were planning a simplified menu for the next week when Father and Gerald walked into the living room. What a surprise! And they looked like the best of friends. Did Gerald propose? And could Father possibly have approved?

Gerald greeted the two of them, then Father said, "Kirsten, there is a problem and only you can solve it." He then looked expectantly at Gerald, who seemed abashed.

"Uh... Just now, Kirsten, I asked your father to approve a betrothal between us."

Mother stood in surprise but said nothing.

"He has not said no but hasn't said yes either. And one of his objections weighs heavily on my mind. He pointed out that marrying me could impose suffering upon you, and that's the last thing I want."

She looked at Father, then at Mother. "I love Gerald and will do anything to make him happy."

Gerald grinned. "The other day, Luke came to me for advice, and I explained the difference between giving love and taking love. His has been taking love. Mine for Kirsten is giving love, and she has just defined that. But, Kirsten, although my family is wealthy, I don't share in their largesse. I'm a poor deacon and can expect to be a poor parish priest."

"So?"

"Your father explained to me, years from now, when life has descended from the heights of first love to ordinary routine, you may suffer, being a poor woman instead of a lady."

She opened her mouth, but Father cut her off. "Have you ever scrubbed clothes, or ironed them? Do you even know how to? I know you learned cooking at school, but can you do it for a brood of children, day after day, year after year? And that's only part of the change."

She had an idea. "Father, Mother, with Mila injured, we're short of a cook. Why don't I apprentice myself to her? I can have all our servants teach me their jobs, and also..." she felt her face blush, "find a poor woman with young children, and have her instruct me also?"

The two men exchanged glances, then Father gave a great laugh that didn't want to stop. When at last he took a deep breath, she demanded, "What's so funny?"

"Hahaha," he was off again, "that was exactly one condition of my approval. If you can do the tasks that are foreign to a lady for six months, Gerald may ask me again."

"And foolish me," Gerald added, "I dreaded asking you to make this sacrifice."

She stood straight and tall, feeling power fill her. "It won't be a sacrifice, or a penance, but a gift from the heart. And twenty years from now, it still will be."

Gerald glowed at her. "I've made the acquaintance of five widows, three of whom have young children of various ages. All are struggling and will be delighted to accept your assistance. One of them is a wonderful cook and supplies me with my regular evening meals."

Luke

Luke was out hunting with three of his friends. They'd ridden out before dawn, each with a packhorse, hopefully to bring home the fruit of their effort. Young Doug McKendrick said, "Charles, you better make sure that hat hides your red thatch. With the sun on it, a kangaroo will see it a mile away, like a lighthouse."

Charles Bell answered through the laughter, "Yeah? Be it known that Amelia feels the need to stroke my hair and is besotted with the colour. And we're both delighted to have a red-haired daughter."

An instant heaviness spoiled Luke's fun. Why couldn't he have a woman like that?

Llewellyn Roberts replied to Charles, "Your sister is satisfied with brown hair, and likes the tickle of a beard." Then he glanced at Luke. "Hey, you look like you stepped in a cowpat."

The sun was well up behind them now, casting long shadows, and Luke detected movement ahead in the distance. Instead of answering, he pointed, pulled on his packhorse's lead and kicked his big hunter into a gallop. He heard the others follow.

The big mob of kangaroos soon detected them and bounded away. Luke stood in the stirrups and leaned forward, and noted they were gaining on the prey, if slowly. He felt the pleasure of his horse as the animal put everything he had into the effort.

Yes, they were gaining, and Mujip Creek would get in their way soon. Luke could see the trees lining the creek.

The kangaroo mob split in two, north and south. Luke tugged the reins to the right, because the slight slope fell from north to south. Cutting off a triangle favoured them also. The prey were now spread out, with bigger animals up front, smaller falling behind. When he reckoned he was well within 300 yards of the leaders, he sat back in the saddle and pulled his rifle from its holster.

Well trained, the horse steadied his movements. Luke aimed, squeezed the trigger, and with a yell saw the lead buck fall. Two more shots sounded, then the fourth, but they resulted in only one more hit, and that one was wriggling on the ground — wounded only.

Luke pulled up next to his prize. He'd got the kangaroo through the head, not even spoiling the hide.

Doug stopped next to the wounded animal and put it out of its misery with a shot from his pistol. He grinned back at the other two. "You married men are too old for hunting," he taunted them.

Luke had two carrots in a pocket, and rewarded his horses, then hobbled them and allowed them to graze. He got busy gutting the carcase, and Charles gave him a hand. "Great shot," he said. "Luck in the hunt, no luck in love?"

"That wasn't luck. Well-trained horse, steady eye. And yeah, I did draw the short straw with Kirsten."

"She's gone crazy, I reckon," Llewellyn called across from the other carcase. "Believe it or not, I saw her scrubbing the Widow Wilson's dirty clothes!"

Charles said, "I had to talk to the captain about something, and when I got there, she was beating a rug on the line, her clothes and even face covered in dust. My friend, you've had a lucky escape, but why did you break up with her?"

Luke straightened his back. "I got sick and tired of constant defiance, always knowing better, every word one of rejection. I talked with Gerald, and he pointed out that after marriage, I could look forward to a life of woe. Who needs that?"

Doug said, "I heard a rumour that you tried to force her, and Gerald stopped you."

Luke managed a convincing snort. "You don't want to listen to servants' gossip. You know how rumours grow in the telling."

"Any idea what the captain's plans for her are?" Doug asked.

Luke grinned at him. "You're too young for her." This got a laugh. "I reckon he'll seek someone out of town, and good luck to the fellow."

Samuel Mogden

With a big mob of steers to organise for Newcastle market, Samuel wished Sunday was just another day, instead of an interruption. But appearances had to be maintained, and here he was in church, his mind still on the practicalities. After all, he knew the ritual off by heart. He knelt and stood and sat at the right places, and went forward to receive Holy Communion, and sang along with the hymns, but actually, he might as well not have been there.

Young Kline started his sermon. The fellow's opinions were certainly refreshingly different from anything Samuel had heard preachers spout, so he sat back with interest. He didn't always agree with the young man, but anything breaking the routine of life was welcome.

"My dear friends in the Lord,

Last week, I discussed what Jesus says about honest repentance. I hope you remember, and now understand, that, since occasionally we all do bad things, repentance is the only road to heaven. And in His eternal grace, the Holy Father does forgive you if you acknowledge a mistake, and are determined never to repeat it, and especially if you then devote yourself to actions that in some way help you to pay back for damage you have caused.

I don't necessarily mean payment in money, but in doing things to reduce that kind of evil in the world. Suppose you've caused hurt by insulting someone, and you realise this was wrong and now want to do something about it. The way is to do your best to be respectful and supportive to all, especially to people you don't like. Stand up for the victims of insulting comments, and gently lead others to realise that we need to respect each other.

Simple enough, isn't it?

Today, I'd like to carry this idea further. Right now, there is a terrible civil war in the United States of America. By all accounts, it's the bloodiest conflict of all time. It has multiple causes, but a major one is that the Northern states want to end slavery, and the Southern ones consider that wrong, because their entire wealth is built upon it.

The funny thing is, both sides support their case by quoting from the Bible. As you may guess, my interpretation of God's word is in favour of those who want to end slavery. Instead of boring you by quoting verses at you, let me just say, Jesus is quite clear, every human being is a child of the Father. Your skin may be white, brown, black or purple. You may be young or old, male or female, speak whatever language, come from whatever place on earth, you are His child. Chinamen, Africans, Russians, Mussulmans, Irish, our own Aborigines, and of course Swedes and Britons are all God's beloved children.

When the bushranger Ben Hall held twelve boys of this town captive, fear consumed their fathers, who did what they could to free them. Although Mr Mogden and Captain Petersen don't have children in the school, they were also there, supporting the fathers, because they cared."

Samuel hid his smile. He'd been there to show his leadership and had not the slightest worry about the fate of those brats.

"What those fathers felt for their sons is what the Heavenly Father feels for all His children. How could He not?"

Samuel had a sudden imagining. What if indeed he did have a son held captive by that savage? Certainly, that'd have been different.

"This is why slavery is wrong, like other forms of cruelty. It's a great evil, and the Northern states of America have my best wishes in their struggle.

But we don't need to look at America to see the evils of slavery. This land of ours has seen it too, though it went by a different name. Convicts are slaves. For example, until recently, it was a law of the land that a master could whip a convict to death for a variety of offences, and the master's word was always accepted. Now, this is no longer so. The law of the British Empire has changed, and for the better.

The law of God hasn't changed. Cruelty was wrong even when it was legal, and as Magistrate, Mr

Mogden can tell you, ignorance of the law doesn't excuse you if you break it."

Kline looked at him, and obligingly Samuel nodded.

"I'm a newcomer to your community, so as yet don't know its history. It's possible that when it was legal, some people in this church today did things that were against God's law. For all I know, some of these actions could have been horrendous, and deserve a permanent stay in hell. However, thanks to God's infinite grace, they'll be admitted to heaven, provided they realise the evil of their past actions, and are truly repentant, and especially if now they act in a way that compensates for these past misdeeds."

The young priest continued to look at Samuel while saying this, somehow causing the most uncomfortable sensation. It was exactly like the reading out of a charge against the defendant in court. But Samuel had never ordered a convict to be whipped to death. Fifty lashes was the most he'd ever approved. He stood for the final prayer.

31

Gerald, six months later

As he rode Gita toward the Petersens', Gerald went over his plans again. Next Monday, 17th day of April 1865, would be the end of Kirsten's six months' apprenticeship. But it would be Good Friday in two days. Gerald had spent many enjoyable hours with Christopher, Kirsten, and Mrs Lorien, the organist, planning and practising the ceremonies for all of Easter.

This morning, after the now customary martial school, he intended to remind the captain of the end of Kirsten's servitude.

Sebastian was at sea, but the other young men soon arrived. Captain Petersen said, "We'll do the run this morning." This was four laps starting at the barn, around the house and back again, covering a total of three miles. They set off, and soon the lighter men forged ahead. Panting, covered in sweat, Gerald barely managed to beat the captain and Emil.

Fencing followed a drink, stretching exercises and a rest. Gerald was in a threesome with Charles Bell and Luke Mogden, two on one, taking turns to defend. Luke was a marvel with a sword, and despite Gerald's improvement over the past six months, he and Charles couldn't get past his guard for maybe ten minutes. Then Gerald managed to lock swords and used his greater strength, while Charles poked the wooden plug on his swordtip into Luke's stomach.

Charles defended next, and Gerald flicked him on the leg with the side of his blade within a minute, while the red-haired fellow was concentrating on Luke.

Now it was his turn to defend. He had this planned out. As his opponents came at him, he delivered a mighty swipe to knock the sword from Charles' hand, using the weapon like a broadsword or battleaxe, then handled Luke by retreating. He was so focused that he forgot about Charles, till he got a whack on his behind from the young man's sword.

Charles was holding the weapon left-handed. "Hope you haven't broken my wrist!" he complained.

The captain came over and ordered him to put his hand in cold water, saying that after ten minutes he'd bind it up in a tight bandage. "One day," he said to Gerald, "you'll surprise me and do what everyone else does. But in a real battle, that'd have been a great trick."

"Thank you, sir. And, Charles, my apology."

"You beware! My wife will come and get you for damaging me."

"Is that why we practise running?" That got a laugh all around.

Luke said, "I'm looking forward to being married, too. Gerald, will you conduct the ceremony, although it'll be in Teralba?"

"I'll be honoured, but we need to clear it with Laura's family's parish priest."

Luke shrugged. "I'll ask Father to make a good donation to their fund."

Gerald hid his instant negative reaction. Even after all this time, any mention of, or contact with, Samuel Mogden got his mind onto the murder of the local Aborigines. And, despite several hints, the man had no idea he had committed mass murder. Perhaps he'd conveniently forgotten it? Gerald asked Luke, "So, my friend, Laura is happy to marry you?"

He got a cheeky grin. "I've been a good student. She thinks I am Sir Galahad in person."

"Back to work, men," Captain Petersen shouted. "Get your rifles."

Douglas and Luke were still the best shots, but Gerald was no longer the worst. After the shoot, while cleaning his weapon, he said, "Captain, if we had some native people here, I could show you how they throw spears. It's marvellous."

"I suppose you could ask my servants, Tom and Dake."

"I guess. They probably know how to make them." He joined the others at the water trough, taking his shirt off along the way. But when every other young man went for his horse, he hung back. "Captain, may I have a private word with you?"

Soon, they were once more in the captain's office. Gerald said, "Sir, Kirsten's six months will be over on Monday. She has faithfully followed the course she took on and could now be an excellent serving woman and mother, and I haven't heard one word of complaint from her."

"You're right there, lad."

There was a silence, and at last Gerald asked, "So, Captain, may I marry her?"

"She has proven that she could live in poverty, but I still don't want her to do so."

"Oh." Disappointment gripped Gerald's heart. The world was a heavy place.

The captain shouted with laughter. "You should see your face! I have a condition."

"You mean..."

"As you know, I'm having a house built in the middle of town, some hundred yards from the church. That's my wedding gift. And I'll pay Kirsten a stipend of 500 pounds a year and put in my will that Emil will continue that after my death. If you accept, I give my approval."

Gerald felt a conflict. He didn't want to bought. At the same time, he appreciated the benefit to Kirsten, and to any children of their union. He stood, grasped the captain's hand and shook it.

The captain laughed, and held on, Gerald's big hand lost in the older man's huge one.

At last, Gerald asked, "But what will this do to the growth of family power and wealth?"

"Well, lad, I thought this might help me through the eye of that needle."

Luke

Luke was sick and tired of Church. Easter dragged on, and here he was on Easter Sunday, sitting still and going through ritual again. This time, Mr Taylor was officiating, and Luke wished he'd get on with it. But then, the old man said something to make him sit up.

"Brethren, I have a joyful announcement to make. Captain Petersen has asked me to let you know that his daughter, Kirsten, whom we all love, has become betrothed again. The lucky man is also everyone's favourite, my delightful deacon, Mr Kline."

Unusually, a great buzz of chatter filled the church, but Luke sat there with a fist in his heart. Sure, he had Laura.

Unlike Kirsten, she adored him, laughed at his jokes, was obedient and compliant to his every wish, and to that of her parents. And Father was pleased with an alliance to a wealthy and influential business contact. But Kirsten...

All he still wanted was Kirsten.

He happened to glance sideways and saw Father's face. He also looked displeased. Interesting, that. *I wonder why?*

When at last the religious rigmarole was over, Luke couldn't face the thought of shaking Gerald's hand, so sidled out of the line and passed behind the two ministers. This of course attracted attention, but he was beyond caring. Not waiting for his family, he rode home at a furious pace.

Some time later, he looked up at a sharp sound. Gerald was outside his window, mounted, and in the process of throwing a second pebble at the glass. Luke strode over and opened the window. "Gerald. This is a surprise. Don't you know where the front door is?"

"Good afternoon, Luke. I have a fair suspicion that if I called formally, you'd send a message that you were not home."

"In that case, should you wish your company onto me?"

"As your friend, I most certainly should."

"My friend? Stealing Kirsten from me?" Anger boiled inside him, and he had to restrain himself from shouting.

"What about the lovely Laura?"

"When old man Taylor made the announcement, I realised, you were wrong when you said I don't love Kirsten. I do, and only her."

"I'm glad your memory spans six months. Do you also remember saying you'd need to go back in time to undo fourteen years of ill-advised action?"

Luke could find no answer for the moment, but resentment and hate boiled within. How could this interloper into the community win the love of his heart?

Still in a friendly, level tone of voice, Gerald spoke into the silence. "Also, I did not steal Kirsten's affections. She gave them, freely. Look, I know there has been considerable ignorant gossip about her recent activities. She chose to undergo an apprenticeship in how to be a poor wife and mother. This was her offer to her father, who was concerned that if she marries me, she'll suffer for lack of the wealth she's been used to all her life."

"I've wondered, what craziness would make her clean a poor widow's house, or scrub pots in her father's kitchen."

"Captain Petersen called it voluntary Cinderella. She chose to do it, freely from her heart, because it was a condition of his agreement to our marriage."

"Hey! You said it was her idea."

"It was both. The captain and I were going to put the possibility to her, and she came up with it herself, without prompting."

"But... why?"

"Luke, my dear friend, when you understand that, you'll become the kind of person who lives a good life whatever happens around him, and who radiates happiness to all. I can see you're angry, and suffering. Insofar anything I've done that causes that, I ask your forgiveness. None of it was done to hurt you." Gerald wheeled his horse and rode away.

Damn the fellow — or bless the fellow. Luke didn't know which. Perhaps both. He had managed to turn Luke's world upside down, yet another time.

Kirsten, Saturday, 27th day of May, 1865

Kirsten looked along the aisle, delighted with the crowd packing the church. She glanced down at her beautiful, long white dress, through a white veil. Father held her right elbow as they walked forward. Mrs Lorien was playing Mendelssohn's Wedding March, accompanied by Mrs Goldberg on violin, Becky — now Mrs Steiner, and pregnant — on viola, and Ben on clarinet.

Everyone smiled. She heard appreciative whispers over the sound of the music, but her eyes were fixed on the front. Standing before the altar was Mr Taylor, with Gerald by his side. Kirsten exchanged a smiling glance with Kathryn — Mrs Cartwright now — as she passed her and wished

Maraglindi could have been present.

"Kirsty, I am here with you," she heard, so clearly she had to resist a compulsion to look around.

She had briefly met all the people who sat to her right, Gerald's family and friends from his hometown, but focused on the front. She was delighted to see signs of nervousness on Gerald's face. No doubt he was worried about dropping the ring, a present from his father. His best man, Peter Mac... looked calm and reassuring though. She'd have to remember his name before the reception.

She stopped, facing Mr Taylor, with Gerald now by her side, and Father still comfortingly steadying her. She heard Susannah and Caroline also stop behind her. The cessation of the music left an expectant silence.

Mr Taylor spoke the ancient words, exactly as during rehearsal. Gerald and she managed to give the right answers, and, to Gerald, she didn't even mind promising to obey. It was all dreamlike, and before she knew it, their lips met, chastely in front of all these people, they signed the certificate, then she found herself outside the church, with Gerald rather than Father holding her arm.

Mr Mogden's present was the hiring of an expert at making photographic pictures, and now came long stretches of motionless posing while a blinding white light burned, and the whiskered young man hid his head under a black cloth. He pronounced himself satisfied with the results and promised to deliver the pictures tomorrow.

Gerald escorted her to their new house, with a crowd of common people lining both sides of the road. Again, Maraglindi spoke within her mind: "They love you because you shared their lives for the past six months." So, she took the trouble to smile, to look as many people in the eyes as possible, and to wave her free hand.

Here they were. Gerald picked her up as if she was a child. Father swung the door open, then they were in. Of course, she'd inspected the house when it was completed, and she and Mother had often been there during the furnishing, but now it seemed different. It was her new home.

Gerald set her on her feet again and kicked the door shut with a heel. Then they were in each other's arms, and they shared a real kiss this time — the second, but certainly not the last.

"My love, you'd better get changed for the reception," Gerald said.

Atan

Tari on one side of him, Mother on the other, Atan sat in the back row of the church, with Father in the corner seat. Sad that Old Mother had gone to the spirits. They did get a few odd looks from white strangers, but the thin man,

Harvey, was there to deflect any problems. Atan watched Gerald up front. *My white brother, may you be happy*, he thought, then, *Froggie, is she right for him?*

Maraglindi answered within his thoughts, with joy, "She is. They're my next parents."

That was fitting, if the girl was worthy. Atan watched the ceremony until the new husband and wife walked out, with the audience gradually following, then at last everyone else was gone. Harvey nodded, and they stood, too. If Gerald ruled the world, this wouldn't be necessary, but it was sensible to avoid conflict, especially at such a happy occasion. They walked over to the inn where the celebration was to continue. Again, thankfully, Harvey escorted them to an inconspicuous place at the back and shared their table. He looked at Atan. "Gerald told me, you and your family are his best friends in all the world, and if it was socially possible, he'd have you as his best man."

"Thank the Lord he didn't! I'd have to make a speech!"

A good meal followed, and Harvey's presence stopped the serving women from showing their disdain too obviously. Then Gerald and his lady cut the cake with joined hands holding a big knife.

Mr Kline struggled to his feet, needing to stand well away from the table to accommodate his big gut. Two years' pregnant, Atan reckoned. "Ladies and gentlemen of

Griscombe, thank you for welcoming my youngest child, Gerald. He has chosen a difficult path, when he could have lived at home in luxury, or entered a well-paying profession, but as no doubt you know by now, he… thinks differently." This got general laughter. "I'm delighted to have acquired a beautiful new daughter and look forward to some grandchildren to join the seven who already link me to the future."

Everyone clapped as he sat. Then the girl's father stood. Though he was grinning, Atan thought he wouldn't want to get on his wrong side.

"My friends all, old and new. Months ago, I said to Gerald, he is the yeast in the bread, and wasn't I right? He has made me into a better person, and I know he's had this same influence on many others. He is such a decent fellow that I decided, I need him in my family. Thanks to him, I now look at everything in a new way, and hope to continue."

Mr Petersen spoke for another five minutes, then Mr MacCartney was next. "Dear people of Griscombe, I do know a few of you from business dealings, and like Mr Kline, want to thank you for taking my dear young friend Gerald into your community, into your hearts. I thought you'll be interested in a story about his younger days."

Gerald looked worried, but Atan was sure Mr Peter wouldn't say anything harmful.

"As a boy, Gerald was one of seven lads, who were as spirited and, let us say, adventurous as boys can be. Then something terrible happened. The other six died in great pain. Gerald survived, barely. It took him months to stop looking like a skeleton. But when he recovered, he was no longer a twelve-year-old boy, but the man you know. His special project was the poor Aborigines of our town. He taught many of them to read and write, and about the grace of God, and in turn they took him into their hearts. I believe he is the only white man to be a member of the Worimi people of this land. His best friends are from among them, which is why you may have noted, a very special family is here. Please look on them as Gerald does, as people worthy of respect, liking and even love."

Every eye turned to Atan and his family. Mother and Tari looked down, but Father confidently smiled around, so Atan did his best to look like he also expected respect.

"So, dear people of Griscombe, let me tell you, you've acquired a jewel."

Mr Peter sat to applause, then it was Gerald's turn, and he managed to surprise everybody. "My dear friends, it's customary at these occasions for the men to do all the speaking. I'd like to ask my lovely bride to say a few words."

The tall, golden-haired young lady stood, her face red. She took a deep breath. "It's not always easy, being married to a man who expects women to act equal to a man!" Atan laughed with everyone. "But think about it. Our Queen Victoria is a woman. During the Crimean war, Florence Nightingale showed that women are highly suitable to nurse injured soldiers, and since then, female nurses have saved many lives, and given comfort to the sick. And Gerald's favourite book is full of stories about admirable women. Think of Jesus' mother, and Mary Magdalena, Esther who rescued her entire people, Judith, and so on. And Boadicea defeated the armies of mighty Rome. I am no Esther or Mary, and certainly no warrior, but I promise to do everything in my power to make Gerald happy, for the rest of my life."

She sat, to enthusiastic applause and shouting.

Gerald stood again. "What can I say after this? I've been upstaged!" More laughter followed. "As my friend and mentor Mr Peter MacCartney has said, I nearly died as a boy, and have since considered my second life to be God's gift, to be used in God's service. That's why I am here, and now with Kirsten by my side, I'll be able to do it twice as well."

32

Samuel Mogden

Naturally, the journey to Teralba had to be during the rains of early winter. If Luke was an honourable young man, he'd now be preparing for his marriage to Kirsten on her twenty-first birthday, instead of having that terribly uncomfortable Kline fellow enter Griscombe society. And with typical impulsiveness, Luke had arranged for Kline to conduct the service.

I really don't know why he keeps looking at me like that. Sense of justice ensured that Samuel did nothing to retaliate, but as the carriage jolted over rocks exposed through the mud of the road, he decided to have a talk to the young man about it. Some time. Now that he was Sven's son-in-law, he had to be handled with subtlety.

When they arrived at last, Hugh Jackson greeted him with enthusiasm, as well he might. While the arrangement would be beneficial to both, Jackson had the more to gain from an alliance with the Mogden fortune and influence. Oh well, his contribution was still an addition, compared to completing the triple alliance with Sven.

Jackson took the religious business more seriously than Samuel, and had paid for a brick church, with a spire and all.

Perhaps it was homesickness, since the man came from England.

All the lesser gentry were housed in the inn, but Jackson had more than enough room to put up the Mogdens and Petersens. After a magnificent meal, the three families were enjoying a selection of wines in the living room, when Elizabeth murmured to Samuel, "It's not as warm here as I like, and I don't want to make a fuss."

Softly, he replied, "And I don't want some strange servant pawing through our things. I'll fetch your shawl." He excused himself and strolled through the door, along a corridor impressively lit by a chain of lamps.

Before reaching his and Elizabeth's room, he passed a part-open door, with voices coming from within. He was not eavesdropping, but all the same, heard a strange girl's voice say, "My dears, I'm coming back as your child."

How odd. Almost against his volition, he stopped. A strange feeling overtook him, as if he were in the presence of something, Someone, mighty, as if he should kneel.

He heard Kirsten say, "Maraglindi, thank you for the honour. We'll love you, always."

The strange voice said, "Until then, I'm always with you."

That feeling of being in a Presence ceased, and Samuel was about to keep walking, when Kirsten asked, "What will we call her?"

"Gerald's answer came, "Or him?""

"No. She is the Mother and will always be female. We can't very well name her Maraglindi, but to white people she was Mary. Will that not do?""

"She always disliked being Mary, even as a tiny tot. But tell you what. During your famous speech at our wedding, you mentioned this lady who made nursing respectable for women.""

"Florence Nightingale?"

"Yes. How does Florence Kline sound to you?""

Samuel forced his legs to softly continue along the corridor, remembering that uncanny feeling. He'd never believed any religious nonsense — but... this was real. What, who, was that Person?

He was soon back with the crowd and handed his wife her shawl. He certainly would need to talk with young Kline, but the prospect was suddenly even more... intimidating. Now, that was a hard thing to admit.

The wedding ceremony went off without a hitch on the Saturday. Kline certainly knew his job. And Samuel was pleased with his new daughter-in-law, who'd be sharing his household. If Kirsten was a summer storm, Laura was the gentle rain of autumn, with her chestnut-coloured hair and willingness to please. And he would keep a firm rein on Luke to prevent any cruelty.

The rain was gone when they emerged from the church, and a beautiful, complete double rainbow captured Samuel's eyes. What a good omen! From the comments flying, he was not the only one to think so.

During the reception, he was pleased at people's reaction to his speech. Afterward, wanting solitude, he went for a walk and soon reached the lakeshore. Legs spread, hands locked behind his back, he watched the antics of the many birds, when he heard a slight noise. Surely, people should know when to leave him alone?

He turned to look. It was young Kline, smiling at him. "Good afternoon, Mr Mogden. God has blessed us with a beautiful world to live in, has he not?" The young fellow stopped beside Samuel, also gazing out over the water.

Now was the time.

"Good afternoon, Gerald. I'm surprised you sought me out. I've noted, you turn the other way when encountering my presence."

"Sir, you're very observant. But after that beautiful wedding, and the beautiful rainbow, I've decided I need to do something about it."

Samuel chose to reply with a silence. They stood side by side, a light, salt-scented breeze breathing into their faces. At last, Kline said, "Sir, I've heard a tale that in the early days of Griscombe, there was strife and conflict between the local

Aborigines and the Europeans who arrived upon their land."

Something clicked into place. Samuel remembered the Aboriginal family at Kline's wedding, and Peter MacCartney saying they were his best friends. "Yes," he answered. "It was a savage time. I can only describe it as full-blown war. I was a young man then, with a young wife who pleased me. When the blacks killed her favourite brother, she fainted, and happened to be holding our only child at the time, my first son." After all these years, he still needed to stop, and strive for at least the appearance of calmness. "The baby died."

"Oh, I am so sorry! And the pain never really passes." There was genuine compassion in the young man's voice. "But how did that war begin?"

"I had a letter of patent from the Governor himself and took up my holding. These savages understood no English, so I was unable to explain to them, but from the first day, they killed my animals. Naturally, I protected my property, and my men shot a few of the worst natives. And from that moment, there was all-out hostility. Certainly, our guns were superior to their boomerangs and spears, but they had an amazing ability to hide, and strike from nowhere."

"I've been inducted into the secrets of the nation of my hometown. They're different people from those of this area, but undoubtedly their customs are similar. They can send a wish to the spirits they revere, and it comes true. I'm sure intelligent use of camouflage, and the self-discipline of absolute stillness have a lot to do with it, but they can in fact do things our European understanding considers impossible."

"Is it not merely superstition?" This was fascinating.

"Not any more, sir, than many of our beliefs. For example, we believe that Albion should rule all, and so we have conquered the world. When you... were engaged in that war, did it occur to you to disengage and admit failure?"

Samuel sighed, remembering. "It did. We had no chance of sleep. All of us were at risk, including the women and children. Never could we expect attacks to be the same twice. I could not farm, and was losing animals, losing wealth. But if I left, I'd have felt shamed in the eyes of my family, of my peers. Defeat was unthinkable. It's as you said. I'm of English stock, and we have conquered everywhere. I needed to try harder, so I did."

"And then you lost your brother-in-law, and your son. Sir, I have an apology to make."

Samuel looked at him.

"As you know, I love the people of this land. When I heard that you were responsible for exterminating those local to what is now Griscombe, I judged you, and considered you to be a monster, a person who'd kill women and children for wealth. But now I've heard your version, and while I still grieve for the massacre, it's for the massacre on both sides. I'm sincerely sorry for having judged you."

The brown eyes looked down on him with honesty and compassion. Samuel held out his right hand, and Gerald grasped it. Samuel said, "But, if I know you, you've got more to add."

Kline gave a rueful laugh. "Indeed, sir, you know me all too well. Suppose you had been one of the leaders of those Aborigines. Your people are living their life, the same as for thousands of years, when strangers arrive. They don't perform the customary ceremony of asking for welcome to country, as any neighbouring natives would, but take the best land. You've always been a hunter and have no conception that animals can be domesticated. Those strange animals are much easier to hunt than kangaroos and emus, so, naturally, you hunt them. And the next thing, completely inexplicably, these strangers start killing people!"

"Hmm. So, you reckon, for them my men protecting my animals was a surprise? They didn't tie it to their killing of cattle and sheep?"

"It couldn't possibly have occurred to them. Their culture has no conception of private property, far less owning other living beings. They wouldn't even have imagined a connection between them killing animals and your people killing them. If I have something that is of use to another of my group, we share it. This is not even generosity, just the way things are."

"So, because I had them all killed, you considered me to be a mass murderer. And, within the point of view you've shown me, that's correct. But it really was a war, kill or be killed."

"They had absolutely no choice. For them, it was also kill or be killed. You see, they don't look on land like we do. If I owned a property, I could sell it and use the money to buy elsewhere. For them, their particular country is life. The greatest punishment they have is to expel a person from the land. That person will die. If you'd gathered them all up and deported them to somewhere else, be it the greatest hunter's paradise on earth, they'd have withered and died."

"All through the months, there has been a theme in your sermons. If I were to feel genuine regret within my heart for all that killing, and asked for forgiveness..."

Kline spoke into the silence. "Then the good Lord would forgive you. I don't know but suspect, the Spirits of the Aboriginal people would also forgive you, for the two sets of myths are backed by the one Truth."

Samuel had to laugh at that. "You don't sound like the typical churchman!"

"Have you ever come across the work of the ancient

Greek philosopher, Plato?"

"I do remember something. You're referring to the shadows in the cave?"

"Yes. We humans can never see the Truth, only its projection."

"Gerald, I am wondering... If I did wrong back then, I don't know that I could have done anything else. Hindsight is the sharpest vision there is, but it seems to me I had to do what I did, or be destroyed myself."

The young man thought, head hanging, then looked Samuel in the eyes again. "Perhaps if I were in your position at the time, I may have done the same. But knowing what I do know, a few ideas have occurred to me."

"Do go on."

"I'd have found a native from an already civilised area who could speak these people's language, and used him as both ambassador and interpreter... Hmm. I might have invited the most important elders to visit Sydney as my honoured guests, so they could see the new world coming, and to be willing to reach a compromise... Negotiate a trade with them: to allow me to farm their land, in exchange for modern tools and implements, giving them horses of their own... They don't like living in the one place but like to travel around. Perhaps gypsy caravans would make their lives easier...

Samuel took a deep breath, and slowly released it. "Well, young fellow, I'll forgive you for your unkind thoughts about me, if you'll forgive me for my unkind thoughts about you."

33

Gerald, Monday, 2nd day of April, 1866

Never before had Gerald seen the captain worried. He did now. "You're good at praying, son," he said. "Pray."

They were in the living room of the new Kline residence. Kirsten, her mother and the midwife were in the main bedroom, and men were banished from there. Only Tillie was allowed entry.

"Anything wrong, sir?"

The captain managed a grin. "Not as far as I know. But Margarita had two stillbirths, and nearly died when Emil was born. We also lost two children in infancy."

Instead of praying, Gerald said aloud, "Maraglindi, please introduce yourself to Captain Petersen."

"What?"

The air shimmered in front of them, between the two windows, and she stood there, in a demure brown dress, still seeming fourteen. "Sven my dear, I'm pleased to make your acquaintance. After all, you'll be my grandfather very soon."

The captain was speechless. Mouth open, he looked at the young girl, made of light.

She continued, "I moved into the little body four months ago, but until I'm actually born, I can do this. After that, Gerald dear, I'll be just a newborn child with no memories of anything before, so in a way this is goodbye."

"Who are you?" The captain still looked like he doubted his own sanity.

She laughed, exactly that laugh Gerald loved so much, a higher version of Glindi's laugh. "I've told you. Your new granddaughter."

"But... how can that be? I've never..."

"You humans live in order to learn the Ultimate Lesson, the Lesson of unconditional Love to all of creation. Listen to Gerald, who has told you about Jesus' real message. When you can achieve that, automatically and without effort, when it is part of your very nature, then you no longer need to live a material existence. I am such a person and have taken on the task of being a guardian spirit to your kind. Only, I've never lived as a human. Maraglindi was my first such life."

She looked at Gerald and laughed again. "That's why I was so awkward. One of the lessons I learned in that life was how to inhabit a human body."

"So," Gerald asked, "the birth will go off all right? We can stop worrying?"

She smiled. "I don't know!" Then she was gone.

It took all of that night, and half the morning of Tuesday,

3rd day of April, before, bleary-eyed but happy, Tillie came for them, and led them to the bedroom. Kirsten lay in the bed, radiant but exhausted, with a tiny bundle in her arms. She passed the baby to Gerald.

The baby gazed at him with eyes the same brown as his, but the slight fuzz on the top of her head was golden, like her mother's. He comfortably held her on the palm of his right hand, and lifted her to his lips, to kiss the soft little face. "Welcome, darling Florence," he whispered.

Finally, a chat

But... but isn't this a Christian story, and doesn't that rule out a belief in reincarnation?

No, this is not a Christian story. Being set in the Victorian era, it accurately represents the beliefs and customs of English-speaking people of the time. In the land that was to become Australia in 1901, the culture was defined by the Anglican version of Christianity. So, Maraglindi's mission needed to be clothed in Christian beliefs. Her message is the same as Jesus' message, but here is a shock for you: Christianity doesn't have copyright on the universal message of Love, which is at the heart of all the great religions. For example, Confucius, has said, "Love others as you would love yourself, judge others as you would judge yourself, cherish others as you would cherish yourself. When you wish for others as you wish for yourself and when you protect others as you would protect yourself, that's when you can say it's true love."

The Qur'an specifies that Jesus is a prophet on the same level as Moses, and therefore accepts the message Jesus was sent with. This is emphasised in some versions of Islam, played down in others — as is the case with different versions of Christianity. How much unconditional Love is there in hell and brimstone fundamentalist Christianity?

Buddhist teachings make no mention of a god at all, but the requirements on a good Buddhist are exactly the same as the requirements on a good Christian. The recipe for a good life, for a good society, is merely adapted to a different culture.

Gandhi was a Hindu, but he was killed because he stated the same message Jesus was killed for: love your enemy. He said, "Suppose your beloved little son was killed by Muslims. Then go out and find a Muslim boy of the same age, both of whose parents were killed by Hindus. Take him into your home, take him into your heart — and raise him as a good Muslim."

All religions and philosophies are human constructions. They all have the potential to reflect the underlying Truth, but all are distorted because of the necessity to be understood by people of a particular culture, and because the human interpreters of the Truth have failings, and the desire for power.

In any case, who says that Christianity and reincarnation are incompatible? Prominent theologist, Geddes MacGregor, has shown that the two belief systems don't contradict each other. Indeed, the Celtic church of Ireland before St Patrick had reincarnation as a central part of its beliefs, as does Rosicrucianism, which has a following to the present day.

A great many people of all religious persuasions have personal experiences they interpret as past life recalls. For them, reincarnation is true, because their memories validate it. This includes Jews, Christians of all denominations, Muslims, atheists, and people with no views on religion.

Finally, scientific investigations have moved the question of reincarnation out of the domain of belief. Belief is an opinion you hold when there is no evidence to guide you. Before Pasteur, a cough and a runny nose were due to breathing bad air if you were European, or to a spell cast by an enemy if you were an African villager. Now, it is part of common sense that it is due to a virus infection. The cause of illness is no longer in the domain of belief, because there is strong scientific evidence for the "germ theory of disease."

If you take the Bible literally, the Earth is flat, and the Sun moves through the sky. Galileo and Copernicus were persecuted for presenting evidence to the contrary. Nowadays, everyone knows the basic facts of astronomy, because of the wealth of scientific evidence that has become part of common knowledge.

In the same way, it is possible to pose the question of whether there is life after life in a way that allows it to be tested by using the scientific method. It needs a search for evidence to prove or disprove testable claims.

Two lines of investigation have succeeded in this. The

first is by a research group at the University of Virginia, initially headed by Dr Ian Stevenson until his retirement, and now by Dr Jim Tucker. Since the 1950s, they have investigated apparent past life recalls by young children. The child will make statements, and/or show abilities that are foreign and unexpected, given their family setting. The investigators elicit testable claims, then look for the evidence. As of 2005, when Jim Tucker's *Life Before Life* was published, the evidence had been found in over 2500 cases. Given the prejudice against this kind of research, the investigators have been extremely conservative in their interpretations. Dr Tucker has restricted his claim to the conclusion that these 2500 children have lived once before. He and his team explicitly demur from claiming that they have proven reincarnation, but this disclaimer is to be understood in terms of the nature of the scientific method. In science, you never prove anything. You may be able to reject the "null hypothesis" that there is nothing but chance operating. However, if there was a court hearing and the defendant needed to have the judge accept that reincarnation is a reasonable belief based on the evidence, then Tucker's book would be considered powerful enough to demonstrate the case for reincarnation.

The second line of investigation concerns past life regression hypnosis. People sometimes experience a slip into what they feel is a different personality, sometimes even a different body. Incidentally, this can happen without being in a hypnotic trance, something that has occasionally been known to occur while processing traumatic memories in an alert state.

Some writers, for example Brian Weiss in his celebrated books, approach past life regression in a non-scientific way, valuable as their reports may be. However, Peter Ramster has done better. He got his clients to do things like drawing the marks carved into a stone laid as part of a floor, or describing the internal layout of a building on another continent. Then Peter, the client and a cameraman went to seek the evidence. In three of four cases, they found it, exactly as the hypnotic recall predicted. In the fourth case, there was a very large overlap, with a few inaccuracies. Any explanation apart from past life recall is beyond belief.

In science, the highest support for a theory is "convergent evidence:" when several different lines of investigation provide independent support. Even if some of these sources of evidence are weak, they add to the total strength of the case.

A third line of evidence is inherently weak in the scientific sense, because it depends on claims by people that in principle cannot be independently verified. They are personal testimony, which can never be scientific. These are recalls of experiences some people have while in a coma, under anaesthetic, or clinically dead. There are many thousands of such reports in the public domain. You can read a very touching clinical death report by Yvonne Rowan, as one of the chapters of *Cancer: A personal challenge* by Bob Rich et al. The content of such experiences is coloured by the person's culture, but there are remarkable similarities, including the presence of a superior being Who conveys unshakable unconditional love, with no judgment. If the coma goes on for long enough, the person reports the start of a process of re-experiencing the just completed (or more exactly, temporarily interrupted) life, from its end toward birth, in the way I've had Derek Johnston experience it in this story. That is, the person feels the emotions and reactions of other people affected by some act. Positive, pleasant reactions by others helps the person build on strengths, while negative reactions are very powerful motivators for seeking to improve.

This only makes sense if there is a further opportunity to build on the strengths, make restitution for the evil acts, and learn new lessons.

The Person Who chose to be Maraglindi needed more lives to learn how to be a human. I hope I have interested you in following Her journey. The next volume will be *The Protector*.

If you enjoyed this book, please write a review. You can contact me at my blog, Bobbing Around https://bobrich18.wordpress.com If you email me your review, you have earned a free electronic copy of any of my other books.

With unconditional love, whoever you are.

Acknowledgements

The Wiradjuri Condobolin Corporation provided both general and specific information on Aboriginal traditional life in the general area. Mr Robert Russell, CEO of the Awabakal Local Aboriginal Land Council, and Mr Bob Syron, who is an Aboriginal expert on the history of the Worimi and related people, have graciously given advice in response to specific questions. Mr Syron has read this story and provided the correct terms in the Gathang language. He also emailed me a copy of his illustrated essay, *Aboriginal Dream Time Stories*, which is full of useful cultural detail including a long dictionary of Gathang terms.

The New South Wales Department of Education sent me a copy of their instructional booklet, *Aborigines of the Hunter Region*, which was also immensely useful, having been written in close consultation with knowledgeable Aborigines from the relevant nations.

Carolyn Harris, and Australian historical fiction writer Margaret Tanner, were both invaluable with their comments, helping me to ensure historical accuracy for 19th Century Australia. Margaret's books are true to life and enjoyable reading.

Talented Canadian writer Rita Toews made very valuable comments on an earlier version of this book.

Emeritus Professor Florence Weinberg is the author of many excellent books of historical fiction. Her beta read of this story was extremely useful.

The Reverend Dr Peter Bolt, author of *Thomas Moore of Liverpool,* was very helpful with historical details, which allowed me to bring religious education of the mid-1800s to life. His several books are well written and illuminating on the period.

Margaret Blair offered extremely helpful advice on the procedures of the Church of England, now and in the 19th century.

Finally, I am very thankful for, and immensely impressed with the amount of work, thought and care, my publisher, Michael Amos of Sleepy Lion Publishing, has put into this book. It was well beyond the line of duty from a publisher.

Naturally, none of these people are in any way responsible for any mistakes or inaccuracies I may have committed.

About the Author

Bob Rich is an Australian storyteller, with 19 published books in a variety of genres including both fiction and nonfiction. Five of his books, and over 40 short stories, have won awards.

He has retired five times so far, from five different occupations, but is still busy as a Professional Grandfather. Anyone born since 1993 is his grandchild; anyone born after 1987 his child. Everything he does, including his writing, is working toward a survivable future for them, and one worth surviving in. This means environmental and humanitarian activism: an attempt to change a worldwide culture of greed, hate and fear into one of compassion and cooperation. He does this work at his popular blog, Bobbing Around, https://bobrich18.wordpress.com

He has been writing since 1980, with a byline column in "Earth Garden" magazine and several other periodicals. His first book, *The Earth Garden Building Book: Design and build your own house*, was published in 1986, and went through four editions, the last going out of print in 2018. He has had four other self-help books published, the latest being *From Depression to Contentment: A self-therapy guide*. A biography, *Anikó: The stranger who loved me* has won four awards.

SLEEPY LION

P U B L I S H I N G

If you are interested in publishing, writing, and you love to read, then head over to www.sleepylionpublishing.com

Otherwise, all questions, suggestions and queries can be sent to enquiries@sleepylionpublishing.com

If you would like to submit any work, whether a short story, article, blog post or even art work, then send us an email at submissions@sleepylionpublishing.com

We offer different paid contracts on smaller pieces, so whether you would rather an upfront payment, or to make money over time, we also personalise our collaborations. So, get in contact now and start earning money from your work!

On our website you will find:

-Our personal editing, illustrating and publishing services with no costs or fees.

- Blog posts

 -Articles on writing and reading

-Short Stories

-Poetry

-Contests (Coming soon!)

-News on any books we are publishing

-Finally, if you are looking for a new or different way to publish your book, then definitely look at our website. We provide a range of different non-binding contracts, we prioritise author power and freedom, and we supply an individual approach to each author's publication.